I wanted to run...

I kept shaking my head, unable to form words, unable to tell Camden how I was feeling. I just wanted him to go away and leave me alone.

"You know how I feel about your scars. They only make you more beautiful," he whispered, now stroking the side of my face. His eyes were searching mine, begging me to open up, but the fear was so big and so damn real.

"You've never seen my scars." My voice was barely audible, even in my own head.

"No, I haven't. But I've seen what they've made you."

His nose nudged the side of mine. I leaned in and kissed him. This wasn't the tender kiss from earlier. This kiss was soft for a moment, then hurried. His lips sucked gently on mine, his tongue ravishing my mouth like he couldn't stop himself. I was suddenly insatiable, each kiss reaching down into my core, making me want all of him, every part. A million thoughts flew through my head and then there was nothing at all. There wasn't even Camden and Ellie.

There was just this hot, primal, crucial need for each other...

Also by Karina Halle

The Artists Trilogy

Bold Tricks
Shooting Scars
On Every Street

SINS & NEEDLES

BOOK 1 OF THE ARTISTS TRILOGY

KARINA HALLE

FOREVER

NEW YORK   BOSTON

Copyright © 2013 by Karina Halle
Excerpt from *On Every Street* copyright © 2013 by Karina Halle
All rights reserved. In accordance with the U.S. Copyright Act of 1976, the scanning, uploading, and electronic sharing of any part of this book without the permission of the publisher is unlawful piracy and theft of the author's intellectual property. If you would like to use material from the book (other than for review purposes), prior written permission must be obtained by contacting the publisher at permissions@hbgusa.com. Thank you for your support of the author's rights.

Forever
Hachette Book Group
237 Park Avenue, New York, NY 10017

Hachettebookgroup.com
Twitter.com/foreverromance

Printed in the United States of America

Originally published as an ebook
First mass market edition: August 2014
10 9 8 7 6 5 4 3 2 1

OPM

Forever is an imprint of Grand Central Publishing.
The Forever name and logo are trademarks of Hachette Book Group, Inc.

The publisher is not responsible for websites (or their content) that are not owned by the publisher.

The Hachette Speakers Bureau provides a wide range of authors for speaking events. To find out more, go to www.hachettespeakersbureau.com or call (866) 376-6591.

ATTENTION CORPORATIONS AND ORGANIZATIONS:
Most HACHETTE BOOK GROUP books are available at quantity discounts with bulk purchase for educational, business, or sales promotional use. For information, please call or write:

Special Markets Department, Hachette Book Group
237 Park Avenue, New York, NY 10017
Telephone: 1-800-222-6747 Fax: 1-800-477-5925

PROLOGUE

THIS WILL BE the last time.

I've said that before. I've said it a lot. I've said it while talking to myself in a mirror like some De Niro cliché. But I've never said it while having a pool cue pressed against my throat by a crazed Ukrainian man who is hell-bent on making me his wife.

It's nice to know there's still a first time for everything.

Luckily, as the edges of my vision turned a sick shade of gray and my feet dangled from the floor, I had enough fight left in me to get out of this alive. Though it meant a few seconds of agony as the cue pressed into my windpipe, I pried my hands off of it and reached out. Sergei, my future fake husband, wasn't short, but I had long arms, and as I pushed aside his gut, I found his balls.

With one swift movement, I made a tight, nails-first fist around them and tugged.

Hard.

Sergei screamed, dropping me and the pool cue to the sticky floor. I hopped up to my feet, grabbed the stick, and swung it against the side of his head as he was doubled over. When I was a child, I was never in a town long enough to get enrolled in the softball team, which was a shame—because as the cue cracked against the side of his bald head, I realized it could have been a second career.

Hell, it could even be a first career. I was quitting the grifting game anyway.

Sergei made some grumbling, moaning noise like a disgruntled cow giving birth, and though I had done some damage, I had only bought myself a few seconds. I grabbed the eight ball from the pool table and chucked it at his head. It bounced off his forehead with a thwack that made my toes curl.

For all the games I played, I'd always been a bit squeamish with violence. That said, I'd never been busted by one of the men I'd conned with my virgin bride scam. I chalked this up to "kill or be killed." Self-defense. Hopefully it would be the last time for that, too.

Not that I was doing any killing here. After the pool ball made contact with his head and caused him to drop to his knees with a screech, I turned on my heels and booked it into the ladies' washroom. I knew there were two angry-looking men stationed outside of the door to the pool room, and they definitely wouldn't let me pass while their friend was on the floor hoping his testicles were still attached.

The ladies' room smelled rank, like mold and cold

pipes, and I wondered how long it had been since it was cleaned. The Frontier wasn't the sort of bar that women hung out at, and that should have been my first tip that something was awry. The second was that no one even looked my way when I walked into the place. It was like they were expecting me, and when a dodgy bar in Cincinnati is expecting you, you know you're on someone else's turf. Third thing that should have tipped me off was the pool room was in a basement and there were an awful lot of locks on that door.

But, as I balanced my boots on the rust-stained sink, I found there were no locks on the rectangular window. I slammed it open and stuck my arms out into the warm August air, finding soggy dirt under my hands as the rain came down in heavy sheets. Just perfect. I was going to become Mud Woman in a few seconds.

Mud Woman was still preferable to Dead Woman, however, and I pulled myself through the narrow window and onto the muddy ground, the cold, wet dirt seeping into my shirt and down the front of my jeans. I heard Sergei yelling his head off and pounding on the bathroom door.

This had been a close one. Way too close.

I scrambled to my feet and quickly looked around to see if anyone had noticed. So far the bar looked quiet, the red lights from inside spilling through the falling rain. The street was equally quiet and lined with Audis and Mercedeses that stuck out like gaudy jewelry among the decrepit meatpacking buildings. My own car, which I reluctantly called Jose, was parked two blocks away. I may have underestimated the situation,

but I was glad I still had my wits about me. When an old friend e-mails you out of the blue and asks you to meet him at a sketchy bar late at night, you do take some precautions. It's too bad I hadn't clued in that it wasn't an old lover of mine but Sergei, out for revenge.

I took advantage of not being seen and ran as fast as I could down the street, my footsteps echoing coldly. By the time I rounded the corner and saw the dark green 1970 GTO sitting on the empty street, the rain had washed the mud clean off of me.

I wiped my wet hair from my eyes and stared at the glistening Ohio license plate. It was time for that to come off, and I mentally flipped through the spare plates I had inside. I knew I'd never set foot in Cincinnati again after this, and now that I knew this had been a setup, I couldn't be sure they hadn't noticed my car. I had a wad of Sergei's money—which I'd been keeping strapped to the bottom of the driver's seat—and apparently he was the type who'd follow up on that kind of thing. He was the type who would hunt me down I should have figured that from our e-mail exchanges. This wouldn't even be about the money anymore, but the fact that I pulled a fast one on him. But what do you expect when you're trolling for virgin brides on OkStupid?

Men and their stupid pride.

I supposed he could try and hunt me down. He could try and follow me from state to state. But I knew as soon as I got in Jose, he wouldn't be able to find me. I'd been hunted before and for a lot more than money.

And they still hadn't found me.

Yet.

Hearing distant but irate voices filling the air, I quickly opened the door and hopped in. My instincts told me to just drive and never look back, and unfortunately I knew I had to listen. I had to leave my pretty apartment, my safe coffee shop job, and my yoga-infused roommate, Carlee, behind. It was a shame, too. After living with Carlee for six months, the flexible little thing had actually grown on me.

I'll mail her something nice, I told myself, and gunned the engine. Jose purred to life and we shot down the street, away from the bar and from Sergei and his buddies, who were now probably scouring the streets looking for me.

It didn't matter. I was used to running and always kept a spare life in the trunk. Spare clothes, spare driver's licenses, spare Social Security numbers, and a spare tire. As soon as I felt like I was a comfortable distance away, I'd pull into a motel under a new name. I'd change the plates on my car. Yes, Jose wasn't the most inconspicuous of vehicles, but I was sentimental about the car. After all, it wasn't even mine.

Then tomorrow, I'd figure out my budget. Figure out how long I could go before I'd need a legitimate job. Figure out that moment when I'd have to stay true to my word and make sure that this truly *was* the last time.

I careened around a corner then slowed as the car disappeared into traffic heading across the Ohio River. With my free hand I opened my wallet and went through my spare IDs. Now that I was going to go legit, I didn't have much of a choice.

I took out the California license that said Ellie Watt.
I'd need to change the expiration date and photo since
the last time I set foot in the state was seven years ago,
just after I turned nineteen. But it would do. I was Ellie
Watt again.

I was finally me.

Oh joy.

CHAPTER ONE

Then

The girl was lying down in the backseat of her parents' rusting station wagon, counting down the minutes as she stared up at the green water spots on the roof. If she had a cell phone, keeping track of time would have been a lot easier, especially since the girl still struggled with math. Of course, you could blame her mother for that—you could blame her for a lot of things—since the girl had been homeschooled her whole life. Division and multiplication were about as advanced as things got for the eleven-year-old. But, according to her mother, you only needed to be able to count in order to succeed in grifting, and at the moment the girl was counting away.

It had been four minutes since her parents left the car and walked up, arm in arm, toward the cold lights that emanated from the sprawling house. The girl had no idea where they were except that they were still in Mississippi. She could smell the swamps. The man they

were visiting was supposed to be an old friend of her mother's, but the girl wasn't too sure about that. She had heard her mother screaming about this Travis man from time to time, and her anger had done nothing except build over the last few weeks. Finally, she had made some phone calls, got herself dolled up in her "special" dress that showed far too much cleavage, made her husband slap on a suit, and dragged the girl out to the car. They were going to have dinner with this old friend of hers, and they needed the girl to do a little breaking and entering while they had the man occupied.

The girl was shocked at first. It wasn't just that she was getting older and developing her own sense of morals that didn't seem to gel with the world her parents had created; it was that no one in their family had pulled a scam in years. Her father had steady work at a casino, and their tiny apartment in Gulfport had become as much of a home as a home could get. Her parents had promised her that they were finished with grifting for good and that they'd try to lead as normal a life as they could, all for their young daughter. Or so they said.

But her mother had her reasons, reasons that the girl didn't understand. If they were friends with this Travis man, why were they robbing him? If he lived in an outlandish house with marble pillars and a driveway full of fountains, why didn't they just ask him for the money? This was another reason why the girl doubted her mother's story. This man wasn't a friend at all.

And the girl was being sent right into his clutches.

When the time was up, the girl slowly got out of the car, careful not to make a sound, and hugged the shadows of the house, moving toward the back. She listened for the telltale buzz of security cameras or the click of motion sensor lights and felt relief when she couldn't detect them. She kept low, quick, and quiet until she was in the sprawling backyard, the manicured grounds lit by the moon. She paused behind a fragrant bush and counted the windows down the side of the house. The plan was for her to go in the second window, the master bathroom, then walk out of the bedroom and take the first door on the left. That was where she'd find the safe; the code for it was written in permanent ink on the back of her sweating hand.

How her mother knew the code to this man's safe, she had no idea. She had stopped asking her mother these things a long time ago.

She scampered over to the narrow, frosted pane window, and just like her mother said it would be, it was open a crack.

The girl would always look back at that moment, the hesitation as she stood below it, the moon behind her. She remembered having a choice—she didn't have to go through with it. She could run back to the car and tell her parents she changed her mind. But fear and pride kept the foolish little girl from acting on her instincts.

Instead, she silently opened the window and went into the house.

When she eventually left the house, her life would be changed forever.

Now

Bright blue skies, rough desert, open blacktop spreading before me.

Cue the music.

I fumbled with my iPod and selected the Desert Playlist I concocted a few days ago in a hotel room in Colorado. The Doors' "Roadhouse Blues" came blaring from Jose's speakers, and I let myself smile as the hot breeze blew my hair back.

It had been two months since I escaped Sergei's fat-knuckled clutches in Ohio. Two months of being on the road and lying low from state to state. Two months of trading in my long, naturally strawberry blonde hair for a choppy black bob. Two months of surviving on Sergei's money until it ran dry. Two months of being Ellie Watt.

Two months before I finally had to return home.

Well, the only place I'd ever called home.

I loved the high desert though, always have, and seeing the Joshua trees as they clung to rocky, chalk-colored hillsides made a familiar thrill run through me. The same kind of thrill I got when pulling off a scam. Only there were probably more repercussions for returning to the Coachella Valley. A scam, yeah, I was usually good at those. Being home again—being me again—not so much.

But I brushed that worry out of my head and gunned the engine. Roadrunners shot out of the bushes at the barren roadside, their little legs kicking up dust onto the rippling asphalt. There wasn't a car or a soul around

for miles. It was just me and Jim Morrison and the extreme landscape. The endless sky, the searing heat, the relentless sun that made the highs pop and the lows sink. This was a high-contrast land and I lived a high-contrast life.

I followed Highway 62 while listening to my favorite Calexico songs and surf music until Joshua Tree National Park appeared on my left.

And that was when I had to pull the car over to vomit.

Ugh. I sat back down on the passenger side, away from the road, and leaned forward on my knees. Jose made a clicking noise under the hood as the engine settled. I tried to breathe in deeply through my nose. My hands were shaking slightly, my heart was running around in my chest as if it were looking for a way out. This was going to be a lot harder than I thought. A semi roared past, making Jose tremble beneath me. Now we were both scared.

You can do this, Ellie, I told myself, even though my own name sounded weird in my head. *No one will know you're in town. You're twenty-six, not nineteen. You don't look the same. You don't even walk the same. And like anyone from high school would still be living here. They all probably left just the same as you did.*

I punched the glove compartment with the side of my fist and it flipped open. I grabbed the bottle of kava pills and shook a few into my mouth. They were the size of horse pills, but I managed to swallow them dry. If you do something enough, your body learns to adapt. I should know.

Another car roared past and we shook again. The kava would kick in soon, and if it didn't, I had a few bottles of Ativan in the trunk. I was trying to wean myself off of the stuff since my habit had gotten a little out of control for a while, but I'd cut myself some slack this time. I just didn't want to be totally out of it when I saw Uncle Jim.

The intense, ovenlike heat was making my thighs stick to my jeans, which were in turn sticking to the seat. I peeled myself off of it and walked around to the driver's side. I gripped the worn wheel until my knuckles turned white then sped off down the road. I hoped I'd left my fear on the roadside with the rest of my breakfast.

Uncle Jim owned a date farm on the outskirts of Palm Valley. My parents and I went to live with him after we fell into a bit of trouble. They thought a fresh start would be a good idea, though I thought it had more to do with Child Services poking their nose around and the fact that my dad lost his job at the casino. So we left Gulfport, Mississippi, and came west. Uncle Jim is my mother's brother and the only living relative I have who hasn't disowned me. And at the time, he hadn't disowned my parents either, which is why he let us stay with him.

They enrolled me in Palm Valley High School, the first real school I'd ever attended. I'm sure high school is a big shock to a lot of people, but to me it felt like I'd stuck my tongue in an electrical socket. And as if I wasn't damaged enough at that point, a year later my parents sort of forgot about the whole "starting over"

To everyone with the scars that have made them who they are—this one's for you.

SINS &
NEEDLES

the same truck I learned to drive in, and it barely ran back then.

I pulled Jose to a stop on the street and approached the house with trepidation, wiping my hands on my jeans. I could hear the far-off cries of Spanish from the workers in the groves and the coo of a few ground doves that were walking across the cracked, tiled driveway. An enormous wash of guilt curved over me like the surrounding palm fronds. The last time I talked to my uncle was two years ago, when I was holed up in Vermont. I told him I'd send him some money, and he said he was fine and didn't need my charity. I meant to send him some cash anyway but I never got around to it.

Now it looked like he was in dire straits. And that would make two of us.

I took in a deep breath at the door, noticing the doormat was the same as it was back then, the same thick embroidery that his wife had done up before she died. It was patched with black mold and barely hanging together. I hoped that wasn't symbolic.

I knocked quickly and snapped my hand back. I waited, taking a moment to look around me. I wouldn't have been followed, but some habits stuck with you. Being extra precautious was a wonderful habit for a girl like me.

I raised my hand to knock again when the door was opened a crack and I spied a familiar-looking eye peering through it.

"Uncle Jim," I said through a broad smile.

He frowned and the door opened fully.

He looked me up and down and said, "Oh shit."

*   *   *

"I'm sorry, but you know you can't stay here," Uncle Jim was saying to me in his dusty kitchen as he poured me another glass of iced tea, the undissolved crystals swirling around the bottom like tornado debris.

I breathed out sharply through my nose, trying to hide my frustration. I'd been talking to him for an hour, and we hadn't gotten anywhere except that I wasn't welcome.

"Look, I get that you're a proud man," I started.

His eyes snapped up. He looked so much older now that it scared me; his dark hair had gone gray, and the sides of his mouth were lined like canyons, but his eyes were still sharp and determined.

"This isn't about pride, Ellie. If you were someone else offering to help me, I'd take you up on it. It's not like I'm not getting enough fucking charity from Betty down the street, bringing me hot meals a few times a week. I know I'm struggling here. But you're not someone else. You're Ellie Fucking Watt."

I wrinkled my nose at his profanity. "I didn't know *fucking* was my middle name."

He raised a caterpillar brow. "No?"

I rolled my eyes. "No, *Uncle* Jim. That's not a very nice thing to insinuate of your niece."

He smiled—ever so briefly—but I caught it. He turned around and pulled open the fridge, looking at it blankly. There wasn't anything in there except condiments. "Well, I beg your pardon for not being an appropriate uncle. I haven't seen you since you were nineteen, you know."

"Oh, I know."

He seemed to think about pulling out a jar of mustard but decided against it. What, was he going to make me a mustard milkshake? He slammed the door shut and leaned against the counter.

"I'm sorry I can't offer you anything to eat."

"I had some beef jerky in the car."

He looked me over and shook his head. "You're too skinny, Ellie."

"It's just my arms," I told him defensively, crossing them over my chest. "Stress does that to you. I've still got enough weight down below."

He nodded and his face pinched in sympathy. My heart thumped. I knew what followed that look.

"How's your leg doing?"

I gave him a tight smile. "My leg is fine."

"And you're still grifting?"

"Sometimes," I said, diverting my eyes. Suddenly the pattern on the faux marble countertop was fascinating. "I've quit for good, though. Had a close call in Cincinnati. Don't want to do that again."

Without glancing at him, I knew he was giving me the "a leopard doesn't change his spots" look.

"What con went wrong?"

I suppressed a smile. "It was just an online dating thing."

"And...?"

"And, well, it just didn't go as it normally does."

"And how does it normally go?"

"Get a bunch of desperate men to fall in love with you. Tell them you'd love to meet them, fuck them, marry them, but you're stuck in Russia and don't have the funds to leave the country to do so. Get them to give you the funds. Close down your online dating account. Simple as that."

I could see him shaking his head out of the corner of my eye. "Jesus, Ellie. That's low."

"Oh, spare me your sudden display of ethics," I said with a wave of my hand. "That's how it works. I don't go after men who can't afford it; I'm not that cruel. Most of them are cheating on their wives, too, so how about them apples? Besides, it's not a quick scam. It takes months to build up a fake relationship. But that's why I usually have six on the go at once. Makes it worth my while."

He gulped down the rest of his drink in a fit of thirst. "All right, well, what happened in Cincinnati?"

It suddenly felt very stuffy in his kitchen. I was tempted to open the window above the sink, but I could tell the breeze had picked up and was blowing around dust from the groves.

I started sliding the razor blade charm back and forth along my necklace. "I just picked the wrong guy. And I got sloppy. I thought he was an American, but he wasn't. He gave me a fake name, and that should have set me off. Who says they're Steven when they're really Sergei? He also had a lot of money to throw around. Too much. That should have also set me off. He kept sending me gifts to my PO box in St. Petersburg, really flashy items that I had to pretend I'd gotten, like pearls and diamonds. Really makes me want to take a trip to Russia and empty it out. Anyway, I got the money from him in the end, way more than I normally get, and then I disappeared."

I took a sip of the iced tea and said, "Everything was back to normal for about a week. The money had been wired to my offshore account as usual. Then I got an e-mail from an ex-boyfriend of mine. Said he was in town and would I meet him for a drink. So, I did. Turns out it wasn't my ex but Sergei, and that big, bald bull was pissed. I barely got out of the bar."

"So what do you think happened?" Uncle Jim looked pained, and I couldn't blame him. I was only twenty-six, far too young to be playing with Ukrainian mobsters.

I shrugged. "The only thing I could think of was him contacting the post office in St. Petersburg about the PO box. I couldn't remember what name I signed up for the account with. He might have traced me to Cincinnati somehow. I lived with my ex for a couple of months, and I'm guessing he went there under false pretenses, got the e-mail of my ex, and impersonated him. I totally underestimated Sergei. I think he was involved in a bunch of bad things."

My uncle's eyes turned hard and flinty. "This ex of yours...is this..."

"No," I said quickly. "No, this was some guy I met at the rock-climbing gym. Jack. It was short and sweet. And what are you getting at?"

He raised his fingers and looked to the side. "Oh, I just heard some things, that's all."

"What kind of things? And from who?" Panic was starting to press on my chest. He couldn't be talking about who I thought he was. I mean, he could not. It was impossible. Oh shit.

"Whose car is that outside?" he asked.

Shiiiiiiiiiiiiit.

"How do you know about all of this?" I asked, shooting to my feet and sending the bar stool clattering behind me.

"Easy there, Hellie." He was back to calling me my nickname from high school. It would have been charming had my blood pressure not been through the roof at that moment. Ativan. I had Ativan in the trunk.

"I talked to your parents a few times, you know. More than you have," he continued.

I blinked stupidly. "Okay, aside from the fact that I can't believe you're talking to them again, I don't know what my parents could possibly know about—"

"You falling in love with a drug lord?" he supplied. "Oh, they know enough. It's a small world out there. If you double-cross enough people, you're bound to double-cross them again."

His words coated me like fine dust. My parents were alive and kicking. They were talking to my uncle. And somehow they knew all about Javier.

"What did they tell you?" I asked quietly, hiding my hands behind me so he couldn't see them shaking.

"Well, they are back in Gulfport. No, maybe it's Biloxi. Somewhere on the coast. And apparently they aren't the only ones visiting their past."

I couldn't believe it. Why on earth would my parents return to Gulfport? We fled from that place like it was a life-and-death situation, and I'd grown up believing it was.

"Didn't you return to Gulfport after you left here?"

he asked me, as if he could read my thoughts. "Maybe they went back for the same reason."

Yes, but I went back for revenge. For what had happened to me all those years ago. For what had scarred me for life.

"So what did they tell you?" I asked. I ground out the words like hard kernels.

He scratched beneath his ear and looked down into his glass, examining the floating crystals. The sun was streaming through it, causing a tea-colored stain to dance on the walls. "They mentioned how you had been living in Gulfport after you left Palm Valley. They hinted that you'd switched sides for a few years, shacked up with one of Travis's men. Javier…something Spanish. Then, for whatever reason, you left. Took his money and his car."

I swallowed hard. I wanted nothing more than to run out of the house and back into that said car and drive far, far away. That was always Plan A, and it had worked out great so far.

"Okay," I said, trying to find an angle in our conversation. "But how did they find that out?"

"Look, I don't know. This was a few years ago, anyway. It hasn't come up since."

"So you still talk to them?" I asked, brows raised to the ceiling.

He nodded. "Maybe twice a year. We ain't close, if you catch my drift. Which is why you can't stay here."

"You still won't let me stay here?"

"I especially won't let you stay here. Scamming men on the Internet? Didn't your parents teach you anything?"

"Yeah! To con people."

"No, Ellie," he said and then licked his lips. He looked so much older than he should have. I wished I could just wipe the wrinkles from his face. "Didn't what they did to you teach you anything? Eventually you're going to get hurt."

I raised my chin, my walls rising up around me like metal siding. "I've already been hurt, as you love to point out. And I told you, I'm done. I'm trying to go legit, and you won't even give me a chance. You haven't seen me since I was a teenager. You don't know me. You don't know when I'm being honest."

"Exactly."

"But I am being honest. I need a job, Uncle Jim. I need a place to stay."

He let out a deep sigh and threw the rest of his drink in the sink. "You can stay here for a couple of days, that's it. If you want to hang about in Palm Valley, that's fine. But you don't hang out here. You need to find your own place. Your own money. I can't give you any money and I can't even give you a job. I owe those men out there money already and there's not enough harvest to break even this year. Sad but true."

"I can help out around the house, clean it up a bit," I offered.

"And I expect you to," he said sternly. "But only for a few days. I suggest you hightail it to town and start looking for employment now."

"Why are you so afraid of me?" I asked him softly.

I thought he'd look perplexed at the question but he only looked chagrined. "I've always been afraid of you, little Hellie. You've got something dark inside you, you always have. I don't want to be around when it comes out. And more than that, I'm trying to make good in this community. I'm trying to make good and get help when I need it most. Do you think people will be so generous to me when they find out I've got my sister's daughter staying here? Do you think a town ever really forgets its criminals? It doesn't. Palm Valley may look prettier, but it's still a stubborn old lady who won't think twice about running you out of town. And me, too.

"Now," he said, making his way to the sliding door that led into the date palm grove, "I've got to make sure my livelihood is alive. I'll see you later."

I watched him go, vowing to myself that I'd never be in financial stress at his age, no matter what the cost. Then I turned and left the house. I had some jobs to apply for.

CHAPTER TWO

I DROVE BACK to town in pure frustration, my ever-present anger swarming up my throat. I gobbled more kava pills with one hand and switched off my music with the other. My mood didn't suit my favorite playlist anymore. This wasn't about desert life and hope and optimism. This was about shit I had no control over. My fucking parents. What the hell did they know about me and Javier, anyway? That was a very long time ago, and it wasn't as simple as a man and woman breaking up, she taking his car and money. This wasn't a Carrie Underwood song. This shit went fucking Anthrax for a while. It still kind of was.

Not many people had an ex that would probably shoot them in the head if they ever found them. And I meant that in the most literal sense.

As I was wondering if Javier would still bother looking for me after all these years, I pulled the car (okay, *his* car) up along one of the many trendy-looking cafés that peppered the street. I couldn't use any of my past references, but I knew my way around an espresso machine. I had a new plan, since my uncle speared my original one through the heart. I'd stick around here for a while, make enough money, and then head out on the road. No, I didn't know where I was going to stay after he kicked me off the date plantation, but I knew I'd figure something out. I always did.

I turned off the engine and let the heat build up inside for a few moments. It was just past one and my stomach was eating itself. I took in a few deep breaths through my nose and wondered if it were possible to overdose on kava. Technically, the root was a mild narcotic, but you could make anything beneficial in small doses. I missed the days when it took only a pill to curb my anger and anxiety. Now it took too much.

I grabbed my purse, a nice leather thing with tassels, and sashayed my way into the coffee shop, the door opening with the tinkle of a bell. I wasn't wearing a sundress like most of the women in the shop, but my jeans were clean, my boots were shiny, and my bright yellow tank top showed off my fading summer tan. I had brushed my hair in the car, smoothing it down to acceptable levels, and did a quick swipe of makeup over my lids. I wasn't anything flashy—I was just pleasant enough to sail under the radar.

Shivering a bit at the air-conditioning, I did a quick survey of the room. There was an older couple in the corner, relaxing in armchairs; the silver-haired woman with cat-eyed glasses was doing a crossword or Sudoku, and her husband was reading a book. Everyone else was pretty young. There were three teenage girls giggling in the corner over frozen blended coffees, wearing tube tops and shorts that made me envious. A smattering of college-aged kids were spread about, typing on their laptops, earbuds in their ears, while two businessmen were making awkward small talk over even smaller cups of espresso. Pretty standard stuff. Even John Mayer was playing over the speakers—but the new Mayer, after his years of exile on a ranch.

I went up to the cashier, a petite woman with a bright smile and skin that matched the smooth surface of the cappuccinos she was doling out with supernatural swiftness.

"Welcome to Currently Caffeinated," she said, and as if her smile couldn't get any bigger, it did. My lie-detecting skills told me she was 100 percent genuine. "What can I get for you?"

I tried to match her smile, teeth for teeth. "A medium soy latte, please. And a job application."

The girl's smile faltered slightly as she punched in the code on the register. "I'm sorry, ma'am. We aren't hiring at the moment. But the Christmas season will be here soon, and we'll be taking on more people then. Would you still like to fill out an application?"

How desperate did I want to look? Was I even going to be in Palm Valley next month? Was I even going to be in Palm Valley by the end of the week?

Still, I found myself nodding, with the smile frozen on my face. She passed me the paper and I gave her money, making sure to tip her extra.

"Your name?" she asked, her pen poised and ready on the cup.

"Ellie," I answered. To my own ears it sounded fake, but she just nodded and scribbled it down.

I walked down the bar and loitered inconspicuously near the counter while I looked over the form. I could easily forge my past references if I needed to. I had some friends spread out all over the country for just that kind of thing, and then when they called me in for an interview, I could show them how skilled I was.

Not that it was a crazy complicated skill, but operating an espresso machine during high traffic could be added to my repertoire along with card tricks and how to fire a Colt .45. But what was the point in getting a job here when I might as well get a job anywhere else in the country? Seattle was the birthplace of coffee in North America, and I'd never lived there yet.

I folded the application haphazardly and tried to stick it in the back pocket of my jeans, but I felt it fall out and flutter to the floor behind me. I turned around to see a man bend over and pick it up.

I saw the top of his head first, saw shaggy dark brown hair that curled down the nape of his neck. Then, as he rose, application in hand, I saw dark, arched brows over crystal-clear blue eyes. A septum ring that acted like an exclamation point at the end of his slim nose. A striking pair of lips: thin and curved on top, full and wide on the bottom. A few day's worth of stubble all over his chin and jaw. He looked like a male model, and I found my breath hitching as I took him in, from his nice height and all-too-firm build to the way he wore his cargo shorts and his aged Iggy Pop tee like a second skin. His arms were covered in tattoos, an intensely colorful mixture of skulls, animals, and campiness.

I finally breathed out when he tucked a strand of hair behind his ears. His ears kind of stuck out like Dumbo. This was good. This stranger had flaws. I couldn't stand perfect people.

Then he was handing me the application and smiling at me. And in that smile, the way it took a few seconds to reach his eyes, an expression that darkened momentarily before brightening, I felt a rush of déjà vu that nearly knocked me over.

I knew him. How did I know him? And how long had I been standing there staring at him like an idiot? I was usually a lot smoother than that.

"You dropped this," he said. He had an interesting voice, low but precise, like he could narrate Rosetta Stone DVDs. It pushed pleasure buttons along my spine.

I took the application from him, our fingers brushing against each other. I felt a spark, electricity.

No, literally.

"Ow," I said, as I snatched my hand and the application away from him.

He grinned sheepishly and shoved his hands in his pockets. "Sorry. I'm a good conductor."

I stared at him while blindly refolding the application. He continued, "Of electricity. You know, the sparks. I just shocked you. I'm not a train conductor or anything. Or like a music conductor. Although I do play guitar."

He was babbling, and if I didn't know any better, I'd say he was nervous. But that would beget the question of why the hell this hunk of man was nervous around me.

I wasn't ugly by any means. I had my mother's Estonian features, which meant high cheekbones, heart-shaped lips, and dark, hooded eyes. But my beauty was always more of a *Hey, I never actually realized how pretty you are*. If I was just standing in the corner of a room, your eyes would pass over me. I'd go unnoticed. And I liked that.

If I was walking, well, that would be another story.

"Ellie!" the barista announced in a surprisingly strong voice. Must have been all the coffee she drank.

I shot the man a quick smile, painfully aware that in the last minute, all I'd said to him was "ow," and plucked the steaming drink off the counter.

"I knew it," he said with a snap of his fingers, and I slowly turned around, bringing the cup to my lips and gauging how scalding it was.

"Knew what?" I asked. Hot. Coffee was way too hot.

He grinned at me as if he'd just solved a Rubik's Cube, and I felt myself get a weird flutter in my stomach. I knew I should have eaten more than beef jerky.

"You're Ellie Watt."

Oh fudgeknuckles.

I turned back around and slapped a lid on my cup with shaking hands.

He knew me. Hot tattoo dude knew me and I didn't know him. This wasn't good.

I turned back to face him and shot him my biggest smile.

"I have to go," I said. When in doubt, just go. My parents had taught me that, along with "Never underestimate your mark" and "Emotions don't win the game." It's too bad they were as hypocritical as I was.

I took a step to leave, my eyes newly focused on the door, but he reached out, grabbing my free arm. I flinched, expecting another spark to flow through me, but it was just his warm, strong hand.

"Wait," he said, lowering his voice and coming a step closer. He smelled peculiar. It wasn't bad—actually it was quite a sensual smell, but it was something I couldn't put my finger on. Earthy and industrial. Cinnamon and...ink?

I dared to meet his eyes. He was so close I could see the contact ring around his baby blues.

"Don't you remember me?" he asked. His eyes flashed between expectation and edginess. Like if I didn't remember who he was, he wouldn't be smiling for long.

Unfortunately, I had no idea who this guy was. And I felt like kicking myself for it. My luck usually had me running into assholes, not hot guys I wanted to lick from head to toe (though they often were one and the same).

He took his hand off of me and I relaxed. I tried to look as apologetic as possible. "I'm sorry, you'd think I'd remember someone like you but I don't. I have a bad memory—don't take it personally."

"Somehow I doubt that," he said under his breath. I eyed him quizzically. Was that to the bad memory remark (which wasn't true) or to the—

"Camden McQueen," he said quickly. The name ran along the length of my brain like rain on hardened soil before really sinking in.

I felt guilt before anything else.

His gaze narrowed on my face, still beautiful but dark. "Oh, so you do remember me."

The Camden McQueen I pulled up from my memory banks did not look like the tattooed and pierced sex on a stick I had standing before me. The Camden McQueen I remembered was tall, yes, but gawky. Awkward. Back when he was a teenager, his broad-shouldered build had gone to waste. That Camden had gross, long black hair down to his midback. He was a fan of dog collars and black lipstick and lace gloves with the fingers cut out. He wore black all the time. He always had mysterious bandages on his arms, something you'd see if he wasn't wearing his trademark long black trench coat. He wore that thing in the middle of the summer when seniors were dying from the heat. He loved music and art and spent long hours in the darkroom. Everyone called him the Dark Queen, and there were a few vicious rumors running around that he was gay, or into bestiality, and that he carried a gun to class. He was the most bullied, most tortured kid in the whole of Palm Valley High School.

"Hi," I said softly, trying to match up the Camden I had known to the Camden I saw now. "You look different."

His face relaxed and went back to looking all model-like. "So do you. Your hair..."

He reached forward and brushed a piece of hair away from my face. My body froze at his touch and my eyes widened.

"It's nice," he said, taking his hand away. "I always thought the long blond hair was a bit too Barbie on someone as...tough...as you."

"Is *tough* supposed to be a synonym for *bitch*?" I asked.

He laughed and that hadn't changed at all. It was

one of those laughs that made you believe the joke was always on him. "Well, I was going to say angry, but I suppose that's kind of redundant, isn't it? So what are you doing here? I haven't seen you since high school."

"Oh, just paying a visit to my uncle. Just passing through."

He raised his brow. "Just passing through and you're applying for jobs at a coffee shop?"

Right. That whole thing.

I shrugged and looked around the store with a stupid smile stretched on my lips. "It's nice here. I was surprised how much it's changed."

"Maybe you're the one who's changed?" he questioned. His eyes were still clear and bright, jovial enough, but I detected something off-putting in his tone. He was testing me. And he was right to do it. We hadn't exactly ended on good terms.

I punched his arm lightly with my free hand. So, so awkward. "You're the one who's changed, Camden. Wow." I almost said *What happened to you?* but thought that was a bit patronizing. "What, uh, what's new?"

He looked behind him at an empty table near the giggling tube-top girls who were now tight-lipped tube-top girls. They had been watching him with googly eyes and quickly averted them as soon as he looked their way.

Now, with his face coming back to mine, he looked hopeful. That was the look I recognized.

"Do you have to be somewhere? Do you want to catch up over some coffee?" he asked.

I almost said no. I almost told him I actually did have somewhere to be, even though I had nowhere to go and would just end up driving aimlessly for hours. But he smiled, and the combination of those white teeth, the septum ring, and that messy hair made my heart beat against my chest, shrugging off the pills like a heavy coat.

So I said yes.

Then

The girl had somehow survived her first week of high school, though as she walked down the dust-heavy road that led to her uncle's house, she felt that was as triumphant as surviving military boot camp. Already she'd earned the nicknames Sir-Limps-A-Lot (which didn't make much sense considering her gender), the Gimp, and Crippled Cow. The cow part, of course, was for the fact that she'd gained a bit of weight since the accident. Something that was somewhat inevitable when you combined the burgeoning hormones of a thirteen-year-old and her limited ability.

To add insult to her injury, her uncle hadn't been able to pick her up from school that Friday. To her, there was nothing as humiliating as walking along the side of a road. People had no choice but to stare at her as she went past, and she could almost hear what they were all thinking: *I wonder what happened to her. Why does she walk so funny? Why is she wearing jeans when it's one hundred degrees outside?* She could see their curious stares as they drove past, see them forming the judgments in their heads.

She kept her head down as she walked, her eyes on the hot, rough pavement of the shoulder. Her pack began to pull on her back, weighed down with new books, and she wiped her sweaty palms on her jeans. A red car roared past, honking as it went, but she didn't give them the satisfaction of looking up.

"Hey, Ellie!" a voice called out from behind her. She stopped and turned, her blond hair swirling around her face.

It was Camden McQueen, her only friend in this godforsaken town. She smiled as he trotted up to her, his figure tall and dark against the stark desert landscape.

"Can I walk you home?" he asked, his voice quietly hopeful against the sound of the cars. Even though he looked deeply disturbed with his long black hair, ghost-white face, thick glasses, and lips painted the color of tar, he was grinning at her, causing dimples to pop out on his gaunt cheeks. Looking contradictory was his game.

"If you want," she said, sounding as blasé as possible. The truth was, she was thrilled. Not that she liked Camden in that way—after all, he was her only friend and she wanted to keep it like that—but when he wasn't in the deep boughs of manic depression, she enjoyed his company. She also felt like people never stared as much at her when she was with someone else, especially someone like Camden. He was the only person who had a worse week than she did.

"So how was your day?" he asked as they walked side by side.

"Oh you know, Vicky Besset told everyone in history class that I walk funny because I used to weigh three hundred pounds and broke my ankles. Now I hear 'Crippled Cow' everywhere I go." The girl said all this as breezily as possible, trying hard to hide the shame and embarrassment that was ripping her apart. It was better to laugh than cry, even though only the latter would be honest.

"Ah, Vicky. The other day she told the teacher that I had a gun in my backpack. She's a special little bitch." And like the girl, he had that same tone in his voice, the one that refused to let the other know how badly these things were tearing them apart.

"She's probably afraid of you," the girl told him.

He looked straight ahead at the distant mountain, his expression darkening like a shadow. "She has a right to be afraid of me. Girls like that never get the karma they deserve. If she's not careful, I'll deliver my own karma."

The girl fell silent, her mouth closing into a hard line. She'd known Camden for only a month, but during that time she was surprised at the things he'd thought and said. She had always assumed she was the only one with such righteous anger, but she was very, very wrong.

She made a mental note to never cross Camden McQueen.

Now

Talking to Camden felt surprisingly easy. I never had a problem getting along with people when I needed to, but I was sure I'd feel vibes of resentment coming off of Camden as he sipped his matcha tea and I gulped down my coffee. But I couldn't detect anything. He was open and relaxed, his hands coming dangerously close to mine each time he lowered the cup of tea on the table. I felt hyperaware of him and his body, brought on by my own guilt and memories, I'm sure.

"Are you all right?" he asked. He placed his hand on mine—no sparks—and my eyes flew up from the empty coffee cup where I'd apparently been hypnotized by the sediment at the bottom.

"Sorry," I said sweetly. "I'm just…"

"Overwhelmed?"

"That must be it."

"The memories…" He trailed off. His hand was still on mine. I was conscious—too conscious—of the weight of it. What it meant. Whose hand it was. My hand was going to start twitching at any moment.

"So," he said, removing it and wiping at his chin. He leaned back in his chair. "So then I became a tattoo artist."

I realized I had been totally spacing out for most of our conversation. That wasn't like me at all. Then again, he was a guy from high school, not a mark.

"Really?" I asked, and my eyes immediately went to his tattoos. Upon closer inspection I found a method in the madness of shapes and colors. Scorpions, skulls, snakes, wings, and pin-up girls all met one another on blue ocean waves. Tiny inscriptions ran throughout.

"I take it you never heard of my tat business?"

"Should I have?"

He nodded at my arm where I had a band of music notes inked all around. "Where did you get that?"

"Some parlor in Mississippi," I said, then quickly clamped my mouth shut.

But he didn't ask me why I went back to the state I

lived in before I moved here. Instead he said, "It sounds familiar. The tune."

"Did you just hum it in your head?"

He beamed at me, looking proud over impressing me and lazy at the same time. If he could have leaned any farther back in his chair, he'd be on the ground. "I told you, I play guitar. What song is it?"

"It's nothing," I told him. "Anyway, so you're a tattoo artist. I'm guessing you got pretty big."

"Big enough." He shrugged with false modesty. "I was one of the top artists in LA. I was even on *LA Ink*. Ever watch that show?"

"I don't have cable."

He nodded, as if he could deduce something about me from that. "Well, you weren't missing anything. You know I'm going to keep humming that tune and eventually I'll figure out the song. Maybe then you'll tell me the meaning."

I frowned at him. "I think you overestimate your skills of persuasion."

"I got you to sit down and have coffee with me when you were ready to bolt out the door."

Yes, well, it helps that you're hot, I thought. "So what are you doing here if your business is in LA? Visiting the 'rents?"

From the way his eyes shifted—changed—I could have sworn a cloud passed over the sun, putting the whole shop in shadow. But it was only in his eyes, and it disappeared as soon as he smiled.

"No. Not my parents. Though they still live here. Dad's still the sheriff, you know."

How could I forget? He ran my parents out of town.

"I actually have my business here. I own a tattoo shop. Sins & Needles," he said. "It's just coming into town from the east. Maybe you saw it? It's in an old house with replicas of Bela Lugosi and Swamp Thing on the porch."

Charming.

"My shop's downstairs, I live upstairs."

"And you make enough to live on?" Despite the proximity to LA and the facelift, Palm Valley still wasn't a place for culture—or subculture, as it were.

His smile went from charming to shit-eating. "I sure do. You'd be surprised how much money a tattoo shop can rake in."

I would have found his cockiness to be off-putting, but the truth was I knew nothing about tattoo parlors. All the ones I'd been to looked half dead, with an artist who looked like he'd been reduced to piercing young girls' ears in order to keep the lights on.

He pulled his phone out of his pocket and glanced at it. "In fact, I have an appointment in twenty minutes. Want to come see me in action?"

Normally, the thought of watching someone get jabbed with an inky needle would have turned me off, but there was something so earnest and open about his handsome face that I found myself nodding. There was also the whole guilt thing over how horrible I was to him in high school. And, let's be honest here, I was curious to see how successful this guy was.

In my business, you had to stick to successful people like glue.

CHAPTER THREE

TWENTY MINUTES LATER, I was pulling up Jose in front of a quirky, two-story house, Camden McQueen at my side. The drive was short, and he alternated between pointing out what had changed since I left town and cooing over the car.

"How much was it, if you don't mind my asking?" he said as the wheels crunched to a stop over loose sand.

A smile tugged at my lips as I took the keys out of the ignition. "I wouldn't know. I borrowed it."

He opened the door and paused, giving me a suspicious look. "Borrowed it like you used to borrow the teachers' books before a test?"

I matched his suspicious look, wondering how much Camden knew about what I did. After my parents became fugitives, everyone in Palm Valley knew they were con artists. People used to point at me and whisper, and I figured it was either over my injury (which was usually the case) or they were placing bets on whether I was in on the con. I hadn't been, not that time. That didn't stop me from pulling a few tricks in high school, but they were just minor things. I'd never gotten caught—teachers just looked the other way when they saw me. I think it was because they felt sorry for me, and they were right to.

"I always gave them back," I told him, and got out of the car. The sun had somehow gotten hotter. On days like this, I hated that I couldn't wear shorts.

He was staring at me, his hand shielded over his eyes. I'd forgotten how much he used to stare. Now it was a bit easier to take since I didn't think he was going to pull the rug out from under me, but it was still unnerving.

I turned my attention back to the house. It was clap-board and a bright yellow with cobalt-blue accents. There really were life-size replicas of Dracula and Swamp Thing on the porch as well as an intricate wooden sign that said Sins & Needles. The garden was of your standard rock, brush, and cacti variety, something that lazy people like myself would fall back on. It was a hell of a lot cheaper than maintaining a lawn in the desert.

"Like what you see?" he asked, his gaze following mine. "The house was built in the 1950s. I think it used to be at the air base, then they moved it over here when the town got started up. It even has a bombproof bunker."

"Seriously?"

He nodded. "Well, Audrey will be here soon."

I guessed she was his client. I followed him up the path, stepping only on the stones as if the ground was lava, and had a nice view as we climbed the creaking steps to the porch. Camden sure had one hell of an ass. That was something I thought I'd never say.

He unlocked the door and flipped over the Open sign

as we stepped in. The place was kitschy as anything. It was like walking into Graceland if it were owned by John Waters. The walls were an obnoxious green, the suede couch was orange, and the coffee table was pink and made out of alligator skins. I had to do a double take. A 1930s scuba-diving suit hung in the corner by a papier-mâché Speed Racer. There was a stack of shiny guitars underneath a flatscreen TV that was showing *Who Framed Roger Rabbit* with Asian subtitles.

But for all the visual diarrhea, I couldn't help but add up the dollar value of the place. He wasn't kidding when he said he brought in the dough. As ugly and campy as half the stuff was, they'd be worth a pretty penny to purchase.

"Can I get you a beer?" he asked. There was a small, retro fridge beside his tattoo chair, and when he opened it, it glowed glass green from all the Heineken.

"Please," I told him. Probably wasn't the best idea since my stomach was still growling and I was strangely nervous, but I could never pass up a free cold one.

He nodded at the couch. "Why don't you take a seat? Here." He reached over and handed me a stack of binders. "That's all my art in there. You know, in case you have a change of heart and let me ink you." His eyes twinkled mischievously.

"I don't recall you giving me the chance to turn that idea down," I said wryly, taking them from him and sitting down on the couch. For all the orange suede, it was really comfortable. While he busied himself getting ready for the client, I flipped through the pages.

His art was beautiful. From soaring owls to photograph-quality portraits and strange symbols, Camden looked like he could do anything. All of his work had a certain shadow, a certain dark quality about it that instantly reminded me of art class. Back when he and I were friends, back when we'd sit next to each other in Mrs. Slevin's class, he'd doodle page after page of his sketchbook with these highly detailed and intricate drawings, all with a skinny black pen. One day I let him draw all over my arm, from my knuckles all the way to my shoulder before Mrs. Slevin yelled at him, throwing around big words like "ink poisoning." I had worn those drawings with a perverse sense of pride like the freak I was.

I peered up from the pages and watched him. He was sitting in his chair, prepping his station, brows furrowed and bright eyes in clear concentration. The package may have changed, but his eyes were still the same. Even now they were as engaged and coaxing as ever, like he was trying to get the ink to tell him its secrets.

"So what do you do for work, Ellie?" he asked without meeting my eyes. He knew I was staring at him.

"I work odd jobs," I said, and went back to flipping through the book.

"You never went to college?"

"Not unless you count the School of Hard Knocks."

"Still funny, I see."

"You gotta be something."

I felt him pause, a heaviness at my back. The hairs on my neck felt like they were being tugged. I was reminded of the electric shock he gave me and I slowly turned my head. He was staring right at me, his expression unreadable. Something strange passed between us, but it felt foreign to me and I didn't know what to make of it.

Finally he said, "Audrey's here."

I turned in time to see the door opening and a girl in her early twenties enter, doing her best Dita Von Teese impression with black retro waves and polka-dot dress. Her arms were covered in tats, a full sleeve on her left and half of one on her right. It was just an outline of cherry blossoms, the color missing.

"Hi, Camden," she gushed. She trotted over to him in her minxy heels, pausing only to give me a dirty look. I was reminded of the way I must have appeared when I first saw him, before I learned who he was to me.

"Audrey, babe," he said, and got up out of his seat. He embraced her good-naturedly and patted the chair. "Take a seat. Oh, this is Ellie, by the way. She's going to watch me color you up, if you don't mind of course."

She gave him a half smile that turned fully fake when she looked at me. For Christ's sake, she even had one of those fake beauty marks on her face. "No, I don't mind. She your girlfriend, Camden?"

I almost snickered but caught myself just in time.

"No, she's an old friend, just visiting," he supplied smoothly. "Or are you staying in Palm Valley now, Ellie? I can't remember."

"Um, just passing through," I said, getting to my feet. I felt that itch to get out of there. Why was I even in his tattoo studio to begin with? One minute I was at the coffee shop and suddenly I was here, hanging around someone I didn't know. I mean, it felt like I knew him, but not really. We weren't the people we were when we were teenagers. God, I hoped we weren't those people.

Then I realized why I was really there. What my subconscious was working away on. I found my eyes resting on the cash register.

He started dabbing cleaning solution on Audrey's arm and noticed my wayward eyes. I tried to cover it up, but he just held my eyes and said to Audrey, "Ellie is actually looking for work. Do you know of any openings at the boutique?"

Audrey shook her head politely. "We're full up."

"That's too bad," he said. "Are you paying with cash or credit today?"

"Oh, cash," she said, and he waited while she fished out a wad of bills from her wallet. It looked to be at least $200. I supposed that was enough to get by on if you had one customer a day, but it would barely pay your bills, let alone all the cool stuff in the place.

"Thank you," he told her, rolling over in his chair to the till and punching in a few numbers. "I'll get you a receipt after."

The register opened with a loud chime, and my jaw unhinged. It was loaded with cash. And I mean loaded to the brim. There's no way the shop could bring in that much. He must keep it for show or something, though I couldn't fathom why. Maybe if he was the lovestruck boy he was back in the day, I could say he was trying to impress me, but he didn't even know I'd be around.

I must have been staring at him with a stupid look on my face because he shot me a coy glance that said *I told you so*.

All right, fine. So he brought in a lot of money. Now that the shock had worn off that the geeky, emo teenager had done well for himself, I started wondering exactly how much money he was bringing in.

And if he'd miss it if any of it disappeared.

The buzzing of the needle snapped me out of my musings. It was crazy, anyway. I told myself I was going legit and I needed to stick to it. More than that, I'd done enough to the poor man all those years ago. On the other hand, he didn't seem to be any worse for wear. He looked like a hot, successful lady-killer. Maybe the past didn't matter if you were making a killing in the present. Living well was the best revenge, wasn't it?

And just like that, I let all the guilt over what I had done to him go. Javier once told me I wore my guilt like a badge of honor, because it meant someone else was suffering the same as I was, or worse. But it was obvious that Camden wasn't suffering anymore. And I was.

"Are you leaving, Ellie?" Camden asked me. I looked over to him, his eyes on the needle as it buzzed along Audrey's arm. She was watching me expectantly, her face a little pale and shiny. Pain sweats.

I had somehow moved closer to the door and now I was standing in the middle of the Technicolor store like I was caught in limbo. I could go. I could go and leave Palm Valley and try to find a new life somewhere else. But I was down to my last $200. I couldn't afford a place to stay for very long or food to eat if I were to leave Uncle Jim. I needed a job. I needed money.

When I couldn't find a job, I was known to create my own.

I realized they were still staring at me, waiting for my response. The needle's buzz was hypnotizing me into a druglike state. Christ, I really needed to eat something.

"I...uh..."

You need to go, I yelled at myself in my head. *You need to walk out that door, tell him it was nice seeing him again, wish him the best of luck, and disappear. You need to go. Go before you do something stupid. Go before this gets complicated.*

"I'm playing a show tonight in Palm Springs," Camden said while taking the gun off Audrey and peering at it. "How about I pick you up at six?"

I blinked. "Sorry, what? You're playing a show?"

I looked at Audrey, who was nearly pouting at our exchange. Was Camden asking me out on a date? The idea was equal parts thrilling and nerve-racking.

"Yes. I told you, I'm a guitarist. It's a Cramps cover band called Kettle Black."

Well, *that* was intriguing.

"Do you remember where my uncle lives?"

"I haven't forgotten," he said, and flashed me that smile of his. I swear Audrey melted into a puddle at his feet. "So I'll pick you up at six."

Before I knew what I was doing, I was nodding and saying, "Yes, see you then."

Then I was out on his porch and making my way to Jose in a daze. It was too hot outside, the sun was too bright, and I felt totally off balance. I opened the car door and let the stale blast of hot air flow out. While I waited for the interior to cool, I stared at the bright shop and wondered what the hell was wrong with me.

I didn't have many friends. Friends are dangerous liabilities when you're a grifter. They're dangerous liabilities, period. I never really had them as a child. In high school, there was Camden, then the fake friends I traded him in for. After I graduated, I decided to do the only thing I knew how and that was grifting. The word rhymes with *drifting* for a reason. I floated like a dead leaf from state to state, and until I met Javier, my ties to people were superficial at best. That's not to say I didn't have some buddies—usually socially unsavory types—I could call up and chat with. I did. I got by. But I never had anyone I could depend on. And aside from my uncle, I never had anyone who knew me back when I was "innocent."

And so there I was, standing outside the house of a guy who knew me when I was still redeemable. Someone who had known me and my parents. Knew exactly what I was and where I came from. Someone who was asking me out on a date to see his show. And I was thinking two things: one, I couldn't afford to befriend anyone, let alone someone I wouldn't mind seeing naked; and two, how much cash could I take from him before I hated myself?

* * *

It was almost six o' clock, and Uncle Jim's kitchen was succumbing to monochrome as the sun lowered itself behind the San Jacinto Mountains. He was leaning against the dishwasher, arms folded across his aging flannel shirt, and eyeing me as I applied my makeup.

I glanced at him over my compact. "What?"

He shrugged. "What nothing. I thought you said this wasn't a date."

I brushed on a few coats of mascara, nearly rolling my eyes into the wand. "It's not a date. It's just old friends connecting. And I like to look nice for old friends, you got that? Here, have some of my bourbon, it'll take the edge off."

I nudged the unlabeled bottle toward him, the mahogany liquid sloshing around inside. He looked at it for a few seconds before sighing and bringing a glass out of the cupboard. He'd been anxious ever since I walked back in his door. After I told him I was going to see a show with the sheriff's son, it only doubled.

He poured himself a glass, took a sip, and nearly spat it out. He winced overdramatically. "Jesus, Ellie, you making moonshine over here?"

I couldn't help but smile. "A friend from Kentucky brews his own. If you have a few shots, you'll forget all your problems."

He pushed the glass over to me, shaking his head. "Yeah, well, I hope that's not what you're trying to do."

My compact closed with a satisfying click. "You think I'm trying to forget my problems?"

"Either that or create new ones. Really, Ellie..." He wiped his mouth, licking his lips with distaste, and turned to the window and the dying light that was settling over the groves.

"Well, I'm certainly not creating any problems with Camden McQueen," I told him, reaching over for his still-full glass. I swirled the bourbon around, watching it, mesmerized. "I mean, he's the son of the town's law enforcement—that doesn't exactly invite trouble."

He grunted in response, not buying it. The truth is, I was looking for trouble tonight. I was looking for someone in particular, a local lackey, a douchebag, a deadbeat criminal. I was looking for someone people would suspect if Sins & Needles were to ever be robbed. I was looking for a way out of the past.

A honk blasted from outside. My heart jumped in my chest, making me realize I was just as on edge as Uncle Jim was. I slammed back the rest of the drink, my throat burning like I was drinking antiseptic, and hopped off the bar stool.

"Have fun," he said without turning his head.

I missed the days when I could kiss my uncle on his cheek and make him smile. But it seemed like the days of smiling had long since passed.

I snatched up my purse and shrugged a worn leather jacket over my shoulders as I made my way out the door and down the driveway. Camden was waiting in a dark, doorless Jeep, its exhaust rising high in the rapidly cooling air. Crickets chirped, and I smiled into the headlights as I made my way around the front of the vehicle.

"Nice ride," I told him, and eased myself up onto the passenger seat.

"Nice date," he answered back smoothly, looking me up and down with a broad grin. I was glad it was dark outside and he couldn't see the flush on my cheeks. Not only at the word *date*, which I had been so certain it wasn't, but the petty fact that he liked how I looked. I was pretty much wearing the same thing as earlier, the same thing I always wore—boots and jeans—but had a flirty white top that showed off a small slice of cleavage. Okay, so maybe I dolled myself up more than I should have for a so-called friend. Damn my uncle for being right.

Naturally, Camden didn't look too shabby himself. He was wearing black pants that were flatteringly tight in the crotch area, badass boots, and a Battlestar Galactica tee that would have looked geeky on anyone else but only made his wide chest and thick biceps more noticeable. Most surprising of all were the glasses he was wearing. It was the only thing that reminded me of the Camden I used to know, even though the glasses now were black rimmed in that hipsterish way.

"Glasses?" I asked. "Looks good."

He grinned and gunned the Jeep in the dark. We roared out of the cul-de-sac, the smell of fresh night air and sagebrush filling my nose.

"I only wear these for shows," he admitted in a conspiratorial voice that made me lean in close to him. "A little thing I discovered as I got older: turns out women love men in glasses. Sure would have come in handy in high school."

I smiled as diplomatically as possible. "Well, girls are pretty stupid when you're in high school. They wouldn't know a good man if they saw one."

If I hadn't been staring at him so intently as we drove under the garish streetlights, I wouldn't have caught the rather malevolent look that clouded his brow like a heavy storm cloud. And like so many of his moods, it passed in an instant, leaving only a pained tightening of the lips behind.

He reached forward and flipped on the radio, blasting us both into silence.

CHAPTER FOUR

Then

The girl and the boy lay beside each other on his trampoline, staring up at the night sky that looked like a sheet of ink with tiny jewels affixed to it. The trampoline wasn't good for jumping anymore, thanks to the hole in the corner that had gone unpatched since Camden broke it years ago, but it was the perfect spot for them to spend the warm summer evenings.

There was one thing that happened that night that made it different from all the other nights they spent on it. That night, Camden had reached for the girl's hand and the girl had let him hold it. That night, in the sweet June air, the girl fell victim to her hormones. She fell to the hopes that maybe she could love this strange beast, even though she was more of a monster than he was. She believed that maybe the affection of the weirdest boy in school—her friend—was better than no affection at all.

But nothing more than hand holding had happened

yet between them. They just lay side by side, staring up at the stars and listening to Soundgarden's "The Day I Tried to Live" on his portable speakers, watching for satellites and enjoying that feeling that they, in their fourteen-year-old tragedies, were the center of the universe. His hand gripped hers, and despite how sweaty her palms felt, she didn't take it away.

She was about to remark, perhaps because it was true or perhaps because his hand was making her nervous, that Chris Cornell sang an awful lot about the sun, when they heard the sound of the back door being flung open. They both tensed up, their hands jerking back to themselves on some untested reflex.

"Camden!" his father bellowed from the door. They sat up, ramrod straight, and twisted around to face the house. His large, formidable silhouette was in the doorway. In that blackness, the girl couldn't see eyes to judge her or features to fear. But she knew that Camden feared him, and that was enough for her.

"What are you doing out there?" he continued to yell.

"We're just laying here," Camden answered anxiously.

"Are you with that Watt kid again? The girl?"

The girl and Camden exchanged a quick look. She'd been over to Camden's house a few times but they usually hid in his room where they could talk, listen to music, and be themselves. His younger half sisters loved annoying him, and his stepmother was so drugged up on medications that she couldn't control them.

"Her name's Ellie!" Camden shouted back. The girl felt a shawl of pride wrap around her, loving his protectiveness.

There was a pause and she could see the man, Palm Valley's sheriff, hesitate in the doorway.

"Well, I guess I should be happy you're not the faggot I thought you were," Camden's father spat out before going back in the house and slamming the door behind him.

The girl's face immediately went red over the father's offensive choice of words. She swallowed hard and looked at Camden. His pale face looked even whiter in the darkness and his blue eyes looked down at his hands.

"Does your father think you're gay?" she asked him.

"Who doesn't?" he said with a laugh, but kept his eyes away from hers. "You forget my nickname is the Dark Queen. If I'm not threatening to blow up the school, then I'm trying to rape young boys."

The girl grimaced, feeling sorry for him. "Even if you were gay—"

"I'm not," he said quickly.

She smiled softly. "I know. But even if you were, that's a terrible way for your dad to act toward you."

He sighed and lay back down on the trampoline. The moonlight glared in his thick glasses. "Yeah, well, that's my dad."

The girl started running her hands over the trampoline's gritty surface. "Have you ever thought about, you know, not dressing the way you do?"

She could hear his breath catch in his throat and knew she'd struck a chord.

"What's wrong with the way I dress?"

"Well, nothing, to me. But maybe if you didn't look so scary and wear makeup, the other kids wouldn't make fun of you."

"But then I wouldn't be who I am. I don't want to hide myself. I'm not ashamed of being Camden McQueen. Are you ashamed of being Ellie Watt?"

"Yes," she said softly.

He sat up and leaned in close to her, his eyes searching her face. "You're serious?"

She frowned. "Of course I am. You have a choice, Camden. You can start acting normal and not like a freak and you'll be fine. I can't hide who I am, even if I wanted to, even though I'm trying to. I can't change the way I walk and I can't get rid of the scars on my leg."

Camden continued looking at her with fervent intensity. It started to make her a little bit uncomfortable and she wiped her hands on her jeans. "You've never shown me your scars."

The girl swallowed hard. "And I'm not about to."

"Can it be so bad?" he whispered. "How can someone as pretty as you have anything that would make her less?"

She glossed over the fact that he had called her pretty. "It can. I'd give anything to be normal, to live a normal life, to be like everyone else."

"Would you really? Give everything just to fit in?" he asked, disbelieving.

She nodded. She would. She prayed for it every night as she lay in her bed, the tears leaking out from the corners of her tired eyes. She would do anything, give everything, just to be equal with everyone else. And if she was lucky, maybe she'd get to rise above them, too. Maybe she'd be able to look down on them one day the way that they looked down on her.

"If I believed in a god, I'd say you should be proud

of the way he made you. You're different, Ellie. Your scars, your injury, they make you who you are. Personally, I wouldn't have it any other way."

Yet the girl could. But before she could dwell on it anymore, Camden moved in closer, until his black shirt was brushed up against her. She froze from his closeness and still couldn't move as she felt his long, cold hands on her face, tilting her chin toward him.

She'd never been kissed before, but she knew what was coming. It both excited and terrified her. She didn't like Camden in that way, and yet she was curious to see if that could change.

She closed her eyes as his lips met hers, surprisingly soft. She was glad he wasn't wearing his black lipstick and almost laughed at the image of black lipstick marks on her face. Now that would confuse his father.

The kiss was gentle and brief, and as Camden pulled back and she opened her eyes, she saw nothing but sadness in his. Perhaps he could already tell that she was going to ruin him.

Now

By the time Camden had pulled the Jeep off the highway and down Palm Canyon Drive, he'd grown out of his mood and was back to being chatty.

"Ever heard of Guano Padano?" he asked me, reaching for his iPod. We bounced along the road, the sky black and star-strewn except near the mountain peaks, where it glowed periwinkle blue.

"What is that, bat shit?" I asked. I leaned in closer to

him as the constant wind swept loose sand off the desert and flung it at the Jeep, coating my hair like styling putty.

He smiled and my heart did a weird skip in my chest. It made me smile back at him, grinning like an idiot, despite the gritty hair flying into my face.

"It's a band," he said. "I remember you being into all sorts of music when you were younger."

"Oh," I said, feeling momentarily stupid. I wasn't very hip with new music, and though I was a big music junkie, I stuck to the stuff I knew and liked. "No, never heard of them. What do they sound like?"

"Spaghetti western rock," he said, and pressed a button. The sounds of slow drumbeats, violins, and a whistling tune worthy of a Sergio Leone film came out of the speakers, enveloping us before disappearing into the night air. It was cinematic and enchanting and right up my alley.

"Sounds like Calexico," I told him, feeling excited about a new musical discovery. "One of my favorites."

He nodded. "They're from Italy. I think the dude from Calexico was involved with the band or something. Anyway, I'd love to e-mail you the tracks. I think you'll like them a lot. They kind of remind me of you."

I frowned, my lips caught in a wary smile. "Reminds you of me?"

He shrugged and changed lanes to get ahead of an old Cadillac. "It's rough and sweet at the same time."

I let out a small laugh and tucked my gritty hair behind my ears. "I get the rough part, not the sweet one, though."

"I see you're still not giving yourself enough credit," he noted with faint amusement. "Fair enough."

I thought about that and sat back. After the way

things had ended between us all those years ago, the last thing he should have thought I was was sweet. Besides, I wasn't sweet. I was planning to scam the poor bastard, which was something I kept on forgetting the longer I rode beside him. Funny how a nice ass, firm pecs, and a great smile could thwart a woman's best plans.

But that's what I got for picking a mark that I knew, a mark I was starting to like. I needed to keep my vagina out of the question and focus on what was really important: money.

We pulled into the small parking lot at the back of a bar called the Coppertank. A few musicians were in the midst of unloading under the orange streetlamp, their small cars packed to the brim with equipment.

"Did you need me to be your roadie?" I asked him, but he only smiled and brought his guitar case and pedals out from the back. As he lifted them out, clear above his head, his shirt rose up and I spied a distinct six-pack with a thin treasure trail leading down to the waistband of his boxer briefs.

I turned away before he could catch me gawking at him and ignored the irony that I'd been staring googly-eyed at him when he used to do the same to me.

Not that I didn't catch him checking me out from time to time. I particularly felt his eyes on my ass as we made our way through the back and into the dark and surprisingly smoky club. Even though California was strict about smoking inside, the patrons of the Coppertank didn't seem to care. And as I did a quick once-over of the place, I could see why. They were a ragtag bunch comprised of goths, punks, rockabillies, and gearheads—and judging by the way they were drunk at seven in the evening and talking trash to one another, it was obvious that this was a bar where the customers called the shots.

That made my plan a lot easier.

"Can I buy you a drink?" he asked me after he placed his equipment in the back room.

"Sure you can," I told him, and I followed him to the bartender. Camden gave him a nod, which signaled the guy to make him what I guessed was "the usual."

I leaned toward Camden, tilting my chin down coquettishly. "Do you play here often?"

"As often as I can." He responded by leaning in closer, his bare arm brushing against mine. There were no sparks, but I did feel a few tingles that shot up along my arm and pooled between my legs. I clamped them shut and tried to ignore it.

"Where's the rest of your band?"

"They probably won't be here till nine or something. We don't go on till eleven."

I raised my brows at him as the bartender pushed two glasses of what looked like Coke toward us. "Eleven?"

He looked a bit sheepish, which was adorable with his glasses. "Yeah, we usually play after the smaller bands finish. I just wanted some alone time with you before the show, that's all. You know, for old time's sake."

He placed a glass in my hand and nodded at it. "It's got booze in there, don't worry. I'm not that much of a saint."

"I never doubted you for a second," I told him slyly, and sniffed the drink. It was strong, fizzy, and fruity. I took a sip.

"Bourbon and Cherry Coke with a splash of lime," he said.

It was good stuff, and I wondered how he knew I liked bourbon, though I probably reeked of the moonshine when I got in the car.

"Want to go get a booth?" he asked. Before I could say yes, he grabbed my hand and led me across the bar toward the red leather booths that lined the side of the stage. I couldn't help but notice the faces of the women as we walked past them. They all needed bibs from the amount of drool that was coming out of their mouths, and I felt a tiny prick of pride that I was being seen with him.

I also couldn't help but notice how firmly he was holding my hand, how warm and strong his grip was. I was met with a rush of cold separation when he finally had to let go once we reached the table.

I scooched in along the squeaky seats and settled back against the shiny cushions that had seen better days. Camden sat beside me, our legs touched, and we had a view over the whole bar. It was a great place to scope out the joint, though his proximity was distracting.

It was always best to steer any potential conversations away from me, so I got the ball rolling by asking him about life in Los Angeles and if he preferred it to Palm Valley.

"I did." He nodded thoughtfully, his full lips wrapped around the straw of his drink. "I loved the beaches and the weather…warm enough in winter, cool enough in summer. I loved the culture, the bars, the shows, even the people when they weren't being righteous assholes."

"So why'd you move?"

His eyes narrowed briefly. "It's a long story. A... complicated story."

"Those are my favorite types of stories," I said, encouragingly.

"In a nutshell, it was cheaper and more advantageous for me to open up my shop here."

I leaned in close and coaxed him with my eyes, trying not to inhale too much of his intoxicating scent.

He looked up to the ceiling. "And I needed to start over. Isn't that why you came back?"

I looked at him quizzically. "What makes you think I'm trying to start over?"

"Isn't that why people return to their past?"

Our eyes were locked together, each of us trying to suss the other out and poke around for the hidden meanings.

"So, then why were you trying to start over?" I asked, ignoring his insinuation.

He licked his lips and slowly twirled his glass around in his hands. I had to stop thinking about his hands, the heavy silver ring on his right thumb, the freckles that dusted over his knuckles. It was like I suddenly had a fetish.

"I went through a bad divorce. I couldn't be in the same city as her anymore."

I didn't know why I found it surprising that he had been married—why wouldn't he have been? Even though we were only twenty-six, he was too handsome not to have been snatched up.

"Oh," I said, unsure of what else to say. "I'm sorry."

"Yeah, well, so am I." He turned his attention to

the stage, where a disheveled band, all its members in skinny jeans, was setting up. "To make things even more complicated, we have a son together."

Okay, now that was surprising. He had a son? I felt a weird emotion slink past me. Disappointment? Jealousy? I couldn't pick it out, except that it was negative.

"How old is he?" I asked.

"Three and a quarter," he said with a smile. "His name is Ben."

"I like that name."

His eyes flushed with pride and his smile broadened. "Thanks. She's got full custody, and she seems to still hate my guts for whatever reason, so I don't see him as much as I would like to. But at least I send more than enough child support each month. I write him letters, too. She can't say I'm a deadbeat dad."

A wave of shame washed over my spine at the mention of child support. I pretended it wasn't there.

"Well, look at you, Camden McQueen. You're divorced and have a child. I think you've reached adulthood." I raised my glass in the air. "I'd say that deserves a toast."

He tipped his head to me and we clinked our glasses. After we nearly downed them, he slapped the table with his palms and said, "You want to see him?"

"Who? Your son?"

He moved over and brought his knee up on the bench. He rolled up his pant leg until I saw the smiling face of a beautiful boy etched permanently on his calf in black ink. It was an extremely lifelike tattoo, with expressive eyes and intricate shading.

"Did you do that?" I asked incredulously.

He nodded.

"Upside down like that?"

He rolled the pant leg back down and resumed sitting normally. "I just worked from the picture upside down." As if that was so easy.

"Well, you're amazing," I told him. I know I was gushing a bit, but I couldn't help it. I couldn't wrap my head around how talented my old friend was, how anyone that I knew could go on to make such beautiful art. Everyone I knew tended to be as shifty as I was.

After we had breached the seemingly harder topic in Camden's life, the rest of our conversation was a breeze. In fact, we were so engrossed with each other, talking about our favorite music and travel spots, that we didn't see his band until they were standing in front of us.

"Hey, man," a guy said from the head of the table.

We looked up, and in one smooth move, Camden slipped his arm around my shoulder and squeezed me closer to him. I knew what that said: *She's mine, buddies. Back off.*

I didn't know how I felt about that. Part of me wanted him to like me; after all, I needed to get close to him to at least get inside his shop and house again to figure out how I was going to pull off the robbery. The other part of me—the moral one—didn't want him to fall too hard. I didn't want to break his heart again. And I guess there was a third part: one that wanted him to like me because I was starting to like him. One that loved the fact that he put his arm around me in a possessive way.

Oh boy.

"Guys, this is Ellie," Camden said, nodding at me.

I gave them a flirtatious smile while checking them out. The one who had spoken was a beanpole-shaped man-boy with shoulder-length red hair and a '70s mustache that looked ridiculously out of place on his baby face. The second guy was broad shouldered and stocky with a toothy grin, paint-splattered jeans, and a gray wifebeater that showed off his tats. The third, his black hair smoothed into a tight ponytail, was wearing sunglasses and a long black leather jacket that coated his thin form. From his tight-lipped smile and air of superiority, I guessed he was the singer. From the Matrix.

Everyone except snooty Neo said hello in that "someone's getting lucky tonight" way and squeezed into the booth with us. Snooty Neo left to get a pitcher of beer, while I learned mustache man-boy was called Randy and Pete was the wifebeater. I didn't remember Neo's name, which was fine because I preferred my name for him anyway.

We talked for about an hour, all the way until it was time for them to set up. By then the joint was hopping with people and I was getting tipsy. Two bands had already screamed their way through mediocrity, and I couldn't wait to see what Kettle Black was really made of. The Cramps had a way of brightening up any scene.

The whole time we sat there, Camden kept his arm around me. Occasionally it would drift down to my waist where he would thumb the hem of my shirt. Once, he brushed it against my bare skin, and I had to keep my body from shivering at his touch. Even with all the people around us, the smoke that lay in sheets in the air, and the loud music that rattled my teeth, it felt like we were the only two people alive.

"Well, we better go get ready," he said to me as they slid out of the booth. Thank God, I had to piss like a racehorse.

I followed him out and he grabbed my hand to help me up, giving it a quick squeeze.

"Will you try and watch from the front?" he asked. Fuck his dimples and his boyish charm. How could I say no to that?

"I'll be your biggest fan," I told him.

For a second there I thought he was going to kiss me. Or at least do something with the intensity that he was giving off. But he just nodded and disappeared into the crowd, following the band backstage.

What the hell was going on with me? I needed to think. I took off to the bathroom, finding it just as pleasant as I thought, with no toilet paper, used pads and tampons hanging out of the sanitary container, and sticky stains on the ground. I washed my hands thoroughly and tried to splash water on my face without ruining my makeup.

A girl with smeared red lipstick and death-by-platforms was looking at me askew as she leaned against the smudged mirror.

"Trying to sober up? Here." She rummaged through her warehouse-size purse and brought out an unmarked spray bottle. She thrust it in my wet hands. "Mist your face with this. It won't smudge your makeup."

I gave her a shy smile and did as she asked. It wasn't

as bracing as the cold tap water, but it was refreshing enough to bring my thoughts around.

"Thanks," I said, giving it back to her. "I hope you don't get that mixed up with your mace."

She looked at me blankly for a second then mused, "I had to mace my boyfriend once."

And that was the kind of bar we were in.

Now that my thoughts were clearer and Camden's hunky tattooed form was nowhere near me, I left the rambling drunk, made my way back into the bar, and started looking for the scapegoat. It was going to be as easy as shooting slimy fish in a dirty barrel.

I leaned against one of the timber posts and surveyed the packed crowd. I had to pick someone who probably should end up behind bars, or at least someone who had enough of a reputation that being blamed for a robbery wouldn't do much to it. Not that anything was going to happen to the dude, not without any proof. I just didn't want the fingers pointed at me when Camden discovered that his money was gone.

I guess the fact that I was going through with it made me a pretty terrible person. Well, that was probably true and, unfortunately, I'd never been able to be anyone else but me. Yes, it kind of sucked learning that he had a kid and an ex-wife to support, but that wasn't enough to stop me from doing what I'd planned on doing. But I wasn't going to leave Camden high and dry. There was no doubt that his shop was insured, and like I noted earlier, he had more than enough pricey crap in there to make up for the loss. It came down to who needed the money more. He had his opportunity to escape and start over. It was only fair that I had mine.

Shitty reasoning, I know. Sometimes I was just all out of excuses.

I found the guy, sitting at the quiet end of the bar. He was sickly pale, an oddity in this part of California, in a hockey T-shirt with mullety hair under a weathered baseball cap. He kept his icy, penetrating eyes focused on his bottle of beer, which he gripped so hard that all the tendons on his forearms stood out. He worked his jaw back and forth on his gaunt face, as if he were trying to calm himself down by grinding his teeth down to the gums. He didn't glance around at anyone and didn't talk. He looked like one of those people who would suddenly pull out a gun and shoot the bartender in the face for pouring him a weak drink.

He was perfect.

I'd pulled the scapegoat scam on a few people in my day, and they'd always fit the same profile. The loner with the piercing eyes, the guy that people glance at and think, *Yikes, one day he's going to blow.* When the crime happens—pickpocketing a few ladies at a café, for example—and there's no clear person to blame, it always comes to *I bet it was that young man, the quiet one in the corner who wouldn't look at anyone. He just smelled suspicious.* No one ever notices me heading out the door. Never commit a crime when you're the only person to blame.

The trick now was to get this guy on Camden's radar, and that wasn't going to be so easy in a bar as crowded as this.

I pulled a notepad out of my purse and found a wedge of space at the opposite side of the bar. I ripped out a page from the back and wrote on it:

You helped me out once before. Just returning the favor.

I folded the note, motioned for the bartender, and slipped it to him with a $100 bill.

"Can you give these to the man at the end of the bar, the pale guy with the hat?"

The bartender looked behind him. "Ol' Scary Eyes over there?"

I nodded. "I'm the girlfriend of one of the guys in the next band, Kettle Black."

He frowned at me, unsure why I was telling him that. "Yes, I served you earlier. Can I get you anything?"

I ordered another one of Camden's specials, dropped him $20, and left the bar with my drink before the bartender had a chance to deliver the message. I moved through the crowd until I was off to the front of the stage and waited.

The scapegoat would get my message and the money and would be confused as all hell. Maybe even a bit suspicious. He'd ask the bartender who gave him the note. The bartender would describe me and then throw in the fact that I was the girlfriend of a guy in the next band. Maybe he'd even describe Camden. That was all I needed. With any luck, the guy would be casting calculating, guarded glances our way for the rest of the night. And since he wouldn't know who I was, the chance of him approaching me over it was too risky for him. After all, this favor I was returning was probably something very illegal.

I stole a peek at the bar and saw Ol' Scary Eyes looking around, already beginning his search.

I smiled before he could see me and looked at the stage just in time to see Camden walk on with his guitar.

CHAPTER FIVE

Then

The girl walked into the cafeteria with her soda and carton of French fries, scouring the hellish landscape that was high school lunchtime. Even though she was now in the ninth grade and things were a little easier than the year before, she still didn't have any friends aside from Camden, and each step she took was like a new nightmare waiting to be unleashed.

She had stopped just after the cashier and knew she didn't have it in her to walk down past the rows of kids, chatter, and flying food to try and find an empty table. She might as well walk down a runway with judges on all sides. She silently cursed Camden for not being at school that day, though she had no idea where he was.

The girl was about to turn and head out into the halls, perhaps to eat her lunch down at the foot of her locker or in a toilet stall, when she heard someone call her name.

She looked around and was surprised to see it was coming from a mostly empty table nearest to her. There was a girl with a short brown pixie cut and dangling chandelier earrings that looked really heavy and far too blingy for high school.

Her name was Janice, and the girl knew her from their Spanish class together. Janice was a new student and hadn't found her place in the ranks yet, which was probably why she was even acknowledging the girl. Birds of a feather flock together and all that jazz.

Janice waved, motioning her to come over. The girl looked around, wondering if it was a trick or a trap, but didn't see anything suspicious. Janice was clearly eating alone and wanted company. The only other people at her table were a bunch of kids who were into skateboarding, and all they were doing was wolfing down their burgers like they had an extreme case of the munchies.

It's just three steps. Make them count, the girl told herself. She threw back her shoulders and tried to walk as if she had feeling in her foot, as if she didn't limp. Sometimes, if she concentrated hard enough, she could pull it off.

When Janice kept smiling and didn't seem to notice anything was wrong with the girl, she relaxed and sat down across from her.

"Hi, Janice," she said.

"Ellie, right?" Janice was from Atlanta and had a peachy accent that made the girl envious.

"Right. So...how are you liking Palm Valley?" she asked, grasping for conversation that wouldn't make her look like an idiot.

"It's dry," Janice said, but she was smiling. "But I guess I'll get used to that. It's hard meeting people, though. Do you find that? You just moved here, too, right?"

"Last year," she said. She didn't bother telling her that she still had a hard time meeting people. That should have been obvious.

Janice went on about her lack of friends and her life back in Georgia and how much friendlier people were in the South. The girl could only nod, knowing all too well.

The two of them talked comfortably for about fifteen minutes before they realized they'd barely touched their food. While they were chowing down, a group of girls approached their table. The girl didn't even have to look up to know who it was—the scent of Angel perfume was way too strong.

"Well, what do we have here?" came the haughty voice of Vicky Besset.

The girl kept eating, though her eyes were now on Janice and watching her carefully.

"Vicky, right?" Janice asked, pointing a fry at her. "And I forget the rest of you guys, I'm sorry."

The rest of Vicky's minions introduced themselves: Kim, Hannah, Jenn, Debbie, and Caroline. From their ironed hair to their Fendi bags, they were all pretty interchangeable.

"Mind if we join you?" Vicky asked. While Janice obliged cheerfully and moved over, the girl was frozen in place with fear. This was going to end very badly with someone getting very hurt.

Vicky took a spot right beside the girl and leaned

forward with her elbows on the greasy table like she had called together a business meeting.

"So, Janice," she began, tossing her silken brown hair over her shoulder. Part of it whipped the girl in the face. "Since you are new here, we've decided to stage a bit of an intervention. You know that it's important to make friends. You must also know how crucial it is to not commit social suicide."

The girl cringed. She knew what was coming.

"Social suicide?" Janice asked, eyeing the girl briefly.

"Yes. For example, it would suck if you were to become friends with someone like Ellie Watt. She's a freak, with parents who are actual criminals, and she'd probably steal your lunch money out from under your nose. She also needs to wear a better bra. Talk about a cow."

The girl swallowed hard, trying to shove down more than just saliva. Anger was flaring inside her chest and she was so afraid she'd either flip out—something that was long overdue—or start crying. The latter was something she did enough of.

There was a hush that fell over the table, punctuated by a few snickers and giggles from the bitches. But Janice didn't look too unfazed.

"I don't really look at a girl's bra when I'm trying to be friends with her," Janice said. "I'm not a lesbian."

One of the girls snorted loudly and Vicky looked shocked. "Lesbian? I'm not a lesbian."

Janice shrugged and took a bite of her burger. "It wouldn't bother me if you were."

Vicky narrowed her eyes at her, unsure what to make of the newcomer. She might have even been impressed. Perhaps intimidated. Eventually, appearances won out and she plastered a fake smile on her face.

"Well, that's good," Vicky said sweetly. "Though the only person who should be a lesbian is Ellie here."

The girl finally looked up at Vicky, utterly perplexed at this newest insult.

"What?" she asked.

Vicky gave her a dry look. "Well, it's no secret that you're having sex with Camden the Queen. And he might as well be a woman."

The girl was outraged, red-hot heat flushing her face. The most she and Camden had ever experienced was that one kiss. "I am not having sex with him!"

"Yeah, right," said one of the girls. "You're totally boning him. He's your boyfriend."

She looked over at Janice, who only raised her eyebrows in curiosity.

"I am not and he's not my boyfriend!"

"Sure, sure," Vicky said with a laugh. "You guys are inseparable. Like total fuck buddies. You know, sometimes I think you're not as much of a loser freak as I thought, and then I see you drooling after that she-man like he was made of chocolate. Makes everyone sick."

The girl pushed her fries away from her, shaking her head, choking with frustration. "You're mad. You're all mad. He's just a friend."

"A friend you're in love with," Vicky teased menacingly. "The only reason we're even talking to you today is because he's not here. If you want some real friends in this town, like us, like Janice here, you better keep that in mind."

"I am not in love with him," the girl said through grinding teeth.

"Oh yeah? Prove it," Vicky said. She nudged the girl on her shoulder and she followed her line of sight. Camden had just entered the cafeteria, apparently back at school for the day, and was walking down the center of it. He hadn't spotted the girl because he would have never looked at the tables at the front of the room. He was heading for the back where the losers and freaks sat.

"Prove it," Vicky egged her on. "Tell everyone that he's not your boyfriend. Tell him that. Because he seems to think it. And everyone else does, too."

The girl watched Camden as he walked by, as if in slow motion. His shiny pants and knee-high patent leather boots, Freddy Krueger shirt, and his dog-collared neck with spikes. His trench coat floated around him like a swirl of crows, his limp hair held back with a rubber band that came with bananas you bought at the store. His eyes were lined with slick blue liner and his lips were painted purple for a change.

Why the hell do you have to be such a freak, Camden? the girl thought bitterly to herself. She was filled with anger that it was his fault now that she was an outcast. She could never help her flaws, but he just flaunted his. He liked pissing people off. He liked being the martyr. And he wanted to bring her down with him.

"Do it," Vicky said. "Or are you just as pathetic as he is?"

Before she knew what was happening, the girl found herself getting to her feet. She found herself yelling Camden's name.

He stopped and was stunned to see her surrounded by their worst enemies.

With his eyes and everyone else's eyes upon her, she swallowed hard, put one hand on her hip, and yelled, "Your mother called! She says she wants her lipstick back."

It wasn't a particularly funny joke, nor was it anything that Camden hadn't heard before. But the fact that his only friend had said it, the fact that the whole cafeteria had burst out in laughter, was devastating. She saw the look on his face, the way it crumpled from within, and it pained her deeply to have hurt him so.

But with that feeling of remorse came another stronger and more peculiar one. It was pride. And acceptance. Vicky, her bitchy clique, Janice, everyone else in the godforsaken school, they were all laughing at something the girl had said. They were laughing with her. And not at her.

The girl sat back down and Vicky gave her a high five and a genuine smile. The girl turned her body away from Camden, who was still standing in a daze in the middle of the aisle, his head no doubt pegged by French fries, and pretended he didn't exist. She pretended that she'd never miss that piece of integrity that she lost that day.

She pretended she had to do what was best for her, no matter the cost to others.

And she never looked back.

Now

I don't know what it is about seeing a musician in his element, but somehow his element (which must be fire, if it has to be any of them) turns him into an animal. It simmers his being into something sexual, sensual, almost primal. Camden was no exception.

From the moment Kettle Black took the stage at Coppertank, all eyes were on Camden. It wasn't that he had the flashy mystique of Snooty Neo, the singer, or the pushy "I call the shots" persona of Mustache Man-Boy, the bassist. Instead he had this quiet command of his own universe. He wasn't the most skilled guitarist I'd ever seen, and he certainly wasn't too involved with the show. But when he was playing, you could see he was 100 percent in the moment. It was just him and his guitar, just him and the music and nothing else. It made you wonder what kind of secrets this man had, because he seemed to only divulge them to the instrument in his hands.

Speaking of hands, just watching his long, delicate fingers work up and down the neck with ease was making me pant a little. I couldn't help it. His arm muscles flexed with power and art, damp stains of sweat forming down his chest, making his shirt cling to him even more. And yet for his septum ring at the end of his nose, the tats, and his steely eyes and his hard body, I knew there was the face of a young boy on his leg, a symbol of his hidden softer side. There were glasses on his face because he was smart. He was like a caring, hulking nerd. And I wanted him.

When the show was over and they had played an encore of the Cramps' "Human Fly" and "Fever" to a rowdy and ridiculous crowd, Camden joined me down at the front of the stage.

He thrust a cold beer in my hand and grinned at me. "Stole them from backstage."

I tried to tell him what I thought of the show, but I just turned into a raving fan instead. "Seriously," I stated, "you're awesome. You're almost better than Poison Ivy."

He looked bashful and wiped the sweat off his brow with the edge of his T-shirt, perfectly displaying his taut abs, lightly sheened and golden in the low bar light.

"Pretty ironic that the guitarist in the Cramps was a woman," he noted.

I was momentarily distracted by his stomach. "Um, well, you're definitely no woman."

"That's not what you used to say. You know, behind my back."

My eyes flew up to him. My gut tightened. He was smiling good-naturedly and drinking his beer. I couldn't tell if that was a dig at me or if everything was completely cool.

My mouth flapped soundlessly as I grappled for words, but he punched me lightly on the shoulder. "I'm just messing with you, Ellie."

He laughed, but I could only give him a closed smile in response. That comment made me extremely uneasy for some reason. I hoped he really was messing with me. But of course, wasn't I messing with him? I had almost forgotten about the scapegoat and was startled as my eyes caught him as I looked around the bar.

He was staring at us a few yards away, taking methodical sips of his drink while giving us the stink-eye. Camden followed my gaze and lightly touched my wrist.

"Who is that guy?" he asked, his voice low even though the bar was too loud for the guy to hear him.

I looked away, not wanting to stir the pot too much. "I have no idea. I noticed him by the bar earlier, staring at you."

He raised his brow. "Staring at me? I think the guy is staring at you. I can't blame him. You're the prettiest girl here."

I gave him a wryly appreciative smile. "Thanks. But seriously, that guy is sketchy as all hell. Wonder what he wants?"

"Should I go ask him?" he asked, moving a step forward. I reached out and grabbed his arm to stop him. That wouldn't be good.

"No," I said, and quickly composed myself. "You know how weird some men can be in places like this. I'm sure he's just harmless. Maybe he thinks he knows you from somewhere. Or maybe he's a customer. You can't remember them all."

Camden rubbed at his chin. "Maybe. Though you'd think I'd remember those googly eyes. Well anyway, is it cool if we leave after these beers? It's getting late and the drive home is killer."

I told him sure, secretly thrilled to be getting out of there now that my plan was put in motion. I was also a wee bit apprehensive about how our date would end. Would I go to his place? Would he come to mine?

Would we drive out to Joshua Tree, which seemed like a different world when it was night, sit on the top of his Jeep, and share a few beers (what, like I hadn't been fantasizing about that)?

We said our good-byes to the rest of the band and a few people Camden knew, garnered one last watchful glare from the scapegoat, and then we were off, roaring down the road back toward Palm Valley.

Guano Padano provided our cinematic sound track, and by the time Camden was pulling his car down the palm-lined road back to Uncle Jim's, we'd been chatting nonstop and were almost breathless. The cold desert wind rocked the Jeep as we came to a stop and messed my hair around my eyes. I was glad he couldn't see them properly. I was nervous as all hell— something new to me—and was feeling as awkward as a thirteen-year-old. I tried to remember that Camden had already kissed me all those years ago, but it didn't change a thing.

I unsnapped my seat belt and twisted in my seat to look at him, pushing some of the hair out of my face.

"Thanks so much for the great evening," I told him, sounding more like a cliché by the minute.

"Thanks for coming." He grinned. A fresh crop of goose bumps sprouted on my arms. Damn, he was going to have to hide those lips somewhere before I stole them.

"Well...," I said. I was starting to fidget, unsure if I should stay and wait for him to either kiss me or suggest we continue our date, but he just kept smiling. And then he put his hand on the gear shift as if he was going to put it in drive.

"Well, I hope you have a great time in Palm Valley. Maybe I'll see you around."

The smile melted off my mouth.

What?

"Uh, yeah, totally," I said, feeling more stupid by the second. I grabbed my purse and hopped out of the Jeep, looking back at him with a stunned expression.

He raised his hand in a wave. "Good night, Ellie."

I copied him. "Good night, Camden," I whispered.

He gunned the Jeep and it took off around the cul-de-sac and down the road. I didn't walk into the house; I just stood there at the foot of the driveway, watching as the Jeep's red lights got smaller and smaller and then eventually disappeared as he turned onto the other road. Then the roar of his engine was gone, and I was engulfed by the sound of crickets and the blanket of stars above my head.

What the hell? What happened to asking me out on another date? Or trying to get laid? Or at least a kiss? I thought the whole evening had been going well, and suddenly it was *See ya.* Not even a *We should do this again sometime* and other polite promises. Nothing!

I slowly turned on my heel and slinked back to the house, feeling like a balloon with its air let out. I had really counted on Camden liking me. I had counted on a lot of things. Now I couldn't be sure of anything.

And for all the effort, for all my plans of scamming the guy, the thing that hurt the most was the rejection. I thought we really had something. Somehow, all these years later, Camden McQueen had managed to put me in his shoes.

To put it mildly, I didn't like it.

*   *   *

You know when you're upset over something and you look forward to the light of morning because you'll have some sort of clarity over the situation, as if you'll work out your problem while you sleep?

Yeah, that didn't happen here. I woke up angry and annoyed. Part of it was that my old bed in the spare bedroom had scratchy, dusty sheets that probably hadn't been changed since I was a teenager, but mainly it was because of Camden. He must have been in my dreams or something, because my first thought as I opened my eyes to the sharp sunlight streaming in my window was *Damn him.*

Apparently I don't take rejection very well. I also don't like it when my plans get messed up. When I have to recalculate. You think I'd be used to the latter and at least some of the former, but when I'd been rejected in the past I never took it personally. I never had time or the nerve to get involved with people, and when I did— such as with Jack back in Cincinnati—I was never really invested. My heart was a shallow instrument.

And yet here I was, lying in my bed, sheets tangled all over me, staring up at the ceiling where I used to tape pictures of my favorite bands, and feeling a little sorry for myself. Where had I gone wrong? I started analyzing every detail from the night before, from the way he smiled at me to the feel of his arm around me.

He obviously wanted his bandmates to know we were an item, or that I belonged to him in some way. Perhaps that was all it was. Maybe they made fun of him for not bagging chicks or something. I had a hard time believing that considering most women were falling all over themselves to talk to the six-two, tat-covered hottie. He could have anyone he wanted, if he wanted them. But Camden wasn't your usual guy. At least he hadn't been.

I mulled it over and over, and the only thing I could come up with was that he just didn't like me like that. Which sucked, both for my secretly fragile self-esteem and for my ticket out of this place. In order for my scam to work, I needed to get into his place and take a look around. I needed to have a better look at his security system—if he had any—and find out where his safe was. Otherwise I'd be setting myself up for major trouble, something I had to avoid in this town for the sake of Uncle Jim.

Speaking of the devil, I could hear him puttering around in the kitchen and could smell the bacon frying in its own fat. My stomach growled and I rolled over into the fetal position. I'd spent $120 last night in the name of the game, which left me only $80 to start a new life somewhere. My options looked bleak.

Soon my hunger won out over my pity party, and I threw on some clothes and shuffled into the kitchen. Uncle Jim was scooping a batch of baked beans onto a plate and pursed his lips as soon as he saw me.

"Thought this would get you up," he said, handing me the plate and a fork. "You came home late last night."

I had to smile at his parentlike interrogation and slid onto the bar stool. "Oh, it wasn't that late. I hope you weren't waiting up for me."

From the way he shrugged I could tell he was. He slid into the seat next to me and started pouring an obscene amount of hot sauce on his eggs. I chose Worcester sauce instead and drizzled it all over my plate.

"So how was it?"

I sighed. "It was really nice, actually. But I don't think it went too well on his end."

"No?"

"I don't know. He just dropped me off. No kiss good night, no plans for the next days."

He chuckled as he delicately sliced his eggs with a knife. "You mean you wait for the men to kiss you, Ellie? Boy, I thought your mother raised you differently."

"Well, we know she barely raised me at all."

He looked at me sharply then said softly, "She did the best she could. You were her number one priority."

"Until..."

"Until...she made a mistake."

"Sounds like you're the one who's coming around, Uncle Jim. Whatever happened to forever punishing us?"

"You're here, aren't you?"

I speared a few beans with my fork and ate them before my appetite totally disappeared. "Not for long."

We sat in silence for a while, drinking our coffees and staring out the kitchen window at the sunny palm groves outside. When I lived up north for a bit, I often thought back to California and wondered how people could ever be sad in such constant sunshine. But the truth is, sadness and anger aren't vampiric. If you let them, they'll follow you around the world, sunshine and stakes be damned.

"I'm sorry your date didn't go well," he finally said after clearing his throat. "It's probably for the best. There's been some rumors about that boy anyway, and you don't want to get roped up in that."

Now that caught my attention. "Rumors? Still?"

He let out a deep breath and shrugged, putting his elbows on the table. "I don't know. I remember that boy being all queer and funny when you were young, but now it's something else. He hangs out with...bad people."

I twisted in my seat and looked him square in the face. "*I'm* bad people."

"Not like you, Ellie. I mean *bad* people. City people. I like to pretend that you have morals somewhere in your skinny little chest. These people don't."

I narrowed my eyes in thought. "How do you know all of this?"

"I hear things. It's a small town still, people talk. Got nothing better to do. And it's probably nothing, maybe he just knows some of the people his daddy arrests. But if you want to give something a reason, maybe it's best that he broke things off like that. You don't need to get dragged into anything."

"I don't think Camden is like that," I mused. Then again, I didn't really know Camden anymore.

"Maybe not," he said, collecting our plates and taking them to the sink. "I'm just trying to make you feel better. Guess it didn't work."

I shot him a smile of gratitude and offered to do the dishes. When he refused, I then excused myself. I went up to my room, shut the door, and started Googling the crap out of Camden McQueen on my phone.

I found nothing. Well, nothing "bad." Just things that reiterated what he'd already told me. He was a talented tattoo artist, he really had been on Kat Von D's reality TV show, and his shop in LA did quite well. Other than that, there was nothing. Only a few pictures that made me feel all quivery inside.

Ugh.

I sat on the bed and hugged my knees and tried to think. I didn't have many options. Since I was already in Palm Valley, I could go back into town and do some serious job hunting. Maybe get a gig at a bar or something like that, since the barista thing wasn't going to happen.

I perked up a bit. Maybe I could get a legitimately great job. And maybe if I did, Uncle Jim would let me stay a bit longer, seeing that I was serious. But then I'd be stuck in Palm Valley, in the same town as Camden, and things could get pretty awkward. I mean, it's not like things ended on bad terms but . . . well, I usually left when places and people got weird.

And that was still an option. Maybe I could barter for a place to stay in another town and get some employment there. Work on a farm for room and board? I'd done stranger things before.

I wondered if there was anyone I knew who could help me out. I wasn't one for charity, but there were plenty of people out there who I'd done favors for and who owed me big time. Jeez, I was getting desperate.

I opened up my e-mail account on my phone.

My heart thumped up into my throat. There was an e-mail from Camden with the subject line *Guano Padano albums.*

How the hell did he get my e-mail?

With a shaking finger I pressed the touchscreen to open it.

Hey Ellie, thanks for coming to the show last night. Hope you had fun. I've attached some zip files of the two Guano Padano albums, in case you wanted to listen to them. I realized last night that I never got your phone number (derp), so if you see this e-mail in time, perhaps you'd like to come with me to the driving range, hit a few balls, and drink a few beers? It's what all the cool kids are doing.

PS if this isn't the fantastic Ellie Watt of Palm Valley fame, please disregard this e-mail. But you can keep the music.

He had his tattoo shop logo and information in his signature, along with his cell phone number.

I felt a sick sense of relief. I say sick because now that I knew he did like me after all, now that I knew I was back in the game, I was getting a little wary of the actual game. It didn't help what my uncle said about the company he kept.

Still, I couldn't imagine Camden hanging out with *bad* people. What was with the older generations thinking everyone who had tattoos and piercings had to be gang members or criminals? Okay, so I had tattoos and piercings (a nipple ring, if you must know), but someone had to start the stereotype, right?

I decided my uncle was too quick to judge, and if Camden was going to be associated with anyone unsavory, it might as well be me. With fingers that were still shaking, I dialed his number.

CHAPTER SIX

"CAN YOU HOLD my balls for a sec?"

I almost did a quite unsexy snort-laugh and took the bucket of balls out of Camden's hands while he bent over and tied up his Converse. Not exactly golf club attire, but Palm Valley's Public Golf Course seemed to attract all the golfers who didn't have the deeply lined pockets to play at the private clubs. And that meant a few golfers wearing clothes that just squeaked under the regulations.

Luckily for me, this meant I could keep my jeans on. I didn't have any other type of pants, and Lord knows I wouldn't wear shorts with the scars I had. Camden looked devilishly handsome with gray Chucks, knee-length black shorts, and a black-and-white-checkered polo shirt. Though his glasses were missing from his face, his hair was spiked up a bit in the front. If anyone could own the trend "golf punk" it would be him.

After I had done my nervous phone call to Camden, he swung by Uncle Jim's and picked me up. He was out

in the groves at the time, thank goodness, so I just left
him a note saying I had gone out job hunting. It was
kind of the truth.

Camden made no mention of the vague way things
ended last night and was back to being his friendly self,
which made me feel like a moronic, crush-bound girl.
One nice date and I'm overanalyzing shit, dissecting
every word and look, trying to figure out what it really
meant. He probably didn't want to make any false promises at the end of a date and decided to take things as
they came. I used to have a guy mentality like that, and I
wondered where it had gone. Being Ellie Watt seemed to
bring about a lot of regression.

"So, are you ready to start Camden and Ellie's Day
of Fun?" he asked, taking the bucket back from me.
Back in high school we used to have these days, usually
on Saturdays. All the cool kids would hang out and do
their parties and shit like that, so we just decided to create days where we did anything we wanted, preferably
weird and random stuff like raiding thrift stores and
making the other person buy an outfit of our choosing,
taking his dad's guns and shooting our failed art proj-
ects out in the desert, or pretending one of our teachers
was a spy and trailing them all over town. For the year
that Camden and Ellie's Day of Fun lasted, it became
our favorite day of the week. And yes, being that it was
the late '90s, we totally ripped off that phrase from our
favorite show, *Friends*.

"I'm as ready as I'll ever be," I told him, as we
walked out of the shop and down the way to our spot.
I'd been golfing a few times before, but I was terrible.

People with anger management issues and impatience do not good golfers make. I swing at the ball way before I'm ready, and then I throw my club and scream. A driving range would be a lot easier, since we wouldn't be holding anyone up, but still. If I had been in charge of our day of fun, this wouldn't have been the first choice.

He put his hand on my shoulder for a moment and gave a warm squeeze that reached all the way into my chest.

"Don't worry, you'll be fine. This isn't about getting the ball as far as it can go."

"No?" I asked, trying to hide the disappointment in my face as he took his hand away.

He shook his head. "Nope. This is about taking control. It's about controlling yourself, getting into that tiny moment in which you can make things happen. It's hard to channel everything you have into Titleist, but when you do, you get...I don't know...Zen."

"I didn't know you were such a golfer, Camden."

"I'm a lot of things, but a golfer isn't one of them," he said with a laugh. "I just like swinging the club. When you take the pressure off and just go for it, it does wonders for your anger."

I chewed on my lip. "You have anger? You're, like, steady as a rock."

He laughed again, but it didn't reach his eyes. He ran his hand through the sides of his hair and looked away. "I'm glad it seems that way. You kind of need to be as steady as something when you have my job." He mimicked holding a shaking tattoo needle.

We took our spot at the range a few sections down

from the other golfers, like troublemakers who sat at the back of the classroom. I told him he was swinging first, and he responded by taking two cold beers out of his backpack.

"First things first," he said, handing me a beer. "In order to get into the Zen zone, you have to be calm. Beer always helps."

We clinked the bottles together and then quickly hid them when a curious golfer looked our way. I stepped closer to him to get out of the golfer's range of sight, and by doing so, my head was almost at Camden's chest. I closed my eyes and breathed in deeply.

Crap. I hope I was subtle about that creeper move.

Camden lowered his head and I was too afraid to look up. I could feel his lips burning just inches away from the top of my head.

I cleared my throat and spoke into his pecs. "Well, now that beer is involved, it looks like this will be Camden and Ellie's Day of Fun after all."

"What was it before?" he murmured. His words ruffled my hair, causing the skin on my scalp to tighten pleasurably.

"Camden and Ellie's Day of Assault with a Golf Club."

I could feel him smile. "Once a spazz, always a spazz."

I put my hand on his chest and pushed myself away from him, ignoring how hard it was beneath my fingers, how I could feel his heart thumping hard. I gave him a wry look and took a long sip of my drink.

"I'll have you know I only spazz when it's called for. And if any game calls for it, it's golf."

He raised his brows and said smoothly, "Well then you better drink faster."

He didn't have to tell me twice.

I was as bad as I thought I'd be. The first few swings were a little rough. I mean, I totally missed the ball. Not even close. And that's when I could feel the waves of anger pushing up through my limbs, wanting some form of release.

I tightened the grip on the club and bit hard on my lip. I briefly shot Camden an embarrassed look and he slowly shook his head.

"Aren't you going to tell me to be the ball or something?" I asked, trying to push the frustration away. Christ, I was a spazz, wasn't I? I wished I could take some of the kava pills I had in my bag without looking like a total junkie.

"Just... stop caring what I think," he said.

I grunted and looked down at the ball, trying to line my club up properly. "I don't care what you think."

"You do. You're trying to impress me."

Okay, that did it. I faced him and leaned with one arm on the end of the club. "I am not trying to impress you."

A small smile tugged at his lips. It was borderline smug, and I wanted to wipe it off his face. "Yes, you are. You don't want to look weaker than you seem. You want to look like you've got everything figured out, everything under control, even your swing."

"You don't know me," I told him with a surprising amount of bitterness. I turned back to the club and the ball and tried to adjust my grip. It all felt wrong. My fingers were stiff. My face was flaring up with heat. I was about to make a ridiculous swing that would have the club go flying across the range.

Then I felt his presence behind me and his arms slowly, softly, slid down on top of mine. He pressed himself to my back, not too tight, and put his lips just behind my ear. My eyes widened and I nearly let go of the club.

"I know what I know of you," he whispered into my ear, his breath hot. "And I want to know more."

His husky voice sent subtle shock waves through me. I was going from angry to turned on in seconds flat, and the friction from my jeans was not helping. He let his hands wrap around the tops of mine, his massive forearms nearly rendering mine invisible. He pressed closer to me, and if I wasn't mistaken, he was as hard as stone. Fuck, he felt large. He felt good. His lips brushed the outer edge of my ear.

"Just like this," he said softly. "Let everything go." He started stroking the tops of my hands with his fingers, slowly, in circles. Back and forth, over every little hair. Somehow, the motion of it was *extremely* erotic. I couldn't help but press my ass back into him, just an inch, and his breath hitched heavily in response. If he truly wanted me to let everything go, I'd flip him over and ride him right there on the range. Screw golf—I'd screw him instead.

"Now..." His voice trailed off and he gradually stepped back. My back felt cold without his body there. "Now swing."

I swallowed hard and willed my legs to stop from

shaking. I took in a deep breath, feeling a headiness that sank into my core, raised the club, and swung.

I hit the ball with a satisfying *thwack* and it sailed across the range. All right, so it didn't go too far, but it went far enough. It bounced merrily among the other balls that dotted the sea of green and came to a stop near the seventy-yard line.

I looked behind me at Camden, who was standing with his arms folded across his chest, grinning in approval. I did my damndest not to look at his crotch and suss out if he still had an erection. If he did, he certainly didn't care.

"Now that's what I'm talking about," he said. He held out his hand for a highfive.

I returned it, wiggling my lips. "That's quite the technique. Do you use that on all the girls?"

His teeth were so white against his perpetually tanned skin. "Only the ones worth the effort. With everyone else I just tell them to be the ball."

He handed me another fresh beer, then guided me by my shoulders and moved me out of the way.

"All right, now it's my turn to impress you," he said, picking up his club.

I stood back and watched him with a smile. I didn't think I could be more impressed than I already was.

*   *   *

My drive improved after that, er, hands-on lesson, but sadly he didn't try his technique again. I could only hope he was saving it for later, but to be honest, that thought terrified me a little. The good news was that he seemed to be able to wet my panties with nothing more than erotic hand holding; the bad news was the whole act of ripping your clothes off and jumping each other involved...ripping your clothes off.

I'm sure the average female has some aversions about being seen naked by a guy they're into—or anyone, really. Maybe they don't like the cellulite on their ass (somehow there's none on mine) or their stomach pouch or they think their torso is too long or maybe their nipples are too small. You name it, everyone's got something. But my something was impossible to hide and it always prompted a story. Every time I had sex with a guy, I had to apologize for the way my leg looked. I had to let them know that I acknowledged my deformity, that I in no way thought I was perfect.

Ironically, most men didn't give a shit. If they saw the horrible ribbons of scars that swarmed my leg, they didn't stare. They barely noticed. They were just staring at my tits and vagina and that was about it. If they were really nice, they'd stare at my face. But it didn't stop me from almost having a panic attack every time I got naked. I was always waiting for that moment when some asshole guy would kick me out of bed for being a freak.

Camden knew about my scars; he always wanted to see them, but I'd never show. I didn't want the only person who liked me to lose his desire or interest in me. I didn't want it to put a barrier between us. It sounded silly, since he was just as different as I was, but I could never forget how easy it was for him to hide—if he wanted to—and how impossible it was for me.

And now, well, now he wasn't a freak. Now he was

a virile young man whose body I wanted nothing more than to run my hands over and get a firm grope in here and there. He was now that and I was still me.

After we left the driving range and headed back into town, the searing heat of the sun and the stark blue sky burning away some of my insecurities, we got started on the next portion of our Day of Fun.

He pulled the Jeep into the parking lot of one of the local thrift stores and peeked at me over his Wayfarer shades. "Are you ready for our next adventure?"

I stared at the store in awe. It was the same damn one we used to shop at when we were young. As high school went on, I kind of forgot about the place, but here it was still ticking. From the smudged front window it looked dimly lit, like it wasn't even open, but then again it had always looked that way.

I took off my sunglasses and slipped them in my purse. "Same deal as before?"

"Yup. I buy you an outfit and you buy me an outfit. And we have to wear it tonight. No matter what."

"Tonight, huh? It would help if I knew what we were doing," I teased. Camden was doling out our day one piece at a time. For all I knew, we could be going to one of the Fabulous Follies shows in Palm Springs, or harassing the camels at the Living Desert in Palm Desert.

"I can give you a hint…it involves dinner. But I haven't quite figured out where yet. I was thinking maybe the restaurant at the top of the gondola."

I grimaced. "The gondola that makes me want to vomit? Good choice."

"Or," he said, louder now, "we can do dinner at my place."

My ears perked up. I smiled mischievously, brushing my hair back behind my ear. Dinner at his place meant I could properly scope out the joint. It also meant sex. I hoped it would at least mean one of those things.

His face went smoothly blank for a split second and his jaw twitched. Then he smiled and was back to his vibrant self. "Dinner at my place it is, then. Now let's make sure we're dressed well for the occasion." He hopped out of the Jeep and made his way toward the entrance. I sat there for a few moments, feeling strangely uneasy, then brushed it away and joined him.

The door was still one of those you couldn't tell if you had to push or pull, and after a failed attempt, Camden was holding the door open for me. The shop smelled exactly as I remembered—like mothballs, potpourri, and brass. The woman behind the counter was younger than the one back in the day, but she was still in her sixties and wore thick glasses with an ugly, beaded neck strap. She snapped her head up from her paperback novel as we came in and gave us a tepid smile. I knew that smile. It was the "oh crap, these kids are going to rob me, aren't they?" kind of smile. She'd be watching our every move.

The shop was almost empty except for an old, hunched-over lady in the housewares section, peering at chipped teacups. Camden and I made a beeline for the clothes, he to the women's section and me to the men's, and we started noisily flipping through the racks.

I was pretty giddy as I flung the hangers down, looking for the perfect outfit for him. In the past we were all about humiliating each other, which was only fair and fun since we'd both look like idiots. Now I wasn't sure what the plan was. But making him look like a goof during dinner seemed like a great idea to me.

I came across an extremely loud pink-and-purple Hawaiian shirt that wouldn't even look hip on him. It was tacky faux silk and two sizes too large. I'd make him wear it halfway unbuttoned, then I could stare at his chest. (Honestly, when had I become such a horndog?) After that winning find, I went to the pants section. Something tight would do the trick, even though he hadn't shown any aversion to tight pants, both then and now.

Then I spotted it. A kilt. Green-and-black tartan. Oh yes, this would look wonderful on my Scottish Hawaiian dude. I rounded out the outfit with a black fedora. Now he was also a private eye.

"Okay," I called to him over the racks. "I have your stuff."

"Already?" he asked, still searching through his end. "Should I be worried?"

"You should be very worried. Unless you've always wanted to be a Scottish detective from Hawaii."

"Like Magnum P.I.?"

"Not even close."

I walked down the aisle and over to him. He was holding a glow-mesh halter top in one hand. Figures. I peered at his other hand. It was a leather miniskirt.

I breathed out sharply through my nose and shot

him an apologetic smile. "Yeah, I'm not wearing the skirt, so you can just put it back."

He shook his head and kept going through some cardigans. "Rules are rules, Ellie. You have to wear whatever I choose for you."

I crossed my arms, the pile of clothes bunching up. "I am *not* wearing a skirt."

He kept on as if he didn't hear me, and the *click click click* of hangers being slid past were driving me insane. I bundled my clothes under one arm and put my hand on his to take the skirt away. He wouldn't budge.

"Seriously, you know I'm not wearing that."

He sighed and turned to face me, his dark brows coming together to create a deep groove between his eyes. "Why not?" He sounded like his patience was being tested, which in turn made my patience feel tested.

I narrowed my eyes at him. "You know why. I have scars, Camden. Still have them."

"So?"

I fought the urge to raise my voice. "So? So I don't feel like wearing something that's going to humiliate me."

"We used to humiliate each other all the time. You're trying to make me look like a cross-dressing Tom Selleck."

"That's different. And we had our own rules back then. You knew how I was, so you'd only dress me in pants or long skirts."

His lower lip moved back and forth as he studied me. "I thought you'd have gotten over it by now."

My eyes nearly bulged out of my head. "That's not exactly something you can get over, Camden." The absolute nerve of him. "I'm not like *you*. I can't just get over every shitty thing that gets thrown my way."

He focused on me intently. "I don't get over everything." His voice had dropped a register or two and flowed out of him like a snake.

I broke away from his gaze and took my hand off the hanger. "Well, so then you know. Look, maybe this whole thing was a bad idea. I mean, we're twenty-six years old and playing dress-up..."

I took in a deep breath and turned to face the changing rooms. My face looked back at me from the mirror. I didn't like that view either.

Suddenly I felt him behind me and his arm going around my waist. He turned me around and pulled me to him, then embraced me in a hug. All our clothes and hangers dropped to the floor, and over his shoulder I saw the cashier getting off her stool to look over at the clatter.

"I'm sorry," he mumbled. "I'm being an insensitive jerk."

He squeezed me tight enough to make breathing hard. I patted him lightly on the back, not wanting to see this side of him, not over something like this.

"It's fine," I told him, trying to sound breezy and not at all caught off guard. "I just get a little touchy over it. It's... it's something I'm working on."

He held me in a pause of silence. I heard the buzz of the dim overhead lights and the rustle of the newspaper as the cashier resumed reading.

"You're still such a brave girl, Ellie," he said softly, sadly. "It's too bad."

I wasn't sure if he meant it was too bad I was brave or the situation was too bad. While I was mulling *that* over, he let me go and scooped up our clothes. To my relief, he stuck the skirt back on the rack and focused behind him where the women's pants were. In seconds he had plucked out a pair of skintight, orange leopard-print leggings. Insanely tacky. It was perfect.

CHAPTER SEVEN

AFTER THE ANTICS at the thrift shop were over and we walked away with a hideous mix of materials, our next stop was to pop into the grocery store and stock up for our meal. Thankfully, we were wearing our crazy outfits only for dinner and didn't have to go into the store looking like total lunatics.

Camden decided on filet mignon, which he wanted to grill on his new barbecue, with a side of asparagus. You couldn't get a sexier meal than that, unless you threw in some oysters. To Camden's brazen credit, he did check at the seafood department, but they didn't have any. I decided to supply the wine and picked up two bottles of deep, bold reds.

"Do we look like alcoholics if we have two bottles?" I asked him, holding them both up, one in each hand.

His eyes sparkled. "Hold on, stay like that."

"Like with wine in the air?"

He put down the grocery basket and came toward

me while I stood frozen. I was like a statue of the world's most enthusiastic wino.

He pressed himself against me, leaving barely any room between us, and with those searing baby blues trailing from my eyes down to my lips, he cupped my face with one hand. I closed my eyes, gripping the necks of the bottles extra hard, and felt his lips press against mine. They were soft, warm, and sweet. It felt like I didn't have a hard bone in my body, just this lightness and sunshine.

Then I felt the wet brush of his tongue along the inner rim of my lip and I almost dropped the bottles.

He pulled back before I could readjust my grip and attack him more voraciously. That was probably a good thing considering we were standing in the middle of Safeway in Conservative Old Person Central.

"What was that for?" I asked breathlessly, finally lowering the bottles. My arms had been shaking, but from the strain or the kiss I didn't know.

He picked up the basket and gave me a nonchalant look. "You looked cute. What can I say?"

"I thought maybe I looked easy, with the wine and all," I joked, hoping my cheeks would stop flaming.

"Oh. Well, that, too."

A half hour later, while my lips still tingled from our first kiss (well, second kiss, if you wanted to get really technical), we were back at Sins & Needles and taking the groceries up to where he lived on the top floor. The front of the house with the porch was the entrance for the shop, while the entrance to the upstairs was from the side of his house, also where he had a small garage. I noted that the garage was used as a woodworking shop instead of for keeping the Jeep.

"I didn't know you were such a handyman," I told him as he unlocked his front door. It was just a simple deadbolt, nothing too fancy. I hadn't heard or seen any motion detectors or cameras, either, though I knew from experience that it didn't mean there weren't any. There was a large hedge of desert rose between the side of the house and the main street, which blocked this door from prying eyes. That was a plus.

He glanced behind me as he opened the door and let me in. "Ah, I'm not so handy, believe me. I dabbled in the sign-making business for a bit and sometimes do it for fun."

The shop had a beautiful sign out front. "Did you do the Sins & Needles sign?"

"Took me a hell of a long time. Luckily when you screw up doing woodwork, the wood doesn't cry out in pain and sue you." He shut the door behind us. "Well, this is the part of my life most people don't get to see."

To the left of us was a door that I assumed led into the shop. To the right was another door that looked like it went into the garage. Then of course there were the stairs we were about to climb. That left three ways to get out of the house if I had to. Not too shabby.

"How do we get to the backyard?" I asked him, as we went up.

"Through the garage," he said, as we paused at the top.

The upstairs was absolutely stunning. Hardwood floors and Mexican rugs, whitewashed walls above peeling-paint baseboards that looked like they were salvaged from a barn. Huge pieces of original artwork hung from the walls, along with a display of guitar necks that went in a diagonal slash from floor to ceiling. The ceiling itself was made of copper panels.

He took me into the kitchen, which was small but homey. To my delight, it was a bit of a mess, with empty beer cans stacked in the corner and toaster crumbs on the counter. Just like Camden's ears had brought him down to earth, the fact that he wasn't 100 percent neat and tidy made his shabby-chic home easier to take.

My eyes were immediately drawn to a painting of a woman above the driftwood table. It looked like Picasso's *Woman in Blue*, except that it was done from a photograph. The woman's face was blurry and covered with a wash of dark hair, but her figure was exquisite.

"I love that." I looked over my shoulder at him. "Did you do that?"

He gave me a small smile. "I did."

Tattoos, sign making, painting; Camden was the epitome of an artist—complete with the occasional mood swing as well.

I was about to ask who the painting was of, but I decided against it. From the tight look in his eyes, I knew it was his ex-wife. I wondered why on earth he kept the artwork in the kitchen. Did he really want reminders of her all over the place?

Of course, that train of thought was coming to you courtesy of a woman who drove her ex-boyfriend's car and had a memory of him permanently inked on her arm.

I whirled around and clapped my hands together. "This is amazing, Camden. Come on, show me the rest!"

He took me out into the living room, which had couches of mahogany leather and white fluffy throws and a wonderful working fireplace. It got shockingly cold in the winters here and many homes didn't have central heating, so the fireplace must have been a major selling point.

Also, a major sexing point. Any date that ended with two people drinking wine near a fire also ended with a woman's thong being thrown across the room.

Before I could fixate on that thought too much, next was the spare bedroom, which had a single bed shoved in the corner. The rest of the room was crammed with paint supplies.

"Not your office, then?" I asked.

"My office is downstairs between the hall and the shop. This is just for Ben, if he ever comes to visit."

"Has he?"

He shook his head and flipped off the light. There was a nice bathroom with a clawfoot tub and a basin-like sink.

Then it was his room. Like the kitchen, it was a bit messy. He looked sheepish before he scampered across the room and started shoving all his clothes into a laundry hamper.

"Sorry, I'm not used to much company."

"You're also a man." With flaws, thank God.

I walked across the room, trailing my hand over the cozy flannel bedspread, and stopped at the window. We were right above the front of the store, and I could see down into the rock garden and the main street. The sun was starting to get low in the sky, casting long shadows in the golden light.

"So does that mean you're neat and tidy, since you're a woman?"

I scrunched up my face. "Are you kidding? I used to buy paper plates just so I wouldn't have to do the dishes. My idea of vacuuming is borrowing someone's dog for the day and having them eat all the crap off the floor."

He laughed, a total belly-aching shake. What a fucking beautiful sound.

"All right, come on," he said, grabbing my hand and leading me away from the window. "Let's keep the Day of Fun moving by going in the backyard and cracking open a bottle of wine."

"I guess the tour's over."

"No more house to see, unless you want to see my office and the garage."

"Sure, whatever." I shrugged like I didn't care.

But moments later, after we had put away the groceries and took two glasses for our wine, he showed me the office. A place I very much wanted to see.

It was small and simple. The door downstairs led into the office, and another door led from the office to the shop. The only locks were on that door. There was also a small window that I could easily fit out of. That would most likely be my escape route. I tried to get a sense of where the window opened up to the outside without seeming overly suspicious, but it looked like it was still on the hidden side of the hedge.

He had a nice, retro-looking desk, mint in color, and a couple of metal filing cabinets beside it. A swanky iPod dock and speakers sat in the corner on top of a thick stack of magazines while a Mac computer ran a slide show of beach photos. A pair of glasses rested on the keyboard. Beside it was a framed photo of a boy on a beach, throwing a rock. You couldn't see his face because of his hat, but I assumed it was Ben.

I didn't see a safe anywhere, not even under the desk. Shit. Maybe I'd be robbing the register, and as crammed as it looked, it almost seemed insulting to steal it from him.

"Where do you keep all your tattoo equipment?" I asked.

He opened a closet that sat between the two doors. This was better organized than the rest of the house, with built-in shelves that housed plastic boxes affixed with Post-it notes and labels. And at the very bottom of the shelving unit was the safe. It was bolted to the ground—not too easy to pick up and run away with—but with only a three-number combination lock. Although three-number locks were easier to decode than six-number ones, they were also easier to remember and usually nixed the need to be written down somewhere near the safe. Eight times out of ten, if someone had a six-number combination lock, they had that code written down somewhere in the room.

I just had to guess Camden's three numbers. I didn't have the time and patience to listen for the contact points and wheels and graph the results, and I certainly wasn't about to do any drilling. I would need to get in, crack the code on only a few tries, and then get out. No fingerprints, no sound. The only thing I'd leave was some sort of sign that made him think a pro didn't do it. Evidence of sloppiness.

Naturally, I was counting on the safe being actually full of cash or something valuable, when for all I knew, Camden used it for mementos and prized comic books. I hoped the bank transaction fees for a small business were high enough that he made a deposit just once or twice a week. I'd just have to chance it. I didn't want to think about Plan B yet.

I made sure to let my eyes gloss over the safe only once and then looked at Camden. "Is this where you come to think? Your office?"

He shut the closet with a click. "Actually I go outside. Care to join me?"

He held out his arm and I gleefully took it, carrying the glasses with my other hand. I fought back the pinpricks of guilt that had started building inside my throat, and by the time we made our way through the garage that smelled like ponderosa pine, we were in his backyard.

The rock garden from the front continued in the back, surrounding a large stone patio that was hedged by sagebrush. But beyond the rocks was a small patch of lawn and two lawn chairs. It looked like it hadn't been mowed in a while, but the grass was so stiff and wide out here that it didn't look unruly. Beyond the lawn was the neighbor's fence, though you couldn't see it thanks to the layers of flowering bushes and the occasional small palm tree.

"This is beautiful," I whispered, taking in the fragrant air. All the night-blooming flowers were opening as the sun disappeared behind the mountains, leaving us in a blue haze.

"Just you wait," he said. He put the wine down on the

wrought-iron table and flicked a light switch on the wall. Suddenly the yard was swamped with small white lights, making it look like we were surrounded by a million fireflies.

"You do realize you have, like, the bachelor pad of all bachelor pads, right? Talk about a babe magnet."

He held his hand out for the glasses. "Babe magnet? I don't know if you'll be saying that once I've got my outfit on."

I grinned and handed them to him. His arms flexed deliciously as he wrestled with the wine bottle's cork. "Well, for the record, cross-dressing Tom Sellecks turn me on."

And at that, the cork came out with a pop. You know, for extra emphasis.

He shot me an irresistible smile. "That's lucky, considering Ellie Watt turns me on. And she doesn't have to be wearing anything at all."

Shit. I was blushing again. "Where is this Ellie Watt? I'll kill her," I joked, looking around and making a fist.

"You tell me," he said softly. "Is she here?"

His tone brought me down to earth. Yes, unfortunately Ellie Watt was here for once. I didn't know how my other identities would handle this.

"I can show you my ID," I said, taking the wineglass from him and swirling the liquid around. I kept my eyes focused on him, and he kept his on me.

He opened his mouth to say something but then quickly closed it. He raised his glass instead.

"To our Day of Fun," he said, voice warm and rich.

"And to the night," I answered.

*   *   *

Some of the best-laid plans are foiled by wine. Though, perhaps in our case, they were made better.

The first bottle of wine went down like a treat and straight to my head. I had only had a hot dog and fries at the driving range, and the copious amount of grease ingestion did nothing to slow the wine. Then someone had the idea to break out the second bottle. It was probably me. Anyway, that went down, too, all while Camden and I lay sprawled in his lawn chairs, staring up at the satellites as they went across the black sky.

I'd be lying if I said I didn't have massive déjà vu about the whole thing, back to the time when Camden and I used to lie on top of his trampoline and listen to music. He must have been reminded of that, too, because when he ran back inside the house to get a third bottle of wine from his rack, he picked up his iPod dock as well.

A few songs into Calexico's *Feast of Wire* (my choice), when the bottle was half drunk, we suddenly remembered we wanted to eat food. So Camden ran back inside to get the asparagus and steak—and a bag full of our thrift-store clothes.

He threw the bag onto the lawn chair beside me and started firing up the grill.

"You know the rules, Ellie," he said. "We can't eat until we're wearing that stuff."

"You just want to get my clothes off, don't you?" I teased, rifling through it. There was my skanky halter top (really nothing more than a bikini top) and Peggy Bundy pants.

"I can get your clothes off in other ways," he shot

back. He buried his devious smile behind the action of squirting lighter fluid onto the charcoals.

I have no doubt about that, I thought. I was fortunate, too, that I hadn't said it out loud. Drunk Ellie needed to keep herself in check. And with that, I made a point of savoring the rest of the wine in my glass. Even though I was having the most fun I'd had in a very, *very* long time, I couldn't forget who I was and the real reason I was there.

Even though every part of me was just screaming to let go.

A few minutes later the backyard filled with the tantalizing sizzle of grilled steaks. I breathed in deeply, my stomach growling.

"You wanted yours medium, right?" he asked. "Not much longer now."

Which meant it was changing time. While he started poking at the foil-wrapped asparagus, I turned the lawn chair around so that the high back was blocking his view of me. Then, after a quick look around at his neighbors and seeing only darkness from their windows, I shimmied out of my jeans. Unfortunately, I was drunk and had forgotten to take off my boots first. I fell over sideways onto the grass.

"What are you doing over there?" I heard Camden yell, and the sound of metal tongs being placed on a rung.

"Stay back! I'm fine!" I yelled, hoping my voice wasn't loud enough to alert the neighbors.

I thanked my lucky stars that my combat boots had a zipper and quickly unzipped them. Lying on my back with my leg bent up to my head, I pulled off the jeans and tossed them to the side. Then I got on my knees and started to look for my ugly Peg pants. Where the hell did they go?

"Looking for these?" Camden asked from behind me.

Swallowing my pride, I turned around on my knees and looked up. Camden was holding the pants in one hand. He dropped them beside him and then walked over to me. He held out his hand.

"Come on," he said gently, a shadowed intensity in his eyes.

I shook my head quickly. "No. I'm just in my underwear."

"I can see that," he said. "Let me help you up."

My heart thumped loudly in my ears, and I looked away from his face and straight ahead at his knees. "I don't want you to see."

Suddenly he was down on his knees, and though there were a few inches between us, he was closer than he'd ever been. "I don't care, Ellie," he said determinedly.

I kept shaking my head, unable to form words, unable to tell him how I was feeling. I just wanted him to go away and leave me alone, let me get dressed in peace. I wanted to run. I wanted the darkness to swallow me whole.

"You know how I feel about your scars. They only make you more beautiful," he whispered, now stroking the side of my face. His eyes were searching mine, begging me to open up, but the fear was so big and so damn real.

"You've never seen my scars." My voice was barely audible, even in my own head.

"No, I haven't. But I've seen what they've made you."

His nose nudged the side of mine and maybe because I'd been thinking about it ever since Safeway, or maybe because I was buying some time, I leaned in and kissed him. This wasn't the tender kiss from earlier. I had no wine bottles held above my head. This kiss was soft for a moment, then hurried. His lips sucked gently on mine, his tongue ravishing my mouth like he couldn't stop himself. I was suddenly insatiable, each kiss reaching down into my core, making me want all of him, every part. A million thoughts flew through my head, and then there was nothing at all. There wasn't even Camden and Ellie. There was just this hot, primal, crucial need for each other.

Before I could stop him, or at least pretend to stop him, he was pushing me back until I was falling onto the grass. I reluctantly slid my knees out to the side, my legs coming into full view. My scars visible in the dark. He didn't notice, didn't care. He kept kissing me passionately, so hot, so sweet, as one of his hands disappeared into the back of my hair, cupping my head. He laid me on the ground, the hard grass tickling the sides of my ears, and that was the last time he was gentle.

He straddled me and pulled my tank top over my head and tossed it aside. Then he leaned back and ripped off his own shirt. As if I wasn't breathing hard enough already, squirming beneath his form, he looked better than I could have imagined. Here was the new

Camden McQueen, shirtless, a tower of defined muscle and gorgeous, darkly dangerous tattoos.

There was a phoenix rising from the ashes along the swoop of muscle of his hip bones, a tiger/dragon hybrid flying up the side of his stomach, scripture peeking out of the top of his boxers. I'd seen only glimpses of them before, and now they glowed before me, lit by the hundreds of warm lights in his garden. He was like a living, breathing painting on an all-male canvas.

I couldn't gawk at him for long. He quickly took off his shorts, and I decided to help him out by removing my bra. I was glad I took the extra effort to wear my matching yellow-and-lace number. By the time I was finished unhooking it and throwing it across the grass, our clothes were scattered everywhere and his extremely erect penis was on full display.

I could only smile in response, stunned at the beauty of it, turned on as fuck at the idea of him thrusting it in me. And a tiny bit scared, to be honest, because it had been some time since I was with a man and it had been, well, never, since I was with a man built like him. Although I had never been a fan of blow jobs, except when it had come to Javier, my first instinct was to lay my lips around his tip and suck him slowly.

But that would have to wait. He leaned forward on me, elbows on each side of my shoulders, his body so wonderfully heavy on mine. His teeth went for my neck, nibbling softly from ear to shoulder while he slipped one of his hands slowly down my side and over my flat stomach until he was teasing the area underneath my thong. Then his fingers brushed against my pubic hair and stopped just as it was getting good. I squirmed, the pressure in my clit building to uncomfortable heights, wanting his hand to go down farther. I felt him smile against my lips, as if he were deliberately torturing me, then finally he gave in and gave me what I wanted. I was slick as oil, and it didn't take long at all before his fingers circled my clit enough times and I came.

I cried out, the orgasm catching me by surprise. If I were a man, I would have hung my head in shame. That took one minute, if that. But I didn't fucking care. I let the waves rock through me, my hand clutched in his hair, until I came to a soft landing.

I cleared my throat and spoke into his kiss. "Sorry, it's been a while."

"You should expect to hear the same thing from me in about five minutes," he murmured.

"Five minutes, huh?"

"I'll make it the best five minutes of your life."

I bit his lip, hard, then released him and looked into those intense blues. "Clock's ticking."

He grinned, dimples and all, then grabbed me by the sides of my arms and flipped me over on my stomach. I tried to turn over but he just pushed my shoulder down into the grass. I felt him go for my underwear, trying to roll it off my ample ass. Then I heard him give up.

It sounded just like a rip.

"That was my only matching pair to the bra!" I cried out, voice mercifully muffled by the grass.

"I'll tattoo you some new ones," he answered roughly. I felt his fingers slide down the crack of my rear, and before I could protest or freak out he slipped his hand underneath my pelvis and pulled me up until my ass was in the air.

I could hear him let out a long breath and could feel his eyes burning a hole through my skin. I was starting to feel uncomfortable, afraid that he'd seen the scars on my leg and was becoming turned off, but all my fears were banished when he brought his palm down across my ass. It stung to high heaven.

Holy shit, did Camden just spank me?

There was another hard slap on my other cheek and before I could start worrying whether I was getting caught up in some wannabe BDSM relationship, I felt his hot, wet lips kiss both of the slap marks. I closed my eyes to the pleasure and let out a groan when his fingers slipped inside me. It didn't matter if I had just come; I was more than ready to go again.

I felt his presence move off of me and heard the rustle of something plastic. Seconds later there was the telltale sound of a condom wrapper tearing. You can almost hear the concentration when a man is trying to put one of those on.

With one hand holding me at the small of my waist, he entered me slowly. With him taking me from behind, I couldn't see what he was doing, I could only feel. And I could feel everything. Pain, mostly. At first. Pain that slowly melted into a wet warmth that seemed to saturate every part of me from my stomach to my nipples. I felt uninhibited, and considering I lived my life by my own rules, I felt strangely free. With each thrust, Camden drove himself deeper. He rocked me against the ground in a rhythm that felt as intuitive as it was pleasurable. He filled me up, the thickness building inside while my own pressure built on the outside. He tightened his grip around my waist, making me feel irresistibly petite and vulnerable, and he pounded me harder, faster.

His breathing became heavier, more laborious, and the occasional moan came out of him that made my urge to come triple. Just when it sounded like he might lose it, I felt his fingers at my clit, working me into a frenzy with him. We came at the same time, groaning loudly, panting quietly, trying to control the volume. But, hell, if a neighbor were to stick their head out their window and see a tattooed god ramming a chick in the neighbor's backyard all lit by romantic lights, they'd probably watch. I'd watch, too.

When the shock waves slowed their roll through me, and my mind and body were coming back to earth, sorting through the delicious high of endorphins, I collapsed on my elbows, too blissed out to move. The grass could have eaten me alive and I wouldn't have cared.

Camden lay beside me, his head propped up by his hand, facing me. Still totally nude, breathing hard but with a smile that matched mine. Satisfied.

"So, I think the steaks are ruined," he said lightly, between breaths.

I sniffed the air, catching a whiff of charcoal from the burned steaks, and made a sad face. "Aw, I'm sorry."

"I'm not," he said. "I've waited my whole life to sleep with you, Ellie Watt. I can't just pick you up from Safeway."

I smiled, kind of embarrassed at that admission, and looked down at the grass. He was staring at me so earnestly, so...obviously...that I felt I should say something like that back. But I couldn't think of anything except, "So if we substitute sex for playing dress-up, does that still count in Camden and Ellie's Day of Fun?"

He grinned. "More than anything."

A light caught my eye and we both turned to look. One of the lights in the neighbor's window had just come on.

"Ah shit," I said. Now that I wasn't in the throes of passion, it turned out that being caught naked would be kind of embarrassing.

But Camden had quickly hopped to his feet and lifted up a wicker trunk that lined the patio. He brought a couple of fleece blankets, wrapping one around his waist and holding the other one out for me. He didn't leer at me as I got to my feet or stare anywhere I didn't want him to. He just wrapped the blanket around my chest and we quickly scooped up the clothes from the garden before we caused a scene. I grabbed the half-full bottle of wine, made another sad face at the overcooked food as the coals died out, and we scampered back inside.

CHAPTER EIGHT

Then

The girl hated gym class more than anything else. Even by the time tenth grade rolled around and she had made a few more friends, the class still scared the hell out of her.

By now, most of the girls in her class knew there was something wrong with her. Not just in the way she walked; they figured out she had something to hide, too. Some would come out and ask her what happened, others would ask why she always changed in the girl's toilet stall instead of out in the open like everyone else.

The girl always had an answer. To the first question, she would tell people she was attacked by a shark. Sometimes it was a bear. Other times it was a tragic skiing accident in the Swiss Alps. There was always an exciting story to think up, and the girl was a natural at lying. The second question was worse. If she admitted the accident had given her scars, the scars, those

burned-red ribbons of horror, they would always ask to
see. So the girl told the others that she was shy, or that
it was against her religion. With high school being the
cesspool that it was, that started a rumor about her being
a frigid prude. Well, it was better than the one that had
her sleeping with Camden McQueen in the ninth grade.

But no matter how used to the questions and the
whispers and the looks that the girl got, every time
gym class would come, she'd be a barrel of nerves. It
didn't help that in the tenth grade she got Mr. Kane: a
tall, paunchy asshole of a man with a balding crew cut
and the desire to make every girl's life a living hell. Mr.
Kane wasn't even a proper gym teacher—he taught law
class to twelfth graders. And yet there he was, barking
at young girls to give him push-ups or a few more laps
around the track.

The girl hated to run. It wasn't that she couldn't, but
she was slow and her run was worse than her walk. She
couldn't do sports like soccer or hockey, either, anything that could involve impact for her scars or required
a lot of balance and quick turns. Consequently, she
was always picked last for teams for the sports that she
could play.

On that particular day it was a game of soccer in
the sun-baked grass field behind the school. As she had
done many times before, she went up to Mr. Kane and
told him she couldn't play and would have to sit it out.

And like the many times before, Mr. Kane turned to
her with nothing short of disgust. "Again, Miss Watt?"
he sneered over his clipboard.

She swallowed hard and hated how she had to prove

her disability when most of the time she was trying to hide it. "Yes. You know I have a disability."

"Actually, I don't know. I never received a doctor's note and you look right as rain to me. I'm a bit tired of these excuses, Ellie. You can walk, right? So you can play soccer."

She shook her head and stood her ground. "It's not an excuse. I can't. I might get hurt and then I won't be able to walk for days." Why did he have to be such an asshole? Couldn't he see from her eyes how sincere she was?

By now a few girls had crowded around him, girls she wished would go back to touching up their makeup on the sidelines. Vicky and the girl now had an uneasy truce, but as the years went on, new mean girls took the reins at the school and didn't ignore her the way that Vicky did now. These girls loved to tease the girl every chance they got.

Mr. Kane folded his arms over his fat stomach, an almost impossible feat. "To tell you the truth, I think you're not giving yourself enough credit. Soccer never hurt anyone. You're just hurting yourself—and your grades—by refusing to play. Maybe you should stop being a little baby about all of this and man up."

The girls snickered, and Mr. Kane looked ridiculously pleased with himself. The girl felt an anger pushing up through her veins like a swarm of malevolent bees.

"I'm not a baby! I have a—"

"—a disability, yes we know. But what is your disability? Does it have a name?"

"Sir Limps-A-Lot!" one of the girls shouted, some-how conjuring up that dreaded earlier nickname.

The girl felt like stomping her pretty red head into the grass. With cleats.

"Hey, be nice," Mr. Kane tossed over his shoulder at her in a vain attempt to look like a diplomatic teacher and not some controlling, sexist moron. He looked back to the girl. "Come on. Tell us what it is. Tell me what happened to you, tell me exactly why you can't play the game, and I'll let you off."

All eyes were on her, watching her expectantly, waiting for her answer. She couldn't tell them the truth, tell them what really happened to her. If she did, she'd shame her parents, and they'd been shamed enough. No one would believe the truth anyway. No one would believe it happened because she'd been caught trying to steal from one of the Gulf Coast's most powerful drug lords.

"I   ," the girl started, but she couldn't find the right excuse, the right answer that would satisfy all of them. She looked down at the ground, her cheeks heating.

"I knew it," someone in the crowd said. "It's prob-ably something lame like she has one leg longer than the other."

"Ha, lame, get it!" joked someone else.

As she stared at the grass, she could see the high noon shadow of Mr. Kane slowly shaking his head. Not believing her.

"All right, well then you'll have to play," he said, sounding so far away. "Or you'll fail the class."

She wanted to scream *You can't do that!*, she wanted

to threaten to sue him, to report him to the principal. She wanted to do all of those things, and she certainly had a right to. She might even win.

But she wanted to put an end to it once and for all. Just to get it fucking over with.

She snapped her head up and glared at everyone, their faces becoming an anonymous blob in the harsh sunlight.

"You want to see? Do you want to see why I can't play? Why I have nerve damage to my leg?" she yelled at them sharply, her voice cracking in places. Everyone, including the teacher, was stunned into an uneasy silence, as if they were afraid the girl would reveal she was some hungry, fire-breathing dragon underneath, ready to devour them all.

The girl stuck out her right leg and with one yank, she rolled up the leg of her sweatpants to the knee.

Everyone gasped. A few covered their mouths. Mr. Kane looked startled and reproached. The girl knew what her leg looked like, knew what an acid burn did when it covered an entire leg. She kept her harsh eyes on everyone else, making sure they saw it. Making sure they got it.

Finally Mr. Kane said, "That's enough, Ellie. You're excused. Please sit at the sidelines and observe the game."

He turned and pushed his way through the girls, who were still staring in horror and disgust, even when the girl rolled the pant leg back down. At least now they understood why she changed in the bathroom stall, why she never wore shorts to gym class, why she wore jeans in hundred-degree heat.

She had to.

"Come on, girls, either we start this game or you're all giving me five laps around the track," Mr. Kane barked as he began unloading the soccer balls. "Now!"

At that, they all jumped to attention and quickly left the girl to her own devices. She could hear them whispering to one another as they scattered, but the girl didn't want to hear what they were saying.

She sighed, her breath shaking like a leaf, and carefully walked across the field and over to the sidelines. She sat down on the bench and watched.

She thought exposing the truth and getting out of class would have brought her a sense of relief. But it only brought her a sense of shame. She'd seen their faces, their reactions. The girl wasn't the fire-breathing dragon, but she was a monster all the same.

Now

The cozy flannel bedspread was wrapped around us, our limbs entangled in its softness and each other. After Camden and I retreated into the house, wrapped only in cheap IKEA blankets, we decided to finish off the bottle of wine and raid his cupboards for something that would make up for the lost steak dinner. We settled on grilled cheese with tomato basil soup. Not exactly gourmet, but after the sex, we didn't really care.

Nor did we bother getting dressed. When dinner was done, Camden decided he was still hungry and proceeded to go down on me in front of the freshly made fire. The man had some serious skill with his tongue and this time, with no neighbors to worry about, I really let go, screaming out his name loudly and gripping the top of his head with each spasm.

Naturally, I returned the favor. He didn't even have to ask; I'd been wanting to take his cock in my mouth the whole night. I'd wanted a nice, clear view of him while I sucked him off, watching his beautiful eyes roll back in his head, his body become more rigid by the second.

And if that wasn't enough to exhaust a person, we ended up in the bedroom for our final course. Nothing fancy here, just the good ol' missionary position. Women may scoff at it, but I'm telling you, when you have an all-male machine of strength and hard muscle primed above you, pounding you to the bed while spearing you with his eyes, there's no better feeling in the world. To me, missionary is all about being taken.

That's probably why I felt a little tender and vulnerable afterward. I wasn't one for spooning, but I let him press me against his naked body, his mouth laying soft kisses on the base of my neck. I was delirious, tired, and a bit sore from all the sexual escapades. And with all that, I felt that little tug at the base of my belly, the one that produced butterflies and caused my heart to burst. One—okay, a few—stints in the sack with this man, and I was starting to get emotionally attached.

I let out a long breath and snuggled my head further down into the soft pillow. I'd let myself feel all lovey-dovey and whatever for tonight. Just for tonight. Then tomorrow, I had to shut off my heart and it was business as usual.

"Do they still hurt?" Camden whispered into my hair. I paused. "What?"

"Do the scars still hurt?"

I raised my head and twisted around to face him. His eyes had heavy lids from the lust and impending sleep, but they were curious and kind. I chewed on my lip, wiggling my jaw back and forth, debating whether I should get into another one of these discussions. But I decided to embrace it and tell the truth.

"All the time," I answered softly.

His eyes crinkled at the corners in sadness, and he gently kissed me on the forehead.

"I'm sorry they still hurt," he said.

I nodded. "Me too."

Feeling brave and honest, I pulled the bedspread back and showed him my leg. He had seen it many times that night, you know, with all the nakedness, but his eyes never lingered; he never reacted and never questioned. Now I wanted him to see.

He took his hand and held it above my leg. I tensed, not knowing what he was going to do. He gently placed his fingers on it and traced the ribbons from the back of my heel all the way up my calf and shin to the knee. I shivered from his touch, the sensitive scar tissue making me feel everything to the bone.

"Does it hurt when I do this?" he asked, tracing his fingers up and down.

"No," I said, barely able to speak. It actually felt nice, pleasurable enough to raise the hairs on the back of my neck. I'd never let anyone touch them before, except the occasional doctor.

"It's like art, Ellie," he said gently and looked up at me. His eyes looked wet in the table lamp's amber light.

"Art?"

"Like an abstract painting. You can find art and beauty in everything, if you look hard enough. But your beauty is just staring you in the face."

I swallowed hard, my throat feeling thick. He gave me a small smile and then pulled the bedspread up over me.

"Come on, we should get some sleep," he said, leaning over and switching off the lamp.

The room went dark but my heart was glowing.

*   *   *

The next morning I got up with the dawn, realizing how worried Uncle Jim was going to be. My phone had gone dead during the night, and he was probably wondering why my car was still outside of his place.

I got dressed in a hurry, already feeling different in the early light. Last night had been a lot of fun but fun was all it would be. It was all it *could* be.

"You sure you don't want to shower here?" Camden asked me as he leaned against the door, watching me smooth my hair down in the bathroom. "I can make you breakfast. Mexican omelet with lots of peppers."

"I would, but Uncle Jim is probably a worried wreck. You don't mind driving me, do you?"

He shook his head no, and soon we were in his Jeep, jutting down the main street. Everything looked peaceful before the shops opened, like nothing bad could happen in this town with its groomed palm trees and bright buildings.

Soon he was pulling up into the driveway beside Jose, and I knew Uncle Jim was going to get a good look at him. I could already feel his disapproval radiating from the stucco.

Camden eyed the house warily, perhaps picking up on my nervy vibes, then leaned in with a smile. "Well, I think it's safe to say that last night was the most fun I've ever had on Camden and Ellie's Day of Fun. I think it was the most fun I've had, period."

"It was certainly one for the books," I told him. Hating good-byes, I quickly kissed him on the lips.

"So you'll stay for a while?" he asked me, all hopeful and cute. He really worked hard at ruining my resolve.

"I think so, for a few days anyway," I said, being careful with my words. Everything was starting to count now. "I have some friends nearby. I may pay them a visit, or I might check out some of the nearby towns if I can't get a job here."

He frowned. "Do you really need a job that badly?"

I grinned awkwardly. "Who doesn't need a job? Anyway, thanks for the lovely time and the fun, and I hope you enjoy your kilt."

He gave me a funny look and it wasn't over what I had said. "Can I call you? Or do I have to guess your e-mail again? I can't believe you still use the same account since high school."

"Well it's all consolidated into one now." But I gave Camden my phone number and told him to give me a ring. I wasn't sure if that was a mistake or not, but perhaps keeping tabs on his whereabouts would help me out in the long run.

My eyes flew to the house and spied the curtains being thrown back. Uncle Jim was up.

I gave Camden a sheepish look. "I better go before he hangs my ass."

I snatched up my purse, suddenly very aware I was doing the walk of shame, and went quickly up to the house. Seeing that he was still waiting in the Jeep, I gave him a short wave, then unlocked the door and stepped in.

I leaned against it and didn't breathe a sigh of relief until I heard Camden's Jeep roar away.

Then I yelped.

Uncle Jim suddenly appeared in front of me.

"Jesus, you scared the shit out of me!" I gasped, hand to my pounding heart.

He folded his arms across his denim shirt and lowered his head in paternal impatience. "Where on earth were you last night?"

"I told you, I was out. Applying for jobs," I said, straightening out my tank top and avoiding his eyes. It's not that I couldn't lie to his face—I could lie to anyone's face—but I didn't want to see the disapproval.

"Without your car?"

"Er, yes," I said, moving past him. I put my purse on the counter and opened the fridge. There was still only mustard.

"Ellie, I don't care if you're with that McQueen boy or not," he explained with a sigh. "I really don't. I know you know how to take care of yourself. You're one of the toughest women I know."

I rolled my eyes and was glad only the jar of mustard could see it. I didn't feel so tough anymore now that the "McQueen boy" had admittedly gotten under my skin.

He went on. "I was just worried. I thought...maybe something had happened to you."

I shut the fridge and leaned back against it to face him, blowing a strand of hair out of my face.

"I'm fine. See? And you just said I was the toughest woman you know."

"I said you were one of them. And...I'm not worried about you and the sheriff's son. I'm worried about *you*. People from your past. About the kind of trouble you get in."

I cocked my head. "People from my past? Like who?"

He waved his hand in the air dismissively. "Oh, no one. I don't know who the people from your past are. I just know you have a past and that people's pasts like to catch up with them."

I had to admit, he was making me a bit nervous. It's not that I wasn't often thinking the exact same thing. When you lived your life scamming people, stealing from them, and making enemies, you tended to have a giant case of paranoia and anxiety in your personal baggage. It was part of the reason I got hooked on Ativan, but then my brain got too fuzzy and I lost a lot of my wits. I needed them.

But I couldn't be afraid of everything all the time.

I had always taken the right precautions. I did certain types of cons under certain types of names and certain types of personas. I had a revolving collection of realistic wigs, colored contacts, and self-tanning lotion. I knew tricks with makeup to make my nose look wider or slimmer; I could change my whole look just by manipulating my brows. No one knew Ellie Watt. Except for the people in this town, people like Camden, no one knew *me*. Even Javier didn't know the real me; he knew me as a bronzed, blond bombshell called Eden White. And yes, I chose to look, and sound, like a porn star on purpose.

"I'm fine, really," I told him, wishing I sounded more confident. "Ellie Watt is a safe bet with a clean record."

He furrowed his brow before walking over to the coffee pot. "Yeah, well, I sure hope she keeps it that way. For both of our sakes."

*   *   *

Later that day, I was walking around Joshua Tree National Park and planning the exact thing Uncle Jim was afraid of: trouble. To be fair, I'd only get in trouble, only tarnish my name, if I got caught. And I wasn't planning on getting caught. I wasn't as impulsive as I used to be. I only took chances when the odds were good. The odds here were in my favor. Camden liked me. He trusted me. He'd never believe I was the one ripping him off.

I couldn't believe I was actually going through with the whole thing, either. That had to count for something.

It was hot as fuck up at Joshua Tree, and two in the afternoon was probably the worst time to go for a hike, but something about the surroundings soothed me. The sky was impossibly blue, like paint pigment. I'd seen a similar color inked on Camden's arm. The boulders were smooth and round, like Camden's shoulders. The scrubby cacti and sagebrush reminded me of the stubble on his chin. And the imposing Joshua trees, the way they rose up out of the earth…well, anyway. Suffice it to say, even though I came here to get some fresh air and clear my mind, my thoughts kept coming back to Camden.

Get through tonight and then you're gone, I told myself, kicking away a small tumbleweed. I had to keep telling myself that or I'd begin to lose my nerve. This was the whole problem with the "knowing your mark" thing. It made things easier and harder at the same time.

Even though I kept thinking back to our lovemaking, to the beautiful things he said to me, to the way he knew the person I had been and didn't seem to care, it was fruitless to even humor the idea of making something out of us. Camden might have known me as a scared little turncoat in high school, but he didn't know me as a criminal. He didn't know the things I'd done and he could never know. What was I supposed to do then? Shack up with him and live a lie? I had done that with Javier and barely got out of that alive.

It was too hard living a lie. I didn't think I could share it with someone, too.

In the sweet shade of a boulder, I parked my ass on

a rock and brought out my notepad and pen. I needed to think hard and think smart. I didn't want to pack up my car to leave tonight, since my original plan had me hanging around town for a few more days. After all, it would look terribly suspicious if I happened to leave town the same time as the robbery. But I had to take precautions, and that meant hightailing my ass out of town if it came down to it.

I wanted to get in the house in the middle of the night. I knew Camden was tired from our early rise that morning and from the wine hangover we were both feeling. He'd probably be sleeping soundly by two in the morning, so I chose four as the best option. Only sordid things happened at four a.m.

I'd go in through the front door. Picking that lock would be easy. Then I'd get into the office and hit up the safe. I had come up with several number combinations that I thought were a good start. If they didn't work, then I could either choose to bail or test my luck and try safecracking. Listening for those contact points took an awful lot of time, however, and time was something that wasn't on my side.

But I'd listened to Camden a lot last night, even when I was drunk. My brain was always reeling stuff in. After trying 007, 311, 911, 411, 187, and 666 (some of the more easily remembered three-number codes), I'd try his birthday (6/11), his son's birthday (10/03), the area code (760), or the last three digits of his license plate (299). Then I'd work through combinations of his lucky number (5) and his phone digits. Yes, I found out an awful lot of trivial information about Camden during our day of fun. Luckily he was the type to just talk and let me ask the questions.

Which, in retrospect, I did find a little weird. He hadn't seen me since high school, and aside from asking how Uncle Jim was doing, what song was tattooed on my arm, and that whole "I've been doing odd jobs" excuse, he hadn't asked me anything about myself. Wasn't I a bit of a mystery to him? Wasn't he at all interested in what I'd been up to in the last eight or nine years or so?

Perhaps he was just being polite. He knew how defensive I could get over the smallest things. I decided to forget about that and be thankful that he had left his questioning out of it. As I said earlier, I'd have no problems lying to him—but it didn't mean I liked doing it.

I had filled up the notepad with a rough map of his house and potential hazards when my phone beeped, breaking through the sound of ground doves and cicadas.

I fished it out of my pocket. It was a text from Camden. Oh boy.

Hey, was wondering if you wanted to catch a show with me tonight in San Bernardino. I know it's kind of far but this band is really good. I think you'd like them. It starts at 10PM.

I pursed my lips, somewhat delighted at this chain of events, and texted him back:

Aw, sorry! I can't, I've decided to go catch up with my friend in San Diego. Just about to leave now. It'll just be for the night though, so maybe we can catch up for drinks tomorrow night? Have a great time at the show!

I pressed Send and waited. The air seemed to get hotter by the second and soon my jeans felt like a sauna prison for my legs.

It wasn't long before he replied back:

Wow, San Diego. That's a long drive. Hope you're careful. Bring back some of that sea breeze for me. Talk soon. Camden.

I thought it cute that he signed his name and exhaled a sigh of relief, tilting my head up to the sky. He was going to be out in San Bernardino all night. That was at least an hour away which meant he'd be gone by nine p.m. and wouldn't be back until midnight at the earliest. I had three hours to do this.

I was going to rob Camden McQueen.

CHAPTER NINE

UNFORTUNATELY, LYING TO Camden also meant lying to my uncle. Their stories had to match, because when the sheriff's son was robbed, the whole town was going to know about it.

When I got back home from Joshua Tree, I packed my bags and left a note for him. He was somewhere out in the date groves, and I didn't have the time to hunt him down. Plus, I felt better lying on paper than to his face.

Basically, I told him the same thing I told Camden; I was going to San Diego for the night to see my friend Cindy. I know, I know. Cindy is totally the name of the girl you make up in your alibi. But I actually did have a friend called Cindy in San Diego, and she was one of those people who owed me big time. Let's just say I did a lot of ecoterrorism on her behalf, and her house is now overrun by the rabbits and dogs we liberated from an animal testing clinic.

I left the note on the counter and made myself

promise that as soon as I had any extra money, I'd make sure that the mustard in Uncle Jim's fridge would never be lonely. The man worked too hard and—in his own way—was far too generous to be missing the finer things in life. He may not have wanted charity, but I was sure he was going to get it somehow.

At about four p.m. I revved Jose and peeled out of the cul-de-sac. If my uncle heard my wheels out in the groves, then the timing would make sense. I took a left onto the highway and headed for the outlet mall in Cabazon. I had a few hours to kill, and that place was as good as any to get lost in a crowd. It would have been more fun if I'd had a few spare dollars to spare, but with my last twenty going to dinner and gas, I was flat broke.

I wasted my time walking around the stores and peeking in the windows, battered by the relentless wind that swept down the I-10 and kept the giant turbines turning. Considering I was forever consigned to pants or leggings, I'd never been too interested in fashion anyway. I wore what I had to and was comfortable with my uniform of jeans, pretty/edgy tops, and boots. When I grew bored of window shopping, I went and sat in my car with my dying Kindle, its battery flashing CHARGE ME for the next hour. Then, when the time was right, I popped a few kava pills to kill my flaring nerves and headed back into Palm Valley.

This time my soundtrack was the album *Sunset Mission* by Bohren und der Club of Gore, a German horror jazz band that was all instrumental. As silly as it sounds, listening to it not only calmed me down but made me feel like a femme fatale in a film noir. It was part of my pre-con ritual. It made me play the character of the grifter. It made me own my lack of morality. Of course when I saw it all in my head, my black hair was curled in a sleek bob and I wore red lipstick. I also drank Scotch on the rocks while safecracking. Hey, whatever gets you ready for the job.

A few blocks before Camden's, I pulled down a side street and went down two blocks. Then I went up another block and parked my car beside a small dog-walking park. If I headed across the street and went through a vacant lot, I'd be on his street and his house would be three doors down. It was a joyous day when Google Maps with Street View came into our lives.

I cut the engine and spent a few moments scoping the darkness. The street was totally empty and very quiet, considering it was only nine fifteen at night. That could work either for or against me. When there weren't many people about, if someone saw you, you were easier to remember. That said, you had a greater chance of *not* being seen.

I was prepared, though. I reached in the backseat and stuck on a blue baseball cap and a pair of thin gloves. The rest of me was dressed in black jeans and a long-sleeved black basketball jersey to hide any sign of femininity. I tucked my notepad into the back pocket of my jeans and removed my car keys from the ignition. On the end of the key chain I had my trusty tiny Allen wrench, which I had ground down, plus a straightened-out safety pin and paperclip, both strong enough to handle the front door's five-pin tumbler lock that kept Camden's house safe. The only other thing I had was a reusable Safeway bag that was tucked into my boots. I traveled light. It was easier that way.

After taking one more pill and a few deep breaths, I left Jose as casually as possible. The last thing I wanted was to be sneaking around and have someone see me sneaking around. I acted unpremeditated, like I lived around here, but I still closed the door quietly. I walked easily across the street and crossed the vacant lot full of sand, rock, and dried-out brush. Just…taking a stroll. Nothing to see here.

Once I reached Camden's street, I walked with the same purpose. I was just a friend, just a friend paying him a visit and oh, look, he wasn't home. Sounded simple when you said it like that, but one house away and I was starting to get really nervous. "Puking my guts out" kind of nervous. "Second-guessing everything" kind of nervous.

I couldn't lose it. I passed by the quaint white bungalow that was his neighbor (thankfully not the ones who we had a close call with the night before) and suddenly there I was. Even though he had kept a light on in the garage and in the kitchen window, his Jeep was gone. I had more than enough time now; I had to remember that.

I did a quick, casual sweep of my surroundings before making my way to his front door. As I thought, it stayed dark and he didn't have any motion sensors. Still, I kept my head down low, just in case there was a camera mounted somewhere. It was extremely unlikely, but it was better to be paranoid than dead.

When I saw the road was deserted, I grinned at the

hedge of desert roses that kept me hidden from the occasional car going down the main street, and I got to work on his lock. All deadbolts were five-pin tumblers, and his was a Kwikset, which was as generic as you could get. Normally, lock-picking took a lot of time and patience, but when you grew up with a family of con artists, you were given locks to practice on more than you were given a Barbie or Legos.

I selected my trusty Allen wrench from the key ring and inserted it, as casually as someone just putting their house key into their house lock. It took only a few seconds for me to locate all the pins from the first to the key pin and push them up past the sheer line inside. The cylinder turned and the door opened with ease.

I knew there wouldn't be any alarms going off, since he didn't have a system, so I quickly shut the door, not locking it, and crept to the office. Even though I knew he wasn't home, it was best to be quiet anyway. It was a habit I didn't like to break.

His office was cold at this time of night. A small lamp lit in the corner cast the room in an eerie glow. I did a quick once-over of the office, trying to see if there was anything else of value. My eyes hesitated on the computer; I thought about going through his files, but I was already invading his privacy enough. Besides, I knew all I needed to know about Camden McQueen. Anything more might work against me.

I opened the closet doors and crouched down to the safe. I turned the dial to zero, then started going through the codes I came up with. I tried the usual suspects, then his birthday, then his son's. I tried his license plate number, then the area code. I tried more things and more things and more things. Nothing doing.

After about thirty minutes, when the sweat began to collect on my forehead, I was about to resign myself to actually trying to crack the safe through the harder and more tedious methods when I had an incredibly vain thought. Camden used to like me...an awful lot. What were the odds of him picking my birthday? I had a single-digit birthday and a double digit birth month, so it would work.

I turned the dial to one. Then two. Then nine.

The safe cracked open.

Shit. Camden had actually used my birthday as his code. I didn't know whether to be flattered or creeped out. I decided on the latter, since any thoughts about the former would only hold me back. I had to stay focused and keep going. I was in way too deep at this point.

And it didn't matter. I had done what I came here to do.

I slowly opened the safe door, and with my heart in my mouth, peered inside.

There was nothing but cash. Ziplock bags of cash. Some of them a mix of notes, others all hundred-dollar bills. There was *at least* twenty thousand dollars piled up in the safe. It was an obscene amount, and I almost started salivating at the sight—which was great, since my tongue had started sticking to the roof of my mouth.

Originally, I was going to take it all. It was the only way I could make the robbery look natural. But perhaps if I threw a couple of bags by the door, as if I had dropped them during my escape, I could make it look like an accident. That way I'd still leave him with something. I mean, serves him kind of right for keeping this much cash in a safe. What, didn't he trust the banks?

I took in a deep breath and with hands that trembled ever so slightly, I pulled my canvas Safeway bag out of my boot and began to pile the money inside in neat little bundles.

I was so engrossed in making the bag look as clean and as inconspicuous as possible, wrapping the excess plastic over on itself, that I didn't hear the door open.

The only thing I heard was a sound that you never forget.

The sound of a Magnum's hammer being pulled back.

The unmistakable cocking of a gun.

It echoed around the small room in slow motion and my actions reflected the pace. When you know you've got a gun aimed at you, everything moves just a little bit slower.

I turned my head in the direction of the sound, knowing it was a dicey move. I saw a blinding flashlight illuminating my face, my hands, my bag of his money, and the empty open safe. I saw his silhouette in the doorway, barely lit by the room's lamp. I saw the glint in his eyes and the matching shine of his smile as he pointed a gun at my face.

"Gotcha," he said. His teeth gleamed white.

CHAPTER TEN

I WAS BREATHLESS. Speechless. Immobile. I could only stare at him, at Camden McQueen, as he held the Magnum like it was just an extension of his arm. This had to be a bad dream. This couldn't be happening. He wasn't in his office, catching me in the act of robbing him blind.

"Put the bag down, Ellie," he said, his voice emotionless. "Put the bag down, then slowly stand up and put your hands in the air."

With the light blinding me, I couldn't see the expression in his eyes. I didn't know how to play this. I tried to swallow but couldn't. "Camden, I—"

"Shut up. Just shut. Up. Put the bag down. Stand up slowly. Put your hands in the air and face me."

Fuck, I couldn't move.

"Now!" he screamed in shaking rage.

The shock of his voice made the feeling come back into my limbs. I put the bag down, raised my hands, and slowly got to my feet. I turned to face him, squinting at the flashlight.

I heard the metal click of a handcuff and saw him bring out a pair from his back pocket.

Oh shit.

He raised them in the air. "Now here's what we're going to do. You're going to turn around and put your hands behind your back. Then I'm going to cuff you. Don't you dare try any funny stuff because I just loaded this gun. The bullets are ready to go. I don't have a problem shooting you if you don't cooperate. Maybe in your other leg to make things more even."

Tears pricked my eyes. *Shocked* wasn't the right word. It didn't convey enough of what I was feeling. None of this made sense. This wasn't the Camden I knew. I didn't know who the hell this was.

He was terrifying.

"Are you an undercover cop?" I asked, picking up my voice from the floor.

"Turn around, Ellie. I cocked the gun to make a point. The next point I make will involve pulling the trigger."

I did as he said. As he walked toward me, I ran through my ways out of this. I could chance it. I could predict where his gun was and turn and knock it out of his hands. I could go low and kick him out at the shins. Or the balls. Anything that would get him to drop the gun, anything to reverse the roles.

But I'd never done that to someone with a loaded weapon before. I didn't trust my reaction time. I couldn't count on my limbs to do the job. It was too much of a risk and I'd already taken too many.

I felt him stop behind me, his breath tickling the

back of my neck. It was no longer erotic—it was horrifying as hell. His hands went for mine, and he slowly placed the cold cuffs over my wrists. When they clicked shut, it was the sound of defeat.

"No, I'm not a cop," he said to my neck. His voice was so flat, so inhuman, he might as well have been a robot. "I'm just a tattoo artist. I'm just a guy who used to be in love with a girl. I'm just a fool who's been fooled too many times before. I'm just a man who's finally getting his revenge."

"You're a monster," I spat out.

He laughed, cold and sharp. Then he placed his hand around my throat and squeezed hard. My windpipe crushed, I could barely breathe.

"Do you ever look at yourself in the mirror?" he asked, his voice rising. "Do you like what you see?"

I fought for breath, trying to squirm away under his hand, but it only made him tighten his grip. Those wonderful, strong fingers would be the death of me.

"I made an assumption about you," he said, his voice calm again. "And I was right. If I'm a monster, then you must be the creator of them all. You're my Dr. Frankenstein."

And like that, he suddenly let go. I bent over, trying to get air into my aching lungs, trying to think past the burn in my throat. My heart was pounding so loudly I was almost deaf.

"Come here," he said, and grabbed me by the elbow. He threw me roughly into his desk chair, where my hands were crushed against the seat. With the gun still on me, he bent down and scooped up the Safeway bag.

"You know, if you needed the money, you could have just asked me." His voice was a little gentler now. "I would have given it to you, no questions asked."

"Why?" My hat fell off my head onto the floor, and my hair obscured my vision.

He walked over to me, putting the bag on the desk, and crouched down in front of me. Through the strands of hair I could see only the shiny barrel of the gun in his hands.

"Because it would have meant that you changed. That you found the decency to be honest. I would have rewarded you for that."

Being busted and cuffed with a gun pointed at you isn't the best time to get annoyed about things outside the big picture. But I couldn't help but snarl at his patronizing tone.

"How did you know?" I asked stiffly. "How did you know I was going to scam you?"

He smiled. Beautiful. Wicked. "Because the moment I told you I was successful, the moment you saw my shop, the moment you saw the money I brought in, I saw the same look in your eyes that you used to give the popular girls in high school. The very same look you gave them that day in the cafeteria when you turned on me. The day you *humiliated* me. The look that said 'opportunity.'"

"So you set me up?" It was too much to take. I couldn't believe that Camden had been playing me this entire time.

"Yes, I set you up. I hoped you'd fail. I hoped that I'd lie on the couch all night and never hear you breaking into my house. I hoped that you'd prove me wrong, that you liked me for me. But I was right. Fuck, Ellie. I've never hated being so right in all my life. You're a con artist. A liar. A thief. An unredeemable soul. You can't be reformed. You can't be saved. You'll die trying to make the world pay for what it did to you. And you'll die alone."

My heart clenched at his words and the inside of my nose grew hot. The tears were back.

He brushed my hair behind my ears, and I flinched at his touch. He observed me curiously.

"Crocodile tears?" he asked with a shake of his head. "You've got to be kidding me."

I swallowed. A hot tear ran from the corner of my eye. "I've never been more serious in my life."

"Good. Neither have I."

He stood up and reached across the desk, bringing out a stuffed animal that had been hiding near the wall. It was a goofy-looking bear. I had seen it earlier but not really *seen* it. I must have subconsciously figured it belonged to his son.

"See this?" he asked, making the bear dance in front of me.

"Is it Ben's?"

"It's a video camera."

Double shit.

"It's one of those nanny cams that you set up in your kid's room. To catch the weirdos. I don't get to take care of Ben and I probably never will, but if I ever had to hire a babysitter, I'd use one of these. You can't trust anyone these days." He smirked at me. "So I pressed Play at about eight o'clock. It's been recording ever since. No matter where you go or what you do, I have all of this on tape. You're done for, Ellie. They're going to lock you up and swallow the key. You're going to follow down the same path as your family, except you won't be able to run. You know, sometimes I look at you and I see this...cornered desperation." The phrase rolled off his tongue like smoke. "Think of how cornered you'll be when you're living in a jail cell."

I'd had some low moments in my life. I'd been scared to death. I'd had the shit kicked out of me on two different occasions. I've had my fingers broken once (a poorly thrown punch). I'd been humiliated, cheated on, cast aside. But other than the moment I got my scars— the moment that put me on the path I was on—I'd never been so scared as I was sitting there handcuffed in Camden's chair with my entire future resting inside the bowels of a teddy bear.

I looked him in the eye and took a steady breath. "What do you want from me?"

"What do I want from you?" he repeated, placing the bear back on the desk, facing me and out of reach.

I sighed loudly. "Yes. What do you want? Are you turning me over to your dad, or do you just feel like torturing me for a bit first?"

He leaned against the wall and bit his lip. "I do feel like torturing you, Miss Watt. I've been waiting for this moment for a very long time."

My face scrunched with despair. "So you've harbored a stupid grudge ever since high school?"

He smiled tightly. "Don't make it sound trivial. Haven't you harbored a grudge since high school?"

"But I have reasons!"

He raised his brows. His eyes looked opaque and glossy like blue glass. "Oh do you? You think because of your leg and your scars that gives you a right to punish people? Rob people? Cheat, scam, and steal? You think you can use that to justify what you do for a living?"

"You weren't me," I said through grinding teeth. "You have no idea what I went through."

"I have some idea. We were friends once, you know." He walked slowly in front of me, holding the gun behind his back like he was deep in thought. "Do you think because you can't see my scars that they don't exist? That's the trouble with pain, Ellie. If you're lucky, you can wear it for all the world to see. Most people have their pain deep inside, in places no one ever goes. Not until it's too late."

I had nothing to say to that. In a way, he was right. I had no idea what kind of scars he had, and just because they weren't visible, it didn't mean they weren't there. I mean, the guy was acting a little sadistic and a little fucking nuts. He was obviously hurting, far more than I would have ever thought.

"Well," I said slowly, licking my dry lips. "I don't know what to say except that I'm sorry."

He stopped in the middle of the room. "Excuse me?"

"I said I'm sorry. I'm sorry. I mean it, I'm sorry I hurt you." I felt like a flood was opening up in my throat. "I...I didn't mean to. I was an idiot back then. I was a bitch, I...I was weak. I wanted people to like me. No one had ever liked me and I just wanted to be normal."

"I liked you," he said quietly. I opened my mouth but he went on. "But I guess I wasn't normal enough for you."

My chest went hollow at the pain in his eyes. "It's not that. I just didn't know how to appreciate your friendship. You were my first friend. Ever. I had no one before you except my parents, and when the thing with my leg happened...I couldn't trust them anymore. I wanted to trust you, Camden, I really did. But then I thought if you liked me then there was something wrong with you. And that you'd hurt me."

"So you hurt me first."

"Yes," I said breathlessly.

He nodded to himself. He seemed to get it. "So why did you try and rob me just now?"

Shit.

"Why"—he started pacing again—"did you try and scam me? Why now? Why me?" He choked on his last words like he was swallowing a bone. "Why did you try and fuck with me again?!"

My hands went into fists behind my back, my body instinctively picking up on the flashes of rage that were starting to flow through him. Flee or fight. Human instinct. In the dull light of the room, with his wild tats and hair that looked like he'd been pulling on it all night, he looked like a crazy person. His eyes were darting back and forth like metronomes.

"You used me," he said incredulously. "You pretended to like me, you went to my show. You fucking paid some drunk-ass one hundred dollars to be your scapegoat. Don't give me that look. The guy approached me in the bathroom before we left. He told me what the note said. I remembered the opportunistic look in your eyes, and I started thinking about things that I didn't want to think about. I've been fucked over too many times to not see the signs. To know when a woman's got something else up her sleeve. And you kept going. We went out on a date. I had to know; I had to see where this was going. We went on a date and you slept with me. You fucked me and fucked me good and you still went through with it. You say you were a bitch in high school. You say you were weak and you just wanted to be normal. Well, guess what? You're not normal. You're definitely weak. And I don't think I've ever met a bigger bitch than you."

I looked down at the ground, trying to keep my cool while the arrows were flung. Some had bounced off of me. The rest stuck in deep. "Are we done?" I said with deliberation.

He sighed and leaned against the wall. Time ticked by. It felt like an eternity.

"Yeah, we're done. I've said what I had to say."

I glanced at him. "Do you feel better now?"

He cocked his head and seemed to think it over. "A little bit."

"So what's next? What do you plan on doing with me? Are you taking me down to the station yourself like Daddy's little hero, or are you calling the cops over here? Or are they already here waiting outside?"

I could have been nicer to him. After all, he had the upper hand and I was totally at his mercy. But he wasn't the only one who was lying. He led me on to set me up. Every nice thing he said about me, about my scars, was just a pile of bullshit used as bait. And let me tell you, shit tastes exactly like the name suggests.

"Well, what's next depends on what you choose. I'm not a total asshole, you know."

I almost rolled my eyes, but the intensity in his gaze kept me motionless. "All right," I said. "What are my choices?"

"You have two. Three, technically. But I don't think you want the third choice."

He was trying to be dramatic. I was too tired for it.

"Then let's hear the first two."

"The first choice is that you go directly to jail."

"No passing Go, huh?"

He shook his head sharply. Boy, if looks could kill, he wouldn't need that gun in his hands.

"This isn't a game, Ellie. I know that's all you're used to playing—"

"Okay, okay. Sorry. So I go to jail. You turn me in."

"Correct. I have more than enough evidence here of your little robbery. I don't know how much time you get for that kind of shit these days, and I suppose it's a bit of a pity that you aren't armed, but anyway, I digress. You go in the slammer for quite some time, that's what I know. You'll do time. Get a criminal record. You'll never be able to con again."

"I got it."

"And your family's name will be tarnished even

more. Your poor uncle Jim. He's going to have a hell of a time with this. Gee, I hope the whole town won't turn against him. Doesn't really look good harboring two sets of Watt fugitives."

I narrowed my eyes, my jaw tense. "What's the other choice?"

"The other choice is that you help me."

I brought my chin into my neck. "Help you? Help you with what?"

He let out a long breath and tapped the gun against his leg, looking up at the ceiling. "That might be better explained in the morning."

"But... but, okay, so then what happens? I can't agree to help you unless you tell me what it is. What's going to happen to me until morning?" The panic was starting to spread inside my lungs at a speed that even Ativan couldn't save.

His look was dry. "Oh, come on and use your brain. You're really going to choose jail if you don't like whatever help is needed? I just gave you a way out. It doesn't matter how you can help me—what matters is that you have the chance to. I'd take it if I were you."

"I don't like agreeing to things without knowing what I'm agreeing to," I squeaked out.

"Well, there's always option three." My eyes darted to his face. He smiled. "I can just shoot you in the head. I'll destroy the tape, make it look like self-defense, and let my father take care of the rest."

The room grew thick with silence as I processed what he had just said. Finally I said, "You wouldn't have the guts. That's murder."

"It doesn't take guts to commit murder. It takes stupidity and passion. You're lucky I'm feeling really smart right about now."

He walked over to the light switch and turned it on. I blinked harshly at the light, feeling more on the spot than ever. Cornered desperation? Yeah, I was sure it was written all over my face, bleeding out from every pore.

I didn't have much of a choice.

"Fine," I said carefully. "I'll help you out with whatever you want, just as long as you promise you won't harm or hurt or defame my uncle in any way. My parents, I don't care. But leave my uncle out of this."

"Deal," he said. He walked to me and lifted me to my feet by my shoulders. He kept his grip tight and his eyes roamed about my face, probably enjoying the eau de cornered desperation.

"Deal," I replied.

He bared his teeth in a smile before leaning into my ear.

"I *own* you, Ellie Watt," he whispered.

The words sounded just like a cell door closing.

Behind me.

CHAPTER ELEVEN

Then

It had been a month since the girl had to show her gym class her scars, and in that month, the rumors had spread. They weren't as harsh and vicious as they had been when kids had nothing to go on, but they were rumors just the same. Some people said she'd been a victim of a chemistry experiment gone wrong, like Bruce Banner before he became the Hulk; others thought that her family were Muslim extremists and she'd been punished for adultery. Of course, none of the rumors made any sense at all. Then again, neither did the truth.

But for the most part, people stopped being so mean to the girl. There was just pity instead. A lot of sympathetic looks, some hushed whispers, and the occasional person backing away from her as if she had some sort of flesh-eating disease. The girl could only assume that was some other rumor going around.

In some ways the girl felt more at peace, because the

others weren't calling her names anymore, but at other times she felt like she'd been ripped open and exposed for all the world to see. With her admission, her deformity belonged to everyone now. She didn't have much else to keep for herself.

At least the girl was feeling confident about her photography class. She loved working with the old-fashioned film, spending the hours toiling away in the darkroom. The only thing she didn't like was the fact that Camden McQueen was in her class. She thought that after giving him the cold shoulder for a year, he would have given up trying to talk to her and be her friend. But he didn't seem to know when to quit, and the girl was constantly dodging him.

That day, the class had their end-of-semester assignments due. They all had to take photos based on their interpretations of the word *justification*. The girl, thinking that she was oh so deep and clever, had taken photos of one of the bums begging on Palm Valley's main street. As the class was invited one by one to put their works up on the board and explain their choices, the girl realized she wasn't the only one who thought she was clever. Four other kids had chosen not only a homeless person but the exact same one. The dude sure did make a lot of extra money that day.

The girl went up and made a half-hearted attempt to explain her views, saying that the bum was justified in his actions because he was homeless and poor. He was allowed to beg for money because the circumstances made it acceptable. Society had shunned him and he was owed that much.

After a few light-hearted claps from her classmates and an approving nod from the teacher, the girl sat back down and watched the rest of the assignments go up. There was another homeless fellow, a picture of a tiny kid beating on a big bully, a Great Dane eating cat food.

Then it was Camden's turn.

All heads turned as he walked up to the board. Now nearly sixteen, Camden was taller, almost six feet. He walked tall, too, with his shoulders back and his face forward. He looked people in the eye, daring them to look back. And look back they did. He still wore his trench coat, though it was a bigger model, and while the full makeup had run its course, he favored sparkly eyeliner. He was pale, as if he was in witness protection from the sun, and his pants were a shiny, tight leather that no teenage boy could wear without getting beaten up for. That day he had on a Cramps shirt, and the girl smiled caustically at the cartoonish coffin, making a joke in her head that he probably slept in one.

Camden walked to the front of the class and looked at everyone. "Good afternoon," he said rather formally. "My name is Camden McQueen."

A few people snickered, probably because of his unfortunate "Camden the Queen" nickname.

He continued as if he hadn't heard them. "The assignment we were given proved to be a bit of a challenge for me. The minute I heard the word— *justification*—I immediately had a subject in mind. But capturing this subject in the state of the word? That was going to be tricky."

Even though most people despised Camden, they

were all leaning forward and listening attentively. Even the girl was pleasantly curious to see what he had in mind. Until his eyes drifted to hers. And stayed there.

"I was fortunate, however," he said deliberately, his eyes never leaving her face, "that an opportunity presented itself to me one afternoon. I had a spare block and was wandering the grounds with my camera."

An immense feeling of dread washed over the girl like soot.

"And while I was wandering about, I noticed the girl's gym class was in session. A soccer game."

Her heart froze.

"Or, it should have been a soccer game. There seemed to be one little problem, and a yelling match between the teacher and a student took place."

Oh shit, the girl thought. Her eyes darted around the room to see if anyone had picked up on it. No one had—not yet. Camden had an audience.

"This girl," he said slowly, finally looking around the room, "the student, was the subject of this project. And as she took to the sidelines and watched the soccer game take place, I started snapping her picture."

The girl started to shrink in her seat, wondering if she could get under the desk without anyone noticing. Maybe, if she willed it enough, she could just disappear.

Camden walked up to the board and started pinning up black-and-white eight-by-tens on it. The girl was too afraid to look.

"Behold," Camden announced like Marilyn Manson's magician, "justification in the form of Ellie Watt."

And there they were, in front of the entire class:

black-and-white photos of the girl. They weren't bad pictures, per se. In fact, Camden had possessed quite a talent for photography. Despite the paparazzi-ish, tele-photo elements to the shots, they were well developed and exposed. The girl looked beautiful with her blond hair cascading down her back, her full lips and sensual eyes. But in that exotic face held more than just beauty. It held anger and it held pain. It held justification.

The teacher cleared his throat, unsure of how to deal with this, while the classroom erupted into excited whispers. Everyone was looking at the girl for her reaction. Everyone.

The girl could only sit there like a deer in the head-lights, the red flames on her face the only sign that she was embarrassed beyond words.

Finally the teacher said, "Camden, I don't think tak-ing pictures of your classmates is appropriate."

Camden shrugged. He obviously didn't care if it was appropriate or not, if he failed or not. He was out to prove a point and he was good at proving them. "You never said it wasn't. Besides, no one in this whole school has the right to act the way that Ellie Watt does. Except for Ellie Watt."

More eyes on her. She wished her school was built over Hellmouth and it would swallow her in one gulp.

Camden continued: "When I see these pictures, when I see this face, this expression, I see someone plotting out their future. I see the bad things this girl will do. And I understand why. That is what I call justi-fication. Thank you."

Before he could take his seat, before anyone could

even think about clapping, the justification took hold of its subject. The girl got up, the stool clanging to the floor behind her. She leaned forward, her eyes, her fury, on the kohl-rimmed boy.

"You stalker!" she yelled, her voice surprising herself, him, and everyone else in the room. It wasn't just that he'd taken photos of her without her knowing, it wasn't just that he was trying to get graded on them, it was what was happening in those photos. It was what they represented; her leg was hidden in those photos, but the scars were all over her face.

"You sick fucking freak!" She screamed the last words, rendering the whole room into silence. "All you do is follow me, pester me, bug me, and now take photos like a fucking creeper! You need a life, a hobby, and a girlfriend. And for the last time, no, it will not be me!"

And with that she slammed her sketchbook down on the table, scooped up her backpack from the floor, and left the room. She didn't care if she was leaving in the middle of class, she had a feeling her teacher would understand. She just wanted to get away from him and that situation as quickly as she could.

The girl ran out into the halls and went straight for the girl's bathroom, the safest place for any teenage girl to hole up and cry. But as she sat huddled above the toilet, the tears wouldn't come. She was so angry, so livid. Justification? Oh, she was more justified than ever now.

She waited until the bell rang signaling the last class of the day. She had ten minutes to get to her social studies class. Ten minutes to get through the halls and put on a brave face.

Only she couldn't go straight to class because she had to get her textbook from the locker. She gathered some strength, pushed her long blond hair behind her ears, and marched out into the hall as smoothly as her leg would allow. She looked straight ahead, avoiding any stares that were coming her way, those predictable glances of pity, and went to her locker. The guy next to her was putting something away and gave her a quick smile as she approached. So far so good.

Then she felt it. That presence. She always felt it, wherever she was. She wished she had noticed it that day during gym class. This whole thing could have been avoided.

With her heart in her throat, she turned around and looked Camden McQueen right into his bespectacled eyes, their brilliant blue color magnified by the glasses. She expected him to be angry or sad or even apologetic after she'd yelled at him in front of everyone. But his eyes were blank, as if every feeling inside him had been sucked away and he was just an empty bag. He was as cold as the metal locker her back was now pressed against.

"You're a bad person, Ellie," he said without a trace of irony.

She watched him carefully, like a trap ready to spring. "I'm not bad. The world is bad and I'm just trying to survive in it."

He smiled, both sad and self-righteous. "And that's why I chose you," he whispered, leaning in so close she had to flatten against the locker.

Then, after he searched her eyes for a few torturous

moments, he whipped around and took off down the hall. He walked as if he'd just won something—but in the girl's opinion, they both had lost.

Now

I never thought I'd be able to fall asleep with my hands cuffed behind my back, but I guess when the body is tired, the body is tired. And I was fucking exhausted.

When I woke up, the sun was already up and birds were chirping outside the window like they were welcoming the day with open wings. I was welcoming the day by feeling scared, stupid, and ashamed. I was lying in Camden's bed for the second time, only there was no hunky, naked man in bed with me. No, the hunky naked man was dressed and sitting in the corner of the room, poised regally in an armchair.

My eyes squinted from the light. From the way he was positioned by the window, he almost looked angelic. But angels don't have tattoos and they certainly don't have guns in their hands.

I sat up slowly with burning abs, the flannel sheets falling away from me. I supposed he had covered me up in the middle of the night. How nice of him.

"Good morning," he said, as if we were old friends. Old friends that *didn't* want to kill each other.

I glared at him. "Is the gun really necessary?"

"No," he admitted. "It's just fun to have one."

"Like an extra penis," I mused.

He smiled unkindly. "Something like that."

I leaned over, rounding my back and letting out a

moan of pain. I'd never felt so sore and stiff before. I was sure the cuffs had carved deep lines into my wrists.

"How did you sleep?"

"How do you think I slept?" I snapped without looking up at him. "You have my hands cuffed behind my back. I'm being held hostage here against my will, and I have no idea what the hell you have planned for me."

He chuckled. "You're not being held hostage. You're free to go. In fact…" I heard him get up and walk over to me. "You're right. You shouldn't be cuffed."

I cocked my head to the side and looked up at him. He had put the gun down on the armchair, brought a pair of keys out of his pocket, and began fiddling with the handcuffs. With a joyous click, they opened up, and my wrists felt sharp air and cool relief.

He removed them and tossed them onto his oak dresser where they landed with a clatter. "There. Better?"

I examined my wrists. They were raw and stung a little but were mainly undamaged. "Not really. I suppose there's a price for letting me go?"

He went into a wide-legged stance with crossed arms and tilted his chin down at me. "There's a price for everything. We still have a deal, remember? You'll help me because I need your help, and because the other two choices are…the greater of the evils. You won't run away, because I've got all the proof to put you behind bars ready to go at the click of a button. If you run, you'll never escape, and all the lives you've tried to create will be ruined."

So basically he was telling me I was already in a

prison. Sure, you couldn't see it, but I was stuck with him, stuck within these white walls until he decided to let me go. If he ever decided to let me go.

"All right then," I said slowly, pulling the flannel sheets up to my collarbone. From where he was standing he had a clear view down my shirt, and I didn't want my hostage taker to be getting any special privileges. Not anymore.

"So," I said, "when you're finished blackmailing me, what do you plan on doing with me?"

"You mean after you help me?"

I nodded brusquely.

"Then we part ways."

I narrowed my eyes. "And is 'parting ways' a euphemism for something else? Say, killing me?"

He looked disappointed in what I said. "No, Ellie. It means parting ways. It means you go one way and I go another. You head east and I head west."

"We're about as west as we can go already," I noted, eyeing him curiously. He seemed as sharp as ever but a lot more reasonable than last night. He was still scarily unpredictable, and I knew I'd never underestimate him again, but I felt like this was as good a time as any to find out what the hell our deal was based around.

"No. There's more west to go."

"So then, tell me. What's the deal? What's your plan? What do you need me to help you with? Is it killing people, because I don't kill people, Camden. You might think I would because I'm a criminal, but not all criminals are the same, and I swear I do have a set of morals somewhere in my body. You might not see it, but it's there."

He gave me a half smile, picked up his gun, and walked out of the room, calling over his shoulder, "Let's discuss this over coffee."

I watched him leave, my pulse quickening at his avoidance of the subject, then eased myself out of the bed. "Can I go to the bathroom first?" I asked.

"Sure," he yelled back from the kitchen. "You won't find any weapons in there anyway, if that's what you were planning."

Actually, all I had was a bladder that was about to burst and hadn't even thought about attacking him with razor blades or tweezers. What would be the use, anyway? Unless I actually killed Camden, which I wasn't about to do, hence my worry over his ambiguousness, I really had no escape. He'd probably let me walk straight out of the house, but I was sure that no matter where I went, the police wouldn't be far behind.

And Uncle Jim. I couldn't, wouldn't, forget about him.

When I came out of the bathroom, he was sitting around the kitchen table with a lined memo pad and pen in his hands, a French press full of dark coffee and two orange mugs beside him. The gun was nowhere in sight. He had his glasses on, the thin-rimmed ones I'd seen in his office, and he looked up at me with such apathy that he could have been an accountant about to go over some numbers. You know, if most accountants had piercings at the ends of their noses and wore fitted plaid shirts.

"Coffee?" he asked, nodding his head at the press.

"Yes, I know," I said in reference to the movie *Airplane!* and took a seat. I pulled a mug toward me and inspected the bottom for any powder or liquids. I couldn't be too careful.

"Do you always make jokes when you're nervous?" he asked. I gave him a sharp look. He smiled and folded his hands over the notepad. "Go ahead, I didn't drug it. I'm not some Bond villain."

I placed the other mug in front of him. "No, you're definitely not. You're just a sadistic freak with control issues." He flinched, barely susceptible. "I'll drink it if you'll drink it."

He sighed and poured my mug before he poured his own. "I guess our trust was broken a long time ago, wasn't it?"

We both took a sip at the same time, our eyes glued to each other. "Actually, I *had* trusted this new Camden McQueen."

"And now?"

"And now I'll never make that mistake again," I said after a mouthful. I still couldn't get over how Camden pulled a fast one on me. I was no stranger to cons getting conned. I'd been conned a few times before, though you learned to read the warning signs as you went along. You get better. More aware. Sometimes, there were just people who were better at your job than you were. But I never saw Camden coming. I never saw his true motives. I never could have predicted his switch. Sure, there were probably a few signs here and there, but I was so wrapped up in my lust for him, my plans for him, and he was always such a strange bird, that they could have meant anything. I had no idea—*no idea*—that I had hurt this man that badly.

"So we're even."

I put down the mug. "Nothing's even when you're being blackmailed. So, tell me, what's the plan?"

"I need you to make me disappear," he said, straight and to the point.

I raised my brow. "Disappear as in . . . ?"

He took a quick sip of his coffee and stared down into the mug. "Ellie, I'm going to be honest with you."

"Oh what a pleasant change of pace." I sat back in my chair, utterly intrigued. Camden had been a master at hiding his emotions, but there was a tiny pulse of life at the corner of his eye, magnified by his glasses. I knew that pulse, that twitch. I had it myself. It was fear.

He ignored my sarcastic remark and spoke to the coffee. "I'm not in any trouble, because that's the first conclusion you're going to jump to. If I just carried on my life like this, running my shop and following orders"—I raised my other brow but let him continue—"then that would be that. My life would go on and no one would probably get hurt."

He paused and picked up his pen and began to click the end of it, in and out, in and out. I waited. It was excruciating.

With a sigh he continued, looking everywhere except my face. "But I'm tired of my life. I want out of it. And it's not the kind of life you can escape from. Not by normal means." *Click click* went the pen. "After Ben was born . . . I did a bad thing. I had my reasons and I have my excuses. But it happened, and Sophia divorced me. But no one's truly free from Sophia. When you marry a Madano, you marry the whole family. And it's a bad family, Ellie." *Click click. Click click.* I eyed the painting of Sophia on the wall. "And they don't let you go so easily, especially when you owe their sister child support. Do they care, really, how Sophia and Ben get on? No. They don't. They'd turn on her in an instant. They just care about their image. Their pride. Their family values. And so they said they were doing me a favor. I didn't have much money back then. Even with *LA Ink* and the increase in business, I barely got by. LA is an expensive city, and they knew I could never make enough there. So they came to me with a deal. They'd give me a shop anywhere I wanted as long as it was in a low-rent town with a couple of paying customers. They'd give me my dream."

"Sins & Needles," I said quietly.

"Yes," he said, finally looking at me. "They gave me this place. But as you now know, everything comes with a price. They said they wanted me to do well and then give most of my earnings to Sophia and Ben. I didn't have a problem with that—I'd give them everything if I could. But I wondered, if they had the money to buy a shop, why didn't they just give her the money outright? Well, they said it was because it had to go through me, because *I* owed her, not them. And then the truth came out, about two weeks into running this shop. Business was slow. Terribly fucking slow. I had a handful of customers and that was it. This goddamn town, it just isn't the place to make a life. It's still not."

"So what happened?" I had a feeling I knew where this was all going, and to be honest, I was starting to feel a bit bad for him.

"I started to panic a little. Vincent came by, that's her oldest brother, that's the guy you never want to see in a bad mood. He flipped the sign over to Closed, and I was so certain he was going to bash my brains in or something. I can do well in a fight, believe me, but that's someone you never want to cross."

This Vincent was starting to remind me of my Javier. That wasn't good. Funny how we had both been wrapped up with bad people at the same times in our lives.

"He asked me about my sales and I told him the truth. I couldn't afford to lie. He owned this building, for crying out loud. But, instead of cutting off my finger, he just smiled and shrugged. Like it was no problem. Then he brought out his briefcase, opened it up, and showed me the shitload of money inside. He told me that it was the real reason this business existed, and as long as I held on to the money for him and made slow deposits into my bank account, *their* bank account, the business would keep going. It didn't matter how many people wanted tattoos. All that mattered was that to the outside, it looked like Sins & Needles was making a lot of dough."

"Money laundering." I stated the obvious. "Of course, *of course* this is just a front."

He glared at me. "I could have done well somewhere else. I could have done really well. I'm not the problem. The town is the problem."

"I think you're at least part of the problem," I dared to say. "You've been cleaning money for a few years now, haven't you?"

He sighed sharply and took an angry gulp of coffee. "I couldn't say no."

"You can always say no."

"Do you always say no?"

"Not lately."

"Anyway," he said, the impatience in his voice rising. "So every week or two a new deposit comes in. I deposit the cash. It looks like I'm making money. Then they take out the cash and they leave me my allowance. I don't have a say in it, but it's enough to get by on. Then they say they're giving so much to Sophia and Ben."

"And you don't believe them…"

"No. As I said, their love of family is only for appearance's sake. I doubt Sophia is getting very much, if any."

"Don't you think she'd let you know if you were stiffing her?"

He pinched the bridge of his nose. "I don't know. She doesn't answer my calls or my e-mails. All I can do is send letters in the mail to Ben. I just hope he's getting them. Anyway, I don't know what would happen if I asked. She might tell her brothers, and they'd get pretty insulted if they knew."

"Right."

"And so that's that. I want out."

I almost laughed at his bluntness. "Camden. You can't just get out from something like this. Money laundering is a very serious crime. What are the Madanos into? Drugs? Guns? Prostitution?"

"Does it matter?" he asked wearily.

"Sort of. You have to know where the money is coming from. You have to know the type of people you are dealing with, because like it or not, you're in business with them."

"I know the type."

"But you don't know *their* type. You're the bank. They're the boss. Who's their client? What's their product? Who's buying what? It all matters."

"I don't know, I don't know. I don't want to know."

I shook my head in thin amusement and finished the rest of my coffee. "Let's just assume it's drugs then. I've had enough experience with that angle. So then tell me what your plan was before I came along. Or were you always just sort of waiting for me?"

His gaze was sharp. "I wasn't waiting for you. I saw you in the coffee shop that day and then everything snapped into place, just as everything snapped into place when you saw me."

"There's been a lot of fucking between us over the last few days," I mused bitterly.

"Don't flatter yourself. I'm the one fucking you, that's why you're sitting here with me, ready to do anything I tell you to."

"And what we did in the backyard and on the floor and in the bedroom?"

He grinned wolfishly. "Oh, you never even had a chance to fuck me back."

I was going to retort something extremely childish like *Oh yeah, that's because you only gave me five minutes*, but the truth was I had nothing to stand on. The sex, believe it or not, had actually meant something to me. I didn't sleep with him to get access—I would have gotten that anyway—I slept with him because I was starting to like him. Because I wanted to. Because he was one of the sexiest men I'd ever come across. And it was a shame he still was. It was a shame that none of it meant anything. It was a shame that despite the rather dire situation I was in, I was smarting like some stupid girl who thought she had something more than a one-night stand.

Get your head out of your vagina, I told myself, and sat up in the chair a little straighter. I smiled at him, trying to get to the root of the matter.

"All right, so then you saw me and you knew I was going to do something stupid and try to screw you over, right?" I asked.

"Right," he agreed simply. "Then I started to think how I could make this all work in my favor. I didn't just want to catch you, to prove that you're not as smart as you think you are. I wanted to get something from you in return. Then I thought of Gualala."

"What the hell is Gualala? Is that another band?"

He smiled at me like I was an idiot. "Gualala is a town north of San Francisco, on Highway 1. I went there after high school, just bumming around the coast for a bit. I fell in love. Gualala has been my motivator. It's the goal. It's the place I'll go when I want to start over."

"You're starting to sound like Morgan Freeman in *Shawshank Redemption*."

I'd said the wrong thing.

Camden grabbed the French press, and in a fit of rage hurled it against the wall, where it shattered into a million pieces of glass and steaming liquid. My heart was fighting with my lungs, my muscles tensed to run. I watched him, eyes wide, afraid to breathe. He was back to being terrifying again.

Definitely not a Morgan Freeman fan.

"Just because we are talking over coffee, do not for a second think that you aren't royally screwed," he hissed at me, eyes blazing. "Don't for a second think I'm going to go soft on you, that I'm going to have a change of heart. You broke my heart, Ellie, all those years ago. That was the last time you'll ever see it." He sat back, took off his glasses, and calmly began to wipe them off with a napkin. I could see from the way his hands were shaking that being calm was taking an awful lot of effort on his behalf, but I was grateful for it. "This isn't a joke. And this isn't a game, no matter how hard you try and figure out the angle and the play. I'm playing you, do you understand me? I'm the one in control."

My voice trembled. "Okay."

"Okay. So now you know what I need. I want to leave this place and I want to leave it with their money. I want to leave and never look back. I want to be able to open a trust fund for Ben, something he can have when he's older. An anonymous donation. I want to live on the Pacific Ocean and eat at my favorite restaurant and work on my art all day. I don't want to be Camden McQueen anymore. I want to be someone else. And I want you to make all of this happen."

It was nearly impossible, extremely risky, completely

dangerous, and the tallest of the tall orders. But I was done making light of it. I was done pretending that Camden was putting on an act and that he just wanted to scare me. This was no act. I would have to help him disappear, or else I'd disappear, too. And not to a place I wanted to go.

"Fine," I said, clearing my throat. "I'll help you. I'll help you get all of that. But I think I'm going to need some of your trust to make this happen."

He grinned at me before pushing back his chair and taking a dish towel over to the mess by the wall. "Ellie Watt," he said as he crouched down to clean, "I wouldn't even trust you if you were dead."

And there was a strong chance I'd end up dead if we didn't play our cards right. Stealing money from drug lords was something I knew a lot about. It was only luck that I was still alive and actually sitting in Camden's kitchen. I had no idea if luck would be on my side this time.

"All right then, don't trust me. But you should at least believe the shit that I'm telling you, because I know a thing or two about this and a thing or two about disappearing."

"That's why I hired you," he said. The broken glass tinkled delicately as he scooped it into a pile.

"This isn't going to be as easy as you make it seem." I exhaled loudly, feeling like I couldn't clear my lungs enough. "There's a chance we'll have to do some... illegal activities. No one takes on a new life without committing some sort of crime. Are your morals going to have a problem with that?"

"Ellie," he said, shooting me a wry look. "My dad's the sheriff of this town and I've been operating a money-laundering business right under his nose. I doubt I'll have a problem with it."

"Good. Because like I said, this isn't going to be easy. I don't know what kind of men you are dealing with, but if they are anything like the men I've dealt with, you can't afford to slip up. Once you commit to stealing from them, you have to follow through. There is no mercy. No one will forgive you or tell you to forget about it. If you have a change of heart, you can't just give the money back. They don't care about the money anymore. They have enough money. They care about making a point. You made a point last night by cocking your gun. These guys won't give you that. They'll blow your face off before you have a chance to say you're sorry."

He had stopped cleaning and was now just staring at me. "Jesus. Who the hell are you on the run from?"

I did a quick shake of my head. "That's neither here nor there. It doesn't affect anything to do with us." When he didn't look convinced, I said, "It was a very, very long time ago. It has nothing to do with Camden McQueen. It has nothing to do with Ellie Watt. I promise."

The last thing I wanted was for Camden to get cold feet about this whole thing and then decide to turn me over to the cops after all. There was no way he'd just let me go free when I had all the knowledge I now had.

He nodded.

"So when were you thinking about doing this? In other words, how much time do we have?" I asked.

"A week," he said. "Actually, six days."

"Six days?" How the hell was I going to round up a fake life for him in six days?

"Yes. Nonnegotiable." He got to his feet and threw the dish towel in the trash. "In six days, one of Vincent's partners will come by and make the drop. I want to take that money, as well as all the money in the safe."

"Whose money is in the safe?"

"Theirs. They like to have some of the cash on hand."

I felt a wash of ice go down my spine. "What would have happened if I had actually robbed you, Camden?"

His smile was sad. "If I hadn't stopped you? They probably would have killed me. No, scratch that. They definitely would have killed me."

Shit. In some backward way, I was glad that Camden had been smart enough to see through me. This alternative was much better than the other. I would have never been able to live with myself if he ended up dead because of me.

"I'm sorry," I whispered, looking down at the wounds on my wrists.

"Yeah, well it's a good thing I'm not one of those guys, because apparently your head would already be blown off."

I gave him a small smile. "It is a good thing."

He sat back down in his seat and stared at me for a few moments before saying, "So now that you know what I want, can you do it in six days?"

"Yes. I can."

"Then I guess you better get started."

I nodded. "What about Uncle Jim? And my stuff, I need the stuff in my car. This basketball jersey is starting to smell."

"Where is your car?"

"Just a block away, by the dog-walking park."

He sucked on his lip in thought. "I'll go with you. I know you're not stupid enough to run, but I can't be sure. As for your uncle, I don't know. I guess you'll have to drop him a line telling him you're still in San Diego, or whatever place you lied about, and that you're not coming back. I know you love your uncle, but I have a feeling he'll be relieved."

I hated that he was probably right about that.

CHAPTER TWELVE

IT WAS WEDNESDAY when Camden told me the details of his plan, six days from the scheduled drop. It's a good thing most con artists don't have banking hours, or we would have gotten screwed over the weekend.

Aside from walking over to Jose and getting all my gear out of the car, I didn't get to leave the house until Friday. Until then, I was holed up in his living room, the couch my new bed. In the living room, I felt open and aware. His spare bedroom was too dark and cramped for me. Like a cell.

It wasn't a bad place to have house arrest. Camden stayed out of my way and spent as much time as possible in the shop or in the office, either inking the occasional client or dreaming about his new future. He was cordial to me when we did cross paths, and whenever he made himself dinner or ordered takeout, there was always enough for me. He even offered me a beer at one point, but I made a point of saying no. I needed to think clearly, more clearly than I ever had to before.

He had put away his gun somewhere and stopped throwing pots of coffee. He seemed a little embarrassed about that, to be honest, and I probably would have done the same thing if I were in his shoes. Sometimes you have to shock someone to get them to see how serious you really are—I knew that all too well. And I saw that Camden was serious beyond reproach. I missed the days we had before this mess, when he was flirting with me and everything was fun. But I guess all of that was a lie, anyway.

There was no fun in the truth.

On Friday, while my friend Gus in Pismo Beach worked on securing Camden some fake Social Security numbers, I was in the middle of making him a fake driver's license. In order to get it done properly, we would have to go to a place to get his picture taken.

"I don't see why I can't go alone," he said while we ate our All-Bran cereal like the world's most fucked-up married couple. "There's a few passport photo places on the strip and in the mall."

"Look," I said pointedly, "you can't keep me cooped up in here forever. I have to go out sometime. I'll go crazy otherwise."

"Too late for that," he mumbled under his breath.

"And I have to make sure you look right and the photos are the right size and the right everything. It's very easy to get wrong. You have no experience in faking IDs. I do."

He obviously thought I was going to make a run for it, but I was beyond that now. I was starting to trust Camden a little bit and trust his intentions. I didn't exactly want to help him escape with a shitload of cash and have more people to be running from, but it wasn't too off from something I'd have been doing anyway. If this was all Camden wanted to use me for, I could live with that.

He sighed and pushed his bowl of cereal away. "Well, if you're coming, we better not let anyone recognize you. If your uncle saw you, it would look pretty bad."

I shrugged. "I have some wigs. It's you we don't want people to recognize. To be more specific, we want you looking as different as possible. Are you sure Vincent or any of his cronies won't be around between now and the drop?"

"Cronies?" he said with a laugh. "You're making them sound like the mafia."

I stared at him. "Yeah? They're Italian, aren't they? They probably *are* the mafia."

"That's racist."

"It's racist if I said all Italians are part of the mafia. The Madanos run drugs or guns or whatever. You're laundering their money. It's probably safe to say they have ties to the mob in some way. My ex-boyfriend is part of a gang. He's Mexican. Guess what? He's part of a large Mexican drug cartel. I'm white trash with an Eastern European background. I'm also a gypsy and a con artist. We're all stereotypes. Sometimes they come from somewhere. Sometimes when people pigeonhole you, you end up being the pigeon."

"You're not a pigeon," he said. "You're whoever you want to be."

"Whatever. So, back to the question."

"The answer is no. I shouldn't see any of them until Monday."

"Then we should get started on your new look now."

"Should I be worried?" A wrinkle appeared on his forehead. I wasn't letting my guard down, but my God he looked adorable.

"Well, aren't we a little vain," I remarked. "You're not going to look like an idiot. I can't do anything drastic with you anyway—you're covered in tattoos."

He raised his hands in the air and wiggled them. I'd forgotten how strong and elegant they were. "I don't have any tats on my hands. They're the last frontier for me."

"Good. Let's keep it that way." At least long-sleeved shirts would do the trick. I peered at him, moving my head from side to side. "You're going to start wearing your Kettle Black glasses, the black ones, all the time. We're going to dye your hair black, cut off all this shaggy surfer dude-ness and make it short and a bit spiky."

He grimaced.

"What?" I asked, leaning in. "That not cool enough for you?"

"Never mind," he said. "Fine. Dye my hair, cut it off, say good-bye to contacts. Anything else? Should I remove my septum ring, too, or do I get to keep some memento of who I was?"

He was being sarcastic and missing the whole point. I almost put my hand over his to comfort him and add emphasis to what I was about to say, but I didn't dare touch him.

"Camden," I said delicately, "you're not going to want any mementos of who you were. This isn't about a disguise; you'll barely look any different than you do now. This is about saying good-bye to the person you are, the person you were, and hello to the person you'll be. You'll have to change, and change is big. Change is scary. You're uprooting everything you have worked so hard to get. You're not going to know who you are for a while, not until you relearn how to live. If you look in the mirror and you don't immediately recognize yourself, then you'll know you're on the right track."

"Is that why you're so sad all the time?"

I frowned. "What?"

"You know when we were in my car, heading to the show, and I said I liked Guano Padano because it reminded me of you? Rough and sweet at the same time? I wasn't lying. I was just leaving something out. It's rough and sweet and very, very sad. When I look at you, I see sadness."

I chewed on my lip and looked away from him. "I thought you saw justification."

"I do. I see a lot of things when I look at you."

I got to my feet, feeling uncomfortable. "Come on. Let's get you a makeover."

*   *   *

It's funny how women underestimate just how vain men can be. Camden didn't really have a problem with wearing his nerd glasses all the time—which, fortunately for him, didn't make him look any less attractive—and he didn't care that he had to dye his hair black. His brows were naturally black, anyway, and the combination would make his icy-blue eyes pop even more.

No, Camden had a problem with having his hair cut short, purely because he didn't like the way his ears stuck out. It was hard to believe that this was the man who was planning to run away with a bunch of the mafia's money, but hey. Someone can look like a tattooed, muscular god and still be terribly insecure because of his Dumbo ears.

Which, by the way, also didn't make him look any less attractive, especially since he didn't get his hair cut *that* short. I had a change of heart. It wasn't fair, really. Somehow, even being a new person and having a new look, he still managed to look hot. I'd stopped swooning over him as soon as I learned that he was borderline insane, but that didn't mean I wasn't still checking him out from time to time.

When we were done with the hair, we made our way to the passport photo place, and I had to explain to the old, deaf man who was taking the pictures that it wasn't for a passport but for an ID. We couldn't say "driver's license" since that was illegal and all, so we made it look like Camden owned a growing business and wanted to get security passes for the staff. That was enough for the old guy, and we got three tiny photos ready to become part of a forgery.

It was surprising how different he looked in the photos. I was standing off camera, looking at the screen and giving him directions. Despite the glasses, the new Camden looked serious and tough, the kind of person who never forgot a face. The kind of person you didn't want to mess with. I wanted for Camden to feel empowered by the new him every time he looked down at his ID and new name.

Now that the hard part was over, we retreated back to his house before anyone could see me and got started on finding his new name. He had picked up a bottle of Buffalo Trace whiskey at the store, and over a glass of it, we were brainstorming.

"Your new name is the most important step in this whole process," I informed him, sitting back on the couch. He was sitting in the leather armchair across from me and swirling his glass. Again, I had passed on the alcohol. "You're going to have to live with this name. You'll no longer be Camden McQueen. Even though that sounds like a good idea right now, it'll hit you somewhere down the road. That you can't go back."

He stared at the swirling bourbon. "You came back. You got to be Ellie Watt again."

"Yeah, well, that's only because that name was clean. It might not be clean when we leave this place."

"That name," he said curiously. His eyes were on me. "You refer to it as 'that name,' but it's your name. You were born with it, were you not?"

"I was," I said cautiously.

"Yet you're treating it like it's made up, like it's not even yours. Like it won't even stick."

I started fiddling with the tassels on the end of the white throw blanket. "It probably won't stick, not until I go legit. Not until I have a home."

"A name is like a home, then. All those years without a name. All those years without a home."

I twisted my lips. What was this, amateur psychiatry hour?

"Be that as it may, you need a name that you like, Camden. And the easiest names to remember, to believe, are the ones that have the same initials as your current name. Or your real name. Either/or. There's something very...reassuring about seeing those initials over and over again, no matter how many times your name changes."

He watched me for a beat, then downed the rest of his drink. The glass was refilled in no time. There was something very cagey about the look on his face, and considering it was only six in the evening, if he kept up at this pace he'd be drunk as a skunk.

"Camden? Now's the time you tell me your favorite names that start with C."

He shook his head. "Does it have to be the same letter?"

"Trust me. It's easier this way."

As he lapsed into silence, I said, "Caleb?"

He made a disgusting face.

"All right, Calum."

"God no."

"Cade?"

"Way too evil. Next."

"Cory."

"Haim or Feldman?"

"Cash?"

"Might as well call me Douchebag."

That can be arranged, I thought. "Okay, Carter."

"Gah. When I hear Carter, I think 'nerd.'"

"Well, if the shoe fits..."

He glared at me over his glasses.

"Cody, then," I suggested.

"Sounds like I should have a mullet. How about Cameron?"

"Oh, I think that's pushing it a bit too close."

"Caithness."

I was starting to worry.

"What?" he said, raising his arm defensively, his drink sloshing over the rim. "It's from *Macbeth*. Hey, there's a last name, too. Caithness Macbeth!"

The drink was obviously going to his head, and I was starting to feel a bit nervous about the whole situation.

Still, I couldn't help but tell him, "That is the worst name ever."

He mulled over it. "Caithness Macbeth."

"People will know it's a fake name," I pointed out.

"People are illiterate. No one will know." He pulled out his iPhone and started tapping on the screen.

"What are you doing?"

"Googling names."

An hour later, Camden was drunk and attempting to make a fire, and we had finally settled on a name. He had wanted to do a nod to some of his Irish ancestry on his late mother's side, so his new persona was called Connor Malloy. It wasn't too similar to Camden McQueen, but because of the pacing, the words rolled off the tongue the same way. To tell the truth, he kind of looked like a Connor.

Though he'd always be Camden to me.

"Come sit with me," he said. He had gotten the fire going and was sitting cross-legged on a Mexican blanket in front of it. The very same place we'd shared some wine and, uh, certain parts of each other. It felt like ages ago. It was amazing how fast everything had changed, even our names.

I hesitated. He was drunk, which was fine. I mean, I'd seen him drunk before. But things were so different and so unpredictable, I wasn't sure who I was going to get. Camden? Connor? Caithness? Today had been the first time we'd been together in a few days, and while things were going smoothly at the moment, I didn't want to push my luck.

"Please," he said, patting the ground beside him.

Feeling he probably wouldn't ask nicely next time, I got up and sat down beside him. The fire wasn't too hot, since it was a Duraflame log, but it was pleasantly warm and toasty. I brought my knees up to my chest and watched the flames dance.

"So when do I start becoming Connor Malloy?" he asked in a dull voice.

I turned my head to look at him. The flames reflected in his glasses, making it hard for me to see his eyes.

"When we run," I said.

"Do you ever get tired of running?"

I managed a weak smile. "Why do you think I came here?"

"I thought you came here to screw me over," he said. It was so emotionless and he watched the fire as if hypnotized.

"I didn't come here to screw you over, Camden."

"Please, call me Connor."

"Seriously, Camden, listen to me. I know you don't believe me or trust me but…you have to know, you weren't why I came here."

"No? Then I'm a bit disappointed," he said sadly.

"I didn't think I'd know anyone here. That's why I came back. I figured everyone was either too old to remember me or had moved on. No one stays in the town they were raised in unless they have a reason. I thought I could just start over. I thought my uncle could help me. Or at least try. But he didn't want me."

"You could have gotten a job like everyone else. A real job."

"I tried—"

"You didn't try." His eyes snapped to mine, taking me by surprise. "You wanted the easy way out. Don't you know by now that there is no easy way out?"

His tone put me on edge. I tried to placate him with kind eyes. "I'm getting out now, aren't I? We both are."

A savage smile slowly spread across his lips. "But you think this is easy. Don't you? You're relieved that all you have to do is help me with something you're good at. Somehow, in the end, you'll walk away. Maybe not any richer, but you'll walk away. And you'll feel great about how much you helped Camden McQueen or Connor Malloy or whatever my name will be. You'll walk away feeling like a winner. That's not fair, Ellie. You don't deserve to feel that way."

I couldn't figure out what to say because what he was saying was the truth. He removed his glasses and put them on the ground beside him. His eyes, heavy lidded with drink, drifted to my mouth. I gulped nervously, not liking the tension that was jagging between us.

"How do you think I should feel?" I asked thickly. My nerves were on fire. Everything was on fire.

"Like this," he said. Slowly, he leaned over and kissed me. His lips were soft and tasted like bourbon. I couldn't kiss him back if I wanted to; I couldn't do anything but freeze. He pulled back a little, his eyes inches away. I could see my frightened reflection in the black hole of his pupil. "See? You're afraid."

"You want to scare me?" I whispered.

He kept his lips an inch from mine. His fingers smoothed the hair off my face, tucking it behind my ear.

"Yes," he murmured. His lips brushed mine as he spoke. My breath hitched as his other hand slid the strap of my tank top and bra off my shoulder. I shivered from his touch, from his eyes, from whatever was buried in his heart and eating him alive.

"Camden," I warned, my voice shaking.

He placed his lips on my shoulder and started kissing down my arm. He was right. I was scared. I was so, so afraid. Yet a terrible part of me wanted him to continue. I was turned on and frightened, ready to run, ready to fight, ready to grab him and kiss him, devour every part of him. I didn't know what was going on, but I was stuck in a cage with something that might or might not harm me, that might give me everything and leave me with nothing.

His lips came back up my arm and across my

collarbone. Slowly. Very slowly. The slowest, softest kisses I'd ever felt. Then his mouth edged down my chest. I was sure he could feel my heart underneath, pounding wildly. With his hand, he pulled down my top and bra and exposed my right breast. My nipple was already hard and now puckered in anticipation. His lips circled it, then his warm tongue lashed it gently, teasing, tempting. He let out a small sigh then tugged at my nipple ring with his teeth. The pleasure traveled along my nerves like lightning strikes.

I couldn't swallow. I felt like I was drowning under his touch. "Camden, please..."

Please stop, I was thinking. *This isn't right. It feels right and it feels wrong, but it isn't right. There's a motive and it isn't lust. It isn't lust. It's revenge.*

Revenge never felt so good.

He nipped at me, and my back arched. A low moan escaped my lips. I wanted him. I wanted the person who didn't exist. I wanted the wrong thing.

I sat up straight and pushed his shoulder back. He slowly raised his head. His eyes were calculating. His mouth twitched up in an unbecoming smile that chilled me despite the fire.

I pulled up my shirt and edged away from him. "I don't think this is a good idea."

"No? And why is that?"

"Because...you're blackmailing me. You threatened to kill me the other night. I'm helping you steal the mafia's money and start a new life and...we don't need to make this any more complicated than it already is."

He looked down at his hands as they were tracing small patterns on the surface of the rug. "Do you know what else I think you should feel, Ellie? Aside from fear?"

"What?" I eked out in an exhale, my body tensed.

"Humiliation." His eyes glittered like a cat before the pounce. "Just like you humiliated me."

Shit. I had to play my cards right here or things were going to get very messy, very fast.

"I already feel humiliated, Camden. You beat me at my own game. You set me up to fail. I got caught because I only saw what I wanted to see. I was following my ego. I don't have your money. I'm sitting here with you and not because I want to. Because I have to."

"Because you chose to."

"And it's humiliating," I admitted, pounding the words out like a stone.

He observed me for a few silent seconds. I could see the wheels of his brain turning, see him fighting something behind those eyes, something deep inside. He wanted to make me feel like he felt. He wanted to humiliate me so badly. To make me feel small, to make me feel weak, to make me feel helpless. Just blackmailing me wasn't enough. He wanted to do something that would really make me understand. I just prayed he wouldn't try it. That he would fight those demons and win. Because the moment he'd try and force me to do something I didn't want to do, I'd be more than humiliated. I'd be ruined. And I'd never be able to look at his face and feel there was someone in there worth rooting for. Despite everything, I wanted to like Camden.

He leaned in closer to me, getting to his knees. The wall was behind me, and beside that, the fire. I was cornered, trapped. I was powerless, helpless. I could fight back and maybe win. Maybe save myself from him. But I wouldn't save myself from my fate, the fate he set for me.

The revenge burned within him. He looked like a man possessed. He put his hand out for my face, his fingers contorted, like he was ready to grab me by my hair and force me to the ground. Like he wanted to cause me pain.

I looked him straight in his eyes, trying to see the good person I believed was still in there. The man who had called me rough and sweet and sad. The one who I'd stare up at the stars with. The one who believed that letting go and moving on was the better alternative to making other people pay.

The good person that I wasn't.

His hand paused in the air, inches from my face, and shaking now. Was it with rage? Was it with control? I was holding my breath in this thick atmosphere, waiting for his next telling move.

A flash of clarity sparked in his rigid features. His hand came down to my cheek where he cupped my face. His hand was very cold, but it was gentle. And it meant me no harm.

"Good night, Ellie," he said, clearing his throat. His eyes were wet, his brow furrowed in wild concern. "I think I've had too much for today."

I watched him, unblinking, unmoving, unable to breathe, until he removed his hand and got unsteadily to his feet. He stumbled across the living room, bumping once into the coffee table and then into the wall, then finally disappearing down the hall. His bedroom door closed with a slam.

A rush of air flowed out of my lungs and the feeling came back into my fingers. I'd been clutching my hands so tightly together that my nails had dug into my palms.

I grabbed the throw blanket from the couch and huddled up by the fire until it went out. It was the only warmth left in the house.

CHAPTER THIRTEEN

SUFFICE IT TO say both Camden and I were in edgy, introverted moods the next day. He was hungover and silent. I was walking on eggshells and trying to give him space. I'd gotten an e-mail from Gus saying he was couriering us the Social Security cards first thing Monday morning before the drop, so at least everything on that end was shaping up.

At some point in the afternoon, Camden had decided to practice his guitar in the living room, just jamming out like a madman. He was singing along, too. I love men who can sing well. Unfortunately, he couldn't. But at least it was on key. No, Camden's skill lay in his guitar playing, and being hungover didn't seem to affect it at all. Maybe it was his way of working things out. I hoped so. He had about as many issues to work out as I did.

Of course, I tended to rely on drugs to get me through that. I was running low on kava pills and was feeling particularly anxious, so I fished out the Ativan and popped a couple under my tongue while I was in the bathroom. Camden had asked me the other day if I liked what I saw when I looked in the mirror. To tell you the truth, I barely looked. Sure, I put on makeup and made myself look pretty. But I was never really looking at myself. I observed the person in the mirror like I was looking through a window at someone else. If I looked really closely, I would have seen glassy eyes, dark circles, and black hair that had a strip of blond roots coming in.

With Camden strumming in my usual space, I retreated to the spare bedroom instead. I left the door open to avoid that whole jail cell feeling, then lay down on the narrow bed. To take my mind off myself and let the drug do the work, I thought about Camden and Ben. I thought about how awful it would be to make a mistake with your life and never see your child again. To keep a room for him in your house just in case you were ever fortunate enough to have him visit. To have that room sit there, waiting and alone, for someone who might never come.

I must have been pulled under into an Ativan-induced coma, because when I woke up, it was completely dark in the room. The only light was coming from the hallway, the light from the kitchen. To my relief, the door was still open.

And through my extremely groggy head and dry mouth, I discovered the reason I awoke. Why my heart was already pounding harder than usual.

There were voices in the house.

Camden. And someone else. A man.

I quietly eased myself out of bed and crept to the doorway. I slowly popped my head around the corner. I saw shadows dancing on the walls, shadows of two people in the kitchen. I jerked my head back around the door before anyone could see me and I listened.

The sound of a chair being pushed back. "I'm sorry," Camden said.

"You're always sorry, aren't you?" a man replied. His voice was deep and emotionless, a bit like the way Camden could be sometimes. "Always sorry for your shit little life."

And now this man was beginning to sound familiar.

"I didn't even think you'd notice, that you'd even care," Camden wailed. Yes, wailed.

"Of course you didn't. Because you're too selfish and too stupid to ever think. I noticed! The whole town noticed! How do you think it looks to me? Huh? Here you are, twenty-six years old with no girlfriend. Just some whore for an ex-wife and a son that I've never seen, and you're using your name—our name—in an ad for gay men!"

What?

"It's not an ad for gay men. It's an ad for the shop. One of my clients happens to be gay. He's one of my biggest supporters and has the most tats and—"

A fist pounded against the table, rattling the items on it. There was no question that Camden was talking to his father. I shuddered at the memories I had of him.

"Look at it!" his father boomed, and I could hear the rustle of paper. "Right in our newspaper. Visit Camden McQueen's Sins & Needles for all your tattoo needs.

And you use a picture of this guy, this *fag*." He said the word with such disgust that I had to fight the urge to run out of the room and hit him. "The name McQueen doesn't just belong to you. I wish it didn't belong to you. It's my name. I'm the sheriff. I rule this town. Do you know how people are looking at me now? They always thought you were one of those fairies. Elizabeth and I were so happy when you got married. Then you screwed it all up!"

"This has nothing to do with Sophia," he said meekly. I'd never heard this big, bad Camden ever sound so small. I swallowed hard.

"This has everything to do with Sophia!" his father roared. Another hit to the table. "Why don't you just admit to me that you're gay, that you're one of them, those fruits over in Palm Springs? God, it's so obvious, isn't it? The way you used to wear makeup and dress like a girl."

"I didn't dress like a girl." His voice was rising. "I dressed like a goth. It's a fucking subculture, Dad. I grew out of it. I'm not gay, and if I were, it would be none of your business."

"Oh, it's my business all right. You live here, in my town, you make it my business." A pause. Another hit to the table. Louder this time. Camden's dad was losing it. "God, the way you never had any real girlfriends in high school, except for that *slut*. No wonder she dumped you—you probably wouldn't sleep with her."

This time the pause could have shattered the room. My jaw had unhinged itself a little. I had a feeling Camden probably looked the same.

"And what slut is that?" Camden asked carefully. I recognized that edge to his voice.

"Who do you think? Ellie Watt. That scum-of-the-earth, conning *whore*." He spat out that word like it was lodged in his throat. "Her parents made me look like the world's biggest fool."

I silently praised my parents for probably the first time ever. I also praised Camden for not immediately turning me over to this guy.

"Ellie isn't a whore," Camden said.

"She's a gypsy tramp, just like her parents. She never belonged in this town, just like you don't belong in this town. I guess I should be happy you never married a gimp."

Now *that* word . . . that was pushing things a little too far; I had to bite my tongue to keep from screaming.

Camden didn't have that problem.

"Fuck you," he seethed.

Another pause. This one slogged on as if through syrup.

Finally his father said, "What did you just say to me?"

Oh, shit.

I heard Camden get out of his chair. His voice lowered. "I said, Fuck. You."

The kitchen exploded in sound. Someone got punched hard. Then punched again. The hit, the sound of fist on flesh and cracking bone, filled the room and shot down the hall. Someone hit the cupboards in the kitchen, and dishes fell to the floor.

I heard heavy breathing, a few sniffs.

"Don't you ever disrespect me again," his father growled.

"I'm sorry," came the very quiet voice of Camden McQueen.

"Sorry? Sorry?" His dad sounded like he was about to let loose again.

"I'm very sorry, sir," Camden whimpered.

The sound of clothes being smoothed, hands being wiped off.

"All is forgiven," his dad said easily, as if they just had a minor spat. Maybe this was a minor spat to them. It would explain a lot of what I saw in high school.

I heard footsteps walk into the hall and I pulled myself farther into the dark of the room.

"Oh, and, Camden? Next time you want to put an ad in the paper," his father said, pausing near the steps, "you make sure to run it by me first, okay?"

I couldn't hear his response, so I could only assume he nodded. I waited in the dark until I heard his father go down the stairs and out the door. Perhaps Camden McQueen would have no problem becoming Connor Malloy.

I tiptoed to the door in time to see Camden storming past me. I caught a glimpse of a bloody lip, a bright-red cheekbone, eyes that didn't dare look at me.

"Camden," I called after him. But he kept going, into his bedroom. He slammed the door behind him, making me jump. Making my heart ache.

I poked my head into the hall and padded my way to the kitchen. A page from the local newspaper was on the table.

It wasn't a huge ad, but it was big enough. Aside from the serious headshot of Camden in the corner, there was only one person in the ad, the man that his father objected to. He had a winning smile and was covered in gorgeous tattoos. He was also fit as a fiddle and wearing a black Speedo, surrounded by oily men lying by a pool. He couldn't have looked gayer if he'd tried.

Camden had known exactly what he was doing. He had chosen this man not only because he probably was one of his biggest clients and certainly one of the most photogenic, but because he knew it would piss off his father. He had done this out of spite. He probably laundered money out of spite, too. I knew a thing or two about that emotion. Spite was the fuel to right all your wrongs. And like any fuel, it could consume you.

I stared at his photo, lost in it. Here was Camden, gorgeous and outwardly successful, but fueled by nothing but spite underneath. All this time later the boy with the lipstick was still inside. Still kicking and screaming. Camden's father underestimated him. Everyone had underestimated him. Especially me.

Then

In the twelfth grade, the girl had found a bit of peace. Perhaps because it was the senior year of high school and everyone knew they were almost out of there. They didn't have much time left with one another, and maybe they were growing up, too.

The girl had never talked to Camden McQueen after

that incident in art class. In fact, he dropped out of that class soon after. It was almost a shame—he received some high marks for his pictures of the girl—but she felt only relief. Every time she saw his face, she felt disgust and, most of all, guilt. When she didn't see him, didn't talk to him, it was much easier to pretend that he didn't exist and that she'd never turned on him in the first place.

She hadn't talked to him until one English Lit class in senior year. It was the only class they had together, but she sat on one side of the room and he sat on the other.

The bell had rung only moments ago. Thanks to her spare block, she always got to class early. She had taken her seat and looked up when a bunch of her classmates—the middle-of-the-run, good-natured crowd that got along with everyone—came in the room talking excitedly.

"I can't believe we have a murderer running around our own town," one of the guys said, slamming his books on the table with enthusiasm.

"Aw, come on, Mike," said the guy in the football sweatshirt, taking a seat behind him. "The guy wasn't a murderer. I think he was arrested for shoplifting or something."

"Nuh-uh," protested a guy who sat in front of the girl. "I talked to Phil Hadzukis, and Phil Hadzukis's cousin's friend works at the police station. They saw it happen. It was a murderer. Or maybe like an assaulter. But he was serious news."

"And now he's gone," Mike said. "Imagine, he could be anywhere."

"What are you guys talking about?" the girl asked. Mike looked her up and down with an appreciative grin. She rarely spoke to them unless she was spoken to.

"Didn't you hear?" Mike said. She shook her head; obviously no, she hadn't. "The sheriff captured some criminal last night, some real bad guy, and locked him up. A few hours later, the guy escaped from his jail cell. Sheriff went crazy, running around town with his guns out like he was Clint fucking Eastwood or something."

She frowned. "Sheriff McQueen?"

"Yeah. He wasn't even drunk."

"I think he was wasted," spoke sweatshirt guy.

"He was pissed off is what he was. Put a perp away only to have him escape later? That's gotta blow, dude."

She bit her lip and anxiously looked to the door as more kids started filing in, hoping she'd see Camden. Hoping he was okay.

"Well, I don't think you guys should worry too much about the criminal," she told the boys. "Whoever he is, he's not stupid. He's long gone by now."

"I forgot," said Mike, "you must know a lot about this. Didn't your parents almost get arrested by Sheriff McQueen?"

She was used to this by now. She gave him a haughty look. "*Almost* got arrested. *Almost* is the key word. They weren't."

"Because they ran," said the sweatshirt guy. But he looked a bit nervous when she speared him with her gaze.

"I wish my parents were cons," Mike mused, looking into the air dreamily. "All my dad does is sit on his fat ass all day."

"'Cuz he's a bus driver," the other guy said.

But the girl was no longer listening. Her eyes were drawn to the front of the class, because Camden was walking in. He no longer wore the trench coat, which made him just a little less scary. But he still wore black nail polish and morbid clothing. His hair was to his shoulders at that point and more neatly kept. But he was still Camden the Queen to everyone.

And he was sporting a black eye.

The girl couldn't help but gasp at the vicious black-and-blue circles that were rimming his puffy eye. The glasses did nothing to hide it. It wasn't anything new to see him looking beat up—he'd often taunt some of the jocks like he was a freaking martyr—so no one was too shocked to see him like that.

"Yikes," Mike said under his breath. "The Queen got his ass beat again."

But the girl knew that wasn't the truth. The girl had seen his father enough times to know that Camden's injuries were a result of his father losing the criminal and taking it all out on him. She had a feeling, deep in the pit of her stomach, the moment the boys had said something.

The rest of the class went by slowly. The teacher didn't even do a double take at Camden, but the girl did. She kept sneaking glances at him at the back of the room. He never looked up at her or at anyone. He kept his eyes on *Lord of the Flies* and that was it.

When the bell rang, however, and class was dismissed, the girl couldn't walk away without saying something to him. She watched him scoop up his books and leave the room. She quickly followed him out and down the hall until she had the nerve to say something.

"Camden?" she asked timidly.

He stopped abruptly. She almost slammed into his army jacket.

He slowly turned, knowing who it was, not wanting to show his face. But he did. It looked even worse up close.

The girl gathered her courage and gave him a small smile. "Hi."

He didn't say anything back, just raised his brow in distrust.

She looked down at her feet, his black eye too much for her to take. She felt drawn to him, pained for him in ways she didn't really understand. As if all of this was somehow her fault. It wasn't, but that was guilt for you.

"I'm sorry," she said.

He cleared his throat. "For what?"

She squinted at his eye. "For what happened to you. Your eye."

He didn't look too impressed. "Is that it?"

"Yes. I mean, no."

He observed her carefully and she squirmed under his microscope.

"I wish we could have stayed friends," she said honestly.

Camden nearly laughed. "You still crack me up, Ellie Watt."

She didn't dare join in. "I mean it."

He shook his head, utterly amused. "You can mean it all you want. It's too late. Look, it's our last year here.

Let's just keep going our separate ways. When this is all over, you'll go one way and I'll go the other."

His rejection stung, but she'd kind of expected it. "Where will you go?"

"I'll go west," he said. He cocked his head, looking ready to say something else. But he didn't. He just turned around and walked away.

"Take care of yourself!" she called out after him, catching the attention of kids loitering in the hall.

"*You* take care of yourself," he said over his shoulder. Then he turned the corner and was gone.

They'd never utter another word to each other until they were twenty-six years old.

Now

Sunday morning was gray and surprisingly chilly. Normally the high desert didn't get this cold until the heart of December and January, but I found myself layering on the sweaters and keeping the fireplace going.

Camden looked terrible. I only saw him briefly at breakfast, where I tried not to look at his bruised and battered face. It felt weird not being able to talk to him normally—even over our plans, which were totally abnormal—but I continued to give him space. He hated pity, and I didn't want to give him any.

Just after noon, he came upstairs from his shop, done with his clients for the day. I'd cracked open a couple of cans of chili, wanting something hearty and warm.

"You hungry?' I asked him, stirring the pot.

I heard him pause. I looked over my shoulder at him. He was standing there and watching me with a small smile. Then it was gone.

"Yeah, starved," he said, and started bringing bowls out of the cupboards, the same cupboards his father slammed him against last night. I didn't dare broach the subject.

He was bringing spoons out of the drawer when we heard the bell ring from the shop below.

I looked at him. "I thought you were done for the day."

"I am," he said, looking confused. "Maybe Chet's dropping off his deposit or something."

He put the forks on the table and ran down the stairs. I heard him open the door to this office and close it. I scooped out the chili from the pot and placed it into the bowls and put them on the table. I hoped whoever it was wouldn't take up too much of his time. His food would go cold.

And more than that, I just wanted to be around him, to make sure he was all right.

After about five minutes, Camden still hadn't come back up. Then I heard the door to the shop open and close. Curious, I scooted myself down the hall and into his bedroom, and peeped out the window.

Camden was leaving the house with two men. Something about the men made my heart skip more than a few beats. I could only see the backs of them, but the men were shorter than Camden, one stocky and the other thin as a reed. Both were wearing well-fitted suits, beige and gray. Both had dark hair, and each walked with a swagger that was designed to look cool and casual. But I knew those men were anything but.

I had no idea where they were going or why Camden went off with them, but it wasn't a good sign at all. I knew I shouldn't leave the house and head into town, since Ellie Watt was supposed to be long gone, but I had to follow them. I had to know.

I grabbed my jacket from the couch and ran down the stairs. I went through his office, looking around to see if there was a sign of a scuffle or if anything was amiss. It looked fine, so I checked the safe, just in case. All the money was there.

I walked into the tattoo shop. The lights were all off and the sign was still set to Closed. Everything looked as it normally did. Except the counter near the register. A folded piece of paper rested there, forgotten and alone. It moved lightly with the draft that sneaked through the thin windows.

I picked it up and straightened it out.

It was a photocopy of a photograph. I recognized the face staring back.

It was me.

It had been taken in Palm Valley, the day of the robbery. I recognized the outfit I was wearing. I had stopped at a gas station on the way back from Joshua Tree and was pumping Jose. I was looking off into the distance, deep in thought, probably too busy planning my con to even take notice of the world around me. You'd think I would have picked up on someone taking my picture, even if they were across the street. But I hadn't.

And there it was. A grainy, black-and-white photo-copy of me from a few days ago.

Below it, it said, "Ellie Watt or Eden White."

Below that it said, "$50,000."

Below that was a phone number with a Biloxi area code.

And below that was the name "Javier."

CHAPTER FOURTEEN

I COULD ONLY stare dumbly at the paper as it trembled in my hands. My thoughts had been blasted into submission. I wasn't even sure if I was breathing or if my heart was beating or if the shock had wiped away everything like a giant supernova. Was I even there in Camden's tattoo shop? Had I died somewhere along the way? Was I in Hell? Purgatory? Was this the end?

Though my first instinct was to flee, to bolt out the door and never look back, I didn't have the strength. Not at first. I sank to my knees behind the counter and put my face into my hands. The picture floated to the floor.

How the hell did Javier find me? All these years later, how did he find me? All those years that he knew me, he knew me only as Eden White. I made up a whole new background for myself and took on a whole new life. The whole relationship was a living lie and I never slipped up, not even once. I was young and in love and way in over my head, but I never slipped up.

You probably shouldn't have stolen his car, though, I told myself. *You shouldn't have been so . . . sentimental.*

I exhaled as slowly as I could to keep the shakes from getting inside me. I sure had a knack for pissing off men and making them hold grudges. They sure had a knack of making me pay for it.

I had to get out of there. I had to go, now.

But before I could, I heard steps on the wooden porch. I froze, then shrank back against the counter, hidden from view.

The door opened, then closed. A lock slid across. Footsteps came across the hardwood floors, slowing down as they approached the counter. The paper. My eyes shot to it, lying on the ground beside me, a picture of an Ellie Watt I'd never get to be again.

The steps came—one, two.

Camden poked his head above the counter, staring down at me.

"Ellie?" he asked quietly.

I couldn't answer him. The fear, it was too much. It was a hand in my stomach reaching for my lungs and squeezing them. It pulled down at my heart until I felt it drop.

"Ellie," he said, a little more loudly. He crouched down beside me. I covered up my face, shaking my head, mumbling, trembling, trying to breathe. I gasped loudly, mouth open, not getting enough oxygen. I couldn't breathe. I couldn't breathe. Gray dots filled my vision.

"Okay, calm down," he said, putting his hand on my shoulder. "You'll be okay."

I didn't hear him. I couldn't breathe. That was all I could think about: the fact that I couldn't breathe.

"Please," he said, now holding my hand. His voice was gentle and soothing but had no damn effect on me. "You're having a panic attack. I can understand why. I know a bit about panic attacks myself. I can get you some pills, okay? You have to come with me. I don't want to leave you here alone. All right?"

He started pulling me up, but I was too weak to move and too terrified. He snatched up the picture of me and crammed it in his pocket. Then he looked around him nervously, reached over, and pulled me up over his shoulders. I went as limp as a rag doll.

He carried me upstairs into the house, and the whole time I wished I had enough breath to get away, to make a run for it. There was no way I'd be getting out of that house on my own free will.

He placed me on the couch and disappeared to the bathroom. When he came out, he was holding a small prescription bottle. He tapped out a few yellow pills into his hand then held them in front of my mouth.

"Open up," he coaxed me. "They dissolve under your tongue."

Except Ativan was white, not yellow. He was trying to drug me.

"No," I tried to say, but it came out like a whisper.

"Ellie, open up. These are for panic attacks. It's like Ativan, but better."

I shook my head but was afraid it was a losing race. I could suffocate to death. Or he could drug me and turn me over to Javier for a cool reward of $50,000.

I wasn't sure which one I preferred.

And I didn't have a choice. Camden opened my mouth for me and stuck the pills under my tongue, his fingers tasting like the latex from the gloves he had worn earlier.

I could have spit them out. I could have tried. But at that moment I just wanted to be able to breathe again. I could worry about my fate better with lungs full of air.

Camden stayed with me, stroking the top of my head while my heartbeat slowed. He told me to breathe in and out, in through the nose and out through the mouth. He held on to my hand and never once let go. I held his hand back, needing something to hang on to.

After some time, I didn't feel woozy. I didn't feel tired. I was calm but I was alert. I gave him a sheepish smile.

"Those are better than Ativan," I said. "I thought you were trying to drug me unconscious."

"I know you were."

I bit my lip, hard. "What are you going to do about me?"

"About you?" He looked at me curiously.

I nodded. "Fifty thousand dollars."

He frowned and adjusted himself on the couch, leaning in closer. "Ellie. I'm not handing you over to some psychopaths for fifty thousand dollars. This doesn't change anything."

"Yes, it does," I said. "It changes everything. It means we have to leave . . . now."

"We can't—"

"Listen to me, Camden," I said, trying to get the

urgency back into my voice. "You have no idea what we are dealing with here. These men...tell me what happened. Tell me exactly what happened."

He rubbed at his forehead anxiously. "Okay. The doorbell rang. I went downstairs and saw these two men standing on the steps."

"Describe them."

"One was about five foot ten, nice gray pinstripe suit. Really shiny shoes. Beaklike nose, a scar at his jaw. Clean shaven. Thick, dark hair, brown eyes. Skinny. Like a male version of Olive Oyl. The other guy was a bit shorter, maybe five eight, same look about him except his nose had a huge bump on it like it had been broken a few times. Tan suit. Dirtier shoes. Both were Hispanic."

"Raul and Alex," I breathed out. Names I thought I'd never say again.

He nodded. "That's right. Raul and Alex. They said they were looking for a girl. I said, 'Aren't we all?' They laughed like assholes laugh, so I knew they were bad news. They asked to come inside and I let them. They asked me a few questions about myself, the shop, how long I've been in the tattoo business, et cetera. Then they brought out the picture. They said the girl had stolen her ex-boyfriend's car and money a few years ago and they wanted it back. The car, especially, had a lot of personal value to the man. They had heard she was in Palm Valley, and considering she had a tattoo on her arm and I was a tattoo artist, they figured I might have seen her."

"That's bullshit," I spat out. "They know I'm here. They've seen us together."

"I don't think they know for sure. It's a good thing your car—his car—is parked around the corner, isn't it?" He continued, talking faster now, picking up on the immediacy of what he was saying. "And so I told them I hadn't seen the girl in the photo, though I knew who she was. I went to high school with her. They looked at each other like I'd said something really interesting, and they asked if I'd come meet someone. I told them I don't normally walk off with people I don't know, and they said he was just at a teahouse across the street. So I figured I better find out what was going on. I followed them to that little shop that sells tea and English pastries and other nasty shit, and they sat me down across from a guy."

I swallowed hard. "And what did he look like?"

"Nice-looking fellow," he said, sounding slightly annoyed, "if you like swarthy-looking Latino men. He was sitting there, cool as a cucumber. And not a false cool—a real cool. Like he owned the tea shop. Like he owned the town. Like he was God or something. Sitting back like he didn't have a care in the world, brown suit jacket, expensive white shirt unbuttoned a bit. Jeans. Shit-kicker boots. Sipping on tea."

"His face?"

Camden wiggled his jaw back and forth. "It... was like the sun. You wanted to look at him and you didn't want to look at him. He looked fine, you know, for a guy. Wide mouth. Square jaw. Shaggy brown hair below his chin. In some ways he looked *really* young. But those eyes... I couldn't look at them for too long. It was like he was staring into my soul or something and looking for things I don't want anyone to go looking for. I couldn't even look long enough at them to remember what color they were."

"They're green," I said absently. "A very light yellow-green."

He exhaled and sat back. "So then you know. It was Javier."

"What did he want?" My voice sounded so far away. Javier. Javier Bernal was in my town. Right down the street from where I was. It was a miracle I wasn't dead. Every second I sat there talking to Camden about him, I was pushing my luck. Javier was like my personal Candyman. There was a chance every time we said his name he would appear.

"He asked me the same questions and I gave him the same answers. Raul, I think, brought up the fact that I knew you in high school. So he started asking a lot of questions about your parents."

"And?"

"And that was it. I told him what I knew, that they were cons that went on the run and never came back. I told him you came from Mississippi, originally."

"I bet that blew his mind," I muttered.

"No." I looked at him sharply but he shrugged. "No, he didn't seem surprised at all. He just nodded like he already knew everything. Everything in the world. He's a...how on earth did you go out with that guy, Ellie? I would have gone insane."

"It was long ago."

"*We* were long ago."

I nodded. "We were. And here we are. And there he is. And we have to go."

I could tell he wanted to argue. That he wanted to talk about the drop and the dream and the plans. But acceptance was coming into his eyes. I knew because it looked like disappointment and defeat.

"He's bad news, huh?" he asked, leaning forward, elbows on knees. The dolphin he had tattooed there look like it was winking at me.

"Remember when you asked me who was chasing me? Now you know. I stole his car, I stole his money. I had my reasons. They still want it back. They haven't forgotten. Drug lords don't forget. Ever."

He looked a little pale. I said, "We can't wait for the drop. They will come back here, they will come into your house, and they will find me. I have nowhere to go or hide in this town. It'll be a miracle if they haven't gotten to my uncle already. You didn't mention him, did you?"

He shook his head. "I didn't. I said in high school you stayed with your godparents. Your uncle isn't a Watt, is he?"

"No, Bespo. Jim Bespo." I breathed out a sigh of relief. "We have no choice, Camden. Either you let me go right now and you stay here. Or you come with me. Or I go with you. Either way, I have to go or I'll be dead."

I said all of this so matter-of-factly that I barely recognized myself. I wanted to give myself a high five for seeming so put together. I wasn't. I was screaming on the inside.

"We can take the money in the safe," he said.

"And we have your ID. That's a start. We can get Gus to send us the rest of your documents somewhere else. But we have to leave now."

He nodded and got to his feet. I joined him, putting my hand on his arm, forcing him to look at me. "Camden, we're leaving and we're not coming back. Ever."

He rubbed his lips together, his eyes scoping out the room, taking it all in, everything he loved. We didn't have any time to pack with thought. We had to throw everything together and go.

"We'll take Jose," I said.

"His car? Isn't that a little obvious?"

"They're watching your car at the moment, not mine. They don't know where mine is."

"They could have seen it at the park."

"Yes," I admitted. "Maybe. But probably not, and 'probably not' is better than a definite 'yes.' If your car is gone, they'll know."

"If *I'm* gone, they'll know."

"But it'll take longer for them to figure that out. I'm giving us five minutes. We've already wasted enough time already. Grab one bag, pack only what you need. I'll take care of everything else. We'll head out the garage door and through the backyard, through the neighbor's. Just in case they're watching the house already."

He stiffened with paranoia. "Should I go to the windows and look?"

I shook my head. "Don't even think about it."

Camden stood in the middle of the living room, looking overwhelmed and stunned, not ready to let go of this life and let in another. He thought he'd had more time. We barely had any.

"Four and a half minutes until we're dead, Camden McQueen," I whispered.

It finally sunk in. We got moving. He insisted on taking his vintage acoustic guitar, but other than that, we made sure he took only what he needed. Documents, money, some clothes, some of his tattoo gear. My bag was small to begin with; everything else was already in the car.

We did a final sweep of the place, Camden taking a picture of Ben from off the fireplace mantle, then we hurried down the stairs and into the garage. After a quick survey of the backyard, we walked quietly across it, helping each other over the fence into the neighbor's yard and then out onto their street before we drew attention to ourselves.

I didn't feel relief until we walked farther up and saw Jose, still sitting by the park. But my relief was short-lived. I couldn't stop thinking about the $50,000 reward for my head and how Camden had passed it up. Just like that. And the funny part was, I believed him. I believed Camden wanted to stay in control of me. I believed he still needed my help. I believed he didn't turn me over to the bad guys because he didn't want to do me any harm.

But the last time I believed in Camden, I got screwed. I was going to have to be a little more careful this time around.

Then

The girl coasted down the street in her beat-up Chevy truck, trying to look as inconspicuous as possible. Considering it was Mississippi in April and everyone had their heads hanging out of their trucks, sweating like pigs, she fit right in.

But she wasn't a local. She'd been back in the state for only three weeks, and during those three weeks, she kept seeing the same people. That was on purpose. The girl had found a familiar house—a rich man's house where bad things happened long, long ago. And she watched that man's house day in and day out. Sometimes from far away. Sometimes from up close. But she made sure that no one ever saw her.

And as she watched his house, this man she remembered as Travis, she watched many men come and go. Some women—some very attractive women—but mostly men. Men who got shit done. Men who wore suits and talked smart. Men who'd cut off your ear with nail clippers.

She watched the men, figuring out which man was the most important to Travis. Which man held the most power. And, over time, she figured out it was a man who looked no older than she did. He was practically a boy, with longish hair that flowed delicately as he walked. When she watched him from afar, you wouldn't think anything of him. But he had a way about him—the way he held himself with such ease, gestured with such control, such confidence, that you couldn't be fooled. That man, as young as he seemed, could not be underestimated. Even Travis seemed to regard him like a snake in a cage, a snake that could easily slip through the cracks.

Once the girl decided that this man was the man she needed to know, she waited until he left the compound, roaring off in a '70s Pontiac GTO, and followed him. She followed him day after day after day. Seeing where he went. Every day he'd leave the affluent suburbs of north Biloxi and head to the quaint town of Ocean Springs. He'd pull up to his small white house, with its curved stained glass windows and sprawling porch, and disappear inside.

The girl never saw anyone else visit the man. She often wondered what he did in there. Did he watch TV? Did he sit on his back porch watching the waves crash against his private beach, the wind rustling the sea grass? Was he lonely?

She wondered all these things about the man and slowly gathered up the courage to find out for herself. One day she followed the man to his favorite café in town, and instead of hiding out in her truck like the stalker she was, she decided to go into the shop. She decided to finally meet this man.

The girl walked in still sweating from the humidity outside. Inside the shop it was cool and surprisingly busy. She spied the man in the corner of the room, relaxing back in a wicker chair, a cup of tea in his hand. He was flipping through a *Men's Health* magazine, seeming bored yet content.

The girl took a deep breath, ordered a coffee at the bar, then took a seat on the couch nearest him.

Up close, the man was just as young as she thought. Maybe twenty-three at the most to her twenty. It was hard to tell, when he was dressed so sharply. He wore a watch like the kind her parents used to get her to steal from rich men. He gave off an air of sophistication and wore cologne that smelled more like tea than the tea he was drinking.

She tried not to stare at him too much, but after a while he caught on. Perhaps he'd always known and had been playing his cards slowly.

He looked up at her, and in that instant he took her heart away. His eyes saw right into her. And he smiled. He liked what he saw.

CHAPTER FIFTEEN

THE SECOND WE got into Jose, we roared off down the street in the opposite direction of the main drag. It would take a little while to get out of town, but I wanted to make sure we weren't being followed, and I really wanted to make sure we weren't about to zip past Javier and his henchmen if they were scouting certain roads.

"Where are we going?" Camden asked, as the houses on the street got smaller and more spread apart. Sand and brush invaded the suburbs.

Why, I thought, *so you can text your new buddies?* I had to stop thinking that way, thinking that Camden could have made a deal with the devil, but my paranoia was at an all-time high, and there was no such thing as being too careful.

"We're going to clean your money," I told him, taking a sharp left onto a street that led out into the desert.

"You know how to do that?" he asked.

I gave him a wry smile. "Of course I do. I'm a con artist. Almost every paycheck is dirty in some way."

"Dirty deeds done dirt cheap."

"Oh, I do nothing for cheap. Not even this. Put your cell phone on the dash."

He was startled. "What?"

I nodded at the dash. "Do it. Put it up there. I don't want to see you sending any covert messages."

There was silence. I looked at him out of the corner of my eye. He was staring at me, seemingly befuddled.

"What?" I asked impatiently. "What's the problem?"

"You don't trust me?" he asked, indignant.

I snorted. "No. You put yourself in my shoes and tell me... would you trust you?"

"Yes," he said right away. "If I were you, I would trust me."

"And I thought my ego was bad," I said under my breath.

"I'm not trading you in for money."

"No, you're just keeping me around for money."

"I was. Everything is different now."

"No, it's not. I still can't get away from you even if I tried," I pointed out. "No matter what, you've still got that evidence on me. Don't think I haven't forgotten. I'm willing to bet that you've e-mailed the file to yourself. You said so; you have it ready to go at the click of a button. But if you turned me over to the cops—over to your father—you wouldn't get any money and you wouldn't be able to run. Now you have money... and the potential to make a lot more." I sighed bitterly. "You don't need me, and I'm more screwed than ever."

"Have I hurt you?"

"What?"

He repeated himself, voice hard. "Have I hurt you?"

"Physically? Not really. Mentally, yes."

"How have I hurt you mentally?"

I bit my lip and started looking for signs for the highway. I hated the way he turned the conversation around. "You said some pretty mean stuff."

He shook his head and muttered, "Unbelievable." His gaze went to the window where the landscape of rolling alabaster and russet flew past. "You tried to rob me, Ellie. I'm allowed to be mean. I have the right to."

"You're justified?" I asked cuttingly.

"Yes." He sighed and took his cell out of his pocket, slamming it onto the dash. "Here. You can keep it if you want. It's of no use to me. I haven't hurt you and I'm not about to."

I hesitated, then took the phone and stuck it in my bra for safekeeping. It made me feel a little bit better, but I wasn't ready to give him the benefit of the doubt yet. It would take a lot more driving without any suspicious vehicles trailing us before I'd even think about letting my guard down.

Once I reached as far as I could go in Palm Valley, I pulled the car onto Highway 62 and headed east.

"Keep your eyes peeled for anyone that could be following us," I told him, though I didn't know what the point was if he was in on it.

He turned in his seat and peered out the back window, which was unfortunately covered in a layer of thick dust. Damn desert living. Everything turns to dust after a while.

He eyed the side mirrors for the next few minutes, as

did I. It was about one thirty in the afternoon and traffic wasn't too bad. If someone was following us, they'd be easy to spot, though we probably wouldn't really know until we made our first stop.

An hour later we pulled into a gas station at Vidal Junction. I began pumping gas, and as Camden went inside to pay, I brought his phone out of my bra and checked his messages. There was nothing, just a few clients wanting appointments and Snooty Neo from the band wanting to discuss the next show. I felt a pang in my heart for Camden: the fact that these clients, his band, they'd all ceased to exist for him. He never even got a chance to say good-bye.

I scoured the gas station, looking for anything out of the ordinary. We were literally in the middle of nowhere, and Vidal Junction was nothing but a ghost town that sat on all four corners of Highways 62 and 95. It kind of gave me the creeps, but at least the lack of traffic and people made spotting the unusual easier. And aside from a family who was bitching at one another as they climbed out of their overheating station wagon, there was nothing strange.

Satisfied, I took out my own phone and checked it. I wanted to check in with Uncle Jim, just to make sure he was okay. The last text I sent him was just thanking him for all his hospitality and that I was off seeing friends on the coast, and that maybe I'd see him again real soon. Short and sweet. He had responded with "Take care, Ellie."

This time I texted:

Hey Uncle Jim, how are things going?

I waited for a bit, and when the gas was done, I put the phone away. I hoped he'd answer soon with a *Fine, how are you?* but perhaps he was out in the palm groves helping with the harvest. It was sunny here in the middle of buttfuck nowhere, but things had cooled down in Palm Valley, which always made harvesting easier.

"Ready to go?" Camden asked as he came out of the store, holding a bag full of crap. I didn't know what was in it, but you couldn't buy anything except crap at a gas station.

I slipped on my shades. "Yep. You buy out the store?"

"Food for the road," he explained, getting in his side.

I eased in, careful of the leather seats and grateful for the shade above the gas pumps. He opened the bag to reveal packages of beef jerky, corn nuts, Doritos, Combos, sunflower seeds, sour berries, honey mustard pretzels, Reese's Pieces, a few cans of Red Bull, and a banana. "The banana is for you," he said.

"Fuck that, give me the corn nuts." I reached in and snatched the bag, along with the sour berries and a can of Red Bull. Who the hell eats a banana when they're on the run?

I put the Dead Weather's *Horehound* on the MP3 player, and the dissonant chords of "Treat Me Like Your Mother" came blaring out of the speakers.

"Getaway sound track?" Camden asked, as we zoomed onto Highway 95 and headed north toward hills of craggy red rock.

"Gotta have fun when you can," I told him with a smile. The getaway was the best part. It was the only time I felt remotely free. I started singing along with the song, doing my best Alison Mosshart impression, which I must say was pretty good. I'd perfected her a long time ago; seemed I was always running from something.

" 'Look me in the eye now, you want to try to tell a lie?' " I sang.

And to my surprise, as soon as Jack White's vocals started, Camden jumped right in. I eyed him appreciatively, impressed that he knew the words. Soon we were singing, shouting, shaking our heads, spelling out "M-a-n-i-p-u-late."

The irony wasn't lost on me.

The sing-along continued until just past the town of Needles. It was nice to pretend we were just taking a road trip or something, fiddling with a playlist and fighting over who got to eat what junk food. It some ways, it felt as natural as the date we had gone on, as natural as the friendship we once had. But, as Mosshart and White had sung, it was all a lie. And it was too late for anything else.

We pulled into a deserted rest area that consisted of a public restroom that had seen better days, a patch of brown grass, and picnic tables surrounded by a chain link fence that protected the place from the barren wasteland beyond it.

"I need to stretch my legs," I told him, shutting off the car and walking with my arms above my head over to the picnic tables. The sun was lower in the sky but it was still hot as hell. I brought out my cell and checked to see if Uncle Jim had gotten back to me. He hadn't. Okay, now I was starting to worry.

"What's wrong?" Camden asked, approaching me. He looked so sincere and concerned, like a sexy, worried nerd. There weren't too many like that.

I straightened out my back and put my phone away. "What makes you think something's wrong?"

The corner of his mouth twitched. "You mean besides the very, very obvious?"

"Haven't heard back from Uncle Jim yet," I said softly.

He walked up to me and grabbed my hand, squeezing. He peered down at me, and with the way his eyes glinted behind his glasses, I had another one of those flashbacks to high school.

"He'll be fine," he told me.

"How do you know? Usually he texts me back right about now."

"I don't know. But I choose to believe he'll be fine, because as selfish as this sounds, we need to worry about us right now. Worrying means nothing if we're dead."

"Are you scared?" I asked him.

"I'm fucking terrified, Ellie," he said. From appearances he looked so strong and put together—tattoos will add toughness to anyone—but I knew better than that.

"Me too."

"We might be scared of the same thing."

"You should be afraid of the people whose money you just stole, not Javier. If he ever catches up to us, there'll be no more us. He only wants me, and I'll do whatever I can to keep you out of it."

He stroked his chin in bemusement. "I was pretty sure you'd bring me down with you."

"Believe it or not, that's not my style."

"Well, I haven't seen any car for quite some time, let alone the same car. I think it's safe to say he's not following us. Do you mind telling me where we are going?"

"Laughlin, Nevada," I said, deciding to trust him a little. Besides, I still had his phone, and I'd keep watching him like a hawk. I pulled my hand out of his and walked back to the car. He followed behind me.

"Doing some gambling?"

"We are. Just try not to bet the house."

*   *   *

The Avi Resort and Casino was just outside of Laughlin in Nevada at the weird corner where the state met California and Arizona. It wasn't anything fancy, just one of those big interchangeable casino resorts that you could find on any Nevada highway. The Avi, though, had a casual atmosphere and was popular with families thanks to its sprawling pool and the mighty Colorado River, which swept past its private, man-made beach. The casino also paid out pretty well and was the perfect place for two ordinary twentysomethings like ourselves to win big.

Of course, we probably wouldn't be winning anything. We'd be losing. But this was the first step toward getting Camden's money cleaned. He could keep the money in cash if he wanted, but it was extremely risky and dangerous, and far too easy to lose. If he wanted to start a legitimate life again, he'd need clean money in a bank account.

After we secured a modest room at the resort, we'd head to the cashier and exchange $5,000 in cash for the same amount on their electronic card. Smaller casinos like this tended to ask questions if you handed them high amounts, but it didn't mean people weren't doing this every day and legitimately. Then we'd gamble for a bit, hopefully losing not more than a hundred dollars—easy to avoid if you just stick to the penny slots—then call it a day and cash in. They give you a check, you deposit the check into your bank account as casino earnings. Your money has been cleaned.

Rinse and repeat.

"Are you sure this will work?" Camden asked, as we locked our hotel door and walked down the dim hall. Despite the casino's nonsmoking policy, the hall still smelled like years and years' worth of built-up smoke and nicotine. You could probably lick the walls and get a bit of a buzz going.

"It will work," I told him. "I've been doing this a long time."

"When was the last time you were here? You've been of age for only five years."

I looked at him oddly. "I was nineteen the last time I left California. Stopped here on the way out. And it's called a fake ID—something you should know about, Connor Malloy."

"I'm not Connor Malloy until I get the Social Security card," he pointed out.

"As soon as I know where we'll be next week, then you'll get your card," I told him.

We took the elevator down to the main floor and

were barraged with casino sounds: blips and bleeps, bells, chimes, the pull of the lever on older models, the smack of buttons on newer ones. A waitress walked by, the ice rattling in the drinks that sat on her tray. Camden quickly plucked one off the tray and slipped the woman a dollar.

"I think I need this," he told me before downing it. We both needed a drink. Several. But first things were first.

We went over to the cashier, and I smiled at the petite, round-faced Asian girl on the other side.

"Hi, I'd like to exchange some cash for a card," I told her with a bright smile, noting her name tag, which said Cammie. I reached into my purse and slid a wad of crisp bills toward her.

She eyed the wad, then me, then Camden, then the cash again.

"It's five thousand dollars," I told her. "Thank God for alimony, right?"

I thought that would bring a smile to her lips but no such luck.

"I'll be right back," she said sternly, and disappeared with my money. Well, our money.

Camden leaned into my ear, whispering, "This isn't going well, is it?"

I turned my head slightly, almost shivering when his lips caught the corner of my ear. "Some people are more suspicious than others. It happens."

When she came back, she was with a thin, balding man with a giant gray mustache. Her manager, no doubt.

"Hello, miss?" the man said, leaning toward the bars. Cammie crossed her arms, watching him intently. "May I see some ID?"

They really had no right to ask for ID at this stage in the game—it was usually when you were cashing out and for over ten thousand dollars' worth. But I wasn't about to argue. I had a clean record, and I knew by law that where I got the money was none of their business.

"Sure," I said, flipping open my wallet and bringing it out. He took it from me under the bars and peered at it closely. I felt Camden tense up beside me. Technically the ID was forged. I mean, it was my old ID, my real one, but I had to add a new photo and change the expiration date on it. It was set to expire next year. Anything later and the card would have been too old to have been issued to me.

"Is there a problem?" I asked as he kept flipping it over. I almost added *officer* at the end of that but didn't want to piss him off.

"No, no," he said quickly, sliding the ID back to me. "Just haven't seen that type of license for a long time."

"I know," I said, peering at my picture. "Mine expires next year. I'm kind of sad to get the new issue. Plus I really like my picture in this one. It's rare you get a driver's license that you're not embarrassed of, you know?"

Cammie nodded appreciatively, and I knew I'd won her over. The man gave me an apologetic smile. "Have fun at the Avi resort," he said, and walked away.

Her smile matched his now. "Sorry about that. We have to take precautions when large amounts come in."

"Oh yeah?" I asked innocently. "I always thought it was over ten thousand dollars."

"That's by law," she told me. "Every casino has their own policy. All the casinos in Laughlin are pretty much the same, too."

Oh, great. Well, it looked like we wouldn't be staying here very long.

She walked away, and I could tell Camden was just itching to tell me something. Instead he sucked back the rest of his drink and tossed it in the trash. When Cammie came back, she had the card in her hands and slipped it to me.

"Good luck," she said, and immediately smiled for the next customers who were standing behind me.

As we walked away, Camden grabbed my elbow and pulled me to him. "Who was that?" he whispered.

"Who?" I asked, playing dumb.

"That Ellie Watt. I know the real Ellie Watt, and she's not that much of a people person."

"Which Ellie do you prefer?" I asked teasingly.

He stopped walking and pulled me closer to him, staring down into my eyes. "Whichever one I've got."

I felt a blush coming on as his stare intensified. I couldn't help but stare back, trapped in his eyes. Thankfully a loud beep came from my phone, making both of us jump and interrupting the weird aspect of our relationship that kept cropping up like a weed.

I quickly fished it out of my purse, heart racing, hoping it was Uncle Jim.

It was. "Fuck, finally," I cried out, opening the message.

Uncle Jim said:

Not much, what's new with you? Hope you're staying out of trouble.

Camden's forehead wrinkled as he read it over my shoulder. "Staying out of trouble? Does he know something?"

I smiled with relief. "No, he's always telling me to stay out of trouble."

"And you never listen, do you?"

"Nope. Though I'm starting to think he might be on to something."

I quickly texted him back, telling him I was just checking in and that the weather was gorgeous in Santa Barbara. Then I put it and part of my worry away. Now came a little bit of fun. Like the getaway, you had to find it where you could.

We invaded the penny slots first, since we both needed drinks and you could sit there for a long time playing. The longer you sat and the better you tipped, the stronger and more regular the "free" drinks were. After our fourth rum and Cokes, our waitress never came back. I guess we'd been cut off.

At this time of the year, the casino wasn't as busy as during peak season, so Camden was able to sit at the machine next to me without pissing anyone off. Only sometimes would we have a local who had to sit at the same machine, and usually we'd just move over. I didn't want to sit next to the crazy gamblers, anyway; they usually smelled bad and had a way of eyeing you down if your machine was paying out more than theirs.

We had the most luck at the twenty-five-cent Wheel of Fortune games. I wasn't that much of a gambler, to be honest—I normally just cleaned my money and got out—but I always had some bizarre luck with these ones. Plus it's fun to yell "Wheel! Of! Fortune!"

I pulled the lever (much more satisfying than hitting the spin button), and as the pictures spun around, Camden whistled a short but familiar tune. A tune that made my heart wrench.

"That was it, wasn't it?" he said. He was watching me expectantly.

"Pardon me?" Another pull, another sip of my drink.

He whistled again. "The tattoo on your arm. The tune. It's from 'On Every Street.' Dire Straits."

Again, I was impressed he was able to deduce it from just the few notes.

"It suits you," he said, quietly this time.

"Rough and sweet and sad?" I joked.

"No," he said. "Just sad. God, that's a sad song."

I don't know why, but my eyes suddenly flared hot with tears. What the hell? A few rum and Cokes and a sad song and I was ready to go.

I swallowed loudly. "I like that song."

"I'd hope you would since it's tattooed on your arm. What does it mean? Are you looking for somebody's face on every street?"

He started singing underneath his breath, going through the lyrics. I blinked hard, shrugged my shoulders, and resumed pulling. I wanted him to stop. He did when he hit the part on my arm, the three notes from the guitar after Knopfler sings the titular sentence. Three notes that never sounded so desolate. Three notes that sounded so much like *loss* in a song that ended with hope.

"That song is not about someone. That song is about you. You still refuse to be traced." He sounded awed.

"There's a cowbell in that song," I reminded him, trying to make light of it while simultaneously wiping away a tear that sneaked out of my eye. "Let's not look into it too much, shall we?"

"Fine," he said. The conversation was dropped and we went back to losing.

CHAPTER SIXTEEN

THE TWO OF us ended up going to bed quite early. Well, early for a casino. After we lost two hundred dollars and earned back one hundred and fifty, we cashed out. I got the same girl as before, and she didn't give me any grief over making up a cashier's check. Nor did she tell me she'd have to report my earnings to the IRS. At least we had that going for us.

With our fancy check in hand, we got two more drinks to go and went back to our room. We had two beds, which was good because I didn't really trust sharing a bed with Camden. I just don't know who I mistrusted more—him? Or me?

After I sent Gus an e-mail updating him on our whereabouts and checked both our phones for new messages (Snooty Neo for Camden, but no one else), I scrubbed off all my makeup, slipped on my boxer shorts and camisole, and crawled into my bed. The sheets were stiff and the comforter had a bizarre smell, but it would do. I couldn't say I felt exactly safe, even though I knew there was security in the hotel, and even though our door was triple-locked. I wondered if I'd ever feel safe with Camden by my side, or if I was going to live in a constant state of anxiety. You'd think I'd be used to it by now.

"Ellie," he called out into the darkness. I had been awake and thinking for such a long time I had assumed he'd be asleep.

"Yes?"

"Tell me the story about your scars."

It was as if the room got darker. Colder. Heavier.

I pulled the smelly comforter up to my face, wishing I could hide. "It's not a fun story."

"I don't want a fun story," he said. "I want the truth. I want to know what happened."

I chewed on my lip, wishing I could buy time, but there was nothing but time on long nights like these.

"I think you owe me that much," he added softly.

And that was true. I did owe him at least that much. I brought my knees up to my chest, full-on fetal position, and told my story to the opposite wall. It was easier than facing him in the dark. It was easier knowing he was behind me.

"Once upon a time," I began, "there was a young girl. The girl lived outside of Gulfport, Mississippi. She didn't call the place home, but she'd been there for two years and it was as close to a home as she'd gotten before. In her home, she believed her life would turn out better and that her family would start acting like a family again. Her parents, or at least her dad, had gotten a real job at the casino. They promised her they were done being grifters and wanted to do things the right away. The girl believed them because they were her parents. She had always believed them, even when they were asking her to steal the wallets of moms at children's birthday parties or distracting clerks while they stole pointless crap. She'd seen the movie *Paper Moon* and was happy someone had made a film about her life, that she wasn't alone. One day, her mother was really angry. Her mother was always an angry person, but this day she was furious. The girl was scared. She loved her mother, but she especially loved her when she was in her rare happy moods. When she was angry, the girl was afraid of her. Even the dad was afraid of her.

"So one day the mom tells the dad and the girl that they're going on a little adventure. Just out to dinner to see an old friend of hers, a man called Travis. Now, the girl knew a lot about this Travis friend of her mother's. She had seen him around the house when her father was at work. The girl was old enough to suspect her mother was having an affair but too afraid to ever ask her mother about it. If her dad ever suspected anything, he was too timid and too kind to say anything about it.

"And so they went out for dinner at his fancy house in the north of town. At the last minute the mother told the girl she was to sit in the car and wait for a few minutes. With a fat black marker she wrote down a combination of numbers on the girl's hand. She told the girl she was to go around to the back of the house, go in the second window, and once inside go for a certain door. In the room she'd find a safe. She'd use the numbers on her hand to open the safe and take the money out. Then she'd leave the way she came in."

I paused.

"I'm listening," Camden said quickly, sounding enthralled.

I took a deep breath and went on. "The girl did as she was told. But she was so nervous that she opened the wrong door. She went into a very black room and before she knew it, there was no ground beneath her. She fell down a flight of stairs and landed on the cold hard floor, crying out from the fall. It took her a few minutes to snap out of it, to realize what had happened. But it was too late. The commotion brought people to the top of the stairs. The light flicked on. It was Travis, with her parents behind him.

"He came running down, waving his arms. The girl's parents were quick with excuses, 'We couldn't find a babysitter,' the mother said. 'We told her to wait in the car.' They yelled at the girl, but it wasn't enough for Travis. He helped the girl to her feet, grasping her unkindly around the wrist, and he looked down at her hand. He saw the combination to the safe written on top. It was all over."

Camden sucked in his breath and I had no choice but to power through the story. It was easier pretending it happened to someone else.

"Travis grew very quiet. For a few seconds there, he didn't say anything. The girl had never been so terrified. The silence choked them all. Finally, he grabbed the girl by her arm, twisting it behind her back until she cried out in pain. Her parents started running down the stairs to stop him, but Travis picked up a container from the shelves behind him. The girl didn't know what it was, except that it had one of those warning labels on it. All the shelves had similar bottles, different colors, shapes, and sizes. The girl had fallen into a sterile, cold basement. It almost looked like a lab but not quite. The man, Travis, threatened her parents. He said that if they told him the truth of what the girl was doing there, he'd let her go. But if they lied, he'd throw the bottle in her face.

"Her parents told him the truth. The mother said she set it all up with the daughter because they were going to rob him. Because Travis deserved it. Because it was only fair. The mother didn't say much more than that. It was enough. Travis smiled, and it looked like he was going to let the girl go. But he didn't. Not at first. Instead he held the girl in place, and while smiling at her parents and telling them 'Thank you for your honesty,' he poured the contents of the bottle on the girl's leg, where it ran down from her knee to the bottom of her foot. She was wearing sandals and shorts at the time. She'd never wear shorts again."

I trailed off, realizing I had a life before all of that happened. That I had been so free and happy once. That I had known what it was like to walk down the street and not have people stare at me. I had so much potential back then and I never appreciated any of it. I never appreciated my future until it was ripped away from me.

"They never found out what chemicals were in the poison," I told Camden before he could comment. "The doctors said it looked like battery acid or methylene chloride, which made them immediately suspicious. To them, it sounded like the girl's parents were operating a meth lab. It made the doctors sic Social Services on them. They asked the same questions about the accident over and over again. And over and over again, the girl had to remember her lie. That she was playing in the dump near her house, searching for car parts for her dad, when she accidently kicked over a bottle of unmarked liquid and it spilled on her. The girl didn't understand why she had to keep lying, why she couldn't tell them the truth. It was Travis's fault. He was the one who did it. Why were they protecting him? But her parents just said, 'No, darling, it's our fault.' And so the girl would spend the rest of her life blaming all of them. She'd blame them until she died."

The story was punctuated by an overwhelming silence. It filled the room to the brim, heavy with the truth and about to run over. Finally, after what seemed like forever, Camden sighed.

"What is it?" I asked, almost annoyed at his response.

"I don't know what to say, Ellie," he said sadly, "and I wish I did. I wish I had the words to take it all away. I am *so* sorry."

"It's all right," I lied. "I'm used to it."

"Did you ever see Travis again?" he asked.

I hesitated. But there was no point in lying anymore. "Yes. I did. That's why I went back to Mississippi."

"And Javier?"

"He worked for him."

Camden took that information and I could hear him

rolling over the bed with it. He exhaled. "So now it's all making sense. You fell in love with one of the bad guys."

"Don't forget, though, I'm one of the bad guys, too."

He didn't say anything, perhaps lost in thought. I settled into my bed and pressed my head into the pillow. My eyes closed, ready for sleep. As I was drifting off, I heard Camden say, soft as air, "You're not bad, Ellie. The world is bad and you're just trying to survive in it."

Or maybe it was a dream.

*   *   *

When the phone rang, jarring me out of my sleep, it took me a few moments to figure out where I was. I sat up in the bed and saw Camden stirring; the sun was just starting to rise somewhere in the east. I snatched up the phone from the table between our beds, remembering I'd asked for a wake-up call.

I eyed the clock as I said, "Hello?" It was seven a.m. I thought I asked for a wake-up call at eight.

There was no one on the line, just a faint humming sound. Then a click.

"Hello?" I asked again. A tiny seed of dread was blooming in my stomach.

"Who was it?" Camden asked groggily as he turned over. He looked over at me, blinking slowly. Without his glasses he looked different. He looked good.

"I thought it was the wake-up call," I said as I put the phone back on the receiver. "But they were supposed to wake us at eight."

"Jerks," he mumbled, and rolled over. The light in

the room was dim, but I could see all the beautiful tattoos down his back. There was so much of him that I had yet to see and explore.

"Yeah," I said absently. I shook my attention off of him. "Jerks."

Still. Something had me on edge. I picked up the phone and dialed the operator.

"Yes, hello," I said when a way-too-chipper woman answered. "I had a call just now to our room, room 416, and I was wondering if that was the wake-up call that I had ordered."

She told me to wait while she tapped on her computer. "No," she said, "we still have you here for eight a.m."

"Uh, is there any way you can find out who just called me? Did you handle the call?"

"Just a moment," she told me. Seconds later a man's voice was on the phone.

"Hello?" he said

"Yeah, hi, I just had someone call my room but they hung up. I was wondering if you could tell me who it was."

"I don't know," he said. "He just asked if there was an Ellie Watt there. I said yes and then he asked how long you were staying. I said two nights and then he asked to be connected."

Oh shit.

"Is there a problem?" said the man on the line.

"Sorry, can you tell me what he sounded like?"

By now Camden was sitting up, the blanket gathered around his waist, watching me anxiously.

"He had an accent. Very faint. Maybe Mexican?"

"Thanks," I choked out into the phone before dropping it on the table. My hands fell limp to my sides. Camden reached over, one hand keeping the blanket around his middle, and hung up the phone for me.

"Javier?" he asked.

I nodded vigorously. "Sounds like it. Yup."

"Time to go?"

"Time to fucking go."

We threw all our stuff together, slipped on our clothes, and ran out of our room. We took the stairs that would deposit us at the side of the building since we wanted to avoid the front desk. They had told Javier I'd be there for two nights, and I wanted it to look that way for as long as it could.

The air outside was cool and clear in the early morning, and by the time we trudged across the never-ending parking lot and reached the car, the sun was above the Arizona mountains on the opposite side of the river. We piled our stuff in and sped off as quickly as we could without drawing suspicion.

"How do you think he found us?" he asked. It sounded like an innocent enough question, but it made my eyes narrow impulsively. I wanted to trust Camden, I really did.

I shook my head, bringing the car up onto the Needles Freeway. "I have no idea. He has his ways."

"So how do you know they aren't tracking us right now with satellites and shit?" he asked. He was gripping the dashboard, his voice on edge, like he was seconds from losing it.

I tried not to laugh. "I'm not Jason Bourne. 'He has his ways' meaning he has a lot of men who do his work for him. They aren't that high-tech; they don't work for the government. He probably just figured I'd be cleaning the money this way and started calling all the casinos in the area."

"That's a lot of casinos."

"He has a lot of men. That's why next time, we're staying under Connor Malloy's name."

"Next time? Where are we going?"

"Vegas, baby."

He sat back in his chair, adjusting his glasses. "Sin City. Seems appropriate."

We left Laughlin in a cloud of dust.

CHAPTER SEVENTEEN

IT WASN'T TOO long until we reached the congested Las Vegas Strip. The car ride there had been somber and quiet. Both of us were tied up in our own heads, pondering our fate. I tried to ignore the fear that Javier was out there, hunting me like a hound dog, and instead focused on our next set of actions. We needed to do this right this time. We had to pretend we were high rollers. We'd stay at a fancy hotel, we'd frequent the casinos like the Venetian, the Wynn, the Monte Carlo. We'd gamble, lose money, and laugh about it over cocktails. We'd play the perfect, rich-to-our-tits couple. And then we'd leave.

It was crowded, glaringly sunny, and warm. Everyone on the Strip was drunk and wearing clothing far too skimpy and bright for before noon. To tell you the truth, I envied them. I don't think I'd ever gone on a vacation my whole life. I was always working, always on. It was a full-time job pretending to be someone else.

I selected where we were going to stay and pulled

into the entrance of the Aria hotel. Camden craned his head to look at the tall, shiny building.

"Impressive," he said. "I'm going to assume Connor Malloy has some money."

"Yes, he does," I said, parking the car at the valet. "Both of us do. We're rich and we have a lot of money to spend here. A lot of money to win."

He nodded in nervous agreement. We got out and I slipped the valet $500, telling him my car was a coveted collectible and needed to have extra special attention away from prying eyes. The valet enthusiastically agreed and told us he'd keep it out of sight. Good.

Once inside, we got a room under his new ID. He obviously couldn't use his real credit card, so I decided to be Ellen Waits and slipped them my (well, her) credit card to hold the room. I thought there was no space on that card, but it still went through fine.

Our room was on the seventeenth floor and beautiful. I pressed a button for the light-blocking, automatic blinds and they withdrew, leaving us a view of the pool area and the impossibly glassy hotel next door. We flopped our stuff onto the beds.

"What's our first step?" he asked, stretching his arms behind his head. Once again, I tried to not look at the tattoos around his abs. Once again, I failed.

"Well, we'll need to go out and get some nice clothing. I mean, really nice. High-roller kind of nice. You're going to look like James Bond."

"Does James Bond wear glasses?"

"If he does, they're probably X-ray vision. You'll have to pretend."

He grinned, the first smile I'd seen on him in a while. "I don't need X-ray vision. Now that I've seen you naked, I can picture it real well."

I rolled my eyes and started going through the bags and sorting stuff. Yep, I'd have to get a whole new wardrobe. And my boots would definitely not do.

Camden walked over to the window and gazed out of it. His broad shoulders and narrow torso made quite a compelling silhouette. "Isn't it a bit early in the day to go gambling?"

"We'll go tonight."

"What are we going to do until then?" He turned his head and looked at me.

I shrugged. "There's a lot we have to do."

"We're going to the pool," he said, and walked away from the window, brushing past me.

"What? We can't go to the pool!"

He fished out a wad of cash from his suitcase and put it in his wallet. "Why not?"

"Because. This isn't a vacation, Camden."

He folded his arms. "I know it's not. But we don't have much else to do and I'm not sitting in the hotel room. Come on, I'm tired and I probably stink. I want a shower; I know you do, too. I want to go to the pool for an hour and relax. What's wrong with that?"

"Uh, everything," I told him. "We don't get to relax. We're on the run."

"You've been on the run practically your whole life," he said, stepping closer to me.

"Yeah, so?"

"So, I think you need to rethink the way you're doing things. It's just an hour."

Now it was my turn to cross my arms. We did have the time. I did feel gross from the day's journey. It probably would do me good to just try to relax and clear my mind. But, aside from the fact that there was no way I could relax knowing Javier was out there...I hated swimming pools. It sounds dumb, but when you've tried your hardest not to show your deformity in public, you tend to avoid situations where your pants are off. Other than as a child, I'd never even owned a bathing suit.

I looked at the clock on the wall. "Okay, you go down and I'll join you soon."

He pursed his lips in suspicion. "You promise?"

I nodded. He snapped his key off the desk and strolled out of the room. Once he was gone, I fell back onto the bed for a few minutes. I didn't understand how Camden could be so relaxed about everything. Lying by the pool? How the hell could you lie by the pool when you knew there were men looking for you? I mean, they weren't looking for him specifically, but still.

I started to get anxious again. What if he was acting all cool because he was setting me up? What if he'd asked me to go to the pool on purpose? He knew about my scars. He knew I wouldn't do it. He knew I wouldn't come down. What if he was planning something with Javier right now? I'd be a sitting fucking duck.

"I'll show you," I said out loud. I grabbed my purse and everything I needed to run, then headed out the door. After the elevator and walking through half the hotel, I found the level for the pool and stormed out

into the overbearing sunshine. It was so damn white
I felt like I was in my own hell disguised as heaven.
The waitresses were in white, the towels were white,
the chairs were white. The pool was such a pale blue
that even it seemed white. My eyes were burning until I
slipped on my shades.

It was a big area with lots of pools to choose from.
I had no idea where Camden could be or if he was
even there, but it was worth checking first. I stayed
along the wall where the change rooms were, observing everyone—buff frat boys, fat tourists, screaming
children, bachelorette parties. Finally I spotted him
on the opposite side of the largest pool. He was alone
and reading a book, although a few chairs down were
a bunch of bodacious blondes tanning their oiled asses.
He kept sneaking glances at them, and I choked back
the streak of bitterness that zipped through me. Now I
was jealous of any girl Camden looked at? I was offi-
cially going insane.

I decided to chance it. I walked around the pool, as
casually as possible, as if most women in Vegas wore
combat boots, jeans, and a slightly dirty tank top to go
suntanning.

I stopped in front of his chair, unabashedly admiring his physique under the security of my sunglasses.
Fuck, damn. He looked good. And those bikini babes
he kept glancing at, well, they were certainly checking
him out, too. When they saw me, they glared a little. I
glared right back. Too bad they couldn't see it.

"Hey," I said to him.

He slowly tore his eyes from his book, a new

hardcover of Neil Gaiman's latest, and broke into a grin when he looked up. I nearly melted. It was hot out.

"I hoped you would come," he said, patting the chair beside him. I smiled a bit too smugly for the other girls' benefit, and with that same smile, did a quick sweep of my surroundings. So far, so good. No one walking toward me like T-1000.

I hovered for a second, watching a bead of sweat travel down the ridge of his abs before sitting down. He picked up a plastic shopping bag and placed it in my lap.

"That's for you," he said.

I peered inside. "What is it?"

"Take it out and look."

If it was a bomb, I was going to be very upset.

"I bought myself some swim shorts, since I forgot to pack any. I knew you probably didn't own a swimsuit."

I held it in my hands like it was a baby (and, just for reference, I hold babies like they are snakes). It was a bikini, pale yellow with adjustable triangles. Not the most modest-looking thing, but it had more coverage than the bikini babes. I'd never wear it in a million years.

I smiled tightly, trying to coax out some appreciation. "It's lovely, Camden. But I don't think I'm going to go swimming."

I began to put it back in the bag but he suddenly reached over and grabbed my wrist. Hard. I'd been fearing the bikini when I should have been fearing him.

"You can't just sit here in your jeans and boots, Ellie," he said. He was startlingly serious.

"Yes, I can," I told him. My eyes darted around. His tone was making me more nervous.

His grip tightened and I tried to pull back but he held me in place. He leaned over and pulled down his sunglasses. "You're wearing the bathing suit. There's no reason for you not to."

I frowned at his hand over my wrist. "Yes, there is a very good reason," I hissed, "and you know exactly what it is. You tried with the miniskirt, and this definitely isn't any better."

"You need to get over your fears. You need to stop caring what people think," he said.

"I don't have to do a single thing you say," I shot back.

He jerked me toward him and I let out a gasp. He didn't hurt me, but he was acting irrationally. I looked around to see if anyone had seen. The bikini babes were sitting up and watching us with concern. I might need their help after all.

He leaned into my face and peered at me, searching for something and being angered by what he found. "You have to do everything I say. I don't care if it was your idea to leave Palm Valley, your idea to come here, your ex-boyfriend who is coming after you. You keep forgetting that you're really here because of me. You keep forgetting that I own you."

So that was what this was about. I matched his look and leaned in closer. "You think you own me? You only own my fate. You don't own me right here, right now," I snarled.

Then I suddenly yanked myself back and he let go.

I kept my eyes on him, afraid to look away, but I could hear the girls whispering anxiously. I didn't blame them. It's never fun to see a couple fighting. And we weren't even a couple.

I stood up, bundling the bikini in my hands.

He glared up at me. "You're so afraid, Ellie Watt. You're afraid to show the world what you're really like. You're afraid to come to peace with your scars, because the minute you do, the minute you accept them, you have to let go of your anger. You have to let go of your quest. And then who would you be?"

I didn't know.

"Fuck you," I said, throwing the bikini in his face. The tears were almost breaking through and I hated myself for them. I hated myself for yelling at him in public but I couldn't help it. "Is that what you meant by trying to humiliate me? Is this what you need to make things even?"

Before he could do anything but stare at me, mouth agape, remorse in his brow, I turned and ran away with a sob. I couldn't stop the tears now. They'd been building for too long. I ran past the white wall of lawn chairs, people turning to look and see. I ran onto the posh interior level with its small food court and all the way to the elevator.

I tried to swipe my card to enter in my floor, but time and time again, nothing would happen. I sank to the floor as the tears blurred my vision until two elderly ladies came inside. They inserted their cards and one of them kindly asked me. "What floor are you on, dear?"

I squeaked out "Seventeen" and they punched in the

number without asking a single question. Bless their hearts.

On my floor I staggered out and went straight to my room, my card working again. I made it to the bed then collapsed into a fit of tears. I cried for all my wrongs that were never righted. I cried that I couldn't just live with the wrongs and find my peace with them. I cried for the childhood I never had, for the future I was robbed of. I cried for my parents, who I knew did love me in their own way, which made not having them around even harder to take. I cried for always being alone, for never having a vacation, for not knowing who I truly was.

I cried until there was nothing left in me to cry. And when I was weakened, exhausted by the tears and anguish, that was when Camden came in the room.

He walked slowly to me and sat on his bed. He waited a few moments before whispering, "Ellie?"

I didn't answer him. I couldn't.

"Ellie," he said again. "I have an idea that might help you find peace."

If he was asking me to meditate, he had another thing coming.

"It will hurt. But the results will be beautiful. More beautiful than they already are."

That was strange enough to make me raise my head and look. He looked solemn, eyes red, hands clasped in front of him. "I'd be improving on your beauty, finding the pattern in the chaos. Making you feel proud of what you've become."

I wiped my nose with the comforter. Totally unattractive. "What are you talking about?" I asked hoarsely.

He went to his stuff and when he came back, he was holding a small silver case. He clicked it open and showed it to me. It was like the briefcase full of his tattoo gear, but smaller. It just had the gun, a couple of needles, ink caps, gloves, and carbon papers, plus a couple of items I didn't recognize.

"A mini-tattoo kit," he said. "I made it a few years ago, decided it was the kind of thing I should keep in the glove compartment. You never know when there's a tattoo emergency."

I pushed myself up onto my elbows and peered up at him. "Is this a tattoo emergency?"

"Ellie," he said, sitting back down. "Let me tattoo your scars."

I didn't know what to say to that. "Is that even possible?"

"With old scars, yes. I've seen some artists turn scars into beautiful works of art. One woman had her mastectomized breast turned into a flower."

"That would fucking hurt." My own scars felt weird and overly sensitive if I touched them too much.

He nodded. "It probably will hurt. But you're tough. And the pain will be worth it."

I shook my head, trying to get some sense into it.

"Don't you trust me?" he asked.

Well, no. I didn't. I wanted to. But I couldn't. That said, I had been wrong about him trying to contact Javier. And I still had his phone, and no weird calls or messages had come through. But did I trust him with my body, with making it into something beautiful? Did I trust his talent and his skill—his passion?

I did.

"How much is it going to hurt?" I asked.

"A little more than your normal tattoo. I have a tattoo on the bottom of my foot. It would probably hurt just the same."

I made a face. "Ugh, you do?"

He slid off his Reef sandal and showed me. It was the symbol for the Wu-Tang Clan.

I had to laugh. "Are you serious?"

"I went through a serious wigga phase and started listening to all this old rap. I think I knew I was going to grow out of it, hence the placement."

I was still smiling at that. It felt good. "Boy, LA changed you."

"Tried to change me. I found myself again."

We exchanged a humbled look.

Then, "Will you say yes, Ellie?"

I looked down at my leg, covered by denim. What the hell. Why not? What difference would it make to me? If he could handle the Wu-Tang Clan on his sole, I could handle his art on my scars.

"This won't interfere with our plans for tonight, will it?" I asked.

He gave me a small smile and started emptying out his kit onto the luxe bedspread. "It should only take about three hours. You'll be able to walk, though to be honest you probably shouldn't wear pants. But it'll be bandaged really well. No one will see."

"Only three hours?"

"I just want to do the front of your leg, where it's more pronounced. I don't want to do too much at once. We can save the back for another time. If you wear a loose and long dress or skirt this evening, you'll be fine."

I swallowed hard, suddenly nervous. "Will I get a drink for the pain?"

He shook his head. "You'll bleed too much. But you'll do fine. I promise."

And so with the curtains open and the sun blaring in, I stripped down to my underwear and lay on the towels he'd spread out on the bed.

He sucked in his breath as he saw me, his eyes traveling from my toes to my hips, as if he hadn't seen it all before.

"Jesus," he whispered, gaze lingering everywhere. "I keep forgetting that you're art already."

I felt strangely shy at his admiration and fidgeted with the corners of the towel. "So what are you going to tattoo on me?"

"Whatever your scars tell me to," he said.

I lay my head back on the bed as he started prepping my leg. I didn't want to watch. I wanted to submit. I looked out the window, the sun glinting off the Rio building in the distance. After a few minutes, the needle buzzed, alive and waiting to transform me.

I put my sins in his hands.

CHAPTER EIGHTEEN

Then

The girl stood outside the tattoo parlor, shaking her head adamantly. She had promised her boyfriend that she'd get a tattoo with him, but she was getting very cold feet at the last minute.

"Come on, angel," Javier crooned to her, taking her hand. "Everyone gets nervous their first time. It's a little like sex, although you should be so glad you don't have to wear the loss of your virginity on your sleeve."

I kinda will, she thought to herself, unable to keep from smiling. Not only had she lost her virginity to Javier, but they had talked for months about getting tattoos together. Javier already had several, a large cross that ran up his spine, and his mother's name scribbled on the inside of his bicep. The girl had none.

They had decided to go with a musical theme based on songs they would pick out for each other. Javier was partial to the song "On Every Street" by Dire Straits.

Being a big fan of the band, the girl loved the song but could never understand why her boyfriend had associated it with her. After all, the song talked about a woman's "injured looks" whose "fingerprints remain concrete," and the man with a "lady-killer regulation tattoo" who was "still on the case" and forever searching for her in "a ravenous town." Javier's answer was always the same, that no matter what happened to them, he'd always come looking for her, on every street.

At the time, the girl thought it was romantic. And perhaps, in some twisted way, she still did. But she couldn't decide how to incorporate that into a tattoo. There was a line in the song about the moon hanging upside down, and she thought that might be a good one. Then Javier suggested she get the written notes to the part of the song that always made her cry. She said she cried when she heard it because it made her feel what the hero in the song felt. And that was alone. Just three simple notes, and she felt all the grief of losing your lover, forever confined to a never-ending search. She told him it sounded like your heart echoing down a black corridor.

Her song for Javier was Nine Inch Nails' "Wish." A darker, faster, more frantic song but one of her favorites. But when it came to the cryptic lyrics, to wishing there was something real in a "world full of you," she wasn't sure who the song was about. Her or Javier?

He decided to get it on his wrist, just the word "Wish." He said he had always wished for a woman like her, and every time he looked at his hand he'd be reminded that wishes did come true.

Still, despite the commitment and support, the girl was having second thoughts. It was more than just the pain; tattoos were forever. Her tattoo spoke of a future that might or might not happen. Did she want it to come to pass, to look down at her arm one day, knowing Javier was looking for her? Did she want to feel that empty, seeking sound?

Javier was making sure she'd always remember the first time she had sex and the first time she got a tattoo. He was imprinted on her body in so many ways. And in the back of her head, buried deep behind logic, hidden behind first loves, sex, lies and power, the girl knew that she was being branded, for him to own, forever.

It took a bit more pleading and coaxing outside the parlor on that day when the clouds pressed down on Ocean Springs like a humid hand. But finally, and as usual, the girl gave in. She had a hard time saying no to Javier. It was one of the reasons why, a year later, her mark became her lover and the master of her heart. She never meant to fall for Javier. She couldn't even understand how she did, how she succumbed to a man who did very bad things, who was part of an organization that had once done very bad things to her.

But when you're twenty, the heart wants what it wants, and if you're dedicated enough, it gets what it gets. Youth and naïveté did so much for this girl who was now calling herself Eden White.

Javier kissed her hand, staring intently at her with the sharp yellow-green eyes that had won her over to begin with. "I hope I'm always a part of you, Eden," he said with conviction. "You'll forever be a part of me. A world without you in it is a song without the music. You need both to make it whole."

She felt her cheeks flush. Javier could be terribly romantic, and the strange part was he was always sincere. He lived his life bravely and with passion, so much so that when he was dispatched by Travis—the man who started it all, the man she had yet to see— he made savagery an art. It made it easy for the girl to forget the type of man she was dealing with, because when he was dealing with her, she was a sacred jewel— his queen.

It wasn't until later, when it was almost too late, that she rediscovered the snake. He was starting to slip through his cage. And it was frightening.

The girl took in a deep, steadying breath, and leaning on Javier for support, entered the parlor. An hour later they came out with their marks forever on each other, sinking into their skin. Her arm was heavily bandaged and soaked through; his song had made her bleed more than normal.

It was her first warning.

Now

To say that the tattoo hurt was an understatement; it hurt so much that I needed something to bite down on. The hotel towel looked like it had been chewed up by a disobedient dog, but it was better than screaming, which I felt like doing on more than one occasion.

Most of the time I just looked straight out the window, imagining I was floating high above the gaudy people at the pool below. Sometimes, though, I would sneak a look at Camden. He almost dissolved into the tattoo, into my body, that was how involved he looked. He was like a sculptor, whittling away my ugliness, leaving trails of beauty behind. What started off as a bare branch growing from the roots of my foot soon unfolded into a leg full of cherry blossoms. Camden made the crisscrossing lines into a tangle of green growth; he coaxed my dead skin into living flowers.

When he was finally done, wiping the beads of sweat from his forehead and snapping off his gloves, I felt like crying. Not just that the pain was over but that something amazing had been birthed from my tragedy. For the first time in my life, I was able to stare at my leg with something other than disgust, anger, and shame. I felt awe and I felt pride. And, whether I wanted to accept it or not, I felt gratitude. Camden...

I couldn't even complete the thought. I stared at him, unable to say anything except "Thank you."

"You're welcome, Ellie," he said. "And thank you. Now you can see what I've always seen."

My throat felt thick and I swallowed hard. Noting this, he got up and came back with a glass of water from the bathroom for me. I drank it down but still couldn't come up with anything to say.

"Are you done admiring my work?" he asked with a wink. The truth was, I didn't think I'd ever be. The pink cherry blossoms were so full, vivid, and lifelike. It really looked like a tree had grown around my leg. "I'm going to have to wrap you up now."

I nodded and winced as he began to wrap my leg

with layers of bandages. He worked quickly and gently, his strong hands treating me like I was precious to touch. It was humbling having him dote on me like that, and for once it felt good to be taken care of. I didn't want to brush him off and tell him I could handle it myself—I wanted him to handle it. I needed him, his touch, his attention. All of it.

When he was all done he ordered me to stay put. By now the sun was setting and casting the Vegas sky coral above the glitzy lights. He thought I should stay off my leg for a little while if I was going to be walking around for the rest of the night.

As he propped my leg up with a pillow, I said, "What about the clothes? I need some nice clothes and shoes for tonight, and we're running out of time."

He looked up at me and shot me a cheeky smile. "Why don't you let me worry about that?"

Pfffht. As if I'd let him shop for me. "You don't know my size. And I don't trust your taste."

He gave my toe a sharp squeeze and laughed. "Wow, so I pick out leopard-print leggings for you one time and suddenly you think I have bad taste. Hey, just trust me. And I know your size. I've felt you up."

A flash of his hands all over me flooded me with warmth. I ignored it, ignored the fact that I was lying in bed in front of him, stripped to my underwear, legs slightly askew. "Shoes?"

He leaned over and picked up my boot from the floor, peering at the sole. "Size eight."

"But I hate high heels. I can't walk in them."

"So I won't get you high heels."

"You'll be able to see the bandages on the top of my foot."

"So then people will see the bandages. People get tattoos all the time here, I'm sure even the high rollers."

"I have to have—"

"—a long dress. I know. Just trust me. I know what I'm doing."

And with that he got himself ready to go out and left me lying in bed, sore and slightly immobile. I flipped on the television and got wrapped up in a few episodes of *Mythbusters* before I started getting worried. Not about what clothes he was bringing me—though I was having visions of stripper platforms, cheetah-printed miniskirts, and bikini tops—but because I wondered if that was all he was going out there to do.

I had to make a decision and I had to do it now. I couldn't live in this indecisive, wishy-washy state of not knowing whether I could trust Camden or not. One minute I thought I could, the next I was afraid I couldn't. It was making me feel bipolar, and in some strange way it wasn't really fair to him. I had to decide how I felt about him and then I had to stick to it. If I got burned either way, then that was the risk.

I studied the patterns in the ceiling, hoping to find a pattern in my thoughts. Camden led me on. He screwed me over as I was screwing him over. He had evidence on me that would put me in jail or at least get a warrant out for my arrest. He had a father who wanted nothing more than to serve me overdue justice. Camden had obvious control issues and his own methods of payback for all the wrongs I'd caused him. He had a meeting with Javier, Raul, and Alex and learned there was a giant price tag on my head. There were many reasons not to trust him.

But despite all my suspicions, it came down to two things. First, he'd had all these opportunities but so far hadn't seized any of them. If he was just biding his time, I had no way of knowing. But it seemed the longer we were together, the more complicated things got. If he wanted to get rid of me, it was easier to do it sooner than later. The other reason was the most simple one, the most honest one: I had reason to trust him because I felt he could be trusted. Call it a gut feeling or primal instinct, but that was what it came down to. I trusted him because I felt that I could, that I should.

Were hunches something to bet your life on? Well, I was in Sin City, where people did it every day. I'd just have to act like the high roller I was pretending to be and take the risk.

With that decision made, I felt a cloud of anxiety lift. It was so much easier to just worry about one thing. I must have been relieved enough to doze off, because when I came to it was dark out and Camden was in the room holding a few heavy garment bags and shoe boxes.

"This game," he announced, placing the packages on the floor with a dramatic flourish, "is a lot more fun when you're playing it at Armani instead of a thrift store."

"Who's going first this time?" I asked as I sat up, my interest piqued.

"You," he said. "I only have a tux. To put it on would ruin my private fashion show."

I felt a little bit like Kim Novak in *Vertigo* as he unzipped all the bags and lay the selection of dresses out on his bed. To my surprise, they were all gorgeous. This man had excellent taste underneath the kinks.

There was a metallic olive-green strapless gown, straight down to the floor, nothing poofy; a slinky material halter dress in gold that seemed to melt into the covers; and a long, black silk dress with the front cut down to the navel and the back cut down to what I guessed would be your crack. A layer of thin black lace covered the open areas, making it seem a more sub-dued dress at first glance, until you looked up close. It was risqué, daring, and elegant. It was perfect.

"I thought so, too," he said, noting the way my eyes were fastened on it. "And I thought it would go well with these."

He opened up one of the shoe boxes and showed me a pair of strappy sandals with a modest two-inch heel. The straps were in the shapes of twisting roses and glit-tering with hundreds of silver rhinestones. Perhaps not so modest after all.

"They're beautiful, Camden," I said in a hushed breath. "I gotta be honest here. I'm starting to feel a bit like Cinderella or something."

"Well, I'm certainly not your Prince Charming," he said, gathering up the other dresses. His arms flexed beautifully against his black T-shirt.

"Thank God for that," I told him, feeling bold. "Prince Charming never had your body or your tattoos."

"Or my cock," he shot in, grinning wickedly.

I bit my lip as my eyes traveled to his crotch and

back. "If he did, Cinderella definitely wouldn't have gone home at midnight."

"And how late are we staying out tonight?" he asked.

"Until the last chip has fallen."

I stood up, cautious with my leg. It felt tight and heavy but other than that it was fine.

"Do you mind turning around?" I asked, making the motion with my hands.

He ruffled his hair with amusement. "I don't think I will. I bought you the clothes, I get to see the show."

He stood there in front of me, surrounded by boxes and bags, the two beds on either side of us. Though the smile on his lips was playful, the look in his eyes was not. It wasn't a mean look, but it wasn't soft. His features stood out in their beautifully masculine way, all hard edges and second chances. This wasn't the time for me to be bashful and he knew it.

Seeing as I was already in my underwear, a black pair that had cheeky coverage, I lifted my tank top above my head and let it drop to the carpeted floor. His gaze intensified, like a heat-seeking missile. I brought my hands behind my back, and as elegantly as possible, I undid the clasp and slipped my bra off of my arms, tossing it to the bed.

Though his gaze, his pose, his very being, reminded me of a wolf about to pounce, he didn't move. I felt his eyes roam up and down my body like silk, sending shivers down my back. He was turning me on without laying a hand on me.

It wasn't necessary for the dress, but I shimmied out of my underwear and stepped out of them. Now I

was absolutely, completely nude, save for my bandaged
leg. To anyone else I would have looked a bit silly. But
not to Camden. I could see in the way he regarded me
that I was nothing short of a phoenix coming out of the
ashes, just like the one on his hips. Now I had become
his tattoo.

I slowly walked over to him, owning my body as I
never had before, shoulders back and head high. I gestured to the dress. "Will you help me?"

He licked his lips; it was probably involuntary, but
it caused heat to flare between my legs, my own lips to
part open. He reached over, picked up the black dress,
and leisurely unzipped the side of it, his eyes never
leaving mine.

I raised my arms above my head, my bare breasts
rising as I did so, surrendering to him. Our gaze never
broke, and the heat only built, connecting us. He took
the dress and carefully slipped it over my arms and
pulled it down. His knuckles brushed against my nipples and I clenched my jaw, supressing the shudder that
wanted to roll through me.

He dragged it down over my breasts and over my
stomach, slowly, so slowly, as if the fabric was an extension of his hands and lips. Every hair on my body was
raised, my skin tense and wanting. He came closer to
nudge it over my hips, letting his fingers rest on them as
gravity took the remainder of the dress to the ground.

Now fully clothed, I lowered my arms. He was so
close to me, too close. His hands burned on my hips.

"Thank you," I whispered, breaking his heated gaze
and looking at the ground.

"One more thing," he said, breaking away. He bent down and rummaged through one of the bags, and pulled out a jewelry box. Before I could say anything, he flipped it open, and I saw a sparkling pair of diamond chandelier earrings nestled in dove-gray velvet. I'd never had such sparkles so close to my skin.

And even though Camden had bought it with stolen money, even though we were only dressing up so we could clean what he stole, this cemented my Cinderella comment. I felt like a princess.

"They're beautiful," I told him, taking the box from his hands, our fingers brushing against each other. "Thank you. I guess I better go make myself look pretty. I think I'll put my hair up."

He beamed and stepped away. "I hoped you might."

I gave him a quick smile and ushered myself into the bathroom with my makeup kit. The minute I shut the door in the spacious, tiled room I exhaled loudly. My heart had been hammering a mile a minute back there, the tension building until I almost couldn't take it. It was like the moment I decided to trust Camden was the moment I wanted to hand my body over to him again. I supposed the tattoo was the first step.

I pinned my hair up in sections then applied some classic makeup. Black-winged liquid liner and red lipstick sealed the deal. The earrings were the world's most beautiful accents, sparkling from the bathroom lights and reflecting on my shoulders like dancing pixie dust.

When I came out, I saw Camden by the bar, pouring a bottle of champagne into two flutes. I thought I'd heard the pop of the cork while I was in there.

He looked . . . well, there was no point describing how he looked. It would never do him justice. It was Camden in an extremely well-tailored, suave, and sexy tuxedo. The sheen of the black lapels, his bowtie coupled with his spiked-up black hair, his nose ring and the glasses—he was one badass spy. I had to keep my teeth pressed together to prevent my jaw from dropping to the floor.

"Well, well, well, Mr. Bond," I said as I slinked toward him.

"Well, well, well, Ms. Watt," he said, handing me my champagne flute. The bubbles sparked and fizzed between us. "I think this town is about to get its hands dirty."

We clinked our glasses.

CHAPTER NINETEEN

DRESSED TO THE nines, Camden and I turned heads in every casino we entered. The cashiers and dealers regarded us with some sort of respect instead of the usual caginess that would put us on their Suspicious Activities Report. We looked the part and acted the part, and that, combined with never cashing in amounts more than $7,000 and actually playing more than a few games, let us slide under their radar. Of course, we didn't stay in one casino. We went to the Cosmopolitan next door to start, then the Monte Carlo, then down the other side of the Strip to the Venetian, the Palazzo, and the Wynn before ending at the Bellagio. We saved the best for last.

Though my leg ached and itched something fierce from the tattoo, and my feet hurt from the rhinestone straps, we made it through by cashing in $25,000 in total and cashing out $24,000 in cashier's checks. We lost only $1,000 during our gambling exploits, which took us from casino to casino so that no one would be the wiser.

By the time we shuffled into the elegant Bellagio, it was one a.m. and we were tired out of our minds. Red Bull and coffee went only so far, even though we kept our drinking to a minimum. We had spent most of the night on edge, and with midnight flying past us—my Cinderella hour—we were letting our guard down a bit.

I was done with gambling for now. We had cashed out, but Camden wanted to play a few rounds of black-jack with some of his own money. Not a lot, just enough to have some fun. It was nice to just sit beside him, perched like the perfect femme fatale, and yell at him to say "Hit me" or not. Plus the blackjack players at the Bellagio were the perfect subjects for people watch-ing. When I wasn't lurking over Camden's shoulder or making sure my nipple ring wasn't poking through the lace inserts, I was watching everyone else, wondering if they, too, had a story to tell.

"Are you thirsty?" I asked him, crooning into his ear as he raked his chips toward him. Oh, I also had a lot of fun with the whole "pretending we were a high-rolling couple" thing. It meant I got to whisper sweet nothings in his ear, breathe in the skin at the back of his neck, and shoot him suggestive glances from across the room. It was all an act and it wasn't an act.

"Last one, I promise," he said, slipping me a twenty. "Something that'll kick my ass for the next hour."

I took it with a sly smile and slinked off through the maze of tables and machines toward the circle bar. I say slink because it was impossible to dress like I had and not feel like Jessica Rabbit.

Almost every casino has a circle bar in it, usually

smack-dab in the middle of the main floor. It's a great place to meet people without paying a cover, especially with the high turnover rate. I had picked Bellagio's circle bar, because the bartender took a liking to me and was giving me strong drinks on the cheap—I'd even scored some Red Bull off him for free. It was a little out of the way from Camden's table, which was hidden in the back behind rows of slot machines, but if we were ever out of each other's sight for too long we'd text each other. Yes, I had given him back his phone privileges.

Some of the clubs and bars must have been emptying out, because suddenly there was a line of drunk frat boys in front of me. I tried to get the bartender's attention, and though he saw me, he couldn't ignore everyone else. I would have to wait.

I stood in line at the bar and debated going to another one, even if it wasn't top shelf for cheap, when my phone beeped. Thinking it was Camden wondering where his drink was, I fished it out.

The screen on my phone showed a text message from a strange number. One word.

Hi.

It was attached to a 228 area code. Biloxi.

I don't think the word *Hi* had ever looked so terrifying. I nearly dropped the phone. But I didn't. I went straight to Camden's number and texted:

Code Black.

I shoved the phone back in my clutch and gulped, dizziness swarming up my arms, toward my head.

I knew whose number that was. It had been left on my homemade Wanted poster. I hoped Camden did exactly what I'd meant with *Code Black*. We'd talked about it earlier, about what to do in a worst-case scenario, the what-ifs, and our plan of attack. And now it was happening.

Javier had my number. He was closer than I had ever thought.

"Miss?" the bartender called out to me. I turned to look at him in a daze. The line had dissipated. I was next.

I was about to wave a "no thank you" at him then get a move on to the elevators, but my vision went right past him. It went to the opposite side of the bar where a man was sitting.

Sitting and staring at me with yellow-green eyes.

The man smiled and I felt a chunk of ice slide down my spine.

Javier.

I wish I could say I turned and ran the minute I recognized his face. But I didn't. I hesitated, perhaps a few seconds too long. Because Javier had a face that compelled you to look at him. Camden had been right with his impression—he really was like the sun. If you stared at him too long, you'd get burned.

He wasn't the world's best-looking guy, and for comparison's sake, he didn't have Camden's classical all-male good looks. His mouth was a little too wide and snaked from corner to corner. His nose had been broken a few times, and when you looked at him straight on like I was doing as I stared at him across the circle bar, you could really tell. But his eyes were beautiful, cunning, and otherworldly. His hair was a controlled mess; wispy dark strands that swooped across his forehead with long sideburns. He had high cheekbones, a strong jawline. When you combined all the parts, they equaled so much more than the sum. He was exotically, dangerously beautiful.

He'd been mine once. He'd broken my heart once.

And he was here to kill me. He only needed to do that once, too.

All the time I'd been staring at him, enveloped in his eyes, caged by his presence, he was staring back at me. It was only when he moved to text something on his phone that I found myself coming back into the present.

My cell beeped again. The corner of his mouth lifted, eyes back on me.

Against my better judgment, I looked at it.

You have no new tale to tell? 26 years on your way to hell.

I felt a hollowness inside, like I was being chiseled out by fear. It was a line from the song "Wish," the song tattooed on his wrist. My song choice for him. At the time I didn't know who the song was about, but now I know he made it about me.

Another beep.

You look beautiful.

I needed to get out of there. I made a quick glance around, looking for Alex and Raul, knowing they had to be close by. I didn't see them, but that didn't mean anything in a casino. I tried to calm my racing heart and think. I needed to walk past the circle bar, past Javier to get to the hotel entrance, to get to Camden. Christ, I hoped he wasn't looking for me and had just done as we planned.

Walking past Javier put me in the line of fire. But he wouldn't dare grab me in the middle of a casino surrounded by people, cameras, and undercover security. He'd let me walk right past him and then I'd be followed. I couldn't have that, either.

I had to have him detained. More than that, I had to have Raul and Alex detained, wherever they were. I had to walk right up to him and engage him because if I ran, there would be no escape.

Sucking back courage like one hundred proof whiskey, I shoved my cell back into my clutch, tightened my grip on it until my knuckles were white, and walked around the circle bar. My eyes never left Javier and his never left mine. I could almost hear "Wish" pounding away in my head, matching its speed with my heart.

I stopped right beside him, beside a drunk couple who were laughing too loudly, a couple who had no idea what kind of animal they were sitting near.

Javier was wearing an unbuttoned suit jacket in a greenish-beige tone that would have looked drab on anyone else but him and a collarless white linen shirt underneath. He smelled like a million misleading memories.

As if in slow motion, I rested my hand on the bar top. I focused on it like obsessive woman possessed, how close it was to his hand as it held on to a drink I knew was Bombay Sapphire and tonic water. His hand was tawny, speckled with scars. I had held that hand many times, marveling at how dark his skin got in the summer, and I'd kissed every bump and mark. Hands that knew my body inside and out. Hands that were so often covered in someone else's blood.

"Ellie Watt," he said to me. His accent was soft and seductive, his voice light. "I have to say I like your real name a lot better. It suits you."

He reached for my hand and I snatched it out of the way before he could touch me. I brought my eyes to his and steadied myself.

"What do you want from me?" I asked.

He tilted his head, observing me with an appreciative smile. "Your hair—it's different, too. I like it. You're far too angry to be a blonde." He nodded at my arm. "I told you I'd be looking for you, didn't I?"

I knew that tattoo would come back to bite me on the ass.

"What do you want from me, Javier?" I said again, trying to keep my voice from shaking. I had to do this fast.

He frowned but somehow he was still smiling, as if I was a child who didn't seem to get the lesson.

"What do I want?" He tugged at his ear, something he did when he was excited. "Oh, Eden, Ellie, you. I want the world from you."

Time to make my move. I kept my eyes cold and

impassive. "I can't give you that. But I can give you a way out."

I opened my purse and took out my pocketknife. Its blade glinted under the casino lights as I brought it close to his stomach. We were so packed in at the bar that no one there could probably see what I was doing. But that didn't mean other people in the casino couldn't see and that's what I wanted. Most people wouldn't be paying attention, but the men who were paying attention, they'd see right away.

He sucked in his stomach to move it out of the knife's way. I kept my hand as steady as possible.

"I'm going to stab you right here," I told him. "Leave you to bleed."

He raised his brows and gave me an anxious grin. It faltered slightly, which meant he was buying it. He was worried, just a little, and it was enough. "I suppose I'd deserve it," he said carefully, his eyes darting between mine and the knife. "As if you taking Jose and the money wasn't enough."

"It wasn't enough," I answered truthfully.

He licked his lips. "Still so much spite, I see."

I edged the knife forward so it pricked the fabric of his shirt and whispered, "You see nothing."

That extra movement was all it took. Suddenly Raul and Alex were beside us, ready to protect their man. I didn't bother looking their way. We'd never gotten along.

Javier jerked his head at them. "If you're planning on killing me, you know they won't let you."

I smiled broadly at him. "Oh, I'm not planning on killing you."

With one quick motion, I put the knife back in my purse, then screamed "Help!" and whirled around to face the bartender, who was just about to pour a drink. "Help me!" I yelled at him. "These men are trying to rob my winnings!"

Javier, Raul, and Alex barely had any time to act. They were surprised, caught off guard, and after the bartender pressed a button underneath the bar and made a few hand gestures to people hidden across the casino, they had nowhere to run. Four big security guys in dark suits and wearing Bluetooths suddenly grabbed them just as they were getting ready to leave.

Javier's eyes could have burned right through me. I felt nothing. I looked at the security guys, aware that everyone in the casino was gasping or watching with interest. "They were trying to rob me, they said they had guns." Raul and Alex objected as the security started patting them down. I knew they'd find guns on them, but I was not sticking around to find out.

I grabbed the closest guard to me. "I need an escort, now!"

The guy nodded and took my arm, leading me away from the scene. That was the great thing about Vegas—you could ask for an escort at any time and you got it just like that. Otherwise, Vegas would be even more of a crime hot spot than it already was.

"Where do you want me to take you, ma'am?" the big-knuckled bruiser of a guard asked. "You might need to file a police report."

"Just take me to the lobby, I want to put my cash away, I feel too vulnerable," I said, as we hurried along.

Once we reached the lobby we heard a cry from behind us in the casino. It sounded like a fight was breaking out.

I nodded at it. "I'll be fine now—you should go help your buddies."

The escort nodded and ran off as the cries intensified. Yeah, that was turning into an all-out brawl. Javier didn't take custody very well.

I walked as quickly as possible through the lobby to the front doors, bringing out my phone and texting Camden frantically:

Where are you???

I stepped out into the cold night, eyeing the valet guy, hoping Camden wasn't up in the room still. We didn't have time to spare. Knowing Javier, they'd find a way to come after me. The man was impossible to contain.

"Excuse me," I asked the valet, who was half-asleep at his post. "Did a man—"

The roar of Jose's engine cut me off. The car came careening around the circular driveway, Camden at the wheel. He pulled up to us with a screech of brakes, leaning forward to push open the passenger door.

"Your pumpkin awaits," he barked at me.

I jumped inside the car and was barely able to shut the door before we were roaring out of the Aria and onto the Vegas Strip.

"Are you all right?" Camden asked me.

I nodded, trying to locate my nerves. "Just get us out of here and fast."

The Strip wasn't as congested at this time of night, but it wasn't empty, either. Slow-moving taxis and limos with people hanging out of them were filling up most of the lanes. Camden zigged and zagged between them, trying to get to the exit for the highway. He handled the wheel with supreme control, looking every bit like an intellectual 007.

"Where are we going?" I asked, keeping my eyes focused on the side mirrors, scanning for cars and anything unusual.

"I thought we'd head to Gualala. It's always been the goal anyway."

It was funny how his goal and my goal were suddenly one and the same.

"So what happened?" he asked as he overtook another limo.

I rubbed my lips together, unsure how to even piece together what had just happened. It was my deepest nightmare come to life.

"I saw Javier."

Camden went silent for a moment. Then he said, "Shit."

"Yeah. It was."

"Fuck you!" He leaned on the horn when a cab cut us off, then turned back to me. "How did you get away?"

"I got security involved. They nabbed him, plus Raul and Alex."

"Do you think there are others?"

"Yes. I can bet there are."

"Do you think it's that white Mustang way back

there?" he asked, his eyes flitting to the rearview mirror. "He just ran a red light and he's been gaining on us."

I couldn't see anything out of my mirror, so I turned in my seat to look out the back. Way behind in the distance was a white sports car. It was getting closer and closer, weaving in and out of traffic and clipping cars as it did so. This wasn't a drunk driver. This was a beast coming for us.

I buckled myself in tight. "Get us out of here. Now."

"I'll do my best," he growled and stepped on the gas.

Jose jolted forward, nearly rear-ending the cab in front of us. Camden deftly wheeled the car around it in the nick of time and I grabbed onto the dashboard to keep myself from bouncing around. From car to car, lane to lane, we jetted in and out of the traffic. He never once let us drop speed, never once hesitated. At first I was worried that Camden wouldn't be able to handle the car, but from the utterly determined draw to his mouth and controlled grip on the wheel, I had no doubt he knew what he was doing. The Vegas lights reflected on his glasses as we flew under the mammoth, glittering buildings.

"Do you think you can lose him?" I asked, looking over my shoulder. The car was still gaining and pulling all the same moves that we did.

"If we can get to the highway first, we can," he told me. The lights in between Treasure Island and the Palazzo went from yellow to red, and we were cars away from the intersection.

Camden grinned and gunned it. We were going for it. I covered my eyes with my hands and let out a scream as Jose shot across the intersection, running the red. I could hear horns honking, tires squealing, and the car careening over to the left. By the time I opened my eyes we were pointed straight again, leaving behind a bunch of disgruntled drivers whom we nearly collided with.

He whipped us left onto Spring Mountain Road, and with our hands clean of the Strip, the highway loomed in front of us. We were almost there.

"Motherfuckers!" Camden yelled at the rearview.

I looked behind me to see the Mustang speeding around the turn, nearly taking out a man on a motorcycle. He was still in hot pursuit, and now with less traffic around us, his pursuit was growing hotter.

"I hope you weren't kidding about that whole 'getting to the highway first' kind of thing," I squeaked out. My hands were digging into my seat belt.

"I hope I wasn't, too," he said. We ran through another red and then rocketed up the on-ramp and onto the highway heading northeast. It was the opposite way than we needed to go, but all we needed to do was focus on being alive.

Once on the highway, Camden switched gears and accelerated even more. I was thrown back, never having driven the car over one hundred miles before. Jose took the speed with ease; in fact, the car seemed to thrive on it. We were fast, going so fast. Our saving grace was that the highway had barely any cars on it.

Unfortunately this meant the Mustang wasn't far behind, either.

"How are we going to lose him?" I asked. Were we

just going to speed forever until the city turned to desert? Then what?

"Don't worry about it," he said determinedly. The car went faster.

Then we saw it. Late-night construction was looming up ahead, just after the intersection with I-515.

"Shit, shit, shiiiiit," I swore. There was no way we could run over a bunch of construction workers. The Mustang was now the closest car behind us. I wondered if they'd be stupid enough to start shooting, then I remembered I had my gun in the back and wondered if I'd be stupid enough to start shooting back.

"Ellie," Camden said, his hand hovering over the gearshift, his polished cuff links glinting in the city lights. "Hold on. And don't scream."

My eyes went wide.

He slammed on the brakes suddenly, and we immediately went into a spin over the burning smell of rubber. Round and round we went, as the car spun toward the edge of the highway.

I screamed.

Somehow, before we hit the concrete barricade and flipped over to our fiery deaths, the car jammed to a stop and shot forward. I nearly hit my head on the dash and gripped it for dear life as the world still spun inside my head.

Now we were driving straight into oncoming traffic. And the first car in our path was the white Mustang.

As we headed toward it—Camden intending to clip the corner of the car—I stared at the man behind the wheel to get a look at who it was. Everything happened in a flash, in a blur, but time slowed down enough for me to get a glimpse. He was Caucasian with a shock of white-blond hair, someone I'd never seen before. He had a gun pointed at my face.

Suddenly Camden was leaning over me, shoving my head down below the dash. There was a distant explosion of glass before the windshield above us erupted. My head smashed into the glove compartment as our car made contact with the Mustang. There was a crunch and spinning tires, but it was just us, still going, cold wind and glass fragments flying over my head.

I felt Camden straighten up. "Keep your head down!" he yelled at me. Despite hitting the Mustang and having the window shot out, Jose kept going. My body went from side to side as he weaved through a maze of honking horns.

Finally I looked up. With no windshield, my hair was blown out of my updo, the glass going with it. We were driving through cars, all heading straight for us but slowing down as we approached.

"Are you okay?" he asked above the roar of the highway.

I looked at him wildly. His glasses were off, lying on his lap with a cracked lens. The wound on his lip where his dad had hit him days ago had been reopened, and blood was trickling out. Other than that, and the adrenaline that was pumping through his eyes, he looked okay.

I looked behind me and saw nothing but a sea of red taillights.

"What happened to the Mustang?"

He shrugged and swung the car around a minivan that was honking like crazy and flashing its lights. "It flipped. That's all I know. That's all I care about. We have to get off this highway before a chopper picks us up."

I guess heading the wrong way on I-515 was a newsworthy event.

"How did you learn to drive like that?" I asked in awe. "And don't say it's because of video games."

He gave me a bloody grin. "Believe it or not, I almost became a cop after high school. Dad was so proud until I failed. The only thing I could pass was the driving test."

"What about the shooting?"

"If I ever get a real-life target, I'll let you know."

He took the next exit, and I couldn't help but scream again as we headed the wrong way down an on-ramp. Soon we were flying across the meridian, and with a deft twist, he got the car on the right side of the road. We sped off down the street until the house and buildings emptied into undeveloped desert. We were safe, for now.

CHAPTER TWENTY

As CAMDEN STEERED the car down the increasingly deserted side road, the realization of what had happened was starting to sink in.

"Pull over," I groaned. I was going to be sick.

He kept driving. "I don't want to stop, not yet."

The road we were on was now completely empty, with no streetlights or development around us, and the sand was starting to come in through the missing windshield. Vegas glowed in the distance against the orange-tinged sky. "We're in the middle of nowhere. He's gone. Pull over."

With a sigh, he coasted us to a stop at the side of the two-lane road. Out here the wind was picking up and coating us with a chill, but I was too on edge to be cold.

I opened the door and ran out of the car, stumbling through the sand and rock in my sandals, gasping for breath. I stopped a few feet away and crouched down, my head in my hands. Javier had seen me. My hand had been so close to his. What happens to love when it turns to hate? Was this it? Did it turn to death?

"Ellie?" Camden called from the car. I heard the car door slam. I waved my hand in the air dismissively. "Stay away!" I yelled, trying to slow my heart and get air back in my lungs.

He must have listened. I didn't hear the crunch of sand under his shiny new shoes. I only heard the whistling wind and the blood rushing around in my head.

When I felt remotely better, I straightened up and walked back to the car. Camden was sitting on the front bumper, looking straight up in the sky like a dejected prom date. A few tiny stars had poked through the light pollution.

I climbed up beside him and sat on the hood, for once not caring that my ass was making a dent in it. The whole front right corner of the car was smashed up, the headlight dangling. I swallowed hard at the damage of my poor car then did a silent prayer of thanks. It was better that Jose got injured than us. Besides, he wasn't my car to grieve over.

"Luck be a lady tonight," Camden said quietly. "I think she'll turn on us soon."

I looked at him sharply, studying the back of his head. "She turned on me a long time ago."

Silence swirled around us. Finally he said, "Oh, why don't you just shut up, Ellie."

My heart squeezed. "What?"

He turned his head so I saw the side of his face. His blue eyes glittered menacingly in the dark, such a change from a few moments ago. "This always has to be about you, doesn't it?"

I was taken aback and struggled for words. Indignation flared hot inside. "Well, I'm sorry I have some psychopath after me. I'm sorry it's such a big inconvenience for you. I didn't ask for this, you know."

"Yes! You did!" he said, bringing his eyes back to the endless black of desert in front of us. "You asked for everything you've gotten."

"Oh, fuck you."

"No," he said, getting up. He turned to face me and leaned forward on the hood, his arms on either side of me, causing me to flatten beneath him. "Fuck you. Why the hell do you have to go fucking with people? Is there anyone else you've pissed off?"

His face was so close to mine, the anger just seething off of him. "What did Javier do to you? What did he do to make you take his car and his money? To get me in this mess? Huh?"

"It's a long story," I spat back. "You wouldn't understand."

"Try me!"

"Fine!" I yelled back. "He cheated on me, okay? He was my first love, my first everything, and I came home one day and . . . well, there you have it. I saw something that ripped my heart out. I overreacted. I was angry . . . I, I would've done anything to hurt him. Don't you see? All this time I was the one pretending . . . I never thought he was pretending, too. Everything was a lie. I was so tired of the lies."

"This is all because of lies?" he asked.

"This is all because of love," I told him, my lower lip trembling. "Or maybe it's all the same. Maybe it will always be the same with me!"

"He hurt you," he said. "You hurt him back."

"The only way I knew how. Javier doesn't have a heart to break. Isn't that what you think of me?"

His eyes narrowed into cool slits, appraising my face. "That is what I thought of you, Ellie. Heartless, reckless, selfish, and cruel."

He was back to shooting me when my armor was down. I turned my face away from him, not wanting to let him see the hurt in my eyes.

He reached up and put his fingers under my chin, bringing my face forward again, forcing me to look at him. "Beautiful, sad, wounded, and lost," he continued. "A freak, a work of art, a liar, and a lover."

His gaze was starting to eat away at my insides. Razor-blade butterflies whirled in my heart.

"I hate you, Ellie Watt," he whispered, lips coming closer to mine, "because I still love you after all these years."

Shock seized me first, the butterflies shredding me to pieces. Then he grabbed my face and kissed me, hard. His lips devoured mine as our mouths pressed against each other in a painful frenzy. It was fire itself, our tongues and lips fanning the flames, our teeth nipping each other like sparks. I ran my hands up and down the back of his head, over his shoulders and back, pulling him to me; I couldn't get close enough. He reached down and pulled my dress up over my waist, leaving me bare, my legs straddling him.

With one hand he began thumbing my clit, rubbing me until I was slick with desire and throbbing for release. He kissed, licked, and bit down my neck. With each groan, his hot breath flared against my skin. Once he reached my lacy neckline, he grabbed it with both hands and ripped it straight down the middle. My designer dress was left in tatters as it fell off my shoulders, leaving me naked. I didn't care.

He worked his way down my chest and stomach, then buried his head in my cleft. He ran his tongue down the insides of my thighs, teasing me until I was grabbing his hair and forcing his dripping mouth onto my clit. He obliged with a grunt and I moaned in response, my back arching into him.

Just when I was about to come, he pulled his tongue away. He deftly unzipped his pants and positioned his cock into my opening. I was more than ready. I grabbed him by the ass and back and thrust him into me. I wrapped my legs around him, holding him until he was deep, deep inside. I ignored the pain from the tattoo and just kept him as close to me as possible while he started pumping in and out of me, my hips in his vise-like grip. He worked faster, harder, and was pounding me back into the hood, deepening the dent. I'd never been fucked so thoroughly before; I felt like I was going to meld into the metal.

"Fuck!" I cried out as we came together, my yelping cries soaring high into the desert sky, joining those of the coyotes. He came hard into me, his fingers digging into my ass as he pumped his load into my spasming body. My convulsions milked him dry until he collapsed on top of me, pressing me to the hood. It felt deliciously cold against my hot and sweaty bare back.

We lay like that for a few minutes until the chill got to us. He pulled up and ran a finger over my lips. I kissed it, smiling, enjoying the taste of me on his fingers.

"We've thoroughly ruined this car tonight," he murmured, planting a kiss on my forehead and down my nose.

"Everyone needs a little excitement," I said, running my hands through his thick, soft hair. "Even cars."

He smiled, soft and sweet, and studied me. I had seen that look before, one we'd shared on his trampoline. I never knew what that look was at the time, but I knew now.

"How can you still love me?" I asked quietly as I traced circles into the back of his head. "After everything I did to you."

God, he was wonderful when he grinned like that.

"There's no one else I wanted to love," he admitted. "No one who deserved it more than you."

I didn't know what to say to that. I didn't know how to feel, other than my heart feeling like it was pressing against my chest, up my throat, until it was stretching my mouth into a smile. I let out a little laugh of joy. He stroked his fingers down my face, peering at me intently. He didn't need his glasses on for me to see the honesty in his eyes.

"I hope one day I'll deserve it, too," he said.

My heart broke, and the jagged, sharp pieces mixed with the warmth that was flooding through me. I held his head tight in my hands and looked deeply at him. "You will, Camden."

I couldn't promise when it would happen. But I wasn't going anywhere. We had time.

At least, I hoped we still had time.

I let go of him and he straightened up. "Time to go?" he asked, reading me.

I nodded. "I might as well get changed here." I sat up.

"I'll get your clothes," he said. He zipped up his fly and dusted off his tux. Aside from his bow tie, which I had yanked loose, he looked calm and collected and ready to take on the night. He went inside the car and came back with a pair of boxer shorts, a shirt, and sweater. "You should probably still keep the area around the leg loose. For now."

When I was done changing, having left the ruins of the dress on the desert floor, we got back in the car and drove off, heading for our next destination, wherever that was. In the side mirror I watched the dress blow away in the night wind, black wings on a black sky.

Then

The girl hadn't meant to go home early. Even though Javier was taking care of her, both physically and financially, she felt strange without having a job. She felt even stranger that he wasn't some sugar daddy that had come into money, but that he got his wealth through criminal means.

In some ways, the girl could relate to her lover. After

all, she had been conning him the whole time they were together. Sure, she never took any money from him, but she was still keeping tabs. She still wanted to get even with Travis, his boss, the man who ruined her all that time ago, but as the year went by, she felt she was less fueled by vengeance. Being loved by Javier—being in love with Javier—stifled the anger she felt inside. For the first time in a very long time, someone was able to take her hurt away.

So, because she didn't like relying on Javier for everything, because she felt he was already giving her so much through his romantic gestures, constant attention, and charming personality, she had gotten a job as a waitress. It was just a local bar, and she worked only weekends. It didn't matter that her weekends were taken up when Javier didn't work business hours, anyway. Breaking fingers and running drugs could be done at any time of the week.

That day, the day that everything changed for the girl, she was sent home early. There had been a small fire in the kitchen, and they were closing it down for the evening to assess the damage. The girl got into her Chevy truck, something she still drove despite craving Javier's car, and went home. She stopped at a minimart, picking up a six-pack for them to split. Javier had been stressed out lately—why, she didn't dare ask—and she thought it might be nice to surprise him. They used to love taking drinks onto the white sand beach and watching the waves roll in, something they hadn't done for an awfully long time.

The girl was pondering why they hadn't been

together as much lately, doing the things that used to bring them joy, when she pulled up to the house. It was completely dark and looked like no one was home, though she had only left him sitting at his computer two hours earlier.

Maybe he's napping, she thought to herself. He often went out into the wee hours of the night to do his business. She didn't once have any suspicions. Why would she? Even though she and Javier weren't spending as much time together as they used to, their sex life always kept them connected. He was a powerful and insatiable man in the sack—dominant, sensual, slightly kinky, and extremely vocal.

For a long time the girl's mind would go back to that moment, the moment she decided to get out of the car and walk into the house. If she'd stayed in the car, perhaps even for a few more minutes, the whole thing would have been avoided. Perhaps her life wouldn't have changed. She looked at that blissful ignorance and wanted it back. The truth was too painful.

But she got out of the car and walked into their house, facing the truth that was hidden in the bedroom. She quietly closed the door in case he was taking a nap and tiptoed through the hall. She gently laid the cold beer on the kitchen counter and pulled one off the ring for herself. She walked down the hallway toward the bedroom—and stopped dead.

She heard him moaning first. For a split second she thought he was having a nightmare. Then the moan became all too familiar. So in the next second, she thought he was whacking off. She liked it when he did it in front of her, or as it often was, on her. But her assumption was short-lived. A woman's cry and groaning were quick to follow.

The sound…she'd never forget the sound of that woman, made her heart bleed in her chest. Her tattoo itched. She was frozen to the carpet, unable to move. She must have stood there for minutes, hearing the whole thing, trying to comprehend how the hell this could happen.

Then they came, her cries drowning out his. The girl finally snapped to attention, just as the beer was about to fall out of her hands.

The woman in the room made some sweet talk to the man, to her Javier, and Javier sweet-talked back. He called her beautiful. His voice was gentle. He was being sweet. That hurt the girl more than their blatant fucking ever had.

The girl was so angry. All her pain, her humiliation, her revenge, came flowing through her. She was going to kill them. Kill both of them.

She crept down the hall, wanting to barge in on them and catch them in the act. She wanted them to be as humiliated as she was. But something happened.

As she pushed the door open a crack and peered into the bedroom—her bedroom—she saw them both naked, lying facedown on the bed. They were facing away from the door, so the girl couldn't see the woman's face. But she looked curvy, silky, with a wild mane of auburn hair that cascaded down her golden back. Javier's foot was hooked around hers and they swung it up and down, like two children who were sitting on a bridge. They looked intimate. They looked...happy.

The girl decided she couldn't do it. She had one thing left—one secret of her own—and that was the fact that she was Ellie Watt. Javier had never known the real her, so he'd never loved the real her. He loved a woman who wasn't a con, wasn't a spy, wasn't there because she wanted to bring down the man who ruined her.

She wanted to hold on to that secret for as long as she could. This other woman, this infidelity, it changed her heart. It made her the cold, heartless person she was supposed to be. The person she needed to be to survive.

The girl quickly slunk down the hallway before she could disturb them, plucking the beer off the counter. She went back to her truck and drove just a few houses down. She cracked open the beer and drank it while crying and watched in the rearview mirror as the woman eventually left the house and drove down the road in her Mercedes-Benz. She never even looked the girl's way.

Later that night, the girl pretended she had worked her whole shift. She brought Javier the beer. She pretended everything was okay, lying through her teeth. She kissed him good night, and they fell asleep like nothing was wrong.

The next morning, Eden White stole the extra cash that Javier kept hidden in the house. Then, while he was off on his morning jog, she stole his car.

She never looked back.

CHAPTER TWENTY-ONE

WE DROVE ALL through the night, heading west while the sun came up in the sky. Though we were both exhausted to the bones, neither of us slept. We didn't talk, either. We just listened to Guano Padano and tried to hold on as long as we could. I was worried about Javier still, wondering how I was going to avoid him down the line. I'd need a new identity again, a new look. He'd never stop trying to find me, I knew that for a fact now.

Camden, too, needed to start becoming Connor Malloy soon. Any day now someone would report him missing, and perhaps that same someone would report the money missing, too. We had checks in his name from the casino, but there was no way he could cash them until he had more ID and papers that could only come from Gus.

Now that it was a weekday, we were closer to getting everything ready. But we couldn't do anything until we picked a place to hunker down for a while. Camden had Gualala on his mind, and at times he seemed convinced we could drive another ten hours to get there. But by the time the sun was high in the sky and we'd passed Tulare, we had to find a place to crash or we would crash ourselves. We would have gotten there quicker, but the headlight and the windshield had to be repaired. We were lucky it was even done in two hours (though we were several hundred dollars poorer).

We pulled into a small motel on the roadside, making sure to park Jose behind the buildings and out of view from the highway. We must have looked quite the sight to the front desk clerk as he observed us behind Coke-bottle glasses; me in boxer shorts and a bandaged leg, Camden in a tuxedo. But he didn't give Connor Malloy or Emily Watson any grief.

Our room was shabby and smelled like too much Lysol, but it didn't matter. Camden and I crawled into bed—now we were sharing—and passed out in each other's arms. Our sleep was deep, and we didn't wake up until I heard my cell phone ringing.

I groaned and frowned at the clock, all messed up from the nap. It was six p.m., and the light outside had faded. I got up and looked for my phone, then remembered it was in my clutch. It was a bit unusual for my phone to ring—everyone I knew almost always texted me.

I peered at the screen, heart in my throat. It was Uncle Jim.

"Hello?" I asked, trying to hide the worry in my voice.

"Ellie!" he exclaimed. "Oh, Ellie, thank God you answered. Are you all right?"

I eyed Camden nervously. He was sitting up, taking off his tuxedo jacket, now all wrinkled from our nap.

"Yeah, I'm fine, Uncle Jim. Why, what's going on?"

"Where are you?" he asked.

I had to remember what the last lie I told him was.

"Santa Barbara."

A pause. "Ellie, I don't want you to freak out, but I…I need your help."

My heartbeat got louder. "What? Why?"

"I'm in a lot of trouble," he said in barely a whisper. "Some men came to my house while I was in town. They…they roughed up one of the workers and lit fire to some of the trees."

"Holy shit!" Now Camden was at my side, trying to listen, his solid grip on my shoulder steadying me. "Did you call the cops?"

"I did," he said. "They got a description of the men from the workers and said they'd look for them, but that's all they could do. Ellie, I'm scared. These men… I think they were after you."

I felt like bricks were being shoved on my chest. "Oh, I…I'm sorry, Uncle Jim, I—"

"It doesn't matter. I just don't know what to do. I left, I got out of there. I packed up some stuff, told the workers to stay away for the week until I figured things out."

"Good, good," I told him, feeling relieved. "Where are you?"

"I'm at the Shady Acres Hotel. It's just outside of Hemet. Do you remember Hemet?"

Of course I remembered Hemet. It was nothing but a town in the green mountains between the Coachella

Valley and San Diego. But it had an amazing music store where I used to drag Uncle Jim when I was a teenager just so I could get some bootleg CDs.

"Okay, stay there. I'm coming to you. What room are you in?"

"Room eight," he said. "Thank you, Ellie."

His voice cracked, bordering on tears. There was a pause, then a click as he hung up the line.

Guilt. I used to wear it like a badge, now I wore it like a ball and chain. I couldn't believe this was happening to him, my only family left, the only one who I could depend on. I was ruining his life with all my past mistakes.

I looked at Camden, his face shadowed in the dark of the room. "We have to go to him. We have to help him."

He didn't nod like I thought he would. His lips were pressed together in a firm line.

"Camden?"

He jerked his head as if saying no.

I frowned. "Look, I know it's out of the way and not part of our plans, but I can't let my uncle hide out on his own. They're after him, Camden."

He licked his lips quickly. "Are they?"

I looked at him askew. "I don't follow."

"Yes, you do." He sighed and ran a hand through his hair. He strolled over to the window then drew the blinds shut and flicked on the light. "But you don't want to think about it."

I crossed my arms. "Think about what?"

"That he's lying to you," he said. He flinched a little

as he said it, as if I'd hit him. I almost did, too. Smart boy.

"How dare you say that," I said to him, seethingly. "He's my uncle."

He raised his palms in defense. "I know he is. And I know it's a terrible thing to even think, but I'm just being cautious. Your life is more important than his."

"Maybe to you! Not to me. He's been there for me when no one else has. My parents left me with him. They basically screwed him over! They left me and ran and they never came back. Sure, they talk on the phone now, but that doesn't mean he didn't sacrifice a lot of his life to raise me. And through high school, of all places. He was there during my deepest, darkest hours. There's no way I can't repay that."

He nodded. "Okay. I just wanted to make sure we're on the same page, that's all."

"Well, I'm not on your page. Shit, Camden. I'm tired of fucking people over! I need to make amends and do things right for a change. If I endanger myself trying to help him, then so be it. He deserves my help and everything else he can get from me." I flopped down on the bed, trying to calm myself, trying to pretend the next words wouldn't hurt. "You don't have to come with me, you know. Go rent a car, go to your Gualala. You don't need to be dragged deeper into this sorry mess."

He sat down beside me and grabbed my hand, giving it a squeeze. "I'm not letting you go on your own. We're in this together, until the ocean waves crash on our feet."

I squeezed back, giving him a shy smile. "You really paint this Gualala as a paradise," I told him.

"If you're there with me," he said, "it will be."

He kissed me softly, his hand getting lost in my hair. I started to fall back onto the bed but he caught me and kept me up. "We can do this later," he murmured into my neck. "We've got your uncle to save."

We got changed into normal clothes and threw our stuff into the car. We hadn't even had the chance to unpack.

*   *   *

It felt completely wrong to be driving south to Hemet when we should have been driving north to Gualala, but my concern for Uncle Jim was too overpowering. Thankfully the drive was just under six hours, even with the rush-hour traffic, and it wasn't long before we were passing Lake Perris and winding through the mountains. With darkness enveloping us, the roads seemed extra treacherous, and Camden was tense as he drove. I'd decided Jose was probably safest with him— they'd been through a lot together.

The atmosphere inside the car was tense, too. I could tell Camden was worried and for different reasons than I was. I was busy planning what to do with Uncle Jim. Telling him we were on the run from Javier wouldn't come as a surprise, but I wanted to leave the whole "by the way, I tried to rob Camden" thing out of it. It would only hurt him that I tried to do it in his hometown, and looking back now, I felt ashamed for even trying it.

Camden, on the other hand, was cagey and silent, because he was expecting the worst. He was expecting Uncle Jim to be compromised, but I just couldn't think that way. I wouldn't. I had to trust someone in my life, and after I had mistrusted everyone and finally took a chance on Camden, my uncle deserved the same opportunity.

We reached the sign marker stating it was ten miles to Hemet when I asked Camden a question I'd been thinking of for a while.

"What had happened to your wife?" I asked gently. I knew it was a loaded question, but he and I were balls deep in loaded questions these days and drowning in our answers.

He chewed on his silence for a few beats, looking romantically pensive in his reading glasses. I looked out the window at the headlights as they illuminated the twisting road, giving him space.

"I hit her," he said. I shrank back in my seat, a bit shocked at his admission, at his bluntness. I'd been in a short but volatile relationship with a man in Nebraska. He hit me—only once, but I packed my bags and never looked back. Sure, I had been trying to con him, but no con was ever worth abuse.

"Why?" I asked, my voice very small, not really understanding how the man next to me could be capable of that.

He breathed in deep and I shot a look at him. His brows were drawn, and his eyes held in some painful memory. "Because I was an angry fool. Our relationship was crumbling beneath my hands. She'd been out a lot. I was the one taking care of Ben more often than not. I never knew where she was or what she was doing, and it was never my business to know. One day I suspected

she was cheating on me. I called her on it. She admitted
it. Actually, she did more than admit it. She flaunted it.
She told me she wanted a divorce, that she didn't love
me, that I wasn't worth anything to her as a man. I was
nothing more than a sperm donor. I think she was back
on drugs again, if you ask me. It wasn't the Sophia that
I married.

"I didn't know how to handle it. She called me
names, Spat in my face. Insulted me with everything
she had. It wasn't until later that I realized what she
had been doing, and I walked right into her trap. She
punched me, called me a name I don't even want to
repeat, and I hit her back. It was just a slap; my fist
wasn't even closed. But it was enough to destroy me.
It was enough for her to get her divorce and custody of
Ben. It was enough to put me in her family's debt."

"So you think she wanted you to hit her?"

He shrugged. "Does it matter? I hurt her, the one person I never wanted to hurt. She loved me at some point,
I know that. I don't know what she must have felt at that
moment, to doubt that I ever felt that way, that everything had been a lie. It wasn't a lie, though, Ellie. I loved
Sophia. She could never replace you, but I still loved her
as much as I could. And I love Ben. I'd give everything
to go back to that moment and make things right."

I stared at him, feeling his pain.

"Would you really? Would you go back in time and
change that, if you could?"

He thought it over and looked at me. "No. No, maybe
not. Because then I wouldn't have this. I wouldn't have
you. I have to live with my mistakes, but I don't have

to regret them. I regret my actions, but I can't regret the consequences. We all make our own paths in life. Everyone we meet, everything we do, it changes us. It makes us who we are. And, if we're lucky, we're given the chance to make things right again."

I completely understood. I stuck my hand out the window and let it snake up and down with the wind. "It's like an IOU you didn't know you'd written."

He nodded. "That sounds about right. I have a feeling we've written a lot of those."

"I think everyone does."

We lapsed into a comfortable silence for the rest of the drive, understanding each other a bit better. Camden lived with his guilt, his guilt that had never let him be free. I wasn't any different than he was. Each day I found myself relating more and more to the only other "freak" in town, the only one who really knew.

Once we passed through the small town center of Hemet, and after I whooped with delight at discovering the Hungry Heart music store still existed, we began our search for the Shady Acres. It was farther out of town than we had both thought, and as the town lights disappeared behind us, I had to admit I was feeling a little bit nervous.

It was terrible to doubt my uncle, but for a split second I thought maybe, somehow, this was a setup. Maybe something wasn't right. I don't know if it was my own instincts or Camden's cynical influence, but it set off alarm bells in my stomach.

It took a lot of courage to say to Camden, "I have a funny feeling about this."

He gave me a smile and kissed my hand. "I know you do. You're a trained con artist, you can't forget that. If you didn't walk into every situation with suspicion, I'd question how you survived so long."

"So what do you think?" I asked him, suddenly doubting everything.

"I think your uncle sounds like an honest man. And I know he took care of you when we were kids, like you were his own daughter. I think he needs our help—that he deserves our help, and I believe that Javier has targeted him. But, I also think to be safe, we don't park at the motel. Just around the corner. We sneak in."

"Better paranoid than dead?"

"You know it."

Once we located the hotel on my phone and spied the flickering signpost in the distance, we took the first side street and parked down by an abandoned house on an overgrown lot. There was nothing but small farms in the area, a place that would probably seem very bucolic during the day but looked lifeless and deserted at night.

"Should we bring a gun?" I whispered as we climbed out of the car.

He eyed me over the roof. "I don't think it could hurt. I'll bring mine."

I liked that idea. I didn't want to have to use my gun in any situation that involved Uncle Jim. I was too close and it would get messy.

We quietly walked up the street, eyes peeled, ears scanning for anything unusual. A few cars puttered past on the main road up ahead, and in the distance an owl hooted, but there was nothing else except the sound of our feet as we crunched through gravel on the shoulder.

When the hotel got closer, Camden gestured for us to head in through the back of the property and scale over the fence. My arms burned from the effort, but I made it over okay. We landed on the ground with a soft thud and observed the scene.

It wasn't a hotel at all but a rundown motel. From the back, it looked like only one of the rooms in the bungalow block was occupied. I did a quick count, and the small bathroom window with the light on was probably Uncle Jim's.

I gestured at it and Camden nodded. We crept closer and tried to look in through the frosted glass pane but couldn't see anything. Camden tried to listen with his ear pressed against it. He heard nothing, either. That could be good or that could be bad.

We went around the side of the block and came into the front. There was a rusted chain link fence surrounding a tiny swimming pool with heaps of leaves floating in it, a small house for the office, and the single row of rooms. There was only one car, my uncle's old truck, and that was it. I scanned the dark street to see if there was anything out of the ordinary, but there was nothing—so far—that made me suspicious. It looked like he'd been telling the truth, which made me feel bad for doubting him and bad for putting him in this position.

With Camden leading the way, his hand hovering near his waistband where he had tucked his gun, we headed for room number eight. I made a sign at him to be careful, take it easy, and don't go in the room guns a-blazin' on my poor uncle. I'm not sure if he picked up on the gesture or not.

I quickly rapped at the door. "Uncle Jim?"

Camden stepped back and to the side, his hand on the gun handle now, like he was playing cops and robbers.

I waited with bated breath, listening hard, until the door opened a crack, the chain lock on.

"Ellie," Uncle Jim said, giving me an odd smile. "Come on in. I'm so glad you came."

He undid the chain lock and opened the door. He looked like he wanted to hug me—he was being quite emotional for my stoic uncle—but first I needed to be sure he was alone. I brushed past him and did a quick sweep of the room. Camden followed, going even further by checking the bathroom and closets.

"Looking for someone?" Uncle Jim asked, his voice shaking a bit. He must have been stressed out of his gourd.

I quickly gave him a hug while Camden locked the front door. "Sorry, you know me, Miss Paranoid."

"I know," he said softly. "Now I can see why you are."

He went and sat on the sagging bed with the tacky green floral duvet and started tugging at his flannel shirt. He let out a sigh. "I don't know what to do, Ellie."

I exchanged a look with Camden. Mine was sympathetic. His was hard. He looked at Uncle Jim with all the warmth of a hawk scouring a field for its next dinner.

I mouthed *What?* to him but Camden ignored me.

"Tell us what happened?" Camden asked in a steely voice.

Uncle Jim glanced at him, surprised. "I already told Ellie everything."

"You never told me," Camden pointed out. "So tell me."

My uncle pursed his lips, looking Camden up and down. "How on earth did the both of you get on the run together?"

Ah shit, I thought. Camden was going to tell him about my robbery attempt. Another thing my uncle really didn't need to know.

"I was in trouble with some people and Ellie agreed to help me," Camden said, keeping his eyes on him. My lungs expanded gratefully.

"You're both in trouble with different people?" he asked incredulously. "Jesus, kids, what the hell is wrong with you both?"

"You tell us," Camden said. He took a step closer to him, his right hand looking anxious and poised. "And while you're at it, tell us what happened."

He frowned but said, "Like I already told Ellie, I went out earlier today, I came home. There was a fire truck there putting out the last of the flames. It was only a row of trees but it had burned right through them. The workers were upset—one, Jorge, was bleeding from his nose, says some people roughed him up. They wanted to talk to me, and when they told them that I had gone out for a bit, they hit him. Then they left."

"What did they look like?"

"They said there were three of them. All Hispanic, although Jorge thought one sounded Puerto Rican or something. But wherever they were from, their English was impeccable. Especially the guy with the longer hair. He had some vivid eyes—they thought he was the one in charge, and maybe a little loco. He didn't say much but he had some sort of authority. Anyhow, I guess that could be your Javier, couldn't it, Ellie?"

I nodded. Vivid eyes, a little loco, and oozing power? Yes, that sounded just like Javier.

"So then what?" Camden asked. The impatience in his voice was rising, and I wondered just what the hell he was thinking. The story sounded tight to me and made sense. Javier had a dramatic flair for lighting things on fire.

Uncle Jim sighed and continued to fidget with his shirt. "Obviously they were gone when I came. I talked to the cops—didn't see your father unfortunately, Camden   and they said they'd keep a lookout. They've at least got arson and assault charges on them. But I know those kind of men. I've been dealing with Ellie and her mother for way too long. They can't be tracked or traced. You won't find them but they'll find you, you know? So I had to run. I came here. Figured it was a good place to lay low."

I eyed the water stain on the ceiling. "You could have picked a better place."

"I'm poor, Ellie," he said. "And now I'm in more of a hole. Losing some of the crop, you know."

My heart stung and I found myself biting my lip hard. He looked so conflicted and sad. I bet he wasn't

sure whether to feel grateful that I had showed up or if
he hated me for ruining everything he had worked so
hard for.

"When did all of this happen?" Camden asked.

Uncle Jim looked up in thought. "Uh, maybe around
one or two in the afternoon."

"And you came straight here."

"That's right," he said. His voice was shaking again.
The man needed a hug and a drink. "Then I called
Ellie. I didn't know who else to ..."

I waited for him to say *trust*, but he didn't. He just
trailed off and looked at the floor.

"What kind of car were the men driving? Did you
ask?" Camden took another step closer.

Uncle Jim nodded. "Of course I asked, I had to
know who to look out for. They said it was a white Ford
Mustang. Looked brand-new. Probably stolen."

The room began to spin as my chest pinched. *What?*

"Are you sure?" Camden asked, finally sounding
calm and patient as hell. "Are you sure that was the car
your workers saw them driving this afternoon?"

My uncle looked him square in the eye. "That's
what they said."

Before I could feel anything else, before I could
even let my brain tussle with the conflicting information we were just given, the fact that there was no way
it could have been the white Mustang since we totaled
the white Mustang last night, Camden acted. As quick
as anything, he whipped out the gun from his waist
and pressed it up against Jim's forehead, finger on the
trigger.

"Why the fuck are you lying to us?!" he screamed, his face turning red, his eyes sharp like blue blocks of ice.

"Camden!" I yelled, going to him. "Put the gun down!"

Camden only pressed the gun harder into Uncle Jim's forehead. He shrank back in shock, eyes wide and terrified.

"Why are you lying to us!? Tell us the truth, Jim, or so help me God I will blow your fucking brains out right here!"

"I'm not...I....I...," he stuttered, shooting me a look to help him.

"If I find out that you've put Ellie in danger by luring her here, I will kill. I will." Camden's voice was shaking now, the anger flowing through him and toward the barrel of the gun.

"Camden, please!" I screamed, trying to grab his arms. But he wouldn't budge. He was going to lose his shit and I was going to lose my uncle.

"Tell Ellie the truth!" he commanded. "Tell her the truth, you owe her that!"

My uncle's eyes fell to the floor and silence overtook him. Then, after a few beats, he burst out into a sob.

"He promised me he wouldn't hurt her!" he wailed.

No. No, this couldn't be. I found my head shaking back and forth, showing my disbelief. Even Camden looked shocked for a few moments before he tightened his grip on the gun, grinding his teeth.

"I'm so sorry, Ellie," my dear Uncle Jim apologized through his tears. "It was so much money. I needed the money. You know I do. Fifty thousand dollars—I could save everything with that amount. I had no choice, I didn't. I need it."

I felt like I was being ripped apart inside, my heart a single sheet of brittle paper splitting down the middle.

"I think you always have a choice," Camden whispered violently, pressing the gun harder, his eyes boring holes into his head. "You were like a father to her."

"I know." He sobbed, eyes tearing and locked on the gun above. "I know. But, Ellie, Jesus, Ellie, how you've made my life so hard. I wouldn't be in this position if it wasn't for you. He promised he wouldn't hurt you, Ellie, he did."

Camden's finger was about to pull back the trigger. Through all my pain, I tightened my grip on his arm and said, "Please, Camden."

His nostrils flared as he tried to regain control of himself.

"Camden, he's still my uncle," I told him quietly, working the pain through my words. "He's still the only family I've got."

With great reluctance he ripped the gun away from his head. "Well now what? How much time do we have?"

Suddenly the room lit up with headlights from outside the gauzy window blinds. We had no time. They were here.

"I'm sorry," Uncle Jim whimpered again. "I wish I could take it back."

Camden shoved him hard. "Well you can start by helping us now."

He ran to the bathroom and I heard him struggle

with the window for a few minutes. "It won't open and it's too small. I can't fit through it."

Meanwhile I just stood there at the foot of the bed, feeling like my life was crashing down on me, reeling from the impossible betrayal by the man I had always trusted.

"Go under the bed, Ellie," my uncle said to me. "I won't break your trust again. Go under the bed."

I looked around the room, thinking there had to be a way out. The car doors slammed from outside. Footsteps.

Camden came back in the room and put his finger to his mouth, motioning for us all to be quiet. Then he pointed at the bed and nodded.

I didn't think I could move my legs. The terror was too great. I heard a knock at the door. Someone tried to turn the knob. I was going to die.

But somehow I did it. I got on my knees on one side of the bed while Camden did the same on the other. We both flattened out and then squeezed in sideways, barely making it. The broken coils of the mattress pulled at my hair but I ignored the pain.

We were both under the bed, side by side. We wiggled as far back as we could go until our feet touched the wall. We tucked our limbs up against us just as Javier called out "Housekeeping" from outside the door.

I held my breath and waited. Uncle Jim got off the bed, the mattress rising in front of us by a bit. I could see his legs, midcalf to his dusty Timberland boots as he walked over to the door and opened it.

"What the hell is this?" Javier asked, his voice collected but with a sliver of annoyance poking through. His sleek leather shoes entered the room followed by Raul's and Alex's.

I could. Not. Breathe.

"I don't know what happened," Uncle Jim said. He was trying to stay calm but his words trembled. "They came and then they left right away. I think they were suspicious, I don't know why."

"They what?" Javier seethed quietly. "They were here? And you let them go?"

Though I couldn't see above his shins, I could tell he was coiling up like a snake. Seeking the right moment to strike.

"I...I don't know what happened," Uncle Jim went on. "I'll try again. It was that McQueen kid; he didn't want Ellie to be here."

"Mmm-hmm," Javier mused. It looked like he turned around to look at the others. His shoes came forward and walked, step by step, over to the bed. Over to us.

Camden's fingers wrapped around mine as we held our arms as close to each other as possible. We were worse than sitting ducks. There was nothing to prevent Javier from dropping to the floor and peering under the bed. He could fire the gun underneath. He could shoot the mattress. We had no way of escape. Even with Camden's gun, it didn't look like we'd make it out of here alive.

He stopped right in front of us. I could see the grains in the leather of his brown shoes, see a speck of gray lint on his black cashmere socks. His feet turned as if he was looking around. Now his heels were facing us, inches away. I didn't dare breathe and I couldn't if I wanted to.

"Do you still want the money?" Javier asked delicately.

"Of course I do," Uncle Jim said. "But I don't know what happened. I don't know why they left. I'll try better next time. I need the money, you know I do."

"You say they believed your story?"

"Ellie believes everything I tell her," he said with a hint of sadness. Another kick to my gut.

"You know you're not a very good uncle, leading her on like this," Javier mused softly. "The poor girl put all her trust in you and you're breaking it. Believe me, I've done it to her before. She can't seem to catch a break."

I could hear my uncle swallow hard. "Ellie made my life very difficult."

"Oh, she made my life difficult, too," he agreed. "But I enjoyed every minute of it."

I knew he was smiling. I could feel it.

"You promised me you wouldn't hurt her," Uncle Jim said. "When I bring her to you, you'll promise, right?"

Javier chuckled. "I don't break my promises." He slowly started walking toward the door. With each step my heart rate slowed. He stopped and turned slightly. "Unfortunately, I once promised to kill any man who'd hurt her. You're here, aren't you? The damage is done."

Javier moved. A gun with a silencer went off. There was a wealth of tension as my world slowed down. My eyes were glued to the legs in front of the bed. Uncle Jim's staggered to the right a step.

Then he fell down to the floor hard, right in front of us. A bullet wound in his head.

I opened my mouth to scream but Camden's hand was suddenly over my mouth, holding it in. I bit down on his fingers, I couldn't help it. I had to bite or I'd reveal us in seconds. He kept his fingers there, letting me, until the scream was swallowed up inside.

"Such a shame," Javier said to Raul and Alex. They left the room and closed the door behind them. I remained frozen in place, unable to look away from my uncle's dead face, the tiny droplet of blood that was slowly making its way down his forehead, the way his eyes stayed open, caught in utter remorse. They stared at me, burning their way into my brain, an image that promised to never go away.

After we heard the car start and drive off, Camden got out from under the bed. He tore the bedspread off and quickly covered my uncle up with it. It didn't matter. I could still feel his dead eyes on me.

Camden's legs went over to the window. "Ellie, we have to go now. They'll be back. Ellie?"

He came down beside the bed in a push-up position. "Please? We have to leave now."

I'd never been in medical shock before, but I knew this was it. I couldn't move. I couldn't speak. I couldn't do anything.

Suddenly Camden reached in and grabbed me by my arm and the belt loop of my jeans. He pulled, dragging me on the stiff, hard carpet until I found enough sense to get out from under the bed with my own strength.

He brought me up to my feet and wrapped me in a

tight hug, his hand at the back of my head, cradling me. "I'm sorry. We have to go. I can't lose you now."

I tried to nod but nothing came out. Camden brought out his gun and kept a firm grip around my arm as he led me across the room. I kept staring at the blanket on the ground, knowing what it was hiding.

He opened the door and looked around to make sure the coast was clear. When it was, we hurried down the corridor and back the way we came in. I don't know how I got over the fence but I did. I don't know how I walked over to the car but I did. I don't know how we got in the car and drove away down the country lane with our headlights off, searching for a hidden way out of town, but we did.

I don't know how we got onto the side roads that took us to Temecula.

All I did know was that my uncle had betrayed me for fifty thousand dollars. And now my uncle was dead.

CHAPTER TWENTY-TWO

WHEN I WOKE up the next morning I had that beautiful split second of peace and warmth where your brain hasn't caught up yet to the events from the night before. You think everything is fine, everything is normal, until that realization hits you like a sledgehammer, shattering your insides, shattering your world. Nothing is normal. Everything is forever changed. It wasn't a dream. You're alive and awake and now you have to deal with putting the pieces back together.

It was a shitty fucking job.

We were staying in a basic cabin just outside the city of Temecula. Camden wanted something that was off the beaten path, some place Javier wouldn't think of checking. The cabins were part of a campground and nestled in hills of ponderosa pine. It was beautiful and quiet, the kind of place where you'd stay for a few days while you tried to make sense of life all over again.

But I wasn't coming up with anything. My life was

rendered senseless. I'd spent the whole night crying, rocking back and forth on the bed.

Camden. I don't know what I would have done without him. He held me in his arms, staying awake with me. He never said a single word, he just held on to me like he was afraid of letting me go. His heartbeat, steady against my back, kept me sane and allowed my grief to flow without consequence.

"Hey." Camden's mouth was at my ear. "It's a beautiful day outside."

I rolled over under the covers and looked around the room, at the stream of golden sunshine that was coming through the windows of the A-frame. It was a lot nicer than a motel room, that's for sure. But all the sunshine in the world couldn't clear up the blackness I felt in my heart.

I leaned back on the down pillow, relieved that no tears were coming. I must have cried them all out. "I can't believe it," I whispered, staring blankly at the wood beams in the ceiling.

"I know," he said, wrapping his arm across my chest. He kissed my temple, letting his lips linger there.

"But you knew."

He shook his head and kissed my earlobe. "I didn't want to believe it. I was just trying to protect us. I didn't actually think he'd do that to you."

"But he did…"

"Some men are weak, and when they're desperate, they grow weaker. I know your uncle wouldn't have let anything happen to you."

I stared at him from the corner of my eye. "He tried to hand me over to Javier. For fifty thousand dollars."

Camden's smile was tight-lipped. "I know. But I think Jim really believed that Javier wouldn't hurt you. You're such a tough cookie, Ellie. He probably thought you'd be fine in the end."

"You're sticking up for him."

"He's dead, Ellie. He doesn't need me to stick up for him. I'm just trying to figure him out, the same way that you are."

I shook my head. "He held a grudge against me, all this time."

"Then you can understand how weak a grudge can make someone," he said softly. I stared up at him, his full lips and the three-day-old beard that was scrawled across his strong face. His eyes were tired, though, with bags that pulled at them, and his brow was lined with worry. Worry for me.

"We're going to have to get you a new pair of nerd glasses," I told him. "Can you even see me right now?"

He raised his brow. "I can see enough. What's wrong with my reading glasses? Not hipster enough for you?"

I shook my head. "They're okay, if you like sexy, intelligent men. But it doesn't do much to disguise you. Remember we need you feeling like as different a person as possible when you start your new life."

His lips twitched. "I already feel like a different person, Ellie. I don't think I can ever go back to the person I was before. I think the real Camden McQueen died somewhere in the night."

I pushed my breaking heart away. "I know. I think Ellie Watt did, too. I think she died right there in the room with Uncle Jim. I think she's died a million times before."

He reached for my hand and grasped it hard. "We can do this, you know. We'll figure things out here, but then we'll be gone. I'm not giving up on a new life and I'm not giving up on you. I don't care if I have to be Connor Malloy for the rest of my life, as long as you are in that life with me."

"But doesn't this seem hard?" I asked. "Doesn't it seem impossible? Day after day our new lives are slipping further and further away from us. We were so close ... so close and then ..."

"And then you decided to save your uncle. You did the right thing and you know it. You had every reason to trust him, and if you'd turned your back on him, I'm sure none of this would have happened. But you'd hate yourself. Now at least you know. You tried to help him. That's all that counts. You tried to make things right, and that's more than you can ask from anybody, let alone someone who has only been burned by life."

Fear ran its cold fingers down my back. "But he'll never stop looking for me. Everywhere I go, he'll be there. He won't stop until he has me in his hands."

"Listen to me." Camden shook me, his voice hard. His eyes were flashing with determination. "I will not let him find you. I will not let him take you. We can do this, you and me. We can live our lives in peace. Maybe you can never be Ellie Watt again. Maybe you can dye your hair red, get a cute little haircut or grow it long, or get a wig. Colored contacts. Different style. We can make you someone else and I'll take her as I take you now. I know the real you is always underneath, still alive, no matter what name you go by on the outside, and that's all that matters. This doesn't have to go on forever. We can shut the door on the past and start over."

What he was saying was so honest, so real, so incredibly romantic. But I couldn't ignore the guilt. I got us into the mess. It should have been my cross to carry, not his.

But whatever I thought, he didn't agree. He wanted this mess. He kissed me passionately, his tongue soothing mine, his lips giving me life, fanning the joy I had somewhere inside, the joy I was too afraid to feel. *I might end up loving this man*, I thought, as his lips caressed the skin of my throat. *It would be so easy to do.*

So, for a moment, I gave in to him and focused only on the physical. I only felt what he coaxing me to feel. His firm, talented hands as they skimmed down my body, his tongue as it lapped behind my ears. He peeled back my camisole, his fingers gently brushing my nipples until they hardened, then he pinched them with delicious pain. I slipped my underwear off as his hand traveled south to join mine. He started stroking me, inserting his fingers slowly, one at a time, until I was open, wet, and begging for him.

He flipped me so I was on my side and brought my back to his chest. He bit my neck, sucking hard; unlike the pain I had inside, his pain was seductive and sweet. I let myself surrender to it, for whatever he wanted to do to me, for whatever he wanted me to feel.

He pushed in between my legs; his hands ran up and

down my ass, pinching here and there, drawing a gasp from my mouth. Then he slowly slid himself inside, filling me with something more than physical. He filled me with light. With effervescence. With hope.

We made love slowly, savoring each touch, each sensation. His hands explored my body like I was a work of art he couldn't quite believe was real. With us on our sides, he pushed in and out in keen deliberation, making me pant, making me sweat, making me want more. He finally gave it to me, his fingers swirling around my clit with precision, his other hand squeezing my breasts until they hurt, his lips enveloping my earlobe.

"I love you," he whispered. "From now until the end, under any name you choose."

That was all it took. The pressure built in my core and I came in dizzying waves, calling out his name. A few tears leaked out of my eyes as I felt everything I could possibly feel.

He came soon after, his groans and grunts filling my ears, filling the room. He gasped for breath and held me close to him, tight as ever. "I'm afraid," he whispered.

"Why?" I whispered back, wiping away the tears, my body somewhere on a cloud.

"I can't ever lose what I just felt." He kissed my cheek. "I'm afraid if I did, I'd come looking for you, too. I'm afraid I can relate...to him."

I turned my head to look at him. "You're not him. You never will be."

He seemed satisfied with that. We lay in each other's arms, staring out the window, at the birds that flew from tree to tree, bustling with the nature of things.

After a while he got up to take a shower. I joined him, making sure to keep my leg as clean as possible. The tattoo looked really good. The scabs were starting to crust over, which is never fun, but even with that the image was stunning. I actually couldn't wait to wear shorts for the first time in my life.

We got dressed, taking our time. There was no hurry now. We needed to come up with a plan, I needed to talk to Gus, we needed to start living again. But there, in that cabin, there was no hurry. It was a hamlet for love and for grief. I let both of those emotions cloak me like layers of silk. I let them slide over me, through my fingers, to the earth, working my way through them. There was no escape from the hurt, but Camden's love made handling it easier.

We were sitting outside on the Adirondack chairs on the porch, bundled in warm sweaters and drinking spiked apple cider, when my phone rang.

My heart made itself known with a single boom. The last time I'd answered the phone...

I exchanged a worried glance with Camden and quickly got up and went inside. I snatched my ringing, flashing phone off the table.

The call was coming from Uncle Jim. Or at least it was coming from his phone. Not many people would probably have access to it.

I answered it. "Hello."

It was time to stop running.

"Hello, angel," came the smooth voice of Javier over the line.

Camden came in the room, shutting the door behind

him. I swallowed hard, my eyes on him as I said, "Hello, Javier."

He chuckled warmly. "So formal with me. You'd think after the other night, we'd be a bit more relaxed. Old friends, you see. That's what we are."

"You're not my friend," I said simply. "You're a sick fucking son of a bitch with way too much time on his hands. Don't you have any drugs to sell or fingers to cut off?"

"Oh, nasty, nasty Eden. Sorry! I mean Ellie. Can I still call you angel? It would make things easier."

"You call me that one more time and I'm hanging up."

"You won't hang up on me," he said quickly. "I have something here of interest to you. To both of you. Angel."

That did it. I was about to hang up when I heard a muffled cry in the background. The cry of a child. I felt like a chunk of ice got lodged in my throat and was slowly filling up my chest.

"What is that?" I cried out pitifully. Camden took a step closer and I put my hand out to stop him. I needed to keep him away from this, I needed to be sure. "Javier?"

"Sorry, angel. I was just adjusting something here. You know you really hurt me with that whole cutting-off-fingers remark. I would never do that to a child."

Oh no. Oh fucking no. Say it wasn't true.

"You wouldn't...," I said, feeling so fucking help-less.

"I just said I wouldn't. But his mother, on the other

hand? I have no problems with that. Hey, do you mind putting Camden on the phone for a minute? I have something I'd like to tell him."

I took in a deep breath through my nose, trying to figure out a way to spare Camden from this pain.

"Now, my bella," he commanded. "Before I grow impatient. I've had a rough few days, and I really don't want to take it out on someone. Especially when a little boy is watching. What's his name again? Ben? Is it Ben? Why don't you put Camden on so I can ask him?"

I couldn't look at Camden. I couldn't prepare him for it. I silently held the phone out for him and huddled down in the chair after he took it.

"Javier," Camden greeted tersely. "What do you want?"

I didn't have to listen to know what was being said. I could tell in the heaviness that rolled into the room like an incoming fog. I could feel Camden's heart come through as he gasped in horror.

"If you fucking dare lay a finger on them...," Camden began, then trailed off. He was choking on his anger, his body tense and ready to strike at something we couldn't get at. We were in the cage now, and Javier was poking a stick through the bars.

"You're disgusting," he muttered in response to whatever Javier was saying. "I won't play your games."

Suddenly the phone was thrust in front of my face. "It's for you," he said to me, his eyes cold.

I took the phone. "Yes?"

"Angel," Javier began, "your new boyfriend needs to learn a lesson or two in compromise. I suppose you're not the best teacher, though, are you? We could have compromised, you and I. We could have come to an understanding back then. You didn't have to leave me."

"What do you want?" I asked, ignoring him. Camden was pacing back and forth across the room, totally enveloped by this madness.

"I want to make a deal. And I think you're smart enough to take it."

My nerves felt electrified, prickles surging through my body. "I've made too many deals."

"I know you have. Did you know you're running with a fugitive? Did you know there are some pretty bad people out there looking for him? I mean, I'm not putting myself down here, but goodness, angel, they seem worse than I am. You know the types. Liars with no remorse."

I heard Sophia cry out in the background. The grip on the phone tightened. "Get to the point!"

"Oh, now you're seeing the hurry. Good, good. We're always best when we're on the same page, you and I. Now, your Camden. Is he your Camden now? We'll see about that soon. But I digress. Your Camden is in some very bad trouble with some very bad people. He stole a bunch of their money. Sounds familiar, doesn't it? The men want it back. They'd kill to get it back. But don't worry, I took care of it."

I hesitated. "How?"

"I paid them off. I gave them the money they wanted, and in exchange they gave me Sophia here and...Ben? Was it? You know I never did ask Camden, and Sophia here, well, she can't exactly talk." I could almost hear him smile. He called into the background, "Hey son, can you tell me your name?"

Ben started crying in response. I wanted nothing more than to reach through the phone and strangle the life out of Javier. "You asshole," "I said, seething."

"Back to the name calling, are we? No matter," he said. "I have them now. I will return both of them to Camden, if Camden gives me you. Why, I'll even pay him the reward money. That's not a bad deal, you know. Fifty thousand dollars and his ex-wife and child back? That's like winning the lottery in some countries."

"How can I trust you?" I asked.

"I guess you can't," he said. "But you know I never break my promises."

"And you promise that everything will go as planned? Nothing funny?"

He laughed. It struck a nerve somewhere, a feeling I didn't ever want to feel again. "You know I'm not very good at being funny. I promise. I don't care about this whore here and her fat little kid. I certainly don't care about the walking tattoo. I just care about you. I want you, angel, and I won't rest, won't leave you alone, until I have you. You do understand, don't you? You do realize how fucking long I've been looking for you!" He screamed those last words, causing my heart to race and the phone to come away from my ear. He rarely got this mad, and when he did…everyone was in danger. I had to make sure Sophia and Ben were okay.

"I do, I understand. I'll do it," I told him. At that moment Camden grabbed my arm and whipped me around, yelling, "What the fuck are you doing, Ellie!?"

But it was too late. The plan was already in motion. The deal had been made.

Javier spoke quickly as I kept the phone to me, fighting off Camden. "Remember, if he messes this up, he loses both of them. And then he'll lose you. Meet me at his tattoo shop in three hours."

I eyed the time on the phone. It was noon. We could be there in two and a half. "How do you know I'll make it there on time?"

"I know you'll figure out a way. And I know you're close. I can feel you. I always have."

The phone went dead. The fuzziness rang in my ear. I gingerly hung it up and stuck it in my pocket. I raised my head, shoulders back, and looked Camden in the eye. He was about to kill someone.

"What the hell did you do, Ellie?" he cried out.

"I'm getting your son and ex-wife back," I said. "You want to pretend like it wasn't going to happen?"

"We have to get the cops. I have to call my dad," he said, pacing again.

"No. We can't involve them. You know we can't. He didn't have to whisper 'and come alone' on the phone for me to know how serious he is. We have to go now, and you'll get them back. I promise you."

He grabbed me by the arm, more harshly than he probably meant to. He was on the verge of freaking out. "I can't let you go with him."

"I won't go with him," I said. "He just wants to see me, to talk to me, that's all."

"They're going to take you away," he said.

I looked him straight in the eye. "I won't let them."

I grabbed his hand and held it, hard. "But we have to focus on Ben right now, okay? Let's make sure he and his mom are safe first. Then we'll deal with me."

I let go and started packing. "Come on, we can't argue about it. If we're not there in three hours..." I wasn't about to finish that sentence. I didn't need to.

In three hours we'd be back in Palm Valley, dust returning to dust.

CHAPTER TWENTY-THREE

WE DIDN'T SPEAK much to each other during the drive, as the rolling green hillsides dissolved into the craggy desert. The moment we hit the I-10, it felt like we were coming home. I felt like I finally had a home. It was too bad home had never felt so frightening.

I felt so bad for Camden, my heart more occupied with his than with my own. It was easier that way. I didn't want to think about what I was going to do or what was going to happen to me afterward. I just wanted Camden to be okay, for his family to be back together with him. I hoped Sophia wouldn't hold it against him; I hoped, even though it hurt my heart to think this way, that she'd forgive him. After all, they had a son together. If anything, their relationship desperately needed to be repaired, more than ours had.

I couldn't believe how easily her brothers had handed her over to Javier, their own sister and nephew. I supposed there was a chance that Javier lied—that he never paid them off with the money we stole, that he kidnapped Sophia and Ben in the night. But here's the funny thing about Javier. As much as I despised him, as immoral of a human being that he was, he rarely lied. And he was right—he always kept his promises. I didn't have to admire him for it, but it was the truth.

That was the only reason I felt a bit of peace as I sat back in the passenger seat of Jose. The only reason why I had some hope for them. I knew Camden, Sophia, and Ben would walk away from this and with the fifty thousand dollars. Camden had the chance to really start over, to become Connor Malloy for good. And after the way her family had treated her, I wouldn't be surprised if Sophia and Ben would join him.

Which reminded me. I brought out my notebook and tore a piece of paper out.

"Camden," I said, trying to write on the dash as he took the exit for Palm Valley. "I'm writing down all of Gus's contact info. You'll need him for your IDs and if you ever get into any trouble."

"What are you talking about, Ellie?" he asked, voice shaking. "If there's any trouble, you're the one calling Gus, because you'll be with me."

"You know we have to be ready for any situation," I said, avoiding his eyes. I folded the piece of paper, leaned over, and stuck it in a pocket of his cargo shorts. "If you want to be a good con artist, you're going to have to start thinking that way, too."

"Ellie," he warned.

"He's an ex-LAPD officer and he lives close by," I went on. "He knows people, he knows everything, and he's always on my side, you got that? He'll be on your side, too."

He gripped the wheel. "I don't like this," he said, shaking his head, his jaw tense.

"I don't think we're supposed to like this," I told him. "That's the point."

"If you try anything stupid...," he said.

"Me?" I asked, managing a smile. "You're the one I'll have to keep an eye on so you don't go all Dirty Harry on him."

"Some guys deserve the Dirty Harry," he muttered.

Together we took in a deep breath as the car sped on. The tattoo on my leg was feeling tight, but somehow the one on my arm was itching more.

Thirty minutes later we were in Palm Valley. My nerves were returning, misfiring. When we passed the road where my uncle's house still was, I nearly choked on my tears. I thought they'd all disappeared, but I didn't think I'd ever stop feeling this way. The pain ran far too deep. It was in the ground, seeping up into me wherever I stood.

"Pull over," I told Camden when we were about two minutes away from Sins & Needles. He did and stopped in front of a For Lease office building.

"You're not going to make me promise you something," he said. "Because that's what they say in the movies, the person who never comes back."

I reached over and grabbed his head with my hands, kissing him thoroughly. When we broke apart, my skin was tingling, my lungs breathless.

"That," he managed to say, sneaking in another kiss,

his eyes exploring mine, "is pretty much the same as a promise. The kiss good-bye." He could barely get out the last words. My heart heaved.

"No," I told him, tracing my fingers along his jaw, "it's not a good-bye kiss. It's just a kiss. I love you, Camden McQueen."

My lip began to tremble, eyes stinging with fire. He looked stunned. I felt stunned. I couldn't help how I felt. I couldn't help the way I was telling him. That I was telling him before it was all too late. It was time for me to make amends, and I'd do so loving him, come what may.

He kissed me so hard I thought I might break. Somewhere in there a sob escaped his lips, or maybe it escaped mine. It didn't matter—we were only one, we'd always been, always been the same. Our lips were wet, the salt of tears hitting our tongue. It wasn't a good-bye kiss, it was the opposite. It was the start of something that would last forever.

Even if we weren't together. Because we wouldn't be together. I knew what I had to do, to give him his life back. And to right the wrongs in mine.

I pulled away, letting the last tear roll down my cheek. I nodded at the road in front of us, the brightly colored shops and groomed palm trees that lined Main Street like a beacon, all pointing us in the right direction. The only direction.

He studied me for a minute, as if memorizing every line on my face. I let him. And I did the same. His quirky full lips, expressive brows, those eyes that knew me, the real me, for everything that I was and everything that I had been. Everything I would be. Even through his reading glasses, he looked like the most handsome man I'd ever seen. I wished he'd gotten a chance to tattoo the back of my leg. I wish he'd made his mark everywhere. I wished everyone could see how much he'd imprinted himself on my heart.

We drove up to the shop and parked in front in visitors' parking. It looked the same as it always did. His rock garden looked tidy, proof that it was the perfect garden for lazy people and fugitives. There was no one around. No other cars. Even the street seemed quiet for three in the afternoon.

He turned off the engine and handed me the keys.

"You might have to give this back now," he said, attempting a joke. His hand closed over mine and we knew it wasn't a joke at all.

I gave him the only smile I could muster. "Here we go."

We stepped out of the car. As we did so, a black Denali SUV roared up beside us and idled on the side of the street. At the same time, the door to Sins & Needles opened and Javier stepped out onto the front steps. He was wearing a tight-fitting white T-shirt that showed off his athletic build and gray jeans. He was going for the "don't be afraid of me" look, which was pretty redundant when you were wearing shit-kicker boots.

He raised his arms wide, like he was welcoming us to his home, with a smile that seemed to split his face in two.

"You made it!" he exclaimed, and ran down the steps two at a time. He clapped his hands together as he walked over to Camden, rubbing them like he was about to eat him for dessert.

My eyes darted between the two men; Camden, who was over six feet and looked ready to bash his head in; Javier, who was five ten and as agile as a reptile on a really warm day. I'd been in love with one of them once and the other now. I couldn't believe the men in my life, and how, deep down, all three of us were kind of the same.

I had met Camden in high school, a place that taught me to kill or be killed better than my parents ever could. I met Javier after. He had helped me perfect the skill.

"So this is the infamous Camden McQueen," Javier said, grinning cordially. That was the thing about him. He was so charming, open and friendly, that you'd never see the strike coming. But Camden did. He'd played with enough snakes in his day. He wasn't fooled for a second.

"Where's my son?" he asked. I almost heard his teeth grinding.

Javier cocked his head. "Oh, you're worried about them? Well, they're right up there."

He jerked his head at the shop.

Camden looked but shook his head. "I'm not an idiot. I'm not going up there until I know they're safe, until I can see them. You let them go."

Javier rolled his eyes in an exaggerated motion. He stuck a thumb at him like *Who's this guy?* while looking at me, exasperated. "Angel, you never told me he was such a stickler for details."

"Do what he says, Javier," I said, sounding a lot more confident than I felt.

He sighed, long and hard. "Fine." He turned around and waved at the house. "Hey, let them out. Someone misses them."

Raul appeared at the screen door and opened it. A petite woman with lovely curves and long dark hair came out. Sophia. The woman in Camden's painting. Her face was bruised, but other than that, she looked okay. She was holding onto a chubby but incredibly cute little boy, quite a bit older from the art on Camden's leg.

"Camden!" she cried out. I would be lying if I didn't feel a pang in my heart at the sound of her calling his name.

He took off to them, running up the stairs. He scooped up the boy first, the boy who had maybe forgotten who his daddy was but still looked pleased to see him nonetheless. Seeing Ben in his arms also made my heart ache.

Javier was watching me and noticed this. He stepped closer and reached out, brushing my hair behind my ears, a disarming tenderness in his eyes. It took everything I had to keep from screaming, to keep from running.

But I was done running. This was the music I had to face.

It sounded a lot like Dire Straits.

"I have you now," he whispered. "Now and forever."

I raised my chin and looked at him. "You're giving him the money."

His lips snaked into a smile. "Of course."

He turned around and looked at them on the porch.

Camden was talking to Ben, who was now crying, trying to calm the boy down.

"Raul," Javier yelled. "Give the family their money."

Raul came back out of the shop holding a small suitcase full of bills that he held open. Sophia, as ruined as she looked, as far away from Camden as she was standing, looked impressed. That was the fifty thousand dollars. That was the price on my head.

Camden whirled around, holding Ben to his side. "What is this?" he yelled.

Javier grinned. "It's the money. For Ellie Watt."

He brushed past me, toward the Denali. "Come on now, we have places to be."

I stood there in the rock garden, knowing what I had to do, but unsure how I was going to force myself to do it.

Camden was staring at me from the porch, openmouthed. "This is payment for *you*?"

"I'm sorry," I told him, burying the hurt inside. "You deserve it. You and your family. To start over."

He handed Ben to Sophia and started running down the stairs. The doors to the SUV flung open and two large men in suits stepped out. They went straight for Camden and held him back before he had a chance to get even close to me.

"What are you doing?" he cried out, trying to fight them and failing. He writhed and squirmed, but he wasn't going anywhere. "You don't have to do this, Ellie!"

I smiled at him, everything vital breaking inside. "I do have to, Camden. I can't run anymore. I'm through with screwing people over, even those who did the same to me. I need to start over, too. I can't let my past control me anymore."

His face was pinched in agony as he tried to get loose. "You're making a mistake. You said it doesn't have to be this way. That you wouldn't let him take you."

I swallowed back the tears. "Yeah. Well, I lied."

Then I turned away from him and walked toward the Denali, the black, shiny beast against the pale desert floor. It was a high-contrast world and I lived a high-contrast life. I gave Jose a final look, knowing Javier would never take it back. It was never about the car. It was never about the money. It was about me. And now he had me.

I looked over my shoulder at Camden just as I was about to get in the backseat. He'd stopped fighting. But his eyes hadn't. They were hitting me, punching me, slicing me to stay. For me to fight back. But I couldn't. Not this time.

My eyes went over his shoulder, over the two thugs who were holding on to him, and to Sophia and Ben. She was clutching the briefcase with one hand and holding Ben in her free arm. She looked beautiful through her bruises, but that wasn't enough to make me trust her. I hoped she knew that if she broke Camden's heart again, it would be my turn to kill somebody.

I took in a deep breath and stepped inside the vehicle. Javier was in the backseat with me, and there was only a large, bald driver in the front. I closed the door, keeping my eyes inside the car. Javier grinned at me, so joyful, it was almost like old times.

"You're here," he said, almost breathless. He buckled in his seat belt and hit the driver on the shoulder. "Go."

The Denali roared off, Sins & Needles disappearing in its wake.

"You better get comfortable," Javier said, patting the leather between us. "We have a long journey in front of us."

"Where are we going?" I whispered.

"Why, to the past," he said with a smile.

I sat back in the seat, watching Palm Valley fly past me. The town disappeared in a cloud of dust.

THE END

ACKNOWLEDGMENTS

I've never been very good at the acknowledgments section. They say it takes a village to build a something-or-other, and while writing is an extremely solitary profession, it does take many patient, kind, and imaginative people to make a book. Especially one of my books—Lord knows I'm a nutcase at times, so even when my friends and family are just being supportive by listening to me rant and bitch and cry and moan, they're doing a *lot*. I came up with the idea for *Sins & Needles* back in September 2012, so, believe me, they've been dealing with me talking about writing the book for a long time. I'm glad they finally convinced me to do it.

Most people start off their Oscar acceptance speeches by thanking the little people first—well, there are no little people when it comes to this book. But there is one big person I have to thank first, you know, before the music comes on and I get dragged off the stage: Scott MacKenzie. I love you. Your belief in me and sheer determination to help me succeed is staggering. I've never known anyone quite like you—you are the Camden to my Ellie, the love of my life, and the one who truly believes my scars, both inside and out, are entirely beautiful. Thank you, thank you, thank you. My life changed the moment you walked into it, and I've never looked back.

All right, now that the big sappy moment is out of the way, here goes the rest: big thanks to my original editor, Kara Malinczak, for her ruthlessness and support (and her hatred of the word *pillowy* and her disbelief that I actually do hold my breath without realizing it); my proofreader, Mollie Caselli, who cut her editing teeth on my EIT novels; my Vegas guru and master beta (NOT masturbator... get your heads out of the gutter), Amanda Polito; Emmy Franke for her tattoo prowess, feedback, and epic forum moderation; Rebecca Espinoza and Megan Ward for being beyond awesome and patient with me as I ferried this book back and forth, piece by piece; my insatiable EIT street team of Megan Simpson, Brenna Weidner, and Robin Prete, who will seriously convince you to read my books (they're great, I'm just worried they might start clubbing people's kneecaps soon); Najla Qambar, my wonderful cover designer; Jamie Sager Hall for her passion and generosity in trying to get people to read my stuff; Maryse Black for being my private cheerleader when I need it the most (and her hubby, Kevin, too!); authors extraordinaire Samantha Young, Nicole Reed, Amber Lynn Natusch, and L. H. Cosway; book bloggers who make my world go around, including Giselle from *Xpresso*

Reads, Janice from *The Demon Librarian*, Laura from *Little Read Riding Hood*, Autumn from *The Autumn Review*, Kristilyn from *Reading In Winter*, Ali from *Ginger-read Reviews*, and many others; my extra-good goodreaders Fathima, Lucia, Nina, Laura, Kirsten P, Lise, and Heidi; Amanda "N" Sanderson for her constant harassment (oh, and superb author photos).

I also can't forget the whole team at Grand Central Publishing for picking up this series and for believing in the story, including my wonderfully fun and passionate editor, Latoya Smith, and my innovative publicist, Julie Paulauski; Wendy and Alan MacKenzie for their tireless support (and having to deal with both me *and* Scott); Kelly St-Laurent for her countless pep talks and encouragement; my agent, Scott Waxman, for taking a chance on me and consistently thinking I'm awesome; and my parents for always believing in me (thank you for not being con artists). Oh, and everyone who has taken a chance on me and my little ol' books. It's a dog-eat-dog world out there, and without my readers, I would be nowhere.

Don't miss the heart-pounding
Artists Trilogy novella!

See the next page for a preview of

On Every Street

CHAPTER ONE

I'D BEEN WATCHING the man for almost a month now, the exotic man with the peridot-colored eyes. From a distance they'd always sparkled like the gemstones, but now that I was in the same room with him, I could see they had an amber tinge to them, rendering them almost reptilian.

That should have been my first warning, that this was all a horrible idea. It was too risky, and I was too emotionally involved. But I felt I didn't have a choice. The man with the yellow-green eyes was just feet away from me, representing the first step toward freedom. Vengeance was a terrible prison.

"Can I help you, Miss Sunshine?" the balding clerk at the counter asked, cutting into my thoughts. I tore my eyes away from the man, who was now sitting with a cup of tea in the corner, and looked at the clerk with an awkward smile. I felt a flush heat my cheeks, knowing I'd been caught staring. What had Gus taught me again? *Never let your thoughts drift.*

Guess at the time I hadn't known I'd be stalking a Latino heartthrob.

"Yes, sorry," I replied dumbly. "Can I get a medium latte? Please?"

He nodded, flashing me a warm smile as I handed over the exact change. I stuffed a dollar into the tip jar, making sure he saw it before he started on my coffee. People in Mississippi were as friendly as they ever were, way friendlier than back in California. It felt as if I was visiting the state for the first time, despite having lived here for a few years when I was a child. But I suppose life colors how you see the world, and the Mississippi I knew back then was completely black and white. Now there was a hue, that dangerous citron I could feel on my back.

I took in a deep breath and resisted the urge to turn around. Instead, I pulled up my long blond hair, which was sticking to my sweaty neck, and glanced out the door of the coffee shop. My rusted Chevy truck was sitting just out of view. I wondered if I was getting too ahead of myself. I'd been following the man from his house to his, well, work, nearly every day, and there was a huge chance that he'd recognize me or my truck. I had been careful, remembering everything that Gus had drilled into my head, even remembering what my parents had once taught me, that there was no room for error in a con.

But this was unlike any con I'd done in the last few months. This was the big one. This was the one that meant something. This meant having my life back.

I could still feel his eyes, though, burning into me, like my back was as flammable as parchment paper.

I had to remind myself it didn't mean he *knew*. I was wearing my most ass-supporting jeans and a tissue-thin tank top that showed off my tan. My hair was naturally blond, but I'd gotten a few layers cut in and champagne highlights added just the other day. My makeup was as natural as I could muster without being boring. I'd prepared for today because I wanted the man to stare at me. I wanted his attention because he sure as hell had mine.

The clerk handed over my coffee, and I took a quick sip before gathering my courage. This would go down a hell of a lot better with whiskey in it. I slowly turned around and let my gaze do a sweep of the room, as if I was looking for somewhere to sit. The man was no longer staring at me—perhaps he never was—and was relaxing in the wicker chair, flipping through a magazine. He held his cup of tea in such a way that it exposed his large watch. Even from where I was standing, I knew the thing had probably cost a fortune. When I was younger, my parents taught me how to spot the real ones from the fake ones. They'd also taught me how to steal them.

The man was the epitome of the word *debonair*. The watch, combined with his smooth linen shirt and clean, dark jeans, suggested understated elegance, a man from money. But his pose, the way he held himself, reminded me of a lion on his downtime, relishing his relaxation, knowing he still ruled the land. I'd had such thoughts about him before, but now, up close, I could just feel the power vibrating off of him, filling the room.

I wasn't the only one to notice this, either. Men in the café shot him curious glances, as if they should know who he was, while the women timidly tucked their hair behind their ears, eyes darting to him and back again. I couldn't blame them. The man wasn't stereotypically handsome, and yet you couldn't stop staring at him. At least I couldn't. And that was going to be a problem.

I spied a couple getting up from the couch nearest to him and took the opportunity. I walked slowly over and gently, ever so casually, took my seat on the couch. I placed my coffee on the table between us, taking a moment to let my eyes feast on him. He was so close now, just a couple of feet between us. I felt like I was at the zoo, and the glass between me and the beast had been suddenly removed.

He was even more striking from this distance. His eyes moved back and forth as they scanned the page, sparking with intelligence, the color of budding leaves. His mouth was wide, twisted in a smirk, and his nose looked slightly too wide for his face and had obviously been broken a few times. His skin was golden and so smooth that I had to recalculate how old he was. Perhaps he was closer to my age than I had originally thought. Still, he didn't look like any twenty-year-old. He didn't look like anyone I'd ever seen before.

He brushed his shaggy dark hair behind his ears, his palm grazing his cheekbones, and I had the chance to look away. To not get caught gawking at him. To save myself. But I couldn't help it. I was naïve and young and caught in the spark that would create the flames.

He looked up from his magazine and our eyes met. I've never believed in love at first sight. I barely believed in lust at first sight. I didn't believe in anything except righting all the wrongs in my life. But at that moment, this man saw me. The real me underneath the bomb-shell mask. I felt like he must have seen everything.

And that was who his smile was for. It reached through me and did something to my heart, to my lungs, to my nerves. It pulled at me, tugged at me some-where deep inside, like a window shade being drawn open. It was dangerous to love that feeling, but I did.

"Hello," he said, his Mexican accent light and melodic. His teeth were white, his smile captivating, and it took every brain cell to remember why I was there and what I was doing. And that my name was no longer Ellie Watt. It was Eden White. And I had a job to do.

I gave him a pretty smile, knowing that damn flush was coming back on my cheeks. I had inexperience written all over my face.

"Hi," I replied, leaning forward to pick up my cof-fee, hoping that he'd get a good look at my chest. I didn't have the biggest breasts, but they looked down-right perky in this top, and I was certain that I could poke his eyes out with my nipples. Thank god for air-conditioning.

But his eyes never strayed from mine. Either this man had manners or he wasn't into women. I'd never considered that scenario in the last couple of weeks. Perhaps my attempt to get to know him would backfire. What use was having womanly charms if he preferred the cock variety?

"I'm Javier," he said, extending his hand with the watch on it, the rich brown leather gleaming under the lights.

Javier. He now had a name. And from the way his eyes were still cutting into mine, how his grin lit up his face like he'd just won the lottery, I knew Javier wasn't immune to women after all.

I ignored the butterflies in my core and placed my hand in his. His shake was strong and warm with confidence.

"I'm Eden," I said, trying to feed off his self-assurance. I *was* Eden now. It had taken me a while to get used to my fake name, but now it was slipping on like fine silk. Maybe pretending to be someone else would be easier than I thought.

His thumb rubbed against my knuckle, softly and sweetly, before he let go of my hand. I fought the urge to bite my lip. The young schoolgirl shit probably wouldn't jibe with him, even though that was really all I was. I wasn't in school, but around men I was as green as a young filly. And this man's touch was igniting something in me that I'd never felt before.

"Nice to meet you, Eden," he said smoothly. I watched his mouth as he talked, feeling a blanket of warmth coat me as he pronounced my new name. Shit. I was supposed to be seducing him, wasn't I? Not the other way around.

"So what brings you here?" he asked, leaning forward on his knees, his hands clasped together.

I swallowed hard and raised my cup at him. "Coffee?" My heart began to beat louder, whooshing in my ears.

He smirked. "I can see that. It's just that I've never seen you here before. I come here every day, and I think I'd remember someone as beautiful as you."

Oh, this Javier—he was *good*. It didn't surprise me, considering the way I'd seen him acting at his "job." Or, to put it better, the way his colleagues acted around him. I should have known he'd be a smooth operator with the ladies.

I quickly recalled my story: "I just moved to Ocean Springs and thought I'd check this place out. Seems to be one of the more popular coffee shops."

The corner of his mouth twitched and his eyes narrowed deviously as he appraised what I said. I swear, my heart could have replaced the drummer for Slayer at that moment.

"Interesting," he commented.

Interesting, *I think I've seen you in your truck, sitting outside my boss's house all day*? Interesting, *I think you've used a fake name*? Interesting, *I think you're lying through your teeth*? I was prepared for him to elaborate by saying any of those.

But he tilted his head, and a small gold chain necklace nestled in his shirt collar caught my eye. He said with a lowered voice, "Do you believe in fate, Eden?"

Well, that caught me off guard. Maybe that was his intention. I frowned and straightened up, unsure how to placate this strange animal.

"Sometimes I do," I managed to say, trying to keep the breeziness in my voice.

"I think it was fate that brought you to me today," he said. The hairs at the back of my neck stood straight up, and I knew I couldn't blame that on the air-conditioning.

"You do?" I asked, my voice barely above a whisper.

He nodded, cool and confident. He sat back in his

chair and drummed his fingers on his leg, watching me so closely, too closely.

"I think you'll look back at this in a few years, and you'll know what I know."

"And what's that?" I asked, forgetting everything I'd been planning to do, just so completely and utterly enthralled.

"You'll have to find out for yourself. Better yet, I can get you started. This Friday."

My face must have looked blank because he went on with a wry smile, "I'm going to take you out on a date."

Shit. That was fast. That was easy. And extremely cocky of him.

"How do you know I don't have a boyfriend?" I asked him, wondering if my singledom and virginhood was stamped all over me.

"Because I don't believe in accidents," he said, licking his lips. "But I do believe you'll say yes."

I had half a nerve to make my lie worse, to tell him I had a boyfriend and that I didn't want to go out with him, a total stranger. But that would defeat the whole purpose of the long con, the reason I had sought him out. Besides, those lips and those eyes, that swagger in his lilting voice, was igniting a fire in me where I'd never burned before.

I was doomed.

"Okay," I said shyly. He gave me that prize-winning grin again and pulled out a business card from his full wallet, then handed it to me.

I turned it over in my hands, feeling the grooved paper.

"Javier Bernal," I read out loud. "Consultant."

And that was it. Just that and his phone number.

"Who do you consult?" I asked, looking up at him.

I could have sworn his face went rigid for a second, but maybe because I was looking for it. Maybe because I knew he wasn't a consultant. Maybe because I knew who he really was: a henchman for one of the most powerful drug lords on the Gulf Coast. Maybe because I knew he had more secrets to hide than I did.

But he just shrugged and said, "People who need it."

He got out of his chair with all the ease of a panther and tapped the card with a well-manicured finger. "Call me. Soon."

Then he left the store, tossing his tea in the wastebasket without looking.

It took a good few minutes for me to calm down and get my heartbeat back to an acceptable level. Ever since I had left California and came here, I knew what I had set out to do. I had prepared for it as much as I could. I was going to find Travis, the man who scarred me as a child when my parents' scam went wrong. I was going to get to him by seducing someone close to him, someone who could get me in close. Then I was going to have my revenge, the only thing that had kept me going over the years.

It was just when I chose Javier as my mark, I never thought my mark would choose me. Because that was what Javier had just done. I wanted to win over his heart so I could get what I wanted. But I had a feeling he was about to get to my heart first.

THE DISH

Where Authors Give You the Inside Scoop

From the desk of Marilyn Pappano

Dear Reader,

The first time Jessy Lawrence, the heroine of my newest novel, A LOVE TO CALL HER OWN, opened her mouth, I knew she was going to be one of my favorite Tallgrass characters. She's mouthy, brassy, and bold, but underneath the sass, she's keeping a secret or two that threatens her tenuous hold on herself. She loves her friends fiercely with the kind of loyalty I value. Oh, and she's a redhead, too. I can always relate to another "ginger," lol.

I love characters with faults—like me. Characters who do stupid things, good things, bad things, unforgivable things. Characters whose lives haven't been the easiest, but they still show up; they still do their best. They know too well it might not be good enough, but they try, and that's what matters, right?

Jessy is one of those characters in spades—estranged from her family, alone in the world except for the margarita girls, dealing with widowhood, guilt, low self-esteem, and addiction—but she meets her match in Dalton Smith.

I was plotting the first book in the series, *A Hero to Come Home To*, when it occurred to me that there's a lot of talk about the men who die in war and the wives they leave behind, but people seem not to notice that some of our casualties are women, who also leave behind spouses, fiancés, family whose lives are drastically altered. Seconds behind that thought, an image popped into my head of the margarita club gathered around their table at The Three Amigos, talking their girl talk, when a broad-shouldered, six-foot-plus, smokin' handsome cowboy walked up, Stetson in hand, and quietly announced that his wife had died in the war.

Now, when I started writing the first scene from Dalton's point of view, I knew immediately that scene was never going to happen. Dalton has more grief than just the loss of a wife. He's angry, bitter, has isolated himself, and damn sure isn't going to ask anyone for help. He's not just wounded but broken—my favorite kind of hero.

It's easy to write love stories for perfect characters, or for one who's tortured when the other's not. I tend to gravitate to the challenge of finding the happily-ever-after for two seriously broken people. They deserve love and happiness, but they have to work so hard for it. There are no simple solutions for these people. Jessy finds it hard to get out of bed in the morning; Dalton has reached rock bottom with no one in his life but his horses and cattle. It says a lot about them that they're willing to work, to risk their hearts, to take those scary steps out of their grief and sorrow and guilt and back into their lives.

Oh yeah, and I can't forget to mention my other two favorite characters in A LOVE TO CALL HER OWN: Oz, the handsome Australian shepherd on the cover; and Oliver, a mistreated, distrusting dog of unknown breed.

I love my puppers, both real and fictional, and hope you like them, too.

Happy reading!

Marilyn Pappano

MarilynPappano.net
Twitter @MarilynPappano
Facebook.com/MarilynPappanoFanPage

From the desk of Kristen Ashley

Dear Reader,

In starting to write *Lady Luck*, the book where Chace Keaton was introduced, I was certain Chace was a bad guy. A dirty cop who was complicit in sending a man to jail for a crime he didn't commit.

Color me stunned when Chace showed up at Ty and Lexie's in *Lady Luck* and a totally different character introduced himself to me.

Now, I am often not the white hat–wearing guy type of girl. My boys have to have at least a bit of an edge (and usually way more than a bit).

That's not to say that I don't get drawn in by the boy next door (quite literally, for instance, with Mitch Lawson of *Law Man*). It just always surprises me when I do.

Therefore, it surprised me when Chace drew me in while he was in Lexie and Ty's closet in *Lady Luck*. I knew in that instant that he had to have his own happily-ever-after. And when Faye Goodknight was introduced later in that book, I knew the path to that was going to be a doozy!

Mentally rubbing my hands together with excitement, when I got down to writing BREATHE, I was certain that it was Chace who would sweep me away.

And he did.

But I *adored* writing Faye.

I love writing about complex, flawed characters, watching them build strength from adversity. Or lean on the strength from adversity they've already built in their lives so they can get through dealing with falling in love with a badass, bossy alpha. The exploration of that is always a thing of beauty for me to be involved in.

Faye, however, knew who she was and what she wanted from life. She had a good family. She lived where she wanted to be. She was shy, but that was her nature. She was no pushover. She had a backbone. But that didn't mean she wasn't thoughtful, sensitive, and loving. She had no issues, no hang-ups, or at least nothing major.

And she was a geek girl.

The inspiration for her came from my nieces, both incredibly intelligent, funny, caring and, beautiful—and both total geek girls. I loved the idea of diving into that (being a bit of a geek girl myself), this concept that is considered stereotypically "on the fringe" but is actually an enormous sect of society that is quite proud of their geekdom. And when I published BREATHE, the geek girls came out of the woodwork, loving seeing one of their own land her hot guy.

But also, it was a pleasure seeing Chace, the one who had major issues and hang-ups, find himself sorted out by his geek girl. I loved watching Faye surprise him, hold up the mirror so he could truly see himself, and take the lead into guiding them both into the happily-ever-after they deserved.

This was one of those books of mine where I could have kept writing forever. Just the antics of the kitties Chace gives to his Faye would be worth a chapter!

But alas, I had to let them go.

Luckily, I get to revisit them whenever I want and let fly the warm thoughts I have of the simple, yet extraordinary lives led by a small town cop and the librarian wife he adores.

Kristen Ashley

♥ ♥ ♥ ♥ ♥ ♥ ♥ ♥ ♥ ♥ ♥ ♥ ♥ ♥

From the desk of Sandra Hill

Dear Reader,

Many of you have been begging for a new Tante Lulu story.

When I first started writing my Cajun contemporary books back in 2003, I never expected Tante Lulu would touch so many people's hearts and funny bones. Over the years, readers have fallen in love with the wacky old lady (I like to say, Grandma Moses with cleavage). So many of you have said you have a family member just like her; still more have said they wish they did.

Family…that's what my Cajun/Tante Lulu books are all about. And community…the generosity and unconditional love of friends and neighbors. In these turbulent times, isn't that just what we all want?

You should know that SNOW ON THE BAYOU is the ninth book in my Cajun series, which includes: *The Love Potion*; *Tall, Dark, and Cajun*; *The Cajun Cowboy*; *The Red Hot Cajun*; *Pink Jinx*; *Pearl Jinx*; *Wild Jinx*; and *So Into You*. And there are still more Cajun tales to come, I think. Daniel and Aaron LeDeux, and the newly introduced Simone LeDeux. What do you think?

For more information on these and others of my books, visit my website at www.sandrahill.net or my Facebook page at Sandra Hill Author.

As always, I wish you smiles in your reading.

Sandra Hill

♥ ♥ ♥ ♥ ♥ ♥ ♥ ♥ ♥ ♥ ♥ ♥ ♥ ♥ ♥ ♥

From the desk of Mimi Jean Pamfiloff

Dearest Humans,

It's the end of the world. You're an invisible, seventy-thousand-year-old virgin. The Universe wants to snub out the one person you'd like to hook up with. Discuss.

And while you do so, I'd like to take a moment to thank each of you for taking this Accidental journey with me and my insane deities. We've been to Mayan cenotes, pirate ships, jungle battles, cursed pyramids, vampire showdowns, a snappy leather-daddy bar in San Antonio, New York City, Santa Cruz, Giza, Sedona, and we've even been to a beautiful Spanish vineyard with an incubus. Ah. So many fun places with so many fascinating, misunderstood, wacky gods and other immortals. And let's not forget Minky the unicorn, too!

It has truly been a pleasure putting you through the twisty curves, and I hope you enjoy this final piece of the puzzle as Máax, our invisible, bad-boy deity extraordinaire, is taught one final lesson by one very resilient woman who refuses to allow the Universe to dictate her fate.

Because ultimately we make our own way in this world, Hungry Hungry Hippos playoffs included.

Happy reading!

Mimi

P.S.: Hope you like the surprise ending.

From the desk of Karina Halle

Dear Reader,

Morally ambiguous. Duplicitous. Dangerous.

Those words describe not only the cast of characters in my romantic suspense novel SINS & NEEDLES, book one in the Artists Trilogy, but especially the heroine, Ms. Ellie Watt. Though sinfully sexy and utterly suspenseful, it is Ellie's devious nature and con artist profession that makes SINS & NEEDLES one unique and wild ride.

When I first came up with the idea for SINS & NEEDLES, I wanted to write a book that not only touched on some personal issues of mine (physical scarring, bullying, justification), but dealt with a character little seen in modern literature—the antiheroine. Everywhere you look in books these days you see the bad boy, the criminal, the tattooed heartbreaker and ruthless killer. There are always men in these arguably more interesting roles. Where were all the bad girls? Sure, you could read about women in dubious professions, femme fatales, and cold-hearted killers. But when were they ever the main character? When were they ever a heroine you could also sympathize with?

Ellie Watt is definitely one of the most complex and interesting characters I have ever written, particularly as a heroine. On one hand she has all these terrible qualities; on the other she's just a vulnerable, damaged person trying to survive the only way she knows how. You despise Ellie and yet you can't help but root for her at the same time.

Her love interest, hot tattoo artist and ex-friend Camden McQueen, says it perfectly when he tells her this: "That is what I thought of you, Ellie. Heartless, reckless, selfish, and cruel...Beautiful, sad, wounded, and lost. A freak, a work of art, a liar, and a lover."

Ellie is all those things, making her a walking contradiction but oh, so human. I think Ellie's humanity is what makes her relatable and brings a sense of realism to a novel that's got plenty of hot sex, car chases, gunplay, murder, and cons. No matter what's going on in the story, through all the many twists and turns, you understand her motives and her actions, no matter how skewed they may be.

Of course, it wouldn't be a romance novel without a love interest. What makes SINS & NEEDLES different is that the love interest isn't her foil—Camden McQueen isn't necessarily a "good" man making a clean living. In fact, he may be as damaged as she is—but he does believe that Ellie can change, let go of her past, and find redemption.

That's easier said than done, of course, for a criminal who has never known any better. And it's hard to escape your past when it's literally chasing you, as is the case with Javier Bernal, Ellie's ex-lover whom she conned six years prior. Now a dangerous drug lord, Javier has been hunting Ellie down, wanting to exact revenge for her misdoings. But sometimes revenge comes in a vice and Javier's appearance in the novel reminds Ellie that she can never escape who she really is, that she may not be redeemable.

For a book that's set in the dry, brown desert of southern California, SINS & NEEDLES is painted in shades of gray. There is no real right and wrong in the novel, and the characters, including Ellie, aren't just good or bad. They're just human, just real, just trying to come to terms with their true selves while living in a world that just wants to screw them over.

I hope you enjoy the ride!

♥ ■■■■■■■■■■■■■■   ♥ ♥

From the desk of Kristen Callihan

Dear Reader,

The first novels I read belonged to my parents. I was a latchkey kid, so while they were at work, I'd poach their paperbacks. Robert Ludlum, Danielle Steel, Jean M. Auel. I read these authors because my parents did. And it was quite the varied education. I developed a taste for action, adventure, sexy love stories, and historical settings.

But it wasn't until I spent a summer at the beach during high school that I began to pick out books for myself. Of course, being completely ignorant of what I might actually want to read on my own, I helped myself to the beach house's library. The first two books I chose were Mario Puzo's *The Godfather* (yes, I actually read the book before seeing the movie) and Anne Rice's *Interview with the Vampire*.

Those two books taught me about the antihero, that a character could do bad things, make the wrong decisions, and still be compelling. We might still want them to succeed. But why? Maybe because we share in their pain. Or maybe it's because they care, passionately, whether it's the desire for discovering the deeper meaning of life or saving the family business.

In EVERNIGHT, Will Thorne is a bit of an antihero. We meet him attempting to murder the heroine. And he makes no apologies for it, at least not at first. He is also a blood drinker, sensual, wicked, and in love with life and beauty.

Thinking on it now, I realize that the books I've read have, in some shape or form, made me into the author

I am today. So perhaps, instead of the old adage "You are what you eat," it really ought to be: "You are what you read."

♥ ♥ ♥ ♥ ♥ ♥ ♥ ♥ ♥ ♥ ♥ ♥ ♥ ♥ ♥

From the desk of Laura Drake

Dear Reader,

Hard to believe that SWEET ON YOU is the third book in my Sweet on a Cowboy series set in the world of professional bull riding. The first two, *The Sweet Spot* and *Nothing Sweeter*, involved the life and loves of stock contractors—the ranchers who supply bucking bulls to the circuit. But I couldn't go without writing the story of a bull rider, one of the crazy men who pit themselves against an animal many times stronger and with a much worse attitude.

To introduce you to Katya Smith, the heroine of SWEET ON YOU, I thought I'd share with you her list of life lessons:

1. Remember what your Gypsy grandmother said: Gifts sometimes come in strange wrappings.
2. The good-looking ones aren't *always* assholes.
3. Cowboys aren't the only ones who need a massage. Sometimes bulls do, too.

4. Don't ever forget: You're a soldier. And no one messes with the U.S. military.
5. A goat rodeo has nothing to do with men riding goats.
6. "Courage is being scared to death—and saddling up anyway." —John Wayne
7. Cowgirl hats fit more than just cowgirls.
8. The decision of living in the present or going back to the past is easy once you decide which one you're willing to die for.

I hope you enjoy Katya and Cam's story as much as I enjoyed writing it. And watch for the cameos by JB Denny and Bree and Max Jameson from the first two books!

♥ ♥ ♥ ♥ ♥ ♥ ♥ ♥ ♥ ♥ ♥ ♥ ♥ ♥ ♥

From the desk of Anna Campbell

Dear Reader,

I love books about Mr. Cool, Calm, and Collected finding himself all at sea once he falls in love. Which means I've been champing at the bit to write Camden Rothermere's story in WHAT A DUKE DARES.

The Duke of Sedgemoor is a man who is always in control. He never lets messy emotion get in the way of a rational decision. He's the voice of wisdom. He's the one who sorts things out. He's the one with his finger on the pulse.

And that's just the way he likes it.

Sadly for Cam, once his own pulse starts racing under wayward Penelope Thorne's influence, all traces of composure and detachment evaporate under a blast of sensual heat. Which *isn't* just the way he likes it!

Pen Thorne was such fun to write, too. She's loved Cam since she was a girl, but she's smart enough to know it's hopeless. So what happens when scandal forces them to marry? It's the classic immovable object and irresistible force scenario. Pen is such a vibrant, passionate, headstrong presence that Cam hasn't got a chance. Although he puts up a pretty good fight!

Another part of WHAT A DUKE DARES that I really enjoyed writing was the secondary romance involving Pen's rakish brother Harry and innocent Sophie Fairbrother. There's a real touch of Romeo and Juliet about this couple. I hadn't written two love stories in one book before and the contrasting trajectories throw each relationship into high relief. As a reader, I always like to get two romances for the price of one.

If you'd like to know more about WHAT A DUKE DARES and the other books in the Sons of Sin series— *Seven Nights in a Rogue's Bed*, *Days of Rakes and Roses*, and *A Rake's Midnight Kiss*—please check out my website: http://annacampbell.info/books.html.

Happy reading—and may all your dukes be daring!

Best wishes,

Anna Campbell